Shadows of the Ironwilde

A.K. Neane

Staten House

ISBN:
979-8-90046-274-5 - Ebook
979-8-89965-903-4 - Paperback
979-8-90046-273-8 - Hardcover

First edition: September, 2025

Published by Staten House

Livingston, Tx.

For more information about the author, visit @a.k.neane.author

Contents

Dedication   1

Triggers   2

Guide   4

Playlist   9

Prologue   11

1. Chapter 1   17

2. Chapter 2   27

3. Chapter 3   39

4. Chapter 4   47

5. Chapter 5   57

6. Chapter 6   73

7. Chapter 7   81

8. Chapter 8   95

9. Chapter 9   103

10. Chapter 10   111

11. Chapter 11   123

12. Chapter 12   137

13. Chapter 13   147

14. Chapter 14   153

15. Chapter 15   167

16. Chapter 16   175

17. Chapter 17   185

18. Chapter 18   193

19. Chapter 19   203

20. Chapter 20   213

21. Chapter 21   221

22. Chapter 22   229

23. Chapter 23   237

24. Chapter 24   243

25. Chapter 25   249

26. Chapter 26   261

27. Chapter 27   271

28. Chapter 28   281

29. Chapter 29   289

30. Chapter 30   299

31. Chapter 31   309

32. Chapter 32   315

33. Chapter 33   321

34. Chapter 34   331

35. Chapter 35   339

Epilogue   349

Triggers list   353

Acknowledgments   356

Small Business Thank You   357

Fullpage image   359

Coming Soon   360

Dedication

To all the sassy, stubborn sunshines out there—
and to those who love them enough to weather any storm.

Triggers

A Note Before You Enter the Ironwilde

Dear Reader,

This is a story forged in both fire and shadow. It carries tenderness, fierce love, and moments of wonder — but it also does not shy away from the darker edges of war, obsession, and survival.

Because your safety matters, I want you to know what waits within these pages:

You'll find battles soaked in blood, grief that carves deep, and a world where power is fought for with blade, magic, and bone. There are deaths — of strangers, soldiers, and even family. There are scars from childhood that still ache in the present.

And there is captivity. An antagonist whose obsession twists into coercion. His scenes carry **humiliation, forced bathing, forced nudity, food restrictions, being paraded as a trophy, imprisonment, and even the forced consumption of gore.** He uses power to strip dignity and choice. There is **no on-page rape**, but there are repeated moments of **sexual intimidation and obsession** that echo its weight.

Amidst this, you'll also find passion. This book is unapologetically explicit: a polyamorous romance, full of heat and tenderness, where fire and storm meet earth and shadow. Intimacy here is raw, rough at times, but always **consensual between the main lovers.**

And beneath it all lies magic — bonds that tug at the soul, shapeshifting into drake form, storms and fire wielded as easily as breath. Even the land itself answers, groaning, burning, healing.

This tale is not gentle, but it is honest. It asks much of its characters, and sometimes of its readers. If any of the themes I've listed are too heavy, please take care of yourself first.

But if you're ready to step into the Ironwilde — know you'll find not only shadows here, but also love, defiance, and hope bright enough to burn through the dark.

With care,
A.K. Neane

Guide

Pronunciation

Note to Readers

Please find below a helpful guide with many of the unique names in this
book and how to pronounce them. That said, if you pronounce a name
differently—whether out loud or in your own head—I truly don't mind. One
of the greatest gifts I gave myself as a child was letting go of the need to
pronounce every word "correctly." I've explored plenty of worlds where I created
my own versions of names for the characters, and that only made the stories more
personal. Still, if you're curious about how I intended these names to be said,
here's the list.

Names—

Lyria (*LY-ruh*) – The last female dragon, hidden in the Ironwilde.

Kiaza (*KAI-zuh*) – King of the Drakarians.

Thalos (*THAH-los*) – Drakarian King Consort bonded to Kiaza.

Ironwilde (*EYE-urn-wild*) – The mist-shrouded mountain range and forgotten woods.

Morgryth (*MOR-grith*) – Rogue Drake believes himself the rightful King.

Natrix (*NAY-triks*) – Abyssian Clan Leader.

Dosha (*DOE-shuh*) – Faelethian Friend to Lyria.

Aiyana (*eye-YAH-nuh*) – Grandmother the Faelethian tribal elder and chieftain.

Novalyn (*NO-vuh-lin*) – Queen of the Crystalians.

Vaelorian Drakmyr (*Vay-LORE-ee-an DRACK-meer*) – [character/lineage details to be added]

Serenya (*seh-REN-yuh*) – Kiaza's Mother.

Dalayna (*duh-LAY-nuh*) – Unknown.

Races—

Drakarians (*drah-KAR-ee-ans*) – Dragon shifters, once the balance keepers of the realm.

Faelethians (*FAY-leth-ee-ans*) – Unicorn shifters, protectors of the Ironwilde.

Abyssians (*ah-BISS-ee-ans*) – Kraken shifters who rule the seas.

Crystalians (*KRISS-tahl-ee-ans*) – Geode-like rock people dwelling in caverns.

Humans— The Five Factions

Rauthen (*RAW-thin*)

Focus: Charisma, politics, and influence.

Color: Red.

Nobles, merchants, and spies, weaving networks of power and persuasion.

Bravarn (*BRAV-arn*)

Focus: Physical strength, warriors, and martial skill.

Color: Blue.

Known for disciplined armies, brute force, and straightforward honor.

Caldenys (*CAL-duh-nees*)

Focus: Mental strength, logic, and innovation.

Color: Yellow.

Inventors, tacticians, and engineers who prize cleverness over muscle.

Velmorin (*VEL-more-in*)

Focus: Intuition and magical sensitivity.

Color: Purple.

Mystics, seers, and scholars of hidden power, tied deeply to arcane arts.

Durnathi (*DUR-nah-thee*)

Focus: Endurance, adaptability, and survival.

Color: Grey/Black.

Hardy clans, isolationist by nature, thriving in harsh lands and valuing resilience.

Places— Names of Asherium

Asherium (*ASH-er-um*) – The known world, divided among humans, shifters, and hidden races.

Ironwilde (*EYE-urn-wild*) – The mist-shrouded mountains and forests where Lyria hides.

Drakorra Spire (*drah-KOR-uh Spire*) – Central Drakarian stronghold, tied to dragon heritage.

Durnathi Fort (*DUR-nah-thee Fort*) – Stronghold of the Durnathi, famed for endurance and survival.

Rauthen City (*RAW-thin City*) – Capital of charisma and politics, a hub of power and intrigue.

Velmorin Citadel (*VEL-more-in Citadel*) – Fortress of the Velmorin, guardians of intuition and magic.

Bravarn Garrison (*BRAV-arn Garrison*) – Military seat of the Bravarn, champions of physical strength.

Caldenys Institute (*CAL-duh-nees Institute*) – Seat of logic, innovation, and scholarly pursuit.

Obsidian Halls (*ob-SID-ee-an Halls*) – Ancient halls carved of black stone, seat of deep knowledge and mystery.

Abyssal Hold (*uh-BISS-uhl Hold*) – Ocean fortress of the Abyssians, kraken shifters who dominate the seas.

Spotify Playlist

Prologue

Kiaza

Pain seared my throat as his clawed hand tightened, crushing the air from me. My vision blurred. Tears burned hot trails down my cheeks as I stared into his dark amber eyes, streaked with red, pupils slitted razor-thin. My body trembled, then locked, terror rooting me in place.

Just as sudden, the grip vanished. I crumpled to the stone, choking, the rough floor slick beneath me where blood spread in a widening pool of crimson.

He was the man I had trusted my whole life, closer to me than my own father, yet he turned and fled the chamber, his shadow stretching long behind him.

I crawled through the gore, knees slipping, until I reached the motionless body at its center.

"Mama." My voice cracked, raw, desperate. I clutched at her yellow dress, now darkened and heavy with blood. "Mama, please. No... wake up." Her arms didn't move. Her chest didn't rise.

I curled against her still form, pressing my cheek to her, breathing in the scent that had always been home—vanilla and warmth—now cut through with the bitter reek of iron.

Her hair fanned around her face in a dark halo, strands catching the torchlight like threads of night. She looked almost angelic, and the sight shattered something deep inside me.

"Kaiza, come here, son." My father's strong arms scooped me up. He held me close as I shook, wiping my tears against his shirt while I nuzzled into him. His stern voice a soft whisper, "Who did this?"

"Mo-Morgryth," I choked out between shuddering sobs, my voice weak and raw from pain. From that moment on, I would no longer call him by any term of endearment. His name would be forever marked on the scars forming around my throat and the wrath in my heart.

"Kai..." Thalos's voice pulled me back to the present, his hand resting gently on my shoulder. I lifted my gaze to the vastness of my kingdom stretching from Drakorra Spire—the ancient fortress carved into the side of Skyforge Summit, the tallest peak of all.

I stood on the outlook of the fortress perched high on the cliffs of Everreach, as the whispering forest spread out below me, these forests were dense, dark, and filled with towering trees. I closed my eyes, feeling the warmth of Thalos's hand on my shoulder. His scent of spice and pine filled my nostrils, calming me.

I took a steadying breath. When I opened my eyes, my skin burned away into scales as the Drake rose through me, smoke gathered. My large, muscular body radiated strength and authority, the regal black scales gleaming in the setting sun with iridescent hues of blue and purple. We Drakarians wore two skins. Flesh and bone, that of a human and the Drake beneath, the truer half of myself. I stretched my wings, Thalos stepped back, sensing my need for solitude, and returned inside the fortress.

Normally, we would patrol together, being the high King of the Drakarian, it was my duty to protect them all. Even as our numbers dwindled, with no younglings born in the last two hundred years, I carried this responsibility alone.

My claws dug into the same stone where my father's had, bearing the weight of his heartbreak. It should have been avoided, but some of our kind bond for life with only one mate, their souls so deeply intertwined that the death of one inevitably leads to the slow passing of the other. That wouldn't me though, not once Thalos and I find our third.

My father, King Vaelorian Drakmyr lived only another fifty years after my mother's murder. A painfully short time for a Drakarian, who, in ideal conditions, can live well over a thousand years before succumbing to old age.

Drakarians come of age at one hundred and fifty years, yet I became King at only one hundred and twenty. In human terms, I was barely twelve, just a boy tasked with ruling a dying race.

My mother, Serenya of the line of Iskara the fate touched, had been one of the last female Drakarians. Humans have hunted our females relentlessly for their prized metallic scales, which can only be taken by killing us in our Drake form. Though males don't hold the same value. Over the last few centuries, humans turned to dark magic and iron, wielding it to annihilate whatever they coveted or feared.

I took flight, soaring over the rippling treetops, their silvered leaves catching the fading light. My thoughts drifted. Once, our world had been home to countless wondrous creatures, but human factions—driven by power and greed—have wiped them from our world with only the trace of their myths left behind.

Not all humans were like this, Thalos reminds me often. A small smile tugged at my mouth, briefly revealing my jagged teeth, before the weight of my thoughts pressed down on me again.

I flapped my massive onyx wings, circling tighter. Thalos had lost his mother when he was just a youngling. He, too, suffered, though he had been spared the memory of her death. Blessed, perhaps, not to have witnessed the horror as I had.

A deep huff escaped me, sending a cloud of smoke into the cooling air. The burden of my thoughts pressed heavily on my chest as I soared higher, seeking solace in the fading warmth of the setting sun, now slipping low behind the mountain range.

I watched as lantern lights flickered across the mountainside, glowing warmly in the small and large homes scattered along the slopes. Some of my people chose to live as humans, others in their Drake forms. Yet all who lived here, beneath the cliffs of Everreach and within the Whispering Forest, were all under my direct protection. It was my duty to ensure their safety.

As King, I had sentinels patrolling our lands, though I preferred to see the landscape for myself. Flying over it daily brought me a rare sense of calm.

The moon rose high, its silvery light mingling with the soft twinkle of stars that greeted me as I took one final circle over my territory. The air was cool for the early days of summer, and a gentle breeze caressed my scales like a soothing balm. I let my eyes drift close for only a moment. Then I opened my eyes again, taking in the sights and scents of the land below.

Ahead, I gazed at my mountain fortress, Drakorra Spire, its carved spires blending seamlessly with the towering peaks and ancient, sprawling trees. It was a hidden marvel—ancient, proud, and strong—camouflaged against the rugged mountaintop cliffs.

I flapped my wings, tilting toward home. Toward my fortress. Toward Thalos. Toward the ever-present weight that haunted me, the slaughter of the last known female Drakarian. The grim news had been delivered with a finality that burned deep into my soul. I would be the last to rule, destined to lead a race now on the brink of extinction.

Chapter 1

Lyria

The morning light spilled through the thin blue curtains, painting the small room in a soft golden glow. I stretched, listening to the morning greetings of the wildbirds and the sound of my roosters crowing in the distance. Outside, the low hum of the wind whispered through the tall grasses that surrounded my homestead, carrying with it the scent of dew-soaked earth and wildflowers. It was the kind of peace I craved. Simple, quiet, and wholly mine.

Through the small window, I watched as sunlight filtered through the dense trees at the edge of my homestead, casting dappled patterns across the clearing. The protective fog clung low to the ground, swirling gently around the fields I had painstakingly carved out of the dense Forgotten Woods. It was quiet here, save for the soft rustle of leaves and the occasional chatter of birds blended with the familiar sounds of my animals. Hidden deep within the mountain valley of the Ironwilde, my home remained undisturbed. A sanctuary protected by the Faelethian chieftains wards and the land's natural seclusion.

I dressed in simple cotton, with cadmium yellow shirt and a pair of worn russet overalls. Then stepped out of my small bedroom into the open space of my family's cabin. Hugging myself, I rubbed my arms, the cool morning air prickling my skin. The familiar creak of the floorboards greeted me as I moved into the kitchen, the heart of my little home. The air carried the faint, comforting scent of dried herbs and fresh earth, which is as much a part of this place as the worn wood and stone that formed its walls.

I set a full kettle of water on the iron-belly stove, still warm from the coals left burning overnight. It cast a steady heat that filled the cabin. I added a fresh log to feed the stove's hunger, the wood crackling as it caught. While I waited, I braided my auburn hair down my back, tying it off with a strip of worn leather. A few loose strands slipped free, framing my face.

The kettle began to hiss softly, and I poured the steaming water into a clay mug, letting the blend of wild mint, lavender, honeyroot, and elderflower steep. The soothing aroma filled the air as I wrapped my hands around the warm mug and stepped onto the porch. My eyes instinctively scanned the horizon, lingering on the edge of the woods where the mist clung low and thick, shrouding the trees in an otherworldly veil.

The fields stretched just beyond the porch, with neat rows of hay, wheat, and tall silvercorn swaying gently in the breeze. To one side of the simple wooden cabin lay a wattle-fenced garden brimming with lush, edible plants. My homestead, a quiet haven nestled within acres of wild land, was bordered by the towering trees of the Forgotten Woods. Beyond them, the mountain range of the Ironwilde rose, their jagged crests peaking thorough the clouds, and their snow-dusted tops gleaming even in the warmth of early summer.

I took a deep breath, the crisp air filling my lungs as I sipped my tea. For now, all was well. Humans had named these lands, and I often found it strange that we, too, had adopted their odd names for everything. My gaze drifted to the goat pen, and I sighed. The fence needed mending, but that could wait until later in the week. Hopefully the goats wouldn't test the weak spot in the meantime. For now, there was other work to be done.

By the time the animals began to stir, the fog was already lifting, curling away from the fields. I set my mug on the table beside the smooth, worn pine door and pulled on my boots over thick wool socks. With a quick tug to secure them, I stepped off the porch and made my way toward the barn.

The big barn door groaned as I pushed it open, the scent of hay and earth greeting me. My donkey, Pip, flicked his ears in my direction, and the chickens clucked noisily as if demanding attention.

"All right, all right," I greeted them with a cheerful smile, grabbing a pail of feed. "Don't get your feathers in a twist."

The pigs snorted eagerly from their pen as I tossed in scraps from last night's supper. Pip brayed, shoving his head over the stall door, nipping at my sleeve until I scratched behind his ears. "Patience, Pip. You'll get your turn."

The goats bleated as I filled their water troughs, and then eagerly gathered at the lumps of grain I threw into their pen. Life here ran on routines, each day blurring into the next. I didn't mind, the simplicity was a comfort.

With the morning chores done and my afternoon meal eaten, I grabbed my basket and knife, heading toward the woods. The dense trees loomed ahead, their trunks thick with moss and their canopies so tall they seemed to touch the sky. The Forgotten Woods were alive in a way most couldn't understand. There was a hum to the air, a pulse in the ground beneath my feet that spoke of ancient magic. They were also dark, and brimming with life, some of which was dangerous if you didn't know how to tread carefully.

I carried my basket in one hand, my knife strapped to my hip. The woods were a place of solace for me, a sanctuary where I gathered herbs, hunted game, and traded with the Faelethian tribes who lived deeper within. They were good people, fiercely protective of their land and traditions. However, they were also fair and kind to those who respected their ways.

The Faelethian chieftain, Aiyana, maintained wards that kept the woods protected, the ever-present fog ensuring no one wandered too close. It was this alliance with the Faelethians that allowed me to live here, isolated and safe. In return, I offered them herbs, select animal goods (since they neither kept nor hunted animals), and the occasional sweet treat.

It was more than just an alliance to me. For my mother, it had been largely transactional, though she would have been the first to call them friends. For me, however, they were like family, the only people I had ever truly known. I was raised here, born in the very cabin I now called home. Aiyana's healing hands had delivered me when my mother brought me into the world. Their traditions and culture, though different from my own, were deeply woven into the fabric of who I had become.

The sound of hoofbeats reached me just before I stepped into the tree-line. I turned, spotting Dosha approaching in her Fae form, she looked nearly like a horse, just larger and her single long, bone horn made her clearly not. Her silver-gray muzzle was the first to emerge from the mist, followed by her sleek white body speckled with black spots, her glimmering silver simmering horn crowning her head. With a spray of fog, her form shifted, and she landed gracefully on two bare feet. She wore simple cotton leggings and a beadwork tunic, her long silver hair flowing freely behind her. She waved, her smile brightening her brilliant blue eyes, that reminded me of crystalline water, as she slowed to a stop.

"Thought I'd find you here," she called, breathing deeply before pulling me into a warm hug.

"And here I thought you'd forgotten about me," I teased, leaning my basket against my hip.

She laughed, the sound light and carefree. "Forgotten you? Never. The elders have kept me busy, though. You wouldn't believe the trouble some of the younger ones get into."

We walked together into the woods, talking about small things for hours. Things like: the babies born to her tribe, how she was helping handle the youngling foals, the stubbornness of Pip, and the coming summer storms. It was easy, comfortable. Dosha Frostwhisper had been my friend for as long as I could remember, and while our lives often pulled us in different directions, we always found our way back to each other. Her presence was a reminder that I wasn't as alone as I often felt.

The woods were alive with sound from the birds chirping, the rustle of leaves in the wind, to the distant call of a horned hare. We stopped near a patch of moonfern, its silver leaves glinting faintly in the light that filtered through the trees. I crouched to pick a few, the soft hum of the woods surrounding us.

"These bloomed early this year," I said, plucking the delicate stems and placing them in my basket.

Dosha frowned slightly, her usual cheer dimming. "It's the weather," there was an edge to her voice that made me pause.

I glanced up at her, narrowing my eyes. "What aren't you telling me?"

She hesitated, her gaze drifting to the tree-line. "Humans. There've been sightings near the lowlands. Hunters, they say."

My stomach tightened. "Are they getting closer?"

"Not yet," her tone didn't reassure me. "The elders are keeping watch. So should you."

I nodded, my grip tightening on the basket handle and the weight of her words settling heavily on my chest. The humans had never bothered me here, not yet. Not with the chieftain's wards and the remoteness of the valley. Dosha's concern was contagious, and I couldn't shake the feeling that my peace might not last forever. Though, the thought of their presence, of what they could do, gnawed at the edges of my mind.

Dosha nudged me out of my thoughts, grinning down at me with a spark of mischief in her eyes. "We should go to the meadow and run." Her smile widened, playful and daring.

I smirked, giving her a side-eye as I shrugged. "Run, huh?"

The meadow ahead stretched for miles, a vast expanse of tall grasses and wildflowers before reaching the large lake we sometimes swam in. We walked toward the edge of the forest, stepping out from the shade of the last tree into the open air. The sky above was endless, painted in soft hues of twilight, and the glowbees drifted lazily above the swaying grasses.

Without hesitation, Dosha began peeling off her clothes, stepping out of her leggings before slipping her beaded tunic over her head. Her tawny skin gleamed in the fading sunlight, her silver hair cascading down her back in stark contrast to her complexion. She shot me a teasing smile as I set my basket on the ground beside her growing pile of clothes.

I exhaled, undoing the snaps of my overalls and letting them drop to the ground. By the time I glanced back at Dosha, she had already tossed her panties into the pile and was spinning in the open meadow, arms wide, stirring the glowbees into an erratic dance around her.

I chuckled, watching her, this was the Dosha I had always known. The friend, the lover, the companion of my reckless youth. We had lived for these moments of wild, untamed freedom.

With a shrug, I slipped off my top, my breasts bouncing slightly with the movement, before stepping out of my panties and matching her abandon. She squealed in delight, grabbing my hand and tugging me further into the open meadow.

"Race me to the lake, Lyria!" she pleaded, eyes glinting with mischief.

Before I could answer, she was already running, her laughter echoing in the evening air. In a swirl of silver fog, her legs shifted, hooves striking the earth as she galloped ahead, her powerful unicorn form slicing through the tall grass.

Determined to win this time, I sprang forward, my body enveloped in a rush of magic as I shifted mid-stride. A burst of smoke curled around me, and within seconds, my human skin gave way to scales of gleaming gold and copper. My wings spread wide, catching the air, and with one powerful beat, I surged forward, closing the distance between us.

We had done this since childhood, racing across the meadow, weaving through the wildflowers, chasing the thrill of freedom before collapsing into heaps of laughter or plunging into the deep pool of the lake. Though, today, I would win.

She darted beneath me, weaving under my belly and between my clawed feet, her speed unmatched on land. I let out a huff, the rush of warm summer air filling my nostrils as I pushed harder, lifting higher above the ground.

With a sharp flap of my wings, I hovered just above her, then surged forward, neck and neck as the lake came into view. The scent of sun-warmed water and wildflowers filled the air, mingling with the adrenaline in my veins.

Then I pulled ahead.

With a victorious roar, I dropped into the lake, my massive form crashing into the water just as Dosha galloped to the edge. A wave of water drenched her head-to-hoof, and she let out an indignant snort, tossing her mane and sending droplets flying like tiny diamonds in the fading light.

Laughter bubbled up from my chest as I surfaced, shaking the water from my scales. "Yes!" I crowed. "I beat you this time!"

Dosha, half-soaked and glaring with mock indignation, narrowed her luminous eyes before breaking into a grin. "Only because you cheated and flew!"

I smirked. "You never said I couldn't."

She snorted, wading deeper into the lake as water lapped at her legs. "Fine, fine. I'll allow it... this time." With a burst of mist, she shifted back into her human form and floated lazily on her back, gliding toward me.

I chuckled and let myself drift for a moment, the cool water soothing the heat still clinging to me from the flight. This was what I needed. What we both needed. A reminder of who we were before the weight of the world pressed down on us.

"Do you ever think about the other Drakes?" she asked softly, gazing up at my larger form.

I let out a chuff, smoke curling lazily from my nostrils around my body as I shifted back into my skin. I kicked my legs through the water and turned my eyes toward the direction of the fog-thick ravine that carved its way through the mountains. "Sometimes, I wonder if the world is truly as dangerous as my mother said. She was old when she had me, and before she died, she made me promise never to leave. But..." My voice trailed off as I stared into the depths beneath us.

She touched my arm gently. "You don't have to do anything you don't want to. If you do ever choose to leave… I'll help however I can."

I squeezed her hand and gave a small nod.

"For now," I said with a soft smile, "I'm happy here. With my home. With our family."

Then I splashed her, earning a squeal and a wave in return. These were the simple moments I treasured.

Chapter 2

Thalos

Moonlight streamed in through our bedroom window as I sat on my overstuffed green velvet stool, gazing at my reflection in the mirror framed by the intricate carvings of the mahogany vanity. My little collection of bits and bobs sat neatly arranged across its surface, ordered just the way I liked them.

A bowl of warm water and lathered soap rested nearby as I drew the blade along my jaw for the final pass. I wiped my face with a soft cotton cloth, savoring the clean smoothness of my skin. My soft green eyes flicked downward in the mirror, tracing over the bronze tone of my features.

The quiet of my nightly routine always centered me. That calm shattered at the sound of stomping boots in the corridor. I turned just as Kiaza's broad frame filled the doorway and stormed into the room, his presence as commanding as ever. His grim, stoic mask did little to dull the sheer force of energy he carried with him.

I watched him for a moment, silence stretching until a smile tugged at my lips. Warm, inevitable.

"Is our kingdom safely tucked in for the night?" I asked, letting my voice come out light and teasing.

Gods, he was breathtaking, his muscular body exuding strength, yet softened by the way his amber eyes lingered on me. His gaze burned into me until warmth rose to my cheeks, and I quickly turned back to the mirror, pretending I hadn't noticed.

He gave a low grunt of acknowledgment. "Yes, Los." I could hear the faint smile hidden in his voice.

I rubbed a balm of camphor and spice into the skin along my jaw, working it up across my cheeks, and caught his reflection in the mirror. Kiaza watched me, unblinking, heat simmering in his amber gaze. Desire sparked low in my chest before he even touched me. His eyes trailed down the navy-blue silk robe that hung loosely over my frame—exposing my chest, concealing everything else. The silence stretched taut between us until I couldn't bear it any longer.

I rose from the stool and crossed the room. He had already begun unclasping the leather straps of his blades. He never went anywhere without them. It didn't matter that he could shift into a fire-breathing, monstrous beast, Kiaza liked to be prepared. Always ready for war, even in our chamber.

Standing before him, I reached out and brushed a hand along the swell of his bicep, my fingers tracing the uneven ridges of scarred skin. His tension melted under my touch, his shoulders loosening just enough to let me in.

"You know," I whispered, leaning closer so my words brushed his throat, "I'd be happy to fly patrol with you. You don't always have to do it alone." My lips lingered against the warm skin of his neck, breathing in the scent of woodsmoke and iron that clung to him. He exhaled slow and deep, and for a moment, his armor of stoicism lowered.

His hands found my waist, broad palms steady, thumbs hooking into the sash of my robe. When his gaze met mine, the amber fire in his eyes softened, his voice rumbling low. "I can't risk you out there if trouble comes. You're the only one I trust to rule if something happens to me, Thalos."

The words stung, though I tried to mask it. I knew his protectiveness would never fade. No matter how fiercely I longed to share his burdens, he carried pieces of himself alone, tucked behind walls even I couldn't breach. Still, I nodded, letting him see understanding in my face, even if my chest ached with the weight of it.

His hand slid up to cup my cheek, rough fingers burning warm against my skin, while the other pulled me closer. "You're the most important thing to me, 'Los. I love you." His voice cracked faintly. "I couldn't bear to lose you, too."

This small vulnerability in him, rare and unguarded, unraveled me. My heart surged, my body aching to strip away every barrier between us and drag him into our bed.

He pressed his forehead against mine, grounding us, steadying us. His thumb traced my bottom lip, and I drew a sharp breath, my pulse stuttering. Tilting my head, I caught his mouth in a soft kiss. His black hair, streaked with flame-red, fell around us like a curtain. My whisper touched his lips. "I love you too."

His hand threaded into my tousled blond hair, gripping with gentle firmness as his lips pressed harder against mine. His mouth parted, and I melted as his tongue swept past my lips, claiming me in a kiss that left me breathless. A small moan escaped me, muffled and lost between us. My hands roamed over his chest, across soft cotton, over the engraved leather of his chest plate. Every touch between us burned electric, the bond a current I could never put into words.

I reached around him, unbuckling the stiff armor he always wore, the royal crest etched into its surface catching faint glimmers of the lamplight. It slid from him with a heavy thud, the sound reverberating in the stillness like a drumbeat. My hands moved to his shirt, tugging it free as my palms traced the solid lines of his chest, his thick muscle beneath skin mapped with scars. Each mark carried its own story, and I lingered over them as if my touch could ease the weight of all he'd endured.

He crushed me closer, his tongue exploring my mouth with deliberate hunger. I melted into it, eyes fluttering shut. He tasted of the rich wine we'd shared at dinner, roasted meat still on his breath, and the sharp cool of mint clinging to my lips. A groan escaped me as heat pooled low, my cock growing hard between us, my need for him stirring deep.

His fingers wove into my hair, tugging just enough to make me gasp. The way he held me—firm, commanding, yet aching with need—left me spinning, my desire spiraling unchecked. Our kiss deepened, fevered, consuming, until I thought I might burn alive in it. My hands dropped to his belt, fumbling the buckle, eager to strip away every barrier until there was nothing between us.

Suddenly he broke away, breath ragged, his forehead pressing to mine as though he needed the contact to steady himself. His hand caught my wrist, halting me.

The sound that left me was small, helpless, I let out a small whimper of frustration and want.

"'Los," he rasped, voice weighted with something more than desire, "we need to talk."

I squeezed my eyes shut, frustration burning through me. I didn't want to talk—gods, not now. Not about duties or destiny or the endless weight pressing down on us. Just one night, I wanted him, only him. No crowns. No ghosts. No war.

Biting my lower lip, I forced a breath steady enough to keep my body still, even as every part of me ached. "Alright, Kia," I whispered, frustration softening into surrender. I would give in. I always did.

I drew back, and he let me go, though his hands lingered against me, reluctant, as if parting was its own wound. I moved to my side of the bed, shoving back the heavy layers of fur and woven blankets. The great feather mattress dipped beneath me, the carved posts of our bed looming like sentinels. This room had always been our sanctuary, yet tonight it felt heavier, suffocating with all that was unsaid.

Kiaza sat on the edge of his side, his broad shoulders bowed, fire dimmed but smoldering. I slid beneath the blankets, studying him in silence. His jaw was tight, the lines carved deep as though chiseled there by years of battle. Whatever he was about to say, it weighed on him.

"You know what I'm going to bring up," he said at last, his voice quieter than I'd expected, it was low, almost somber.

I nodded, the ache in my chest tightening. "The Ironwilde."

His amber eyes flicked to me, ruby fire subdued but still burning. "It's no longer rumor, Thalos." He leaned forward, forearms braced on his thighs, hands clasped tight. "The whispers spread farther every day. They say she's there. Alive, hidden, trapped in her Drake form." His breath hitched, the faintest break in his control. "If it's true... if there's even the smallest chance, I have to go. I leave at week's end."

The words landed sharp, though I'd half expected them. My throat tightened, but I forced my voice even. "You've spoken of this before. But leaving in days, with the kingdom already splintering?"

He turned then, his gaze scorching, magic flickering hot in his eyes. "I know what I ask of you. But if she lives... she is the key. The last female could save us. You've seen it yourself... The losses, the dwindling numbers. Not a youngling in over a century. If we let her slip away, if we do nothing..." His hands clenched tighter. "We may already be too late."

I swallowed against the knot in my throat, his words cutting deep because they were true. Too true.

My mother's face flashed in my mind, though it had been so long that memory blurred at the edges. She had been one of the last females to fall. They said hunters found her, slaughtered for her scales, leaving only scraps behind to mark her end. I had been a youngling then, still clumsy in my Drake form, too small to understand, too old to forget. That wound had never healed. It never would.

Now, here I sat, one of the youngest Drakarians left. Born just before the great decline. Born to inherit ashes. I knew I wasn't alone in that grief we all had lost mothers, sister, and daughters.

Still, the thought of Kiaza leaving, of facing dangers unknown while the burden of the kingdom fell squarely on my shoulders, made my chest tighten. "You just expect me to stay here and deal with everything while you go chasing legends in the wilderness?" My voice came out sharper than I intended.

"It's not chasing legends, 'Los," he said steadily, rising as his fingers went to the ties of his pants. "It's survival. If I don't go, we could lose everything." His tone softened as he glanced at me. "I trust you to hold it together while I'm gone. Especially with Natrix coming."

Her name hit like a stone in my gut. I leaned back against the headboard, staring at his bare chest and his scarred skin catching the moonlight. "Natrix," I muttered, tasting the weight of it. "Of course. She's still pushing this alliance?"

"She is...as long as it's you she deals with," Kiaza confirmed, a small smirk tugging at his mouth as his trousers fell away, leaving him in nothing but thin cotton. "The Abyssians are critical to controlling the seas. Their spies, their ships, their reach... we can't afford to lose that. Besides, she respects you. She never had much fondness for me."

"Respect isn't the word I'd use," I said dryly, raking a hand through my hair. The memory of Nati's sharp tongue and fire-bright temper flickered through me. She was relentless, uncompromising, a sea storm all her own. It made her a brilliant leader, yes. But it had made her impossible for us.

"She still carries feelings for you," Kiaza said, his voice calm, without jealousy, as though simply stating fact. He was always so observent but she didn't sugar coat or hide her feelings. He slid into bed beside me, his bare shoulder brushing mine, the heat of his body a steady presence.

"She does," I admitted, though my own feelings had cooled to nothing but history. "Though we both know she was never right for us. She couldn't share. Selfishness is poison in a bond like ours. Trying to tie her into us would have broken what we built instead of making it stronger." I reached for his thigh and rubbed him gently I needed to touch him, be close to him.

Kiaza inclined his head, slow and sure. "It was the right choice. If fate has someone else in mind for us, we'll know when the time comes."

"You're right," I conceded softly. "Still, the Abyssians' alliance matters. I'll make sure it holds. I'll deal with Natrix." My fingers drawing small circles on his thigh. Kraken like her were tidal waves barely leashed, even in human skin. She would test me.

Kiaza's shoulders eased a fraction, though his gaze stayed flint-hard. "I know you will. I just hate leaving this in your hands while I go. Not with humans pressing deeper into our lands, carving the forests with their machines, and stripping away all that is scared to us piece by piece."

He reached down, covering my hand with his, and I gave his thigh a gentle squeeze. "I can handle it. She knows where we stand. I agree this mission matters more right now. And you..." My voice softened. "You need to do this."

His fingers curled tightly around mine, his amber eyes steady and full of fire sparking with a ruby glow. "I do, 'Los. If she's alive, we can't lose her. Our kind won't survive much longer without hope."

He settled down amongst the pillows and blankets in our bed, and I followed leaning my head against his shoulder, letting out a long sigh. "You're impossible," I murmured, no heat behind the words. Just longing.

"I wish I could take you with me," he whispered, pressing a kiss to my temple. "Our kingdom and I need you here more."

I turned slightly, my cheek brushing against the warm skin of his neck, inhaling the scent that always clung to him, with a hint of something more primal beneath, like embers trapped in a vessel. "You always say that," I whispered. "I know it's the truth, but I still hate being left behind."

His hand moved into my hair, his palm spreading across the back of my head, fingers threading through the strands like he was memorizing the texture. "I know," he said, voice thick with the weight of what neither of us wanted to say. "And, I hate leaving you."

I tilted my head just enough to meet his eyes. The air between us shifted; it was warm, heavy with the ache of separation not yet come. The bond thrummed between our chests like a second heartbeat, heat coiling in my belly.

"Then don't leave so soon," I whispered, even though I knew he would and I would let him. My hand slowly moved up his thigh and grazing his hard length waiting for me.

His gaze darkened, and the last of his restraint cracked as he surged forward. Our mouths collided in hungry, deep, desperation. His lips tasted like everything familiar and everything I was afraid to lose.

A low groan rumbled from his chest, vibrating through mine, as his arms tightened around me and shifting me onto his lap. The hard line of him pressed against me, only the thin cotton between us, sending a shiver through me. I rocked my hips, grinding slow and teasing, while my fingers traced up his chest, nails dragging lightly over the warm, solid plane of his chest.

"Gods, I'll miss you," he rasped, kissing along my arm, beard scraping deliciously against my skin.

"Then don't waste tonight," I murmured, biting at his lower lip before claiming his mouth again.

He yanked the belt of my robe loose, and I arched back, letting the fabric slip from my arms as he hands teased down my chest and belly. I smirked down at him, sitting exposed and straddling him, heat pulsing between us.

I leaned in, kissing his neck as I rolled my hips against his, our bodies perfectly aligned, separated only by the last thin barrier of fabric between us.

"Tell me my fire... do you want my mouth first or my ass?" My voice low and husky against his ear, as I sucked his lower lobe into my mouth.

His growl vibrated through me as his hands clamped hard on my hips.

The firelight flickered golden across his torso, shadows dancing with the bond's thrum. The air around us grew thick with woodsmoke, sweat, and the heady musk of arousal curling together, clinging to our skin like incense.

As his hand slid between us, wrapping around my cock, thick and aching with need. "Kia—" His name left my lips and I arched with a gasp. His touch was slow, torturous, teasing, each stroke making my toes curl and my breath stutter.

"You're always so hard for me, my fucking good boy, my storm," he murmured, his voice low and rough, like thunder rolling over distant peaks.

"Only for you," I panted, threading my fingers through his hair and tugging him up to capture his mouth in another kiss. Our tongues tangled, teeth clashing with hunger, and our bond flared bright, wild, and undeniable.

He pulled the last scrap of fabric pulled aside, as the final barrier gone. As he shifted us slightly I felt his cock, hot and wet with pre-cum, as it slid between the curve of my ass. My hips rolled in response, eager, desperate. I throbbed in his grip, every nerve alive with wanting.

Then he pressed forward, slow and deliberate, his cock sinking into my tightness with one claiming thrust. We moaned in unison, as he sank into me, my nails digging into his chest, I arched and he stroked my hard dick in rhythm with his thrusts. The stretch, the burn, the fullness, for me it was everything.

My thighs clenched around his waist, anchoring him to me. I rode him, matching each deliberate thrust with a roll of my hips, letting his rhythm fill me, claim me, worship me with the press of muscle and the pull of his hand.

The cadence built, raw and relentless. Skin on skin, the bed creaking, our moans braided into one breathless song. Each gasp, each kiss, each hard, sweet buck piled on the last until there was no room in the world for anything but him.

"Fuck, Kia...right there. Make me...make me come, my King." I poured the words through the bond and felt it flare in answer, bright hot threads snapping tight between us. My right hand closed hard around his left wrist, his hand guided my hip, steadying and driving me. With his other hand he stroked up my cock to the tip and back, a cruel, delicious tempo that drove me higher.

The room narrowed to the press of our bodies and the thunder of our blood. He filled my mind through the tether, *"Cum hard for me. Give me something to remember while I'm gone...something I'll have to come back for."*

I couldn't catch my breath. I braced back on my hands, and the world split open—pleasure tearing through me like wildfire. I howled his name. "Kia." Heat folded in me and I came, hard and blinding, ribbons of release soaking his sweat-slick stomach while we still moved, still clung to the last, raw connection.

He followed, with one final thrust deep inside me, and his growl was low and primal. "Los." Magic arced between us—raw, incandescent—igniting each tether that bound us until the bond sang louder than our ragged breathing.

I bent then, licking at his chest, tasting salt and him mixing with the sweet tang that clung to my tongue. He grinned, satisfied, and threaded his fingers through my hair as he drew me close and kissed me, sharing the taste of us.

Silence folded over the room, but the bond still hummed, loud and warm against my skin. I collapsed onto him, our bodies glistening in the firelight, heartbeat pressed to heartbeat. He stroked my spine with feather-light touches while I traced lazy circles across his chest, letting the aftershocks recede.

"You have to come back to me," I murmured into the hollow of his collarbone.

"I will," he breathed. "Always."

Chapter 3

Kiaza

The fresh morning air was cool for early summer, and the scent of rain lingered in the moist foliage below. The world was painted in rich, deep hues—lush greens, dark browns, and vibrant specks of purple, pink, blue, and yellow scattered across the ground like jewels. It would take about two days of flight to reach the Mist-clad Peaks of the Ironwilde, soaring over rolling meadows and dense, sprawling canopies. Fortunately, I wouldn't have to pass over any large human cities. If I did, I'd be forced to shift into my human skin and travel by horse or train, which was a tedious and inefficient use of my time.

Flying was faster, more freeing. It spared me the discomfort of mingling with humans, an experience that always left my skin crawling and my jaw clenched. Being so close to them—their hunters and trappers—sickened me. They treated killing my kind as sport, using our scales in their magic potions or as gaudy decorations in their homes. To them, we weren't people; we were a resource to be exploited.

Smoke curled from my nostrils as I snorted, my irritation simmering just beneath the surface. My jaw tightened at the thought. Perhaps it was our long lives that set them against us, or their envy of the magic they lacked. Whatever the reason, their cruelty knew no bounds.

They were cunning, and their sheer numbers alone made them formidable. Their reproduction rate was absurd—like wildfire spreading unchecked—and now they had mastered black powder and lead, their gunslingers more dangerous than ever.

No longer did you have to be a skilled swordsman or possess the courage to face your prey. A coward could hide behind a wagon or crouch on a rooftop, taking aim from a safe distance and ending a life with a single pull of the trigger. Firearms had replaced the age-old clashing of steel with the deafening crack of gunshots, and where once battlefields were won by strength and honor, now they were decided by speed and powder.

Their technology extended beyond weapons. Railways stretched across their lands, iron beasts belching smoke as they carried humans farther and faster than ever before. Factories churned out tools and goods at a pace that rivaled their insatiable need to consume. Even in remote towns, you could find signs of their so-called progress: telegraph wires strung between wooden poles, steam-powered mills grinding grain into flour, and oil lamps lighting streets long after the sun had set. It was as if they sought to tame the very world itself, bending nature to their will without a thought for the consequences.

My wings beat harder as I climbed higher, the air thinning and cool against my scales. I shook the thoughts from my head, focusing on the journey ahead. The Ironwilde waited, and with them, perhaps, the key to saving what remained of my kind.

There was one settlement I'd have to pass through in my human skin. Just a few miles East of the Ironwilde lay the town of Brakthollow, where I planned to gather a few more supplies for my trek through the mountain range itself. The thick forest bog stretched along the base of the southern mountains, where the fog never lifted. Humans avoided the area, their fear of the so-called evil spirits within, keeping them at bay.

The mountain range curved from the south along the east, wrapping around a central valley that was visible only from the sky. Stories, myths, and legends surrounded these peaks, their reputation enough to deter most from exploring. The cool summers and punishing winters made the region undesirable to humans—for now.

Every year, it seemed their towns and cities grew larger, spreading out. They dug up more of the land, claimed more space, and bred endlessly. In the past hundred years alone, I swear their numbers had tripled, their insatiable expansion threatening to swallow the wild places of the world.

The sun dipped low over the horizon, painting the sky in streaks of amber and crimson. My body was flight-heavy and sore. I hadn't flown this far in years. To make matters worse, I was certain Thalos had packed everything we owned into the massive bag strapped to my back. It dug into my scales with every beat of my wings, making the journey even more exhausting.

My magic allowed me to absorb smaller items into my body when I shifted—clothes, armor, accessories, even the knives I kept strapped to me. But larger bags or packs? Not a chance. If only it worked that way. Life would be so much easier if I didn't have to carry all this weight.

Some Drakarian believed it was bad luck to shift with anything on you. They claimed it could disrupt your magic, throwing it off balance. Personally, I thought it was bullshit. I hardly used my magic for anything beyond flight these days, so I wasn't about to drop my drawers, strip naked just to take flight. Plus, if I needed to shift back for any reason and I would end up butt-ass naked in front of random strangers? No, fucking thank you.

So, I ignored the superstition and shifted with my gear, magic-disruption risks be damned. Honestly, I think the whole thing was just an excuse for public nudity—some ridiculous tradition for Drakarian who wanted to let their dicks hang out.

I spotted a clearing in the forest near a winding creek, the perfect place to set up camp for the night. I descended slowly, my large wings stirring up leaves and debris as I flapped them in steady, measured beats. My back talons touched the moist grass first, sinking slightly into the damp earth. My tail swished behind me, scattering the fluffy seeds of wishstar flowers into the air. Glowbees buzzed angrily, their delicate lights flickering as they darted around, disturbed by my arrival.

Shaking myself off, I carefully pulled the massive canvas bag from my back and set it down with a tender talon, mindful not to tear it. I stepped forward and, with a puff of smoke, shifted into my human skin. A groan escaped me as I stretched my arms high above my head, easing the tension in my muscles. My fingers scratched absently at my groomed beard, and I exhaled deeply, taking in the serene surroundings.

I bent over and unbuckled the leather straps securing the pack, digging through it until I found the sandwiches Thalos had made for me before I left this morning. They were neatly wrapped in waxed cloth to keep them fresh for a few days. After that, I'd have to hunt, forage, or pick up supplies in the town before heading deep into the mountains. I wasn't even sure how long I'd be searching the Ironwilde—a fact I'd been honest about with Thalos.

I sighed, remembering his cool anger when we discussed it. Thalos wasn't quick to temper; even when rage simmered beneath the surface, he kept his composure, his patience seemingly endless. I'd never understood how he could be so forgiving. I'd spent my whole life keeping others at arm's length, yet when Thalos came to serve as my adviser after his father's death, he broke through my walls. He was smart, capable, and far better at handling our people—and outsiders—than I was. We'd fallen in love quickly, though it took me forty years to admit my feelings and settle into a life with him.

My fingers brushed over the mate bond mark on my left wrist, the faint lines warm beneath my touch. A small smile tugged at my lips as I reached back into the pack for my canteen, then carried it and the sandwiches to a nearby boulder. Settling down, I unwrapped the sandwich—a simple yet satisfying combination of salami and cheese—and took a bite. As I chewed, I let my magic channel through our mate bond, reaching out to Thalos.

"How was your day, 'Los?" I sent the thought, the connection between us humming faintly in the back of my mind.

"Long..." came his reply, his tone laced with a quiet weariness. There was a pause, the silence stretching before he added, *"I miss you already. How was yours?"*

I leaned back against the boulder, letting the connection through our bond linger, warm and steady. It wasn't the same as having Thalos beside me, but it was enough to chase away the ache of distance. I took another bite of my sandwich, savoring the salty richness of the salami paired with the sharp tang of the cheese. Simple, yet it reminded me of home, and of him.

"I'm already sore from the flight," I sent through the bond, keeping the tone light. *"You could have packed a little less, you know."*

A soft chuckle echoed in my mind. *"If I left it up to you, you'd be living on dried meat and water. You need real food, Kia."*

I huffed, though a small smile crept across my face. *"I could have hunted. I do know how to survive, you know."*

"I'm sure you do," he replied, the faint humor in his voice carrying through the bond. *"This way, you don't have to. Besides, I made sure to include something sweet for later. It's in the side pocket of the pack."*

Curiosity piqued, I glanced back at the pack. *"What did you sneak in there?"*

"Not telling. You'll have to wait and see." His soft teasing made me long to taste his lips.

I shook my head, as my lips curled into a smile. *"You're insufferable."*

"That's why you love me," he teased, the warmth of his presence flickering in my mind like the embers of a fire.

I let the bond go quiet for a moment, enjoying the connection and the faint hum of his thoughts still brushing against mine. The quiet of the clearing surrounded me, the rustling leaves and soft babble of the creek blending into a soothing backdrop. The glowbees, now calm, hovered lazily over the wishstar flowers, their light faint but steady.

"How are things at the Spire?" I finally asked, my tone shifting to something more serious, finishing the last bite of my sandwich and washing it down with a swig from the canteen.

"Busy," he admitted. *"The council meeting dragged on longer than expected. Everyone has an opinion about the upcoming talks with Natrix. Most of the council supports the treaty, though a few still think it's too risky."*

"It's not risky...it's necessary," I replied, my tone sharpening. *"The Abyssians are the only ones who can control the seas, and with Morgryth and his rogue Drakarians hiding gods-know-where, we need their help. If Natrix and her clans can strengthen the trade routes and cut off the humans who work with him, it could save countless lives."*

Thalos's voice softened through the bond. *"I know, Kia. That's why I've been pushing this. Nat understands what's at stake as much as we do. She might be difficult sometimes, yet her loyalty to her people—and to us—is real."*

"She does have a way of getting things done," I admitted, leaning back against the boulder. *"Even if she's still her usual fiery self."*

Thalos chuckled lightly. *"She wouldn't be Nat if she weren't. She really isn't the problem some of the council makes her out to be. We both know she's more capable than most of them combined."*

I let out a huff, my thoughts turning back to the council's endless bickering. *"They don't see the bigger picture. They focus on what's comfortable, what's known. We simply can't afford that anymore. Not with Morgryth out there, and not with the humans pressing harder into our lands."*

"They'll come around," his voice was calm, his confidence steadying me. *"They always do."*

I nodded, running my hand over the mate bond mark on my wrist. The soft hum of our connection gave me a sense of grounding I didn't often allow myself. *"This treaty could shift everything,"* I sent the thought to him, after a moment I continued. *"If it helps us find where Morgryth has been hiding, we might finally be able to stop him—and his hunters."*

"And bring our people some peace," Thalos added. *"That's why it matters. It's not just about survival anymore, Kia. It's about giving them a future."*

His words settled over me like a weight, one I carried willingly. *"That's why I need to find her,"* I closed my eyes, my resolve firm as I continued. *"If she's out there—if the last female is alive—I can't leave her in danger. Not with the humans, not with Morgryth. She deserves safety. She deserves to come home."*

"I know," Thalos' words were gentle. *"I understand why you had to go."*

I closed my eyes for a moment, letting the truth of his words sink in. *"I just wish I knew how long this search would take. "*

"If she is real, you'll find her," Thalos replied, his certainty in me unwavering. *"If anyone can, it's you. Just be careful. Don't get lost out there. You have to come back. I can handle Nat, the council, and everything else for a while... Kia, this kingdom...and I...need you."* I could feel his longing and sadness through our bond.

"You'd manage just fine," I answered with a small smile tugging at my lips. *"Don't worry. I'll come back. Always."*

"You'd better," he teased lightly, though I could feel the depth of his sincerity. *"You promised me forever."*

"And I don't break promises," I sent that truth firmly through our bond, the resolve in my tone was as much for him as for myself.

Chapter 4

Lyria

I sat on a small wooden stool at the yellow-painted milking stand, the warm, hay-scented air of the barn wrapping around me. A welcome summer breeze brushed the loose strands of my hair across my sweat-dampened brow. I breathed in deeply, wiping my forehead with my arm before returning to milking Stella, my little black-and-white goat.

Her udder was warm and firm, full of milk that streamed into the bucket below with each steady pull of my fingers. Stella stood contentedly in the milking stand, happily munching her grain. She let out a soft bleat, and I murmured, "That's it, girl. Don't worry about me. I know I've been on edge lately, just relax." My voice was meant to soothe her, though I suspected I was saying it more for myself.

Suddenly, the rooster darted past, chasing a hen down the dirt path outside. I flinched, startled by the ruckus. My heart raced for a moment before I sighed, shaking my head. I'd been so tense these past few days. Dosha's warning about the human hunters growing bolder and venturing closer to our sanctuary weighed heavily on me.

We had been in hiding long before I was born, and even though I was 318 years old, nearly 32 by human standards, the fear of discovery lingered. Our kind aged so much slower than humans, our magic gifting us incredibly long lives.

That same magic made it rare for our kind to reproduce, even though we could choose when and with whom to procreate. Our pregnancies lasted as long as a human's, but multiples were unheard of. My mother had warned me of the dangers many Drakarian mothers faced in the early years of raising younglings. Around their first year of life, the first shift would come. From then until roughly their tenth year, a youngling remained almost entirely in their Drake form, their bodies still learning to balance the pull of both shapes. Only after that age could they shift between forms with ease. Because of this, most Drakarian females chose to remain in their Drake form while raising their young, guarding them fiercely and teaching them survival until shifting became second nature.

I couldn't imagine doing it in my human skin. "Could you picture that, Stella?" I asked, chuckling softly. "Me chasing after a youngling Drake, my hair singed from fire?" My laugh grew louder, and Stella let out a bleat as if in agreement.

Buttercup, my tri-colored goat, nudged my arm impatiently, clearly ready for her turn. "Alright, Buttercup, hold your horns," I teased, giving Stella a gentle pat before setting the full bucket aside and freeing her, she moved off of the stand. My eyes drifted to the baby goats, watching as they leapt and kicked in the hay, their tiny hooves scattering golden straw. Their carefree energy brought a much-needed smile to my face, a fleeting moment of peace in an increasingly uncertain world.

My smile lingered as I finished milking Buttercup, her contented bleats filling the quiet barn. I set the second bucket beside Stella's and wiped my hands on the hem of my apron. Tonight was the Full Moon Circle with the Faelethians, and I needed to prepare.

The Full Moon was sacred to the tribe, a time for reinforcing the protective barriers that kept these woods hidden from the outside world. Aiyana, the chieftain and shaman, led the rituals with an authority that seemed to resonate from the earth itself. Dosha always teased me for my awe of her, I couldn't help it, there was something otherworldly about Aiyana's presence, as if the moonlight danced just for her.

I closed the barn doors behind me and carried the milk buckets to the cabin. The soft clink of glass jars echoed in the quiet as I poured the milk into them, setting aside what I'd trade with the Faelethians tomorrow. They rarely asked for much, just a few herbs, some honey, and sometimes fresh milk. I always brought more than they needed. It was the least I could do for their protection.

As the sun dipped lower, casting the sky in hues of pink and orange, I bathed quickly in the small wooden tub by the cabin, the cool water shocking against my skin. I scrubbed away the day's work, rinsing the sweat and dust from my hair. Clean and refreshed, I pulled on a simple dress of soft green wool, its hem embroidered with swirling patterns of vines and flowers. A small shawl of spun silk, dyed in shades of twilight blue, wrapped around my shoulders.

The Faelethians always looked stunning during these ceremonies, their beadwork catching the moonlight like scattered stars. My simple attire seemed plain in comparison, it was comfortable and practical, and just how I liked it. I slipped on soft leather boots and tied my hair back with a strip of green ribbon, letting a few curls fall loose around my face.

I grabbed my basket of offerings—jars of honey, bundles of dried herbs, and a small pouch of sugar. The Faelethians loved sweet things, especially Dosha, who always begged for extra honey to drizzle over roasted roots.

By the time I reached the edge of the woods, the moon was rising, casting silvery light over the trees. The fog shifted around me as if alive, parting to reveal the faintly glowing path that led to the Faelethian village. Their magic hummed in the air, a low, steady thrum that sent a chill up my spine.

Dosha was the first to greet me, her silver hair catching the moonlight like a halo. She grinned, reaching out to take my basket. "You're late," she teased, though her tone was playful.

"I'm always late," I replied, returning her smile. "Blame the goats."

"They're lucky you love them so much," Dosha said, peering into the basket and pulling out the pouch of sugar. "You spoil us."

"Not as much as you spoil me," I said, nudging her shoulder as we walked toward the clearing.

The circle was already forming when we arrived. Faelethians stood in quiet reverence, their tunics and dresses adorned with intricate beadwork and feathers. Aiyana stood at the center, her tall, commanding figure framed by the glow of the fire. Her long white hair cascaded down her back, her wrinkled hands and face showed her wisdom, and her voice, soft yet powerful, carried over the gathering.

She welcomed each of us in turn, her sharp eyes meeting mine as I approached. "Lyria," she said, her voice warm. "It is good to see you."

"And you, Grandmother," I replied, dipping my head in respect. Everyone called her Grandmother, as was tradition.

The ceremony began as the moon reached its peak. Aiyana's voice rose in song, leading the tribe in a chant that resonated through the trees. The barriers around the woods shimmered faintly, their edges glowing as the Faelethians poured their magic into them. I felt the power ripple through the air, a protective force that wrapped around us like a cocoon. The fog grew thick around the edges of the circle and moved quickly outwards.

When the chanting quieted, Aiyana stepped forward, her staff gleaming in the moonlight. "Tonight," she began, her voice steady, "we share the story of the Ironwilde—a tale of loss, strength, and survival."

My heart quickened at the mention of the mountain range. I leaned in slightly, eager to hear more.

"These peaks," Aiyana continued, gesturing to the distant range visible through the gaps in the trees, "were once the fertile nesting grounds to Drakarians. Proud, mighty beings who ruled the skies and guarded the balance of our world. Then the greed of human kind brought destruction to their kind. Few remain now, and even fewer remember the truth of what was lost."

Her gaze swept the circle, her words resonating with quiet authority. "Legends speak of the return of the Drakarians, led by the one destined to restore balance to nature—a female, hidden within the mists. Some say she is cursed, trapped in her Drake form as she awaits her mates. Others believe she slumbers, waiting for those worthy to share her bond and seed her soil. Whatever the truth may be, she carries the last hope for her kind."

Aiyana's voice grew softer, yet no less powerful, as she continued. "She is not alone. Many seek her. For power, for revenge, for greed. Yet those who love her, who see her for what she truly is, will protect her with all they have. For she is more than hope. She is life itself, and with her, the balance of nature."

A chill coursed through me as her words settled over the gathering, their weight pressing against my chest. Her sharp eyes found mine, holding my gaze with an intensity that stole my breath. In that moment, I knew her words were more than legend. They were a reminder of the promise she had made to my mother and to me.

Dosha sat beside me, her quiet presence grounding. As I pulled my shawl tighter around my shoulders, she slipped her hand into mine, her fingers warm against my skin. She gave my hand a gentle squeeze, a silent reassurance.

I couldn't ignore the unease stirring within me—an instinct, a subtle ripple in my magic that refused to settle. Something was coming; I could feel it. Dosha's touch was steady and calm, soothed the edges of my frayed nerves, reminding me that Aiyanna's words rang true, I wasn't alone.

However, I wanted to speak with Aiyanna in private. Her story lingered in my mind. She'd spoken of *mates*, not a single one, multiple? Though I'd had relationships before, I had never truly mated. Not with a blood bond sealed in magic.

You could fall into a love that felt destined, that was written in the stars, but fate never *forced* your hand. In the end, it was always a choice. Here, we chose our mate—or mates. Having more than one could offer protection, stability... though it also meant dividing your magic between them all.

Aiyana stood near the edge of the glowing circle, her silhouette haloed by moonlight as she murmured to one of the younger Faelethians. When she turned to me, her lavender eyes found mine with unsettling precision, like she had been expecting me all along.

"Walk with me," she said, her voice low and certain.

I followed without question, letting the hush of the forest swallow us. Glowbees floated lazily through the trees, their golden light flickering across Aiyana's pale silver hair. We stopped in a secluded grove where moonlight filtered through the branches like strands of spider-silk thread.

"You heard the story tonight," she began without preamble, "what you may not know is that it was never just a legend. It is a prophecy."

My stomach tightened. "Prophecy?"

Aiyana nodded slowly. "The return of balance. The restoration of lifeblood to the land and all magic-kind. It will not come from power alone, it will come from connection, through a bonded triad. Three souls, linked not by chance, but with purpose. By fate."

Her gaze held mine, sharp and ancient. "The one at the center of it will not be a king. Nor a warrior. It will be a female. A Drake bound by magic and blood, hidden in mist until the time is right. She will choose her mates, not only one. Only together can they awaken the true magic that will restore our people and revive the land."

I opened my mouth, though no words came.

"You carry the blood of the ancients," she continued softly. "Though you haven't met them yet, your mates will find you. The bond will not be easy. It never is. When it comes, you will know. You will feel it in your bones. Your choice will shape more than just your life. It will shape our survival."

I stared at her, my pulse a wild beat against my ribs. "How do you know it's me?"

Aiyana smiled faintly, brushing her fingers over a faded braid charm at her wrist. "Because I made a promise to your mother. Because I saw the glimmer of your golden aura as you grew in her belly and because the land itself whispers your name in the roots."

Silence stretched between us, thick with the scent of moss and moonflowers.

"I'm not ready," I admitted.

"No one ever is," she said. "The magic will know. It always does."

The night air clung to my skin as I made my way back to the homestead, the soft rustle of wind through the trees a gentle hush behind me. Lunar moths fluttered by, and star mushrooms glowed lazily in the darkness. My steps louder than I cared for as I walked the path, each step grounding me back in the now, away from the weight of prophecy and ancient promises.

My cabin came into view, its silhouette sturdy against the moonlit backdrop. Warm orange light flickered in the windows from the embers I'd banked in my fireplace before leaving. I pushed open the door and was greeted with the comforting scent of woodsmoke, barn musk, and chamomile. Home.

With a sigh, I hung my shawl by the door and moved quietly through the room, checking that the latch was fastened, the kettle set to heat again, and the hearth still glowing. My body moved on instinct, even as my mind was still stuck in Aiyana's words—bonded triads, fate, magic restoring the land…

I snorted softly to myself as I stripped down to my slip and crawled under the thick quilt on my bed. "Sure," I muttered aloud. "Me. Center of some ancient prophecy. Why not throw in a wicked queen and some pixie dust while you're at it."

I rolled onto my side and tucked the blanket around my shoulders, staring at the knot in the ceiling beam like it might answer me.

"I'm not some wide-eyed youngling," I grumbled. "I've got goats to milk and fences to mend, weeds to pull. Not time to play chosen one."

Still… the idea lingered, like the scent of rain just before a storm breaks.

My mother had always told me I was different, that there was something special in me, and warned me to be careful who I trusted. Honestly though, I'd planned to live much like she had: quietly, tucked away in our little slice of paradise. Maybe one day I'd have a daughter of my own. I didn't need a mate for that. Truly, any male Drakarian would do.

Wasn't that what my mother did? She found a rogue, took what she needed, and disappeared before he ever knew I existed. Simple. Practical. No fuss. I let out a loud huff, amused and annoyed in equal measure.

My multicolored cat, Furgas, jumped on to my stomach, purring like a contented old man. I scooped him up and pressed my face into his warm fur.

"Alright, Furgas," I murmured with a smirk. "Next Drake I meet. He's giving me a baby."

I giggled to myself, the absurdity of it all tickling my ribs as I breathed in the familiar scents of hay, milk, and woodsmoke. I set Furgas on the pillow next to me and he curl up in his spot falling asleep.

Turning again on my other side settling further in to the cozy comfort of my bed, my mind still a swirl of thoughts. Triad bonds weren't unheard of, they were just rare. Powerful. Dangerous, even. Sharing magic between three was no light thing. Bonding? I'd had lovers, yes, and flings that meant more than I liked to admit… but a true bond? One sealed by choice and magic?

I sighed and shut my eyes, chasing sleep before the thoughts could get too heavy.

Let Aiyana chase omens and fate. I had chores in the morning, and I'd be damned if I let some ancient whisper steal my peace tonight.

Chapter 5

Thalos

The salted wind hit me long before the sea came into view, where large wooden docks housed vast ships, and crests of crashing waves.

After a two day ride through the switchback trails of the mountain pass, the sharp scent of brine and smoked fish that marked Driftshore made my nose twitch. I eased my mare along the muddy road, keeping to the shadows of the cliffside buildings. In this port city, a man with a mountain drawl and a worn coat passed easily as Durnathi—one of the reclusive human factions, known for their rugged strength and distrust of the coast.

No one looked twice, so long as I didn't wear the royal crest or shift beneath the open sky.

My Drakarian blood stayed quiet beneath my skin, banked like low-burning coals. Hidden. I bore no visible markings that gave me away as a Drake, thanks mostly to my magic. Some of us, those born with strong magic, couldn't suppress it even in human form. The few rare mixed-bloods? They were different. Born fully human, without a true magical form, and without the lifespan of our kind. Their magic, if any, was a flicker, weak, and unstable. That's why most of us didn't mix-breed. The cost was too high, but it did happen for love or alliances.

I dismounted just beyond the old customs house and led the horse to a stable tucked between two crumbling fish stalls. The stable boy was human, likely of the Bravarn faction, barely past thirteen. He didn't even ask my name, just took the reins and nodded like he'd seen ten of me that morning already.

Good.

I pulled my hood up, with hands too soft to be a mountain man, and made my way toward "The Tipsy Tentacle" an Abyssian-owned watering hole carved into the bones of the old dockside. A place that reeked of fish oil and secrets.

A large kraken tentacle was carved in wood above the entrance as the rusted metal hinges creaked when I pushed open the heavy door, stepping in my eyes adjusted to the low light.

Inside, the air thickened. Salt, smoke, and fermented seaweed clung to the walls, the dark corners had barnacles clustered on the soggy wood. The pub was dim and damp, lit only by globes of soft-blue light that pulsed, glass jars filled with bioluminescent algae, hung from the ceiling every few feet. Music was low, droning sea-pipes as it hummed through the space like a heartbeat. The patrons barely looked up. Abyssians didn't start fights without cause, though they always finished them.

I spotted her immediately. Natrix Dravessai.

Reclined like she owned the damn room, well, because she did. Her boots kicked up, beads rattling in her wild hair as she took a long sip from her tankard. Her dark storm-gray skin shimmered in the low light, and her eyes gleamed like deep ocean sapphires.

Her gaze met mine, sharp and unblinking, like a predator spotting something interesting.

"Thalos," she purred, her voice a rasp of waves over gravel. "I thought you'd make me wait longer."

I slid into the booth across from her, my hands folded calmly on the table. "I know better than to keep a Dravessai waiting."

She grinned, sharp and crooked. "Smart boy."

The waitress who was a lithe Abyssian with opal-scale eyes, dropped a bowl of dried kelp chips and a mug of seawater-infused ale in front of me. I offered a polite nod in thanks.

Natrix took a swig from her tankard, then leaned forward, resting her arms on the table. The teasing smile faded.

"Morgryth's on the move," she said, voice low and cold.

I didn't blink. "Where?"

"East. Past the Coral Divide. He's gathering scaled mercs, your kind. The ones who broke from the fold." She tilted her head, studying me. "He's not working alone."

"Humans?" I asked, though dread already twisted in my gut.

Natrix nodded, slow and deliberate. "Not just raiders or poachers. These ones are organized. Funded. They've got gear I've never seen before."

I frowned. "Made by the Caldenys faction?"

"Possibly. They're preparing for more than war," she said, and for once, the edge in her voice dulled. "Their numbers are growing too. Abyssian scouts spotted camps along the northern shore. These weren't Bravarns, the usual human scum who run with him. These humans looked different. Softer." She wrinkled her nose in that way that meant she was thinking about stabbing someone.

I drew in a steady breath. "Kiaza needs to hear this."

She reached across the table, her fingers brushing mine—cool, calloused, grounding. "I knew you'd say that. Though, I wanted you to hear it first. I trust you... more than I trust him."

I didn't flinch. "You don't have to like Kiaza to know he's trying to keep our kind alive."

She snorted. "Maybe. That mountain bastard carries too many ghosts. You? You still believe in something."

I met her gaze evenly. "Nati, I just have clarity. And the sense to know this fight's bigger than pride."

A flicker of something passed across her face—respect, maybe. Or regret. She leaned back again, tossing a kelp chip into her mouth.

She swirled the contents of her tankard, the faint glow of bioluminescence clinging to her fingertips like living sparks. "So..." she drawled, voice sliding between playful and dangerous, "is your brooding mountain king still sulking at the summit then, or has he finally remembered that there is more out there then just his kingdom?"

I exhaled slowly, dragging a hand through my hair. "Kia's not sulking."

"Mm." She leaned in, elbows on the table, her wild hair cascading like a tide of kelp and curls. "So he *is* brooding."

I gave her a look. "He's searching. For the last female Drakarian."

Nat's smile vanished, the storm behind her eyes sharpening. "Ah."

"He left me in charge for now," I continued, my tone steady despite the ache in my chest. "He didn't explain it much at first. Just... said it mattered. That if there's even a chance, it changes everything. He believes she's real."

She leaned back again, chewing the inside of her cheek, her fingers drumming on the table. "I've heard the whispers. Every port from Driftshore to the Bone Shoals has someone with a cousin who swears they saw something with wings slipping through mountain fog."

I tilted my head. "You believe it?"

"I believe in patterns," she replied. "And this one's getting louder. Rumor has it Morgryth plans to head inland for her. Though, it is just hear-say right now."

That sank in like a stone. "He wants to claim her?"

Nati nodded once, sharply. "Make her his. Breed her, bind her. Anchor his bloodline before the rest of you fall to dust. You think he's wild now? Imagine what he'll do when he's desperate."

I rubbed my temple. "Kia's chasing myths, and Morgryth's chasing ownership."

Nati's voice softened. "What are you chasing?"

I met her gaze. "Peace, maybe... or at least survival. You think Kiaza's wrong?"

"No," she said, then, quieter, "I might not believe in these rumors myself, but I think he's too noble for the world we live in."

"Maybe," I admitted, tipping my tankard toward hers. "You know, I'll follow him anyway."

She clinked hers against mine with a wicked grin. "Of course you will. Always the good little Drake boy."

I smirked. "And you love me for it."

She moved forward, close, her breath cool against my jaw. "I like that you *try* to stay good. Makes it more fun when I drag you into something terrible."

I laughed, despite myself, even as my stomach knotted. "Nati... if Morgryth is heading to the mountains..."

"I'll confirm it," she interrupted, serious now. "I'll also get you maps. Intercept messages. Movement reports. Anything I can scrounge from my informants. If Kaiza wants to find her first, he better move faster than fate."

The sound of gulls echoed from outside, harsh and hungry.

I met her eyes again, and this time there was no teasing between us. I studied her for a moment, the way her shoulders squared even when her heart cracked. Natrix had never been one for softness, though I could feel it there—threadbare, stitched under all the bravado and ocean salt.

"We should formalize our alliance," I said, voice low. "Ink on parchment. No more shadow pacts or whispered promises in dank bars."

She rolled her eyes and leaned back, the chair creaking beneath her. "Funny. Now you want signatures. Where was this push when we could've sealed it in blood and magic?"

I winced. Not because she was wrong, but because she still cared.

"That bond wasn't what any of us really wanted and wouldn't have changed the outcome," I said, gently. "You and I both know it was only me you wanted, not Kai or the bond he and I share."

Her fingers stilled on the table, curling slowly into a fist. "Yeah, well, tell that to the part of me that still wonders what it would've been like." She laughed, bitter and too quiet. "Didn't want me tied down, and now you want treaties and terms."

"I wanted you to be happy," I replied, my voice firm. "I still do. *We*, didn't make you happy, Nati."

She stared at me a long moment, storm in her eyes, then finally—she exhaled, the tension uncoiling. "Fine. We'll write your pretty alliance." She flicked her fingers in mock ceremony. "Dravessai Clan recognizes the sovereignty of the Drakarian Peaks. We'll share information, resources, and defense pacts if shit hits the fan. But if your people, your king, go back on it—"

"We won't," I said firmly. "I'll make sure of it."

She snorted. "There's that honor again. Like the scales under your damn skin."

I offered a crooked smile. "It's why you keep inviting me back."

Her gaze softened, just a flicker. "It's why I haven't dragged you into the deep and kept you."

"There was a time I'd probably let you." I give her a small smirk.

She raised a brow, then leaned closer, her voice velvet-dipped steel. "You say that like it's a joke."

The tension between us lingered, electric and ancient. However, it wasn't the kind that led to a bond, it was what remained when a bond never fully formed. Familiar. Sharp-edged. Yet still real.

I cleared my throat, breaking the moment. "The treaty should go before both councils. You'll need to sign it in Driftshore and I'll take it to the Peaks."

She nodded, pulling a battered leather pouch from her side. "Then let's make it official."

As she rolled parchment and handed it off to her second, a dark skin large Abyssian, I felt the weight of what we were doing. A hope of a new beginning.

"And Thao," she said, without looking at me.

"Yeah?" I rolled my eyes.

"If this girl—this last female—is real…" She paused, then met my gaze. "Don't let Kaiza be the only one chasing her. You might be the only one who can remind her why we're worth saving."

Maybe, I stood, the weight of the moment settling across my shoulders like a familiar cloak.

She remained seated, but her gaze followed me with a sharp, unreadable softness. "I'll send anything I find. Whatever washes up, I'll make sure it reaches you."

I gave a single nod. "I know you will."

She didn't say goodbye. That wasn't her style. Instead, she lifted her tankard with a parting smirk. "Have a little fun while your king is away, won't you?"

"Try not to have too much fun," I shot back with a half-smile.

The moment I stepped into Driftshore's lamp-lit streets, the scent of salt and night fog met me like a memory. I closed my eyes. My whole body buzzed with nerves. The sound of drunken laughter and whispered secrets drifted through the alleyways, dredging up long gone nights of pleasure and easy leisure.

I exhaled and opened my eyes, walking the slick cobblestone path toward the warm glow of the corner inn. I clutched my jacket. The coarse and utilitarian fabric scratched. Not my usual soft, luxurious, and tailored garb. I longed for my own bed, my own room. Tonight, I'd sleep alone in this place thick with memories now turned bittersweet.

I wouldn't trouble Kiaza with tonight's news. Not yet. We both needed rest. Tomorrow, I will reach out as I return to the mountains. To our castle. To the seat we ruled from together.

I pushed open the inn's worn oak door. Warmth spilled out, bathing the space in orange firelight. Overstuffed lounge chairs, polished dark wood floors, and woven rugs surrounded a stone hearth crackling with steady flame. The air smelled of fresh bread, lavender, and woodsmoke. The warmth of it was comforting like a mother's embrace.

A tall table stood between me and a short gray-haired woman whose smile reached her eyes. She turned a page in the thick ledger before her, dipping her quill into the inkwell with practiced ease.

"Good evening," she said with a cheerful lilt. "What can I do for you, love?"

"Just a room for the night," I said, stepping up to the table and placing a handful of coins on it.

The innkeeper raised an eyebrow, then glanced down at the ledger. "Name?"

"Los," I answered simply.

No need for anyone to know that a crowned royal of the Drakarian was staying in a seaside inn and whispering with the leader of the most ruthless Abyssian clan in all of Asherium. That kind of rumor would set every human faction on edge—especially the Rauthen, the ones who held the reins of human politics and stirred fears of looming war. Likely because they wanted it themselves.

The innkeeper gave a small nod, closed the ledger, and swept the coins into her palm before tucking them somewhere beneath the counter. She retrieved a key and slid it across the table to me. "Upstairs. Last door on the left."

I took it with a nod and climbed the stairs, the old boards creaking under my weight. Once inside, I locked the white-painted door behind me and sat on the edge of the bed before tugging off my boots. The room smelled faintly of lavender and old smoke.

Morning would come soon enough.

I stripped off my outer layers, folding my travel-worn clothes over the chair in the corner. The mattress gave a soft sigh beneath me as I lay back, one arm behind my head, staring at the cracks in the plaster ceiling. The scent of iron and smoke washed over me, it was faint, but enough to remind me of Kia. I missed his weight beside me. The steadiness of his presence. The way his silences felt like home. Tonight, that longing twisted with something sharper. If he found her, the last Drakarian female, what would that mean for us? For her? For our kingdom? I told myself we would do the right thing, that he would do the right thing. Still, the thought of her stirred something brittle in my chest. I closed my eyes, even though sleep didn't follow swiftly.

Finally I fell into a fitful sleep. Sleep never came easy on the coast.

I woke before dawn, the faint light just beginning to bleed through the edges of the shuttered window. The warmth from the hearth below had long faded, leaving only the chill of sea air and the weight of everything I carried. I dressed in silence, fingers lingering on the brooch that kept my cloak pinned. The royal crest etched in obsidian and silver, hidden beneath the folds of cloth. It reminded me of Kia and what he trusted me to do for him. No one in Driftshore had noticed. I intended to keep it that way.

I made it to my horse before the weight of the next step settled in. The climb back to the peaks would take a full day's ride, and the distance gave me time to plan, to think.

The narrow roads that twisted up the cliffs were soaked with mist and shadow, familiar terrain to anyone born of stone and sky. The wind whipped through my short hair, messing the tousled strands, and my hands flexed on the reins as hooves clattered over ancient stones.

When the first tree line broke and the cold began to bite, I let my thoughts stretch outward. Past stone and silence, past the sky, toward the bond that still tethered me to him.

"Kai..."

There was a flicker of resistance at first, like tapping a sleeping flame. Then—

"Thalos". His voice bloomed through the bond, low and steady, like the pulse of the mountain itself. *"You made it to Driftshore?"*

"I did. Met with Nat. She took the alliance to her council. She's sending intel... and there's more."

A pause. I could feel him stilling wherever he was, likely on some wind-bitten ledge, staring into cloud and purpose. *"Go on."*

"She's hearing the same things. Wings in the fog. Morgryth heading inland. She thinks he's not after a skirmish. She thinks he means to claim the female."

Kai's answer didn't come in words, just a burst of heat through the tether, full of anger, fear, purpose.

"He won't get to her first," Kai finally sent the thought hard and sharp. *"I won't let him."*

"Then you'll need to move faster," I sent back, not as a challenge, just as the truth.

I felt his acceptance settle between us like a shared oath. *"Thalos..."*

"Yeah?" I sent my sense of calm to him with my response, as my horse turned the next bend in the path and whinnied.

Our bond flared with warm and tenderness, like Kia was holding me close. *Thank you. For keeping things steady. For believing in me.*

I exhaled, the cold cutting sharp through the trees as the mountain path widened ahead. *That's what I do, remember? Someone has to anchor us while you chase a ghost.*

A pause on the bond. Then came his reply with warm amusement. *She's not a ghost.*

No, I agreed, letting the wind carry my words through the evergreens.

The steady clop of hooves filled the quiet as I let my thoughts drift. By the time I reached the clearing, the sun had crested high—just past midday. Our outpost unfolded before me and sat nestled between stone and sky. It was a small farmstead meant for Drakarian travel outside our territory while in human form. What had started as a simple outpost, now, it looked more like a small town.

Wide meadows stretched open enough for several Drakes to land at once. The cabins were a sturdy pine and slate, which lined the path like old sentries. The barn still smelled of hay, iron, and magic, faint present. Stocked with everything we needed for trade routes, resupply runs, or to pass as human in the border towns and port cities. It all sat tucked into this little mountain basin.

Truthfully, the place had grown. With so many of our kind passing through, it resembled a fledgling town more than a simple camp. Trade routes crossed here now. Some stayed. Some passed through. Our people were adapting, rebuilding, surviving.

As my mare picked her way toward the main path, a flash of movement caught my eye. A young boy burst from a field of dry grass, laughter tumbling after him like wind-chimes.

"Sam," I murmured, recognizing the boy by his mop of windswept curls and bare feet.

He ran straight for me, waving, with wild, uneven strides, dirt smudged across his cheek and joy lighting up his eyes. He was ten years old now, and growing fast, faster then I would like.

His mother, Renae, had returned to us seeking sanctuary years ago. Her father had been Drakarian—gone long before Sam's birth. Her human husband, though, had been a monster. When he raised a hand to Sam, not just her, she'd fled in the night. Sam had been four then. Too young to understand, but old enough to remember.

Renae had helped Kiaza and me keep things running at the castle, and here when we traveled. Quietly strong. Loyal. She kept the fires lit, food on the tables, and Everything in order. She made this place feel like more than just a kingdom. She made it feel like home.

Sam reached the path, waving both arms. "Uncle Thalos! You're back!"

I dismounted with a soft grunt, catching him mid-run as he barreled into me. "Careful," I said, ruffling his hair. "You'll knock me over one of these days."

His grin only widened. For a moment, my heart ached even as I smiled down at him.

Would I ever know what it was like to love and raise a child of my own? The possibility lingered like a fragile dream I didn't dare cradle too tightly. Not just the idea of having one, but of that child being *ours*, truly. Not burdened by fleeting years. Not human.

I knew I could at any time, though it wouldn't be like me. It would be *fragile*. Loved, cherished... and heartbreakingly mortal. Like Sam who would grow. Laugh. Stumble. Love. And then, one day, he'd fade—long before I even looked a decade older. I'd be left with the memories, like watching fire burn bright and disappear before the chill returned.

What I wanted deeply, achingly, what I barely dared whisper even to myself, was a child with *Kia*. One like *us*. A miracle child, one that would be the hope of our race.

Did I truly believe that the last Drakarian female existed?

Maybe. Just barely.

Sam clung to my waist for a moment longer before pulling back, eyes gleaming with excitement.

"Did you bring anything cool this time?" he asked, already peeking at my saddlebags.

I chuckled, tugging one free and kneeling beside him. "Depends on your definition of *cool*. No firecrackers or smoke bombs this time."

He gave a mock sigh of exaggerated disappointment.

"But," I added, opening the flap, "I did trade for something in Driftshore."

I pulled out a smooth piece of carved bone. A tiny sea serpent wrapped around a compass rose, its eyes painted a shimmering green.

Sam's mouth fell open. "Is it really for me?"

"Of course it is just for you." I placed the item into his small hands. "The artist claimed it brings good luck on journeys."

He took it gently, fingers brushing reverent over the ridges. "I'm gonna keep it in my box of treasures."

"You'd better," I said, ruffling his hair again before rising to my feet. "Where's your mother?"

"In the kitchen. She said you'd be back today," he said, already racing toward the nearest cabin with the bone carving clutched in his hand like sacred gold.

I followed at a slower pace. The scent of baking bread and something herbal wafted through the open window—familiar, warm, grounding.

Inside, the hearth glowed low, and Renae stood near the counter, rolling dough with the kind of steady focus only a woman keen on her task, seemingly unbothered by our entrance.

She glanced over her shoulder, brushing a few strands of golden brown hair from her face. "You look tired."

"I am," I admitted, setting my bag down by the door.

"Supper's not ready yet," she said, eyeing me with amusement. "And you smell like you could use a bath."

That earned a quiet laugh from me as I passed her, brushing a dusting of flour from her hair. "Fine. I'll bathe before we eat."

She nodded, smug. "You better. Or you can join the pigs and their slop if you don't."

After washing off the road and changing into fresh clothes, I stepped back into the small room, now warmed by the glow of lanterns and the hearth. The scent of herbs and roasted meat drifted through the air, rich and familiar.

Sam had already laid out three plates, his small hands having done their best to line everything up neatly. A pot of stew steamed on the trivet, the lid just slightly askew to let the aroma escape.

Renae served us each a bowl and sat with a quiet grace beside Sam, her big brown eyes softening as he dug into the food with enthusiasm only children could muster.

We ate in near silence, the kind that felt earned, not awkward. The kind that existed between people who didn't need to fill space to feel connected.

The fire crackled low. The scent of rosemary and woodsmoke hung in the air. I let the warmth settle into my bones as I took another bite.

Across the table, Sam yawned mid-chew, and Renae reached over to smooth his curls.

"Long day," she murmured.

"For all of us," I said, my gaze flicking to the window. The stars had begun to pierce through the darkening sky, sharp and cold like truth.

Renae met my eyes. "You'll tell me in the morning."

It wasn't a question.

I nodded. "In the morning."

She stood and ushered Sam off to wash up, his laughter trailing down the hall as he showed off his new carving to the shadows.

Alone again, I sat back and let the silence stretch. My mind turned to Kiaza, to Natrix, to the girl we hadn't yet found, and a longing for a family of my own. I didn't know what tomorrow would bring. Tonight, here in this quiet place of refuge and memory, I let myself be still. Even if it was just for a little while.

Chapter 6

Kiaza

Hearing from Thalos that morning did nothing to still the storm beneath my ribs. His voice had been steady, his report thorough. Underneath it though, I heard the tension, the same worry that coiled like a serpent in my chest. Morgryth was on the move. Hunting. Searching. Just like me. For her.

The difference was I'd save her and protect her. He'd cage her. Breed her. Break her. If our paths crossed, there would be no words, no negotiation. I'd rip the breath from his lungs before I let him lay a single hand on her. He wouldn't do to her what he had to my mother.

By the time the sun reached its apex, I spotted the faint silhouettes of chimney smoke and rooftops through the thinning trees. The human settlement. It stretched like a bruise along the valley floor, built around the base of the mist-clad mountains. The wind carried the scents of smoke, coal, and something sharp and metallic, like rusted iron soaked in sweat. I slowed my pace, my pulse thudding harder with each step.

To fly over would've drawn too many eyes, not to mention the weapons. Human cities had become smarter, more watchful. They lined their borders with sensor wards now that pulsed with stolen magic, some kind of mechanical thing, buzzing faintly against the skin of the world like biting insects. No, the sky wasn't safe today. I would go through, disguised. Walking.

Rail lines crisscrossed the lower hills like veins of blackened steel, groaning beneath the weight of distant cargo. I landed softly on a ridge, my claws digging into the stone and soil, I watched steam lift into the sky from the train moving below, the bell clanged once, twice, echoing into the still air. Sparks spat from the wheels. Men shouted, laughing rough and low, their voices carried by the wind.

Setting my pack down on the rocky ground, I exhaled slowly as smoke coiled around my legs. I was already shifting. My bones compressed with a quiet crackle; wings sank back into skin, and scales folded away like petals withdrawing to a bud. My form narrowed, soft skin overtaking armored muscle, until I stood clothed in thick leather and a weather-worn cloak that concealed every weapon and secret I carried. Simple. Human enough.

Magic pulsed faintly in my palm as I focused, reshaping the pack with effort I hadn't summoned in years. It shrank under my hand, the large straps tightening, fabric folding into itself until it was no bigger than a loaf of bread. A manageable burden. The magic wouldn't hold long, maybe a day if I was lucky. I was out of practice, and spells like this were always fragile.

I fastened the miniature bag to my belt, the weight oddly familiar despite its altered shape. Everything inside had shrunk as well which was useless in this state, but that was fine. My path lay ahead as I made my way down from the ridge to the worn dirt road. The mountains were calling.

The town of Brakthollow lay just ahead, huddled like a cluster of stones around a square marketplace. Slanted roofs clung to crooked houses. Laundry flapped in the breeze from lines stretched between windows. Children darted through alleyways, their laughter thin and shrill. The stink of boiling fat and animal hide drifted from a tannery on the far end, battling the sweetness of baked bread wafting from a stall near the square. My sharp senses overwhelmed me. Human life. Raw. Loud. Unfiltered.

Rauthen flags hung over one building, golden crown with a sword inside it, stamped on deep crimson cloth. The mark of rulers. Of merchants and nobles who bought their influence as easily as they bought steel. The Rauthen thrived on coin and power, their reach stretching through trade houses, council halls, and shadowed networks of spies.

Right beside it, a rough-hewn stone tavern bore the Durnathi crest: a black axe over mountain peaks. Isolationists. Clan-bound and suspicious, but forged strong and proud of it.

I kept my eyes forward, the shift in my posture subtle—head down, shoulders broad but relaxed. My gait quieted with practiced ease, no different than any mountain-born wanderer.

Here, the two factions coexisted in a way that baffled outsiders. Gold and grit. Wealth and stone. Together, they'd carved out a balance that was neither soft nor savage. Just... survivable.

Human towns, even the quieter ones, had a way of pressing in around you. The stale smoke. The feeling of ever-watchful eyes. The bone-deep ache of too many lives lived too fast. I didn't belong in places where time moved like a storm and lives passed in a blink.

My eyes flicked to the horizon beyond the town, where the jagged peaks of the mist-clad range pierced the clouds like ancient teeth. The wind shifted again, carrying a different smell now, earthy and cold, tinged with pine and stone. The mountain.

The Ironwilde.

Getting there would mean cutting through the heart of this settlement and finding the footpath that wound behind the smithy on the far end. It would lead me to the old trailhead, up toward the base of the range.

It would take another day at least, longer if I met resistance. I didn't care about resistance. I cared about time.

Each step through this place would be a step closer to her.

The closer I got, the more I felt it, that pull in my chest, ancient and unknown. Like the fates themself called me closer to her, and our destiny.

The town sprawled before me in crooked lines and muddy ruts, built more from necessity than beauty. Wood-planked storefronts leaned like tired men in the wind. Smoke curled from stone chimneys. Horses snorted from where they were tied to railings outside saloons, general stores, and smithies, their tack damp from the lingering fog. My nose filled with the scent of tobacco, sweat, and hot iron that rolled on the wind, mixed with the faint bitterness of old magic long buried beneath the stone.

My boots hit the packed dirt road with a steady rhythm, and I pulled my cloak tighter around me, the hood casting shadow across my face. Another town, another settlement pretending it wasn't teetering on the edge of its own chaos. My eyes scanned every face. Farmers, blacksmiths, and a few rail workers near the station yard. None of them looked twice, even though it felt like they could see through my skin and knew who I was. I acted like I was just another traveler passing through nothing more than a hired blade or mountain trapper.

No one here knew who I was. I reminded myself.

Vendors hawked root vegetables from muddy carts while barkers called out from under canvas awnings, peddling snake oil and false promises. The church bell struck noon with a hollow clang that echoed through the valley.

I passed children dueling with wooden swords in a garden beside the gunsmith's shop. Others chased a hoop down the path, their laughter sharp as crows. They scattered when a woman hollered at them to leave well enough alone.

"Where ya headed, stranger?" an old man called from a rocking chair outside the saloon, squinting against the sun.

I didn't break stride. "East."

His chuckle followed me. "Ain't nothin' east but fog and ghouls."

A dog barked at the wheels of a rickety cart. A woman in a patched green dress scrubbed the steps outside a brothel, her gaze flicking to me, then away. I didn't smile. Smiling invited questions.

A bell jangled behind me as a man stepped out of the barbershop, smelling of bay rum and soap. He tipped his hat. I returned only a short nod. Courtesies in towns like this were thin masks. I'd seen enough of humanity's "civil" frontier to know the knife often came after the handshake.

The main road ended in a T-shaped square framed by the tallest buildings in town. There was a bank, a church, and a three-story inn with warped shutters and a coat of whitewash trying too hard to look respectable. The heart of the town.

I stopped at a food stall wedged between the dry goods shop and a butcher's that reeked of blood and smoke. The woman behind the counter, her bare arms thick and scarred from kitchen work. She eyed me like she wasn't sure I was worth the bread and stew she ladled into a dented tin bowl. I paid in coin without a word and ate leaning against a wall, watching the town churn around me. Humanity survived on noise and motion. Never still long enough to notice the world watching back.

The stew was hot, heavy with root vegetables and salted beef liver. It wasn't good, but it was filling. I chewed slowly, letting the steam rise into the already thick air, and watched the ebb and flow of the town.

Two women argued over a bolt of cloth outside the general store. A preacher hammered up a notice on the church post, his mouth moving like he thought someone cared. Across the way, a drunk stumbled out of the saloon and pissed in the alley without bothering to hide it. No one looked twice.

I finished the stew, wiped the bowl clean with the crust of bread, and set the tin back on the counter with a quiet thunk. The woman behind the stall gave me a grunt and nothing else. That was fine. I preferred silence anyway.

By the time I reached the far edge of town, the buildings had thinned to lopsided shacks and scrub-lined fences. The main road turned to gravel, then dirt. A weather-worn sign leaned at an angle where the path split. One arrow pointed north to well worn trade routes I wouldn't take. The other pointed east, no name, just a streak of chipped paint.

I took the eastern road.

The noise of the town fell behind me, swallowed by cicadas and the low hush of wind through dry grass. Each step forward carried me closer to the mountains. Closer to stories no one dared speak above a whisper. Closer to her.

The east road sloped up out of town and became more overgrown than the dirt path. Beyond it, farmland faded into rocky scrub and pine. Mist clung to the distance like it had teeth.

I would walk straight into it.

I'd seen many of the wilds in my life—deserts that howled with dead voices, caves full of gemstones where the ancients had once burned their names into the stone—but none of them haunted me like the Ironwilde.

Once, they said, it had been the heart of Drakarian lands. Ancient, sacred, and brimming with power. We ruled there before we learned to covet the skies beyond it. Before our kind fractured. Before those who were slaughtered made the magic turn against the very soil that bore it. Now it stood swathed in fog, a land no one dared to tread.

I tightened the strap on my satchel and stepped off what some called the road, following an even narrower path that led toward the waiting mists. My muscles were tight. My magic coiled low beneath my ribs tighter. Every legend warned against setting foot in the Ironwilde. They spoke of whispers that turned sane men mad, of trees that bled when you cut them, of ghosts that wore your face.

I didn't believe in ghosts. I believed she was there, somewhere beyond the veil of mist and stories. The last of our kind. The last hope of the Drakarian.

I pressed on, the town falling behind me, swallowed by distance and smoke. The fog rose like breath from the bones of the land, and I didn't look back.

By the time the sun dipped westward, I was already beyond the last rusted mile marker and the clatter of wagon wheels had long gave way to silence. The dirt road narrowed into a path not even hunters or fools followed. The trees thickened, darker, wilder. Moss clung to the bark like old ghosts refusing to let go.

I took in the Ironwilde again, where she was in the old lands. Drakarian lands. Before the war with humans, before the factions, before our great kings of old, and even our greatest rise to power. All this had been ours.

Carved from stone and magic, mist and fire. My father told me we left it willingly, abandoning the cradle of our kind in search of purpose beyond the peaks. He warned it was greed that drove us out. Greed for conquest, knowledge, and the love of mortals who would never live long enough to understand us.

Then the Faelethians, those mystical wild unicorns with nothing but love for the land and others died.

Slaughtered by human hands for the magic found in their horns and blood. The last of the unicorn kin. Their magic soaked into the ground, wild and untamed. The mists that followed swallowed everything. Fields, ruins, whole sky-forged temples. The Ironwilde disappeared beneath it.

No one came back. Not humans. Not Drakes. Not even scavengers.

Until now, until me.

My boots sank into loamy earth as I approached the tree-line. The mist curled low, clinging to the grasses and creeping along the broken path towards me like it remembered me. Like it knew what I was.

I'd be lying if I said I wasn't afraid. But fear had never stopped me before.

The thought of her, the last Drakarian female, the heartbeat in every dream I couldn't explain. It pulled at something deeper than instinct. It wasn't just duty anymore. It was *need*. The idea of her, alive, alone, powerful enough to survive what none of us could... it undid me.

I reached the edge of the woods. Mist coiled around my boots, thickening with every breath I took. The mountain path ahead wound through bramble and stone, vanishing into a fog that glittered faintly with magic.

I paused there, the weight of it settling around me.

"She's not a ghost," I muttered to the mist. "I will find you first."

I took my first step forward, into the Ironwilde.

Chapter 7

Lyria

The sun warmed my skin as I yanked a stubborn choke weed from the soil. Damp earth clung to its roots, the scent of warmed dirt and musky oak thick in the air. A bead of sweat slipped down my temple, soaking into the brim of my floppy woven hat.

I crouched among the cabbages and kale, fingers brushing over garlic sprouts and curling moon bean vines. Carrots pushed up in tidy rows, and the purple aster corn stood tall, their stalks rustling in the breeze.

The wind shifted and I sensed it then, something was near.

The kind of presence that made the hair on the back of my neck raise. I froze, my breath shallow. Across the pasture, my goats bolted from their grazing spot and fled toward the barn in a panicked flurry. My confirmation that something had crossed into my land.

I stood slowly, my trowel held tight like a dagger. My eyes scanned the tree line. An owlbear, maybe? A curious sprite deer? Or something worse?

Then I saw him.

At the edge of the south pasture clearing, a figure moved. Bronze skin and long dark hair streaked with crimson. He held a large curved bow drawn taut, arrow aimed forward as if hunting. His frame was massive with broad shoulders, thick arms, the muscles flexing with the tension of the bowstring.

He looked every bit the predator.

My nostrils flared. If he so much as looked at my goats the wrong way, I'd show him exactly what kind of creature he was dealing with. I stomped across the field, fists clenched, dirt on my hands, trowel gripped like a blade. If I had to, I could shift and swallow him in two bites.

Not that I would, not unless absolutely necessary.

He didn't seem to notice the sound of my Ogre-like steps, as I stomped across the field or the steam practically rolling off me. What kind of idiot wandered into someone's land without checking his surroundings?

The closer to him I got, the more I could see of him and my breath caught.

His white cotton undershirt clung to his chest, soaked through from the rising mid morning heat. Each ripple of his muscles showed clearly beneath it, like a statue carved by a god with very specific ideas about beauty. His trousers were practical, fitted, and belted with a leather strap that held a canteen. At least that was smart, I noted.

Once I spotted the knives—five, maybe six—of varying lengths strapped around his wide hips. I slowed, stopping a few paces away, planting a hand on my hip and fixing him with what I hoped was my best stern glare.

"Hey!" I called. "You better not hit any of my animals with that arrow."

He turned instantly, bow now aimed at me.

Well. Shit.

I raised my trowel like it might actually do something. "If you know what's good for you, you'll get off my property and go on your way without any trouble."

He stared me down, unreadable, unmoving.

Then—finally—he lowered the bow by an inch.

My hat flopped in the breeze, my cotton overalls clung to my bare skin, and I suddenly became painfully aware that I hadn't dressed for confrontation. These first weeks of summer had brought an early heat, and I hadn't expected company out here at the edge of the world. Or at least any that would mind my loose, barely covering practical wardrobe choices.

"Do you live here?" Came his low gruff voice.

"Yes," I snapped, gesturing around us. "This is my land. My goats, my garden, my barn. All of it."

As if on cue, the goats began to shuffle lazily back out of the barn, returning to graze.

He slung his bow around his shoulder and took a slow step toward me. I raised the trowel again, daring him.

He raised both hands—not quite surrender, but not aggression either. Still, I knew better. If he wanted to, one of those knives could be buried in my chest before I blinked.

My gaze dipped for half a second too long, tracing the line of his hips to the hard plane of his stomach and the curve of his chest.

The closer he got, the more I could see the sharp edges of his jaw, the sweep of his lashes, the intensity in his amber eyes. With flecks of gold and flashes of ruby.

He wasn't just handsome, he was devastating. He was also not human, he was a Drakarian.

I swallowed, my throat suddenly dry.

I lowered my trowel, spun on my heel, and headed straight back toward my garden.

Nope. I wasn't doing this.

He could go on his merry little way.

Call it denial. Call it stupidity. Honestly, it was just how I handled things that freaked me out with avoidance, plain and simple.

I started to hum a soft tune, sweet and idle, pretending he wasn't there. Still, I felt him behind me. Every step he took echoed mine, shadowing me, close enough to make my skin prickle.

"I have some questions for you, ma'am," he said to my back.

I opened the wooden wattled gate and stepped back into the garden, closing it behind me with a satisfying thump. We stood there with a modest four-foot fence between us, but he still towered above it, and me. I had to tilt my chin to meet his gaze.

"You get one," I said sweetly, a small smile curling my lips.

"One question?" His eyes flashed, with an unmistakable ruby glow. Magic flared behind them. Drakarian. That same, stupid vow stood six inches from my fence, wanting to "question" me.

"Yes. And there you go. That's your one," I replied with a smirk and turned away, stepping deeper into the garden.

Farther from the man who could offer the world, or at the very least a daughter. The one thing I'd dared to want and feared just as much.

Just a child I could raise like my mother had me, no I would raise her differently. Not a tool. Not a prophecy. Let her dream. Let her live. Love. Without the weight of ancient races or dying bloodlines.

I yanked another weed from the earth, fingers tight around the stem.

"That wasn't my question," he growled behind me, low and rough. The wood creaked beneath his grip on the gate.

Still, he didn't step inside. Maybe he sensed I needed space. Or maybe... he needed it, too.

I flicked my gaze toward him, sucking my lower lip into my mouth to muffle the sharp gasp threatening to escape. No way was I letting him see how much he affected me.

Gods, why did he affect me like this?

Every part of me wanted to rub up against him like a goat in heat. *Nope. Not thinking about that.* I forced my attention back to the soil and plants, pretending the sudden bloom of heat in my chest hadn't happened.

I fussed with a weed, the last one in the garden, and dragged it out, fingers idly toying with the stem. Anything to buy myself another second.

"Have you seen..." His voice dropped softer now, a subtle weight in it as he leaned against the surprisingly sturdy gate. "Any signs of Drakarian?"

A full-bellied laugh burst out of me as I yanked the weed free. *Was he serious? Asking me about Drakes?*

He looked... confused. Maybe even a little disappointed.

Then—CRACK!

The wattled gate gave way with a snap of wood and wire, and he landed in a pile of broken sticks and churned-up mud.

That made me laugh harder. Gods, I couldn't help it.

The scowl on his face was the grumpiest thing I'd ever seen, and damn it, I found myself smitten by it.

There was just something about him. Something in the way he stood there, covered in muck and bristling with pride and frustration, that made something in me melt.

Which scared the hell out of me. Because I knew better. There were no happy endings for someone like me. Not with the prophecy hanging over my head. Not with the weight of all magic balancing on my back.

I tilted my head and rested my hands on my hips, watching him with a grin I didn't bother to hide.

"You alright there, handsome?" I asked, barely holding in another laugh. "The ground come up and surprise you?"

He groaned and pushed himself upright, mud streaked across his shirt, a twig stuck defiantly in his hair. "The gate gave out."

"I noticed." I stepped closer, pretending to inspect the wreckage with mock concern. "Huh. Guess it wasn't built to handle a full-grown man in a sulk."

His eyes narrowed just a tick. "I was not sulking."

"Mmm. Of course not," I said sweetly, tucking the trowel into the waistband of my overalls. "You're just brooding. Very different."

He shook off the worst of the dirt and straightened to his full height, towering over the broken fence and me alike, a walking sculpture of smolder and scowl.

Damn, was all I could think, as I fought the urge to fan myself with my hat.

"Well," I said lightly, turning abruptly and walking toward the barn. "Seeing as you've already flattened my poor gate, you might as well come wash up. You can't go hunting Drakes or what not, with half the field stuck to your ass."

He hesitated, then followed, one muddy boot squelching slightly with every step.

As we neared the barn, Pip my donkey raised his shaggy head and let out a loud, offended bray from where he stood by the trough.

"Relax, Pip," I called. "It's just a little mud bath for our guest, not the end of the world."

Pip huffed, ears flicking, and stomped off in a slow, dramatic protest.

I pointed toward the stone trough under the lean-to's shade next to the barn. "There. Water's cool, but clean. Don't worry, I won't peek."

He gave me a confused look, still not sure if I was serious.

I winked. "Unless you want me to."

That earned me the smallest, reluctant curve of his mouth, half a smile, all brooding and wariness.

I left him to it, my steps light as I crossed the barnyard towards my cabin. My heart, though, wasn't quite so steady. I'd just invited a Drake into my space. A male Drakarian.

He now stood barefoot in my barnyard, and had come stomping mud into my world. And I wasn't sure if I wanted to stop him. This might be my only chance at what I wanted, but why was he looking for Drakarians? Was he a rogue, one who hunted his own kind? Luckily, my magic concealed my true nature from those around me, he must think I am only human.

I pushed open the front door and decided I would need to make a stew if I was going to feed a Drake of his size and hopefully get more answers. I removed my shoes and hat, before I gathered the things I needed to cook the meal.

Sometime later, I was chopping carrots and leeks for the stew, the rich broth already simmering with two rabbits and a handful of herbs. The scent of rosemary and wild garlic filled the cabin, mingling with the warmth from the hearth.

The floorboards creaked behind me, and I looked up—only to be met with the sight of a nearly naked brute standing barefoot in the doorway, holding a bundle of clean but dripping clothes and boots. His bow, arrows, belt, and knives piled in his arms.

I pointed the knife at him, arching a brow. "There's a clothesline off the porch. Use it. And set your things in the basket by the door. Don't bring those soggy things in here." My voice was sharp, but the smile tugging at my lips gave me away.

He grunted, but didn't move. Just stood there, water dripping from the ends of his hair, chest rising with every breath. The way the firelight danced across his bare skin should've been illegal.

I turned back to the cutting board before I could get caught staring. Again.

"Unless you want me to throw those clothes in the stew, I suggest you start moving." My voice light, tossing the carrots into the pot with a satisfying hiss.

"I wasn't sure where the line was," he muttered, still not budging.

I glanced over my shoulder, catching the faintest curve of a smirk tugging at the corner of his mouth.

"Oh, don't play helpless with me," I teased. "You've got more knives than I've got goats, and you stalked across my pasture like you owned the place. I think you can find a string with wooden pegs on it."

He finally huffed through his nose and turned for the door.

By the time he came back in, his damp hair curled at the ends, still clinging to him around his neck. His barefoot steps were quiet as he walked closer and he'd clearly chosen not to put on anything more than a pair of long silk underpants.

Well. Stars save me.

I didn't miss a beat. I stirred the stew with one hand and nodded toward the bench by the door.

"There's a quilt folded on the bench," I said, sweet as honey. "Grab it before you drip on my floor again. Then sit. Lunch'll be ready in five."

He blinked at me like he hadn't expected the sass. Or the lack of judgment.

Then he moved—slow, solid, silent. Wrapped the quilt around himself like he'd done it a thousand times, then lowered himself down at my small table with that heavy grace of someone who knew exactly how dangerous he was and didn't bother pretending otherwise.

I slid a bowl in front of him, then set mine across the table. "Eat up. I don't want to hear any grunting at it like you're suspicious. I haven't poisoned anyone all week."

That earned me the ghost of a smirk.

He took a bite. Chewed. Swallowed.

"It's good," came out in a low and rough voice. Like thunder murmured in a summer storm.

"You sound surprised," I grinned, resting my cheek in my hand. "What, do I look like someone who can't cook?"

"You look like someone who'd stab a man with a trowel for looking at your goats wrong." His smirk twisted into a small grin, still no teeth though.

"Fair. I've done worse for less." I couldn't help the wryness in my tone.

He glanced around the cabin, gaze sweeping the handmade chairs, the dried herbs hanging from the rafters, the open window letting in mountain breeze and birdsong. When his eyes met mine again, something unreadable flickered behind them. Curiosity, maybe. Or restraint.

"So," I said, cocking my head. "Do you usually wander onto private land with weapons drawn, or am I just lucky?"

"I didn't know it was private." He took another bite full of meat this time.

"Sure you did," I teased, grinning over the rim of my bowl. "You just didn't care."

He set his spoon down with a soft clink. "You're not afraid of me."

"Nope," I said with a pop of the 'p'. "Should I be?"

He didn't answer.

I leaned back in my chair, eyeing him. "You've got that look, you know. Like someone carrying a heavy truth and pretending it's just a pack on their back."

He didn't respond, so I let it go with a shrug. The silence stretched between us, long and charged as we finished our meal.

"Well," I paused, pushing up to collect the now empty bowls. "You've scared my goats, broken my gate, used my trough, and eaten my strew. Least you can do is tell me your name."

He hesitated, just a beat too long.

"Kai," he said.

Just that. Short. Sharp. Not a lie exactly, but definitely not the full truth either. I could see it written all over his face.

I offered him a knowing smile over my shoulder. "Well, Kai... I'm Lyria." He nodded.

I grabbed two plates and the half-filled pie tin of blackberry pie from the counter, where it had been resting beneath a waxed cloth. Setting it on the table, I dished him a generous slice and slid a fork across to him.

"So... Drakarians, huh?" I said lightly, settling into my seat and pulling my plate closer. I twirled my fork between my fingers, watching him shift in his chair before his posture stiffened and his gaze turned serious.

Before he even glanced at the oozing, dark-berried pie in front of him, his eyes locked onto mine. His jaw tensed as he studied me with a weight that pressed against the air between us. My magic hummed quietly beneath my skin, cloaking me—just as it always had. Even as I could feel our magic mingle, I knew to him, I looked like a simple young human woman, though we were likely the same age. Three, almost four hundred. Both of us were wearing the illusion of thirty-somethings human.

"I'm searching for the last female Drakarian," he said at last, his voice a low, grave whisper. "It's vital I find her, *soon.*"

A beat passed before he added, "I am the Drakarian King. Kiaza Drakmyr."

I nodded once, slowly, and lifted a forkful of pie to my mouth. The burst of ripe, juicy berries, balanced by tart citrus and a hint of vanilla, bloomed across my tongue. I closed my eyes and savored it.

Surprise sparked in my chest at his admission, followed swiftly by a slow-building wariness. Still, none of it showed on my face. I looked calm. Unfazed. As if I heard confessions from kings over pie every day.

"You're not... surprised?" he asked, clearly thrown.

I shook my head. "I've seen a lot in my years—and with those silk underpants, should I be?"

I grinned as a faint flush colored his cheeks.

He huffed, a shadow of a smirk tugging at his mouth. "No, I suppose not. You must be used to strange things, living all the way out here in the Ironwilde."

He leaned back, eyes sweeping over me like a touch, lingering for half a breath too long on my barely covered chest before meeting my gaze again.

I ignored the heat that sparked low in my belly and instead latched onto the word *Ironwilde.* He used the ancient word for my forest, and most didn't call it that. The surrounding towns simply call this place Mist-clad Peaks.

"You're right." I cut into my pie, lifted another bite to my mouth, and smiled. "I've seen all kinds of strange and beautiful things living here my whole life."

His gaze flicked to my chest again before he cleared his throat. "Yeah, well… probably nothing as strange as me."

I shrugged. "Definitely not as *grumpy* as you."

His face soured, and a huff slipped out. "I'm not grumpy. I'm just serious."

I took another bite of pie, licked a streak of berry from my thumb, and gave him a lazy smile. "Seriously grumpy. You haven't even touched your pie or cracked a proper smile."

He gripped his fork like it had offended him, eyes lingering on my mouth. A scowl formed—like he knew I was teasing and wasn't quite sure what to do about it.

"I'm not grumpy, for fuck's sake. I just have… a stoic *demeanor*," he muttered, then stabbed his fork into the pie, scooping up a huge bite like he was proving a point.

The moment the berries hit his tongue, his breath hitched, and a flicker of a smile betrayed him.

Before I could fall head over heels like a fool, I stood, scraped my plate, and pumped water into the wash basin. I glanced over my shoulder at him, still caught in quiet bliss, and smirked.

"Well, *Your Majesty*…" I said, drawing the title out sweetly. "If you're looking for Drakes, you've come to the wrong cabbage patch."

Chapter 8

Thalos

The stone beneath me was colder than usual, even through the folds of my cloak. The weight of the throne never felt heavier than when I had to sit still in it.

The Grand Hall of Dakorra Spire echoed with the low murmur of voices—petitions, grievances, requests. A hundred torches lit the carved walls in flickering gold, casting long shadows across the faces of the gathered Drakarian. Elders, merchants, clan-bound warriors. All seeking something.

I listened. Because that's what Kiaza left me to do.

Two months. That was the last time I'd heard from him. Just before he entered the Ironwilde, his voice brushed my mind like a comforting caress, then vanished. The bond between us, once bright and sure as lightning, had gone silent in the mist. I told myself not to worry. Told myself the old magic simply interfered with the link.

So I ruled. I bore the crown in his absence, steadied the Spire, calmed the restless wings. If I let my thoughts drift too far, I'd lose myself in them—and we couldn't afford that.

"...my livestock were taken, King Thalos," a young female was saying, her voice sharp with frustration. "Two calves, one goat, no tracks. Not even ash. This reeks of sorcery."

"Or cowardice," someone muttered.

I raised a hand, and silence followed. "You'll be compensated," I said, my voice even. "Have your steward file the loss with my quartermaster. If sorcery is involved, I'll see to it personally."

She bowed and stepped aside, fists at her sides clenched in frustration. The next in line approached.

And then the doors slammed open.

A hush fell, heavy and instant. I didn't need to look to know who had arrived. The air changed with him—colder, slick with something oily. Shadows clung tighter to the stone.

Morgryth.

He entered alone, without guards or entourage, which made his presence all the more pointed. His silver hair long and pulled back in a tight braid, and stolen scales shimmered like scorched steel beneath his open coat, and his expression was carved from smug stone. Every step he took echoed like a challenge.

"I see you're keeping my throne warm," he said, voice smooth and sharp as a dagger's edge.

My knuckles tightened against the carved arms of the throne, but I didn't rise. "That sounds of a dying Drakes final wish."

He laughed hard, mocking, theatrical. "Oh, I don't doubt you'll try to kill me. But your time is ending, Thalos. You can feel it, can't you?" He stepped closer, his boots heavy, and his eyes flashed ruby as his fingers slowly showed claws. "The world shifts. The bloodlines thin. The last female Drakarian—she's more than myth now. I've flown over the Ironwilde more times than I can count. She's real. I have felt her. It's only a matter of time."

The silence that followed was taut and biting.

He tilted his head. "My soldiers will find her. Sooner than you think. And when they do?" His smile was a slice of poison. "There won't be a kingdom left to stop me."

I stood now, slow and deliberate, letting the power roll off me like heat from smoldering coals. "If you step foot on our soil with intent to claim what's not yours," I said, voice low, "I will burn your bones to ash and scatter them into the sea."

Morgryth's gaze glittered with amusement, but something in his jaw twitched. He gave a shallow bow, mocking again. "Until then, king ... Thalos."

He turned and walked away as casually as he came.

The doors closed behind him, and only then did the hall breathe again.

But I didn't sit.

I stood there, heart pounding, jaw clenched, knowing damn well that the moment we'd feared was finally circling overhead like a vulture.

The moment the great doors sealed shut behind Morgryth, the murmurs began—low at first, then rising like the wind before a storm.

"He threatened open war—"

"He means to challenge the line—"

"Should we prepare the Skyguard?"

"My clan will not bow—"

I didn't shout. I didn't need to.

I let my eyes close and inhaled through my nose, drawing deep into the well of calm that lived beneath the flame of my power. I reached inward and let it rise—not heat, not fire, but stillness. Serenity. The ancient magic born into my blood and bone. I let it pulse from my chest like a silent wave.

A hush spread over the hall.

Voices quieted. Feet stilled. The panic pressing at the edges of the room melted into a strange quiet. Drakes blinked, breathed easier, some with confusion, others with reverence. I opened my eyes slowly and stepped down from the throne.

"I understand your fear," I said, voice steady but low enough they had to lean forward to hear. "He is a snake. A vulture circling, waiting to strike while our King is away."

I felt it again—that unbearable silence where Kiaza's presence should've been. The bond between us had once been a star in the night, constant and guiding. Now it was only fog and ache.

Kia… please.

Nothing answered but the quiet throb of my own heart. Still, I stood taller.

"But we will not let him have what our ancestors died to build. Kiaza entrusted me with our kingdom, and I will hold it."

A ripple of nods and low affirmations passed through the gathered crowd. Some council members approached, others stayed back, uncertain. I could see it in their eyes that they were waiting for direction.

High Chancellor Sareth stepped forward first, all crimson robes and steel-threaded feathers, worry etched into his brow. "We can't wait for him to strike. If Morgryth is hunting the female… then we must consider allies. Immediate ones."

"The human factions won't turn on him now," Lord Vare muttered. "He's been their biggest source of magic for far too long. They are unlikely to change their minds now."

I turned to the war table at the side of the hall, dragging a finger across the etched map of the realm. "Then we must look elsewhere. The Crystalians hold the key to balance. If Queen Novalyn still remembers the old accords, she may see that helping us is helping herself."

"You would ask the Queen of stone, to side with fire and wing?" General Harth scoffed. "They spend their days among humans, guarding secrets, not kingdoms."

"While that is true, General, that hasn't always been the case, we were once allies." I replied sharply. "The fact she knows both sides makes her powerful. The Caldenys and Rauthen factions trust her. If we can sway her, we might sway them too."

More murmurs. Some hesitant. Others grudgingly approving.

I looked to Sareth. "Send her a formal request. An invitation to the Spire. Tell her we wish to discuss peace, trade... and the future of magic."

He hesitated, then bowed his head. "As you command."

The days dragged on, one after another, as we waited for word from Queen Novalyn. Now I stood where I always had with Kia, just outside our chambers, overlooking the valley that cradled our kingdom. The sun had only just begun to climb, gilding the peaks in pale gold. I closed my eyes and breathed in the warm summer air.

Then I felt it. Him, Kia.

A flicker of his magic, it was like a heartbeat echoing across distance and veil. There was more though there was *her*. As if I stood within that very garden. Wisps of her deep chestnut hair catching the wind, sun-kissed skin and generous curves wrapped in simple fabric. Her warm brown eyes sparkled with something wild and unbroken.

She was *breathtaking*.

And I knew.

She was the one. The missing piece. Our fate.

The vision vanished as quickly as it came. The tether between us frayed, but for that heartbeat, I *knew*. No matter how distracted or distant he might be, Kiaza wouldn't be able to resist the bond.

A bond like this wasn't something that could be ignored. We liked to pretend there was choice of who and when we bonded, though a *fated* bond?

It was death to deny it.

From the beginning of all things magic and Drakarian, the fated triad—though rare—was sacred.

...And *never* to be fought.

I stayed there, unmoving, letting the vision echo through me like a bell still ringing long after the strike.

Was this what it felt like for fate to speak?

It wasn't just that she was beautiful. It was something deeper, more primal. Something *ancient*. She felt like fire and earth, storm and stillness. Like the kind of love that could bring any king to his knees. The kind of bond that could either save us... or unravel everything.

Kiaza had found her.

I *knew* it in my bones. Even without words. Even without the connection fully restored. I could feel the weight of her presence pressing against him, wrapping around the thread that still bound the three of us, even if faint. The bond was waking.

Gods help us all if Morgryth found them now.

A cold dread coiled low in my gut, curling tight like smoke.

I couldn't lose him. I couldn't lose *either* of them.

My hands clenched against the stone railing, jaw tightening as I forced myself to breathe slow and steady.

Kiaza... please. Stay alive. Don't push her away. Not this time. Not when it matters.

The door behind me creaked open, and soft feet tapped briskly against the stone floor.

"Los," Renae called, her voice sharp and breathless with urgency. "A raven arrived from the Crystalian Court. Queen Novalyn has responded."

I turned, the weight of duty settling over me again like a mantle I could never take off.

"Good," I said, already moving. "Summon the council. Let's see if the Queen of Gems is as wise as the legends say."

As I left our chambers, the echo of their presence still lingered in my chest. Hers was like wild honey and sunlight, his like steel and storm. I couldn't hold onto them, not now. There were wars to prevent, alliances to forge, and a kingdom to protect.

As I walked away, I carried the weight of them with me. The pull of our bond. The promise of what we could be, the three of us, together. Only if fate was kind, if time allowed, if we survived long enough to find our way back to each other.

Chapter 9

Kiaza

The blackberry pie was obscene.

Warm, tart-sweet, and perfectly nestled in a flaky crust that melted on my tongue, it had no business being this good. I took another bite without meaning to, lips parting on a low exhale I would never admit sounded like pleasure. My fork hovered over the next sliver before I glanced up and saw her watching me.

Lyria.

Sunlight filtered through the cabin's narrow windows, catching strands of her wild hair and gilding her skin in soft gold. She wasn't graceful. Not in the way fae queens or sirens were. No, she was something that felt older. Earthy. Real. She moved like the forest moved, unbothered by observation, powerful in her stillness, with hands stained from soil and an expression always two seconds away from mischief or challenge.

I had been searching for sixty-five days. Sixty-five days of wind, mist, and endless pine. Not a single trace of the last female Drakarian. No tracks. No scent. No magic signatures. Just fog and the growing weight of failure. Until this.

Until her.

A woman. Alone. With goats and a trowel like a dagger. Living in a place no one should. Her land sat at the middle of what used to be Drakarian territory, what humans now whispered about as the mist-clad mountains. A place said to be cursed with ghosts and magic that swallowed men whole.

And she'd built a fucking vegetable garden in it.

"Do you always glare at your food before devouring it, or is that pie special?" Her voice cut through the quiet like a spark.

I blinked, caught. She smirked.

"I'm not glaring," I muttered, forking another bite into my mouth like I could silence her with my chewing. It didn't work.

"You've got a look," she said, propping her chin on her hand. "Like you're in love. Or constipated. Hard to tell."

I nearly choked.

Her laugh was soft, unbothered. Like the woods outside, ever present and deeply uninterested in my rank, my power, or the ache in my chest where Thalos should have been.

I couldn't feel him. Not since stepping into the Ironwilde.

It was like the mist itself had clawed between us and dragged silence into our bond. I didn't like it. I didn't like the emptiness. Thalos had always been my center, my calm, my tether. Without him, the edges of my control frayed like thread in flame.

My eyes drifted to Lyria again.

She asked questions with her gaze. Pushed and poked in ways I didn't know how to shield against. One moment sweet as honey, the next cutting through my words with maddening logic. She was frustrating.

And wonderful.

But she wasn't the one I came for.

The last female Drakarian was out there. Somewhere beyond the barn and the trees and the quiet pull I felt every time Lyria hummed while cooking or pulled weeds like they owed her money. I was supposed to be searching for the one who could save my people. Not daydreaming about a woman with a nose full of freckles, a toothy grin and bare feet who smelled like lavender and iron-rich earth.

Yet here I was.

Watching her.

Wanting to know if her hair was as soft as it looked, if her lips tasted like blackberries and rebellion.

I scraped the last of the pie from the plate and sighed. "That was... dangerously good."

"I knew you'd like it." Her hands were still wet, little bubbles of soap clinging to her skin. I gathered my plate and walked it over, setting it gently into the soapy basin. She tossed me a towel without looking. "I wash, you dry."

I grunted, catching the handmade indigo towel, and began drying each dish as she handed them to me. I stacked them neatly on the tall wooden table at the center of the room, it was rough, worn, and full of nicks. A lot like my skin.

I worked in silence, trying to ignore the dull ache in my chest, the weight of failure pressing against my ribs. But her voice, soft and melodic, cut through the heaviness.

"So... the Drakarian you're searching for. The one who can't shift. What do you want with her?"

I paused, watching her hands move through the water, then spoke, low and stern. "I want to protect her. Find her. Bring her somewhere safe. She's the last female of our kind, and if anything happens to her…"

I swallowed hard. *Morgryth would ruin her. Doom us all.*

She handed me a plate. Our fingers brushed—just a moment of contact—and something like a spark flickered down my spine. Gone in a breath, but I felt it.

She met my eyes, searching. "Protect her from what?"

"Hunters. Humans. Other Drakes. Anyone who might try to harm her." My voice was quiet, steady, absolute. I focused on drying the plate in my hands.

The water trickled down into the wooden bucket beneath the sink, louder than my thoughts. She turned and leaned back against the counter, her hands on either side of her hips, bracing herself, her gaze square on mine. "What makes you think you can?"

I snorted, barely stopping myself from letting smoke curl out of my nose. "Because, Sunshine, I'm the King of the Drakes. I've protected my people for centuries. I can protect her too."

She smirked, her lips twisting in amusement or defiance, I couldn't tell which. "And what if she doesn't want to be found, King?"

The words landed like a blow. Too sharp. Too real. Too frustrating.

My fingers clenched the towel. My jaw locked tight. I searched for Thalos's calm in myself, any flicker of his steady presence.

Finally, I spoke, voice low and full of quiet resolve. "Then I won't find her. But I have to try. I have to *know* for sure."

"I see... so if you find her, you'll ask her?" Her voice was light, teasing maybe. However, her eyes held something sharper. I couldn't tell if she was playing with me or truly testing me. My gaze caught on the curve of her lips, the line of her throat, the soft swell of her breasts beneath the worn straps of her overalls. I dragged my eyes away and focused on her words.

"Yes," I meant it with everything in me, desperate for her to understand me, and why I was doing this. "If I find her, I'll ask. I won't force her. But I'll do everything in my power to protect her... whether she wants me to or not."

She straightened, arms crossing over her chest. "What makes you think she needs protecting if she's been 'lost' this long?"

My jaw clenched. I could feel the familiar crease forming in my forehead. Thalos always told me that was my flame-mark, proof of how tightly I held the fire in, and that I needed to relax. I didn't feel like relaxing. Not with this woman asking impossible questions.

"What do you mean, *what makes me think she needs it*?" I snapped, frustration rising. "She's been alone, hiding, probably cursed. Vulnerable. This world is full of dangers lurking in the shadows that would destroy her if given the chance."

She stepped closer to the kitchen island, grabbed the utensils and began arranging them in a drawer. Calm. Casual. Dismissive. "Maybe *you're* one of the dangers lurking."

The words hit like a slap. I tossed the towel into the basin, and heat surged through me as I scowled at her. I stepped in close—close enough to count each of her darkened freckles on her sun-warmed skin that dotted her nose and cheeks.

"I'm not," I said, voice low and cold. "I've spent my life protecting my people. I would never hurt one of my kind, especially not a female. *She's our last hope.*"

Her chin lifted as she met my gaze. "And what if finding her... *is* hurting her?"

I ran a hand through my hair, pulling in a breath, trying not to shout. I looked around her home, it was simple, handmade, full of quiet comforts. A place made for peace. Not prophecy. Not war.

My voice dropped into a quieter, rough edge of frustration. "How could finding her harm her? I'm trying to *save* her. There are worse things coming. She'll need me."

Her eyes lingered on me a heartbeat too long, her lips quirking into something unsettling and serious.

"So..." she drawled, tilting her head, "you don't plan to bond with her, then?"

The question stunned me, why was she so curious, wanting so much from me, though it wasn't like Thalos hadn't asked me some of these questions too, but he at least knew what was at stake. I tried to breathe to keep my tone even. "You think it's that simple? Find her. Claim her. Bond her. Tie a neat bow around the last hope of our people?"

She gripped the pan hard and put it away.. "Isn't that what kings do?"

Gods. If only. I let out a long breath, dragging a hand through my hair. "No. Bonds aren't... contracts. They're magic in the blood, threads of souls in the marrow. All involved must choose it—unless fate decides otherwise. And even then, if she doesn't want it, there is no bond. Not one that would ever be safe, anyway."

I meant every word, but her gaze fixed on me and sharpened, probing deeper as she smirked. "So you've never thought about it?"

My jaw flexed. I should've lied. Should've said I had no designs beyond duty. Instead, the truth slipped like smoke. "I already have a bond. Thalos. He's been my other half since we were very young. My storm, my calm. Everything I'm not, he is."

Her smirk faltered, just slightly, curiosity flickering across her face.

"And yet," I continued, quieter now, "a bond doesn't end where it begins. Some Drakarians... we've always known it can stretch wider. More than two. Three or more, sometimes. Balanced magic of the right fit stabilizes the bond. A triad, though rare, is powerful." I swallowed the knot tightening my throat. "If the last female is found, if the fates allow it... if she chooses it... maybe the three of us."

Her brows lifted. For once she didn't have a quick retort, just that soft smile again, edged now with something sad.

"Is that what your consort wants? A triad? To share you with her?" The words came sharper than before, almost disappointed. Jealous, even. We'd only just met.

My calm faltered. I rubbed my beard, weighing how to explain love and magic to someone raised under different rules. "I can't teach you a few thousand years of Drakarian bond-lore in one night, Sunshine. But yes, Thalos wants a triad. He keeps me from being reckless; he always has a plan. He has his reasons."

She stacked the bowls idly with a shrug. "Sorry," she murmured, "I'm just a stupid human. What do I know about Drakarians... or your last female?"

That hit deeper than I expected. Her voice was soft, but the bitterness behind it stung. I could swear I saw a flash of gold in her eyes but it must have been the setting sun catching in them. She wasn't stupid. Far from it. She was challenging me in a way no one else dared—especially not lately.

"You're not stupid," I muttered, leaning back against the basin. "You just... ask a lot of hard questions."

She stepped into my space again, close enough that I inhaled deep and held it. The scent of her—hay, lavender, soil, and something sweet—wrapped around me. She held the bowls in one hand and looked up, eyes steady, like she could see too much.

"I'm surprised you haven't asked yourself these questions already," she said softly.

She reached up, stretching to place the bowls on the high shelf above me. Her warmth brushed against me, and I caught the glimpse of the soft curves of her peaked breasts beneath the gap in her overalls. The contact was light, almost accidental—though the effect was anything *but*. I went hard in a breath, overwhelmed by the nearness of her. My focus cracked.

The bowls clattered into place above my head.

She stepped back, giving me room. I blinked, remembered to breathe, and dragged a hand across my face.

What the fuck is happening to me?

How does this *human* have this much power over me? Being near her felt like standing too close to a fire I didn't want to leave. Gods, Thalos is never going to go for a bond with a human. Even if it was possible—not that this is even that.

Right?

Except... the feeling of her brushing against me felt a hell of a lot like a bond. Like home.

Shit.

Chapter 10

Lyria

I needed to pull myself together.

Kiaza—if that was even his real name—had taken the quilt I'd handed him and muttered something about getting fresh air. Good. Because I couldn't breathe with him in the kitchen, couldn't think with those amber eyes tracking my every move, or how the curve of my hip brushed him when I reached for the shelf. The man carried tension like armor, and wore purpose like a blade. Yet... something in him trembled. Something uncertain. Something I understood.

The moment he stepped out, I exhaled a shaky breath. I took steady steps toward the barn to do chores and for room to pull apart the knot he'd twisted inside me.

He landed on *my* doorstep. Out of all the hidden hollows, forgotten paths, and cursed trails, he found me. That wasn't fate. That was trouble with a chiseled jaw and a Drake-sized ego.

And gods help me—I was starting to like it.

The sun dipped low, painting the sky in swaths of fire and lavender as I slid the chicken coop door shut and latched it with one hand. The hens clucked sleepily, already roosting, not even bothering to protest the early bedtime.

Evening settled across the homestead with the quiet weight of routine—warm, familiar, and predictable. Unlike the man currently occupying my porch.

I tossed a scoop of feed into the pig pen and watched the greedy snouts dive into the trough. The goats bleated in demand until I filled their buckets too. Pip, my judgmental old donkey, glared at me from behind the fence like I was late for an appointment he had scheduled.

My boots crunched on dry dirt as I made the last rounds, but my thoughts didn't follow.

They were back in the kitchen where we were. On *him*.

That look in his eyes—feral and focused—when I got close. The heat between us had hummed like tension in a summer storm, and I knew, *knew*, he'd felt it too.

And maybe... maybe that was enough.

Maybe I didn't need more than this moment.

Maybe I didn't need a prophecy, a bond, or fate.

Maybe I just needed *him*. One time. One night. One chance—to have what my mother never got to choose. A daughter. A future not tied to thrones or riddles or dying bloodlines. Just a girl who could live *free*.

I swallowed hard as I carried the empty bucket back toward the cabin, heart pounding like I'd already decided. Maybe I had.

Then I saw him.

Kiaza sat sprawled in my old rocking chair like he'd belonged there for years, shirtless and barefoot, freshly dressed in clean, sun-warmed pants. Then of course, there was my cat, Furgas, betraying me, rubbing against his leg with shameless purrs.

Of course. Even the cat wanted him to stay.

I paused just before the steps, the air thick with dusk and decision.

Tonight... I was going to make the first move.

I stepped onto the porch and crossed my arms, raising a brow at the scene before me.

"Traitor," I muttered, eyeing the cat, now curled shamelessly in his lap, purring like he hadn't just spent the last three years pretending to hate everyone.

Kiaza looked up, and for the first time all day, a slow grin tugged at his lips. Not a smirk. Not a scowl. A real, lazy sort of smile that made something low in my belly twist tight.

"He came to me," in a low and smooth voice. "I think he likes me."

"Oh, he *definitely* likes you. He only does that to people he wants to murder in their sleep." I leaned against the porch rail, the last pink glow of the sun catching in my hair. "Should I warn you now or let it be a surprise?"

He huffed softly, and the grin didn't quite fade. "I'll take my chances."

We stayed like that for a moment, the quiet settling around us. The kind of silence that wasn't uncomfortable. Just... charged.

I glanced toward the door. "You want some tea?"

His brow arched. "Um... Do I have a choice?"

I barked a laugh. "It's just tea. Plants in hot water. Yes of course you do, but good to know where your mind is at."

He gave a one-shoulder shrug, trying for nonchalant but failing miserably. "Hard not to wonder, the way you look at me."

I rolled my eyes and made a dramatic show of opening the door. "Come on then, Your Majesty. Let's see if you can handle tea before we move on to real danger."

He stood, gently nudging the cat off his lap, who gave him a betrayed glare before trotting to her perch near the door. As he stepped inside behind me, I asked, over my shoulder, "So... how long have you been searching for your lost Drake?"

"Sixty-five days." His answer came without hesitation. "Through woods and fog and mud. Nothing but silence until I found this place while hunting for dinner."

I nodded slowly as I set the kettle on the stove and lit the fire beneath it. "Before that? What made you even believe she was real? The last female Drakarian?"

"I didn't believe," he said. "I *knew.*"

There was no bravado in it. Just certainty. Bone-deep, unshakable truth.

I leaned against the counter and watched him sit down awkwardly, he looked large on my small sofa taking up more than half the space, while the kettle heated. "Do you always trust your instincts like that?"

"Only when they scream at me." He huffed slightly like he was offended.

I bit my lip, eyes narrowing playfully. "And what are they screaming now?"

He hesitated. Just a beat. But that beat told me everything.

"They're screaming you're dangerous," he murmured.

My smile turned slow and syrup-sweet. "Well. At least they're smart." The kettle whistled and I poured two mugs, adding in some glow bee honey.

I crossed the room without a word, the soft creak of floorboards the only warning I gave him. I carefully handed him his mug before moving slowly to the side of him. His eyes followed me the entire way, that strange storm behind them flickering as I settled onto the small couch beside him. Close. Not touching. But close enough that I could feel the heat rolling off his skin. The kind of heat that made you want to lean in just a little further, just to see if you'd burn.

I tucked my feet up beneath me, cradled the mug between my palms. "Can I ask you something?"

He huffed, rubbing the back of his neck. "You're going to anyway."

"Fair." I let the silence stretch for a beat, before, "How open is your bond?"

His brow furrowed, slow and deep. "Open?" He took a long sip of tea.

"Yeah." I looked at him, watched the way the question visibly ruffled his feathers. "Like... Do you and Thalos ever just let things happen? Or is it all very planned and closed-off, carefully chosen?"

His jaw worked as he searched for the right answer—or any answer at all. I bit back a smile.

"You ask the strangest questions, you know that right?" He deflected my question before taking another sip.

"You avoid the most interesting ones." I smirked and nudged him softly.

He glanced at me, exasperated in a way that somehow made him even more handsome. "We're bonded. That doesn't mean we're... closed. But we don't just—" he paused, clearly wrestling with the words, "—entangle ourselves with anyone who looks at us sideways, if that's what you're asking."

I sipped my tea. "Sounds very... practical."

"It has to be," he said, voice low. "It's not just about emotion. Or lust. In the end it's magic. Because we want to bond a third to be in a triad. Once a bond is forged, it's permanent. It's power shared, fates linked. We can't afford to take it lightly. Not in the way humans can, falling in and out of love or lust at will."

"Even if you feel something unexpected?" I lifted my eyes, meeting his gaze fully now. "Even if it sneaks up on you, out of nowhere, and fits before you have a chance to question it?"

He stared at me like I'd peeled back his ribs and peered inside. "Do you always do this?"

"What?" I cupped both my hands tightly around my warm clay mug. Trying not to smile.

"Get into people's heads." His tone was flat. I fought my giggle by taking another sip from my mug letting the flavor of the soft herbs quench it. I watched Furgus settle on Kia's lap again, the cat's soft purr filling the space.

"Only when I like them." I shrugged simply.

That got a breath out of him, half chuckle, half sigh.

"Do you?" I asked.

He blinked. "Do I what?"

"Like me." I tilted my head and studied him closely for every shift in him.

He looked at me for a long moment. Then down into the depths of warm amber liquid in his mug.

"I don't know what this is," he said finally. "But I know it's dangerous."

I leaned in, just a little. Let my thigh brush against his. "Sometimes the dangerous things are the only ones worth chasing."

He didn't pull away.

Didn't speak.

Didn't move.

But the air between us? It crackled like lightning in the dark.

I watched him wrestle with the weight of silence, his body tight and coiled like he didn't trust himself to relax. So, naturally, I pressed a little further.

I offered a bright smile, feigning innocence as I took another slow sip of tea. "So… this last female you're searching for."

His brow lifted. "What about her?"

"You're hoping she's the one, aren't you?" I tilted my head, curling one leg beneath me. "The missing piece of your great fated triad. The one you and Thalos have been waiting for?"

His body tensed beside me. I could see him trying not to react, trying not to let the truth show on his face. That only made it more obvious.

"I'm just curious," I went on, swirling my tea, letting the steam brush my cheek like a secret. "Is that why you've been searching so long? Because you want to bond with her?" I paused, letting the next words hang like bait. "You want heirs, right?"

He choked. Literally.

One second, he was taking a careful sip of tea, the next, he was coughing like I'd stabbed him in the throat with a pitchfork. The cat—who had once again been curled contentedly in his lap—yowled and launched itself across the room, tail bottle-brushed and furious.

I blinked wide, batting my lashes. "Oh, gods, was that too forward?"

He glared at me, sputtering, hand over his chest like he might never recover. "What—what kind of question was that?"

"A fair one," I said, lifting my mug to hide the grin that threatened to break free. "You're the king, after all. Save your people, continuation of the line and all that."

"I wasn't expecting—" He coughed again. "—to be interrogated about heirs over tea."

"Well, I wasn't expecting you to show up on my land, break my gate and become half-naked in my barn, so I guess we're even." I rolled my eyes taking my last swallow of the sweet soothing mixture from the bottom of my mug.

He stared at me, stunned, his mouth slightly open like his brain hadn't caught up yet.

I held my empty cup in my lap and leaned in slightly, warmth in my voice. "You haven't answered, though."

His jaw flexed.

"I don't know what I expected," he muttered, eyes fixed on a point just past me. "Maybe... I thought finding her would fix everything. That the bond would make things easier. That she'd want the same things."

"Like what?" I asked gently.

His gaze met mine, softer now, but guarded. "To keep our people alive. To make something better. To build something that lasts with *US*."

The answer settled in my chest like a stone skipping across water. Not heavy. Just deep. But I wasn't done teasing.

I nudged his knee with mine. "Well, I don't know about her, but you've got a cat's approval. That counts for something."

He looked at the empty spot where the cat had been, then narrowed his eyes at me.

"You're so odd."

I beamed. "I try."

My smile faded just a little—not gone, just tucked behind something quieter. I watched him closely, watched how he didn't quite meet my eyes now.

"All jokes aside, though..." I looked into my empty mug between my hands, letting the lingering warmth ground me. "You say you want to protect her, but is that really what this is about? Protection? Or purpose?"

His shoulders stiffened like the question struck bone.

"I mean," I continued, my voice soft, "it sounds like a lot to put on someone you haven't even met."

He stared into his mug the small bits of leaves might rearrange themselves into the answers he sought.

Then, after a long breath, he said quietly, "You're right."

The honesty in his voice caught me off guard. I blinked.

"I miss Thalos." His words came slow, like peeling bark. "I haven't felt him—not even a flicker—since I entered the Ironwilde. It's been sixty-five days." He paused. "Sixty-five days of nothing but mist and trees and silence. And I've started to wonder if I'm chasing just some impossible dream."

His gaze lifted, locked with mine. It was the first time I saw something fragile under all that heavy armor.

"I want to find her," he said, "because I believe she's out there. But I'm not sure how much longer I can keep doing this. The winter storms are coming. If I don't turn back before fall..." His voice trailed off, but the meaning hung in the space between us hard and real.

As if the world agreed with him, a crack of thunder split the horizon. I glanced toward the darkening clouds just beyond the trees as fat, warm drops of rain began to spatter the windows.

"Well," I said, nodding to the window, "looks like the gods made your choice for you tonight."

He looked up at me, brows furrowed.

"No dry trail back to your camp in that mess," my voice a bit stern. Not that I knew where that was. "You're staying here."

"Lyria—" He started.

"No arguments," I said with a raised brow, I looked at him squarely. "Not unless you want to wrestle Pip for space in the barn."

As if on cue, the donkey brayed somewhere out back in indignant agreement.

Kiaza stared at me for a beat, rain patting harder, soaking the world in summer's heat and steam.

Then, at last, he gave a low sigh and a nod. "One night."

I smiled. "One night."

Though the moment stretched longer than that.

Long enough for thunder to roll again.

Long enough for my heart to do something stupid.

Chapter 11

Thalos

She straddled my lap on the worn little couch, soft brown overall barely containing her full bare breasts. Heat pooled between us, her breath a whisper against my ear.

"Just tonight, Your Majesty." Her voice was full of mischief and promise.

The words curled down my spine like smoke. My hand slid into the tumble of her long, loose hair, silken strands catching between my fingers. I caught her mouth with mine, and gods—her lips were warm, sweet, dangerous.

She pulled back just enough for me to see her eyes, deep brown shot through with molten gold, like sunlight melting into earth. Magic shimmered in them, and I felt it, felt *her*, the raw, perfect pull that reached past bone and blood and straight into my soul.

My chest tightened. I didn't want to breathe. I didn't want to let go.

Light flared.

Not magic—sunlight.

I blinked hard, the couch, the gold in her eyes dissolving into the pale stone of my chambers.

Renae's voice cut through the haze, brisk and bright. "Up with you, Thalos. The day won't wait."

I groaned, rubbing the grit from my eyes. She swept across the room, pulling back the curtains and pushing open windows until warm summer air spilled through them, carrying the scent of blooming vines from the walls below.

A tray clinked onto the table beside me, the steam from the tea curling upward in soft ribbons.

The dream still clung to me, her voice echoing in my mind. *Just tonight, Your Majesty.*

I wasn't sure whether to curse it or crave it. I knew she would be my undoing.

I pushed upright, the cool stone floor grounding me, but the dream clung like smoke—her weight on my lap, the heat of her lips, that flash of gold in her eyes. It was nothing I'd ever seen before, nothing I could forget if I tried.

Renae fussed with the windows, letting in more light than I cared for. "You'll want to eat before the council gathers," she said, her tone layered with that quiet authority only she could wield without rank.

I reached for the tea first, letting the heat seep into my palms. The taste was bitter and grounding, but it did nothing to still the restless edge inside me.

I missed Kiaza. The bond was still severed, the Ironwilde's cursed mist holding him beyond my reach. Two months without his presence was too long—long enough for doubts to creep in, long enough for me to feel the weight of the Spire's throne pressing harder each day.

Now Morgryth's shadow hung over us, his claim still ringing in the council chamber like a distant thunderclap.

I forced my focus forward. Today, maybe we would receive word back from Queen Novalyn. If the Crystalians had any sense, they'd see the value in standing with us. She might keep her strongest ties to the human factions of Velmorin and Rauthen, but I had to believe reason would sway her.

Because if it didn't, our line—and our future—would narrow to nothing.

I set my cup aside, rising to my feet, already hearing the murmur of council voices down the hall. The dream still whispered in the back of my mind, wrapping its heat around my thoughts, but I pushed it down.

There was no room for fantasy in war. Not while Kiaza was gone. Not while the fate of our kind balanced on a blade's edge.

The council chamber was already warm when I entered, the sun pouring in through high slits in the stone walls. Voices dipped the moment I stepped inside, replaced by the scrape of chairs and the shuffle of boots.

Renae took her seat at my left, parchment and quill at the ready. Across from her, two of the elder Drakes watched me closely, as if they could see the remnants of that dream clinging to my skin. I straightened my shoulders and set my face into the calm mask they expected.

"Queen Novalyn has agreed to meet with you along with an envoy of her choosing," Renae announced before anyone could open their mouths to pry. "She requests terms in writing before she departs the Obsidian Halls for our Spire."

A ripple of murmurs passed through the room. One of the younger councilors leaned forward. "If she comes, she'll bring her human allies with her."

"Let her," I said, my voice even. "If it gains us her ear, I'll hear them too."

Another cleared his throat. "What if she refuses our request?"

I held his gaze. "Then we find another way. I will not let this kingdom weaken while our King is beyond my reach."

The words came harder than I meant, edged with the ache of that empty bond. Kiaza had been my constant—my anchor—since the day we first joined magic. Now, the silence between us was a weight I carried into every decision.

Still, the dream lingered.

The warmth of her body. The gold in her eyes. The taste of her lips when she whispered *just tonight, Your Majesty.*

I shoved the memory down deep where no one could see it, where it couldn't tempt me. There was no time for distraction—not with Morgryth circling, not with our people's survival at stake.

I looked back at the council and continued. "If she's willing to talk, I'll make damn sure she sees the value of standing with us."

The council nodded, but I could feel their unease in the air, sharp as a blade's edge.

Because they knew, as I did, that time was running out.

High Chancellor Sareth was the first to speak. Tall and lean, with hair the color of white-gold pulled neatly back and fastened with a silver clasp, he moved with the deliberate grace of someone who measured every step. His dark blue robes, embroidered with curling Drakarian runes, whispered against the marble as he rose from his chair.

"She will not come cheaply, my lord," he said, voice smooth as still water. "Queen Novalyn guards her people's neutrality as fiercely as her crystal gates. We will need to offer more than promises of alliance if we expect her to leave her Obsidian halls at all."

On the far side of the table, General Harth leaned forward, forearms braced on the polished obsidian. He was broad in the shoulders, his tunic stretched tight across a chest built from decades of armor and battlefields. His dark hair was cut close, streaked with iron gray, and his weathered face bore the kind of deep lines carved only by war and loss.

"I'll not give her our troop movements," Harth rumbled, the baritone carrying across the chamber. His thick fingers tapped an unhurried rhythm against the map spread before him. "Or our supply routes. If she's as close to the humans as they say, it'd be as good as handing the Rauthen scum our throats."

"Noted," I said, letting my tone carry enough weight to still the argument before it began.

Lord Vare cleared his throat—a sharp, papery sound that matched his narrow frame. The treasurer's bronze-brown hair was thinning at the crown, his beard kept immaculately trimmed. He wore a layered doublet in muted earth tones, and his long fingers were smudged faintly with ink from the ledger at his elbow.

"Our coffers can support aid in materials, not gold," he said crisply. "If you wish to entice her, offer trade. Access to the silver veins along our western ridge, perhaps. But coin?" He shook his head, the corners of his mouth pinching. "That, we do not have to spare."

The council table was a massive oval of black obsidian veined with threads of gold that caught the morning light filtering through the tall, narrow windows. The scent of cedar smoke lingered from the braziers lit at dawn, curling upward into the vaulted ceiling. Beyond the open balcony doors, the summer air was warm, carrying the faint hum of the city far below the Dakorra Spire.

I leaned forward, resting my hands lightly on the table's edge. "We'll offer her trade rights to Dros Vale's gem market and access to the ridge's silver mines. In exchange, she brings her voice to our cause—and her fleets, should we call for them."

Harth's jaw tightened, but he gave a short nod. Sareth inclined his head in quiet approval. Vare made a sound that could have been either agreement or disapproval.

It didn't matter. This was the only offer I was willing to make, and they all knew it.

Harth's nod was slow, reluctant, his gaze fixed on the map between us as though he could will the Crystalians into proving him wrong. His fingers curled into a loose fist against the table's edge—habit from a lifetime of gripping a sword hilt whenever he didn't trust the company.

Sareth sat straighter, his hands folded in a precise, almost ornamental clasp atop the table. But his eyes—sharp as frost—shifted toward me and lingered there a moment too long. I knew the look. It was the silent weighing of whether my trust in Queen Novalyn was strategy... or hope.

Vare busied himself with the ledger at his elbow, the fine tip of his stylus tapping against the parchment. He kept his gaze low, but the slight twitch in his jaw betrayed the calculation running through his mind—the tallying of what this alliance would cost against what it might save. He'd sign off on it, yes, but only because the alternative was worse for our coffers.

The room itself seemed to hold its breath with us. The flicker of torchlight against the gold-veined obsidian table caught on the polished curves of the council's chairs, the shadows long and reaching. Outside, the wind shifted, carrying the faint clang of hammers from the forges below, a reminder of the war creeping closer with every day.

"We'll draft the terms for Queen Novalyn before midday," I said, letting my gaze travel from one councilor to the next. "If she accepts, we will meet her here. If she refuses…"

I let the words trail off. No one needed me to finish that thought.

Harth straightened, shoulders squaring as though bracing for a blow. Sareth inclined his head in a courtly gesture that was too measured to be entirely genuine. Vare made another neat notation in his ledger, the scratching of ink against parchment loud in the stillness.

This was an agreement, yes—but it was brittle. If Queen Novalyn misstepped, the fracture would run deep.

Before anyone could speak further, the heavy oak doors swung open without a knock.

Natrix strolled in like she owned the place, her hips swaying under a fitted leather coat that caught the torchlight. A sly grin curled her mouth as her gaze swept the table, lingering on each of us with open mischief before she claimed the empty chair to my right. I was just as surprised as the rest she rarely left the sea or the shoreside town. Let alone up here in our Spire. I looked her over once deciding whether to call her out on it or not.

She leaned back at ease, unhurried, propping her booted feet on the edge of the obsidian table as though it were a tavern bench instead of the heart of Drakarian diplomacy. The crossed ankles made her spurred heels catch the light, a lazy display of defiance.

"Ello, boys," she drawled, the smirk deepening. "What are you up to?"

Sareth's brow tightened, though he didn't dignify her with a reply. Harth gave a long-suffering exhale, muttering something about "storm-bringers" under his breath. Vare glanced up from his ledger just long enough to give her a look that could have curdled milk before returning to his neat rows of figures.

Nat only grinned wider, clearly enjoying the ripple she'd sent through the room.

She didn't move her boots from the table, even as Sareth's voice went cold. "This is a closed council session."

"Mm-hm," she said, flicking a speck of dust from her glove. "Yet, here I am. Guess that means I'm not here for the wine."

I caught the way her eyes darted to the stack of parchment between Sareth and me. She'd already sized up the conversation without hearing a word of it.

"So, you're talking about the Crystalians, aren't you?" she said, almost lazily. "Queen Novalyn's the only one who'd make you all look like you swallowed a sour plum. Let me guess, you want something from her, but you're too afraid she'll ask for more than you're willing to give."

Sareth's jaw locked, his knuckles white against the carved arm of his chair. "This is delicate—"

"Everything worth doing is a calculated risk," Nati cut in, tipping her head back against the chair. "The trick is knowing what you're willing to lose before you start bargaining."

General Harth's mouth curved into a reluctant grin, though he tried to hide it. Vare muttered something about "meddlesome women," but his quill slowed on the page, as if her words had lodged in his mind despite himself.

Nati's smirk softened just enough to turn thoughtful. "If Queen Novalyn is smart—and she is—she'll want proof of strength, not desperation. Send her an offer that makes her think you can walk away from the table at any time... even if you can't."

She let the words hang in the air, daring anyone to tell her she was wrong.

Nat had always been good at slicing through courtly posturing, even if she used a blade instead of a scalpel. Her methods were rough, unapologetic—but effective. It was one of the reasons I'd admired her from the first time we met, long before she became an ally. Even without an official bond between us, she'd stood beside the Drakarian throne when others hesitated, cutting through the tangle of politics in ways my council could never manage without drowning in formality.

She moved then, boots hitting the stone with a thud and rattle. She reached into her jacket, pulled out a rolled sheaf of parchment, and let it drop onto the polished table with a satisfying *thud*. The weight of it made the inkwells rattle.

"Well," she said, leaning back in her chair again, "besides, you might not need Queen Novalyn at all." Her grin widened as she tapped the documents with one finger. "More than half of the Abyssian clans have already signed. And—" her voice lowered, turning sly, "—there's the land witch, and her little gift of magic she peddles to the humans."

She rose with slow, deliberate poise, pushing the scrolls towards me, and stepping close enough that I could feel the heat of her. Leaning in, she tilted her head as though she might press her lips to my neck, but instead her breath grazed my ear.

"And you didn't even have to bond me to do this, Thao." Her hot breath made a shiver run up my spine.

Before I could react, she straightened, her smirk sharp enough to draw blood. Louder now, so the entire council could hear, she added, "Just needs your seal, King Thalos."

The room seemed to breathe in and hold itself still. All eyes slid towards me. The treaty lay between my hands, smelling faintly of salt and deep-sea ink, the signatures of the Abyssian leaders curling in black across the parchments like tentacles.

I inclined my head to her. "Thank you, Nat. Getting them to sign my proposed treaty wasn't a small feat."

Lord Vare was already moving with his usual quiet precision, setting out the seal, a stick of crimson wax, and the inkwell. Together, we pressed the molten wax to the parchment and stamped it with the Drakarian crest, the double Drake's wings spreading wide in relief. One by one, I separated the copies—one for each Abyssian clan, one for our records, and one to send with Nat as proof of the alliance.

I was reaching for the final document when the air around me shifted—thick, charged. My breath caught.

Lyria.

She was there in my mind, though not as she had been in my dream this morning. She felt...sad. Distant.

And then Kiaza's presence hit me like a solid wall. His magic roared in my chest, heavy with anger maybe sorrow, his voice deep and quietly firm, *"I have to go. I have to find the last female. I have no choice."*

I was no longer in the Spire's throne room, it was as if I stood there *with* him, in the same room, her home alone as he left the door closing.

Before I could speak, the connection fractured, fading like smoke through my fingers.

A sharp snap brought me back. Nat's fingers were in front of my face, she was leaning over the table, tilting her head, and her eyes narrowing in faint concern.

"Are you okay, Thao?" Her voice was lowered so only I could hear.

I swallowed the lingering pulse of magic and locked my expression into something steady. Whatever I'd just felt, whatever it meant, this wasn't the place to unravel it.

"I'm fine," I told Nat, the words even, if a shade too clipped.

Still, the unease clung to me like a shadow. Lyria's sadness, Kiaza's anger, both still coiled in my chest, a knot I couldn't shake. Forcing my focus back to the council table, to the faces watching me for direction.

I straightened in my chair, hands resting on the sealed treaty. "Now," I said, letting my voice carry, "Let's get back to drafting the terms for Queen Novalyn and see if she will consider our offer. If she won't, then with the Abyssian clans at our side..." I gave a small nod toward Nat, "...I believe we still have enough to keep Morgryth from making any more bold moves. At least for now."

The murmurs that followed were measured—less tense than earlier, though far from relaxed. That was as much peace as I was going to get from them today.

Inside, I could still feel the faint echo of Lyria and Kiaza in my magic. And for the first time in a long while, I wasn't sure if I should be more hopeful...or more afraid.

The council bent their heads to parchment and ink, voices layering over one another as the first lines of our offer took shape.

"Access to the silver veins along the western ridge," Vare murmured, his quill already scratching. "And limited trade through Dros Vale's gem markets."

"Add joint patrols of the border forests," Harth rumbled. "Not troop counts...just the promise of shared steel when it's needed."

Sareth inclined his head. "And language that binds us as equals. The Queen will not stomach subservience, nor will we."

Nat gave a dry laugh. "Dress it up however you like, but make sure she knows you're willing to walk away. That will tempt her more than any promise of coin."

I listened, then spoke, letting my words cut through the noise. "Write it all down. Trade rights, shared defense, equal footing. Enough to prove our strength, not our desperation."

The scratch of quills filled the chamber, each stroke a fragile tether to hope. By the time the last line was inked, a rough draft lay before me, sealed with wax still warm from the flame. It wasn't perfect, but it was a start.

The council shifted into smaller conversations while Vare quietly noting the courier routes for treaty copies, Harth speaking in low tones to Sareth about defensive patrols along the southern border. Nat lounged back in her chair like the meeting was already over, but her sharp eyes missed nothing.

I let them talk. Let the voices blur into the background hum of court. It gave me a moment to breathe, to steady the pull in my chest.

"Enough for today," I finally said, rising from my chair. The words cut clean through the low chatter. "We've done what we can here. Now we wait."

Chairs scraped back. Papers were gathered. Lord Vare tucked the sealed copies into leather tubes, bowing slightly before leaving with a measured step. Harth left more abruptly, his boots striking the polished floor in quick, military rhythm. Sareth paused long enough to incline his head toward me which was half-respect, half-scrutiny, before following.

Only Nat lingered. She gave me a look that was part knowing, part warning, then tipped her head toward the great doors. "You'll tell me when you're ready," she murmured, and was gone before I could say anything.

Alone, I stood in the quiet chamber. The summer air drifted in through the open windows, carrying the scent of sea salt and stone.

Beneath it all, I could still taste the sharp, electric thread of connection. Lyria. Kiaza. Both pulling at me from somewhere far beyond these walls.

Still somewhere deep inside, I knew, whatever came next, the waiting wouldn't last long.

Chapter 12

Kiaza

The rain echoed on the tin roof above us. I set my empty cup on the small table to my right. This couch was far too small for my frame—and she was far too close. Her warmth bled into me, every shift of her body an unspoken invitation.

Fuck, Los... I wish you could hear me. Feel this. Tell me she's just a human. Just a woman with perfect breasts, round hips, curves that make a man forget himself... Not to mention skin I'd bet is soft in every place that matters.

And *fuck, Thalos, you'd love her too.*

No. Not love. I'd just been alone for more than two months, my hand my only companion. That would drive anyone mad.

She smiled at me, and her eyes, *Gods*, those eyes were warm and beautiful. She was sunshine made flesh, and I was the earth starving for light after a long winter.

Without a word, she leaned over me to set her cup beside mine. Her body brushed mine, thin cotton the only barrier between us. Sparks shot through me, heat pooling low and hard. The sway of her breasts beneath her loose overalls was its own kind of torment. She reached farther until the cup landed on the table with a soft clank, her left breast grazing my resting hand, my thumb catching on a taut, peaked nipple.

Fuck.

She started to move back, but I caught her arm, holding her gently. My magic churned, glinting in my eyes, as I knew I couldn't hide it well. Not now. She didn't look away. If anything, she met my gaze deeper.

I brought my other hand up, smoothing down her braid until I found the tie. I pulled it loose, working my fingers through the deep chestnut strands until they spilled freely. She leaned into my touch, and I cradled her head, tangling my fingers in that softness.

Then she kissed me.

Soft, but with purpose. *Fuck*, I melted into her. Her lips tasted like honey, her mouth like sweet berries and herbs. My tongue swept into hers, teasing, claiming.

She shifted her body, straddling my lap, and the solid weight of her warmth made my cock strain hard against the rough fabric of my pants. I held her head as she moaned into my mouth, that sound sinking into me like molten rock. Her hips rolled against my hardness and I broke the kiss just long enough to breathe her name.

"Lyria?" It was more a question than a statement.

She kissed up my collarbone and neck, her breath hot in my ear. "Just tonight, Your Majesty."

One night. That was all. Enough to burn this madness out of me. She was only human, so there was no real risk to it. Thalos would understand. He'd never been threatened by our primal instincts. Sometimes, need simply had to be met.

And gods, I needed her.

Like I hadn't needed anyone since the first night with Thalos, which was primal, fated, inevitable.

No, I told myself. This wasn't that. Couldn't be. She was human. We couldn't bond to someone without magic.

I was just touch-starved. Just lonely.

"Just for tonight," I breathed, my heart pounding.

I unsnapped her overalls, freeing her breasts. Gods, they were the most perfect, plump, creamy things I'd ever seen. I leaned down, tasting each one, licking, nipping, savoring her gasps. She arched into me, my hand leaving her hair to trail down her hip, my other cupping her right breast, holding it steady as my mouth closed over her nipple.

Her center pressed harder against me, the friction was like sweet torture.

Her body moved against mine in slow, deliberate rolls, her breath coming faster with each pass. The storm outside rumbled, as if it, too, felt the tension snapping between us.

I wanted to grab her hips, hold her there, grind her down onto me until I forgot my own name, but I didn't. Not yet. Because this wasn't just about release. This was turning into something more dangerous.

I brushed my mouth up her throat, over the curve of her jaw, until I found her lips again. Her fingers curled into my shoulders, nails scraping just enough to make me growl into her kiss.

She pulled back, just an inch, eyes locked to mine. "You look like you're thinking too much," she teased, voice low and breathless.

"I'm thinking just enough," I murmured, brushing my thumb across her lower lip. "Every thought is about you."

Her mouth curved, but her gaze didn't waver. "Even the dangerous ones?"

"Especially those." I couldn't hold back my smirk when I said that because everything about this felt like danger, but I needed to taste her, feel her, and make her mine.

Lightning flashed through the windows, the brief light catching in her hair, turning the deep chestnut to fire. I wanted to bury myself in her. I wanted to feel her come apart around me, hear my name on her lips like prayer and sin.

But a small, treacherous thought slid in— *What about the last female?*

I shoved it away. Tonight wasn't about fate. It wasn't about duty or kingdoms. Tonight was about her warmth, her breath, her heartbeat thudding against my chest.

"Just tonight," she repeated, like a promise... or maybe it was a warning.

I slid my hands down her back, gripping her hips and finally pulling her flush against me. She gasped, her lashes fluttering, and I swallowed that sound with my mouth on hers. Her scent—lavender, hay, soil—wrapped around me, grounding and intoxicating at once.

The storm outside broke fully, rain hammering the roof in a relentless rhythm. It was the only sound besides her soft, uneven breaths and the pounding of my own heart.

If this was madness, I would let it take me.

Her hands slid over my chest, mapping every ridge of muscle through the thin shirt. She didn't rush, and gods, she *took her time*, like she needed to feel every part of me, not just see it.

Then her fingers dipped under the hem, nails grazing my skin as she pushed it up, up, over my head. The air hit my bare chest, but it was nothing compared to the heat radiating from her.

"You're warm," she murmured, palms pressing flat against me, like she was soaking in my heat.

I huffed a low laugh. "I suppose, I run hotter than most."

Her smile said she knew exactly what I meant and exactly what I didn't.

When she leaned in to kiss my neck, her lips lingered just enough to make my breath hitch. She caught it and smirked against my skin. Then she sat back, still straddling me, and tugged on the buckle of my belt, in a deliberate pull.

Metal clasps clicked. The fabric loosened. My hands twitched, wanting to help, but she kept control, sliding the leather strap out of my pant loops, the pants stayed a tight barrier between us.

"You're taking your time," I said, my voice rougher than I meant.

"Would you rather I didn't?" She tilted her head with mischief and smiled with amusement.

"No," I admitted. "Gods, no."

She stood just enough to shimmy the overalls down, the movement brushing her thighs against mine. The cotton slid past her hips, revealing smooth skin, then the curve of her underwear. They were simple, dark, and already testing my restraint.

I hooked a finger into the fabric, tugging her closer. "You're dangerous, Sunshine."

"Was my trowel your first clue?" she teased, before leaning down to kiss me again. This one was slower, deeper, her tongue sweeping against mine like she meant to draw every ounce of control from me.

My hands roamed her back, down to the small dip just above her hips. She pressed herself against me, rolling her hips once, it was deliberate, testing, and I nearly groaned.

"Patience," she whispered, though her breathing had quickened.

She slid her hands between us again to the edge of my pants, undoing them with maddening precision, popping each button of my pants like she enjoyed the sound. When her fingers brushed against me through the fabric, I caught her wrist, holding it there.

Her eyes lifted to mine, all warm brown and mischief. "You planning on stopping me?"

"Not a chance," I said, my grip loosening to let her do exactly what she wanted.

The storm outside deepened, thunder rolling low and steady. Inside, the world had narrowed to her scent, her touch, the way her hair spilled loose around her face as she worked me out of my pants.

She wasn't rushing. Neither was I. This wasn't just hunger—it was the slow burn of two people who knew they were about to cross a line they couldn't uncross.

And I wanted to take my time falling.

Her hands were on my rigid length. I hissed out a breath. It wasn't greedy, no, she was far too calculated for that, but she touched me like she wanted to own every inch of me before the night ended.

She let go and I missed the feel of her immediately, my cock throbbed with the ache of it. Her fingers trailed up my ribs, slow enough that each pass made my breath grow heavier, before her nails skimmed down again, light as the brush of air. She was studying me—*testing me*—like she knew exactly how far to push before I broke.

I wanted to grab her, flip her beneath me, and claim that teasing mouth. I didn't.

Instead, I sat back against the too-small couch, letting her straddle my lap, letting her dictate the pace. The storm outside rattled the tin roof, wind sweeping the scent of rain through the open window, mixing with the lavender and earth clinging to her skin.

She leaned in, close enough that her breath tickled my ear. "You always this patient?"

I swallowed hard. "No."

"Good." She kissed the corner of my mouth—just there, not quite giving me what I wanted—before pulling back, her smile sharp and knowing.

Every movement was a game, and she was winning. She shifted on my lap, slow enough that the pressure of her hips against me made my jaw tighten. I could feel her warm wetness through her panties against the length of my bare cock.

"Lyria..." My voice was a warning. Or maybe a plea.

She ignored it, dragging her hands over my shoulders, down my arms, mapping me like she might get lost if she didn't learn every contour. Then she caught my hand, brought it to her thigh, and held it there, like she was daring me to move higher.

I didn't. Not yet.

"You're very... contained," she murmured, her gaze fixed on mine. "Is that how you always are? With him?"

My breath stalled. "Thalos?"

"Mhm." She rolled the word over her tongue like she already knew the answer. "Do you ever just... let go? Or is everything between you two planned? Calculated?"

I narrowed my eyes. "You ask too many questions."

She smirked. "And you avoid too many answers."

The push and pull between us was starting to burn. My magic—restless, hungry—shifted under my skin, responding to her nearness. She felt it, I knew she did. But she didn't back away.

Instead, she traced the line of my jaw with one finger, then my throat, then lower, until her palm splayed flat over my chest. Her warmth sank through me.

"Tell me," she said, her voice softer now, "if you find her, the last female, are you hoping she'll be the one? That missing bond?"

The question hit like a blade under my ribs. My grip on her thigh tightened, and for a moment, I forgot to breathe. "That's not..."

She tilted her head. "So... yes?"

Before I could answer—before I could even catch my breath—her lips were on my chest, then my stomach, each kiss pulling another thread from the frayed edge of my control. She slid down to the floor between my knees, her presence there more dangerous than any blade at my throat.

Her mouth found the sharp edge of my hip bone, kissing it, claiming it. Then—*fuck*—she licked the tip of my cock, slow, deliberate, swirling her tongue in a spiral that sent lightning up my spine. She didn't look away as she took me in her mouth—her gaze locked to mine, all molten challenge and knowing delight.

My hand, which had been resting on her hip, slid to my knee, gripping so hard the golden-brown skin of my knuckles blanched white. My other hand clutched the couch, desperate for an anchor. The storm outside raged harder, but it was nothing compared to the one breaking loose in me.

She's human. This can't matter. This can't mean anything.

My magic flared in my chest sparked like dry tinder at her touch, and I could feel that dangerous edge of my primal instinct, the one where want bleeds into need.

Her mouth closed over me fully, heat and velvet wrapping my rigid length, and I let out a growl so low it rattled through my ribs, the thunder answering in kind. My hips twitched despite my effort to stay still, to keep this slow, but every instinct I had screamed to take, to claim, to make her mine.

Just tonight, I reminded myself. *Just tonight, and then you walk away. Then you find her, our fate.*

As I watched her head move in a slow rhythm, felt the slick pull of her throat and the way her hands gripped my thighs like she belonged there, I knew I was lying to myself. She was undoing me with every stroke, every look, every soft hum of pleasure against me.

I knew—whether it destroyed me or not—I was going to take her. Claim her. Make her mine.

If only for tonight.

Her mouth worked over me in slow, deliberate strokes, each one dragging my restraint thinner until it felt like a single thread about to snap. Every time she drew back, her tongue teased the underside of my cock, and every time she sank down, that perfect, molten heat wrapped around me like she knew exactly how to ruin me.

My fingers ached from gripping the couch, from holding myself in place when every part of me wanted to shove deeper, harder, until she forgot everything before this moment. The storm outside had settled into a steady roar, rain hammering the roof in time with my pulse, thunder rolling low and close like it was listening in.

"Lyria..." My voice was rough, strained, almost unrecognizable. I didn't know if I was warning her, begging her, or both.

She hummed around me, and the vibration made my hips jerk, my self-control crumbling faster. I bit back a curse and dragged my hand from my knee to her hair, threading my fingers through the loosened waves until I had a firm hold. She looked up at me with those eyes—deep, warm, flecked with gold—and I swore she could see every thought I was trying not to have.

Don't. Don't push. Don't take.

She drew back just far enough to lick me from base to tip, slow and wicked, and then her smile—gods, that smile—broke me.

My grip tightened in her hair, and I felt my control snap like brittle glass. "Enough," I growled, the word thick with everything I'd been holding back. I stood, pulling her with me, the heat between us sparking like the lightning outside.

I kissed her hard, no pretense left, my tongue claiming her mouth as my hands roamed—up her spine, down her curves. She pressed against me, soft where I was hard, her body fitting mine like it had been carved for it.

The storm surged again, wind rattling the windows, and I didn't care. I had her in my arms. "Fuck it." I murred into her hair, for tonight... Tonight she was all mine.

Chapter 13

Lyria

His mouth crushed against mine, hot and unrestrained, the taste of him sending a shiver straight through me. I'd been teasing him for what felt like hours, dancing around that edge just to see how far I could push the Drakarian King before he snapped. Now I had my answer.

His hands were everywhere—spanning my back, cupping my hips, sliding up my ribs, leaving trails of heat as he went. He kissed me like I was air after drowning, like I was the one thing he refused to lose.

The gods help me... I wanted to be that for him. Though, I would only give him tonight. I didn't want to be a queen to save the fate of all of magic, I just wanted here, now.

The storm outside rose to match us, rain pounding the roof, wind thrumming in the walls. His body was solid heat against me, his hard length pressing into my belly, reminding me exactly what I'd been coaxing toward all evening.

I slid my hands up his chest, feeling the tense flex of muscle under my palms, and then higher—curling my fingers into the thick long hair at his nape. He made a low sound, almost a growl, and deepened the kiss, his tongue stroking mine with deliberate, claiming sweeps.

This wasn't calculated courtship. This wasn't some careful dance for a crown, for politics, or even for fate. This was raw and hungry and real.

And I wanted more. He moved and his face was in my hair, his lips against my neck and I heard the ever so faint whisper, "Fuck it."

With one decisive movement of his hand, his pants hit the floor in a heap beside mine. The only thing left between us was the whisper-thin barrier of my dark cotton panties—already soaked through from how badly I wanted him.

Before I could draw another breath, he shifted me, turning my back to the solid wall of his body until my ass pressed to the hard, unyielding line of his cock. His heat bled through the fabric, sending shivers racing up my spine.

One of his hands found the base of my neck, firm but not cruel, guiding me forward until my palms braced against the couch. The position left me open, my hips tilted, my body a silent offering to whatever he wanted.

His other hand slipped between my thighs, fingers sure and unhurried as they coaxed me apart. The first drag of his fingertips along the damp fabric had me gasping, my knees threatening to give. He traced a slow path from my clit to the curve of my ass, not pushing, just teasing. I am sure it was in return for all the teasing I had been doing to him. I groaned, as my smile grew.

I pushed back into him, my body betraying every ounce of my restraint, my hips rolling into the maddening rhythm of his touch. A small, needy sound escaped me that I couldn't bite back.

Gods. I didn't care if this never happened again. I had never wanted anyone like this—never felt such an ache low and deep inside me, my body felt as though I had known him long before I did. I had been with others before but not like this, it was as if my soul had been starving for this. For him.

"Kia…" My voice was breathless, ragged. "Please."

The word hung between us, far too raw, far too needy, but I didn't care. This night was not about love. Not about magic. Not about fate. Not about the feelings swirling inside me. This was about what I wanted.

I wanted a daughter.

For the life we could have together. For what I could give her, free from prophecy, from destiny's cruel hands. A life where I could be what my mother never was. A life where I could finally have someone who was mine to love completely for the rest of my life.

His growl rumbled low in his chest, vibrating through my back where we touched. The sound was primal, answering something buried in me.

His thumb hooked under the edge of my panties, dragging the fabric slowly, deliberately down until the night air kissed my wet skin. Then—finally—he pressed forward.

The head of his cock slid through my slick folds in one long, torturous pass, testing me. Moaning, I arched, seeking more, but he kept the slow pace excruciating, the heavy weight of him promising everything I craved but holding it just out of reach. As he moved his cock back and forth, my hips rocked, pressing and begging for more.

"Kiaza," I gasped, twisting my head enough to catch his eyes over my shoulder. I saw the small smile just as his gaze darkened.

Whatever he saw in my gaze broke his restraint. His hands gripped my hips like they belonged there, and in the next breath he pushed inside me, inch by inch, claiming me with a slow, commanding drive.

The sound that left me was nothing I'd ever made before—low, trembling, threaded through with pleasure so sharp it hurt. His fingers dug into my hips as he drew back and then slammed into me again, deeper this time. Rougher.

I welcomed every demanding thrust, pushing back against him. The need for more of him ignited a fire inside me, burning hotter as I rolled my hips. I wanted him deeper, until he was completely filling me.

His right hand slid along my hip, across my belly, then down to my pelvis without breaking the rhythm of his thrusts. His fingers found my aching clit, circling in slow, torturous strokes. I moaned, breath quickening, my whole body tightening as he kept working me closer to the edge of my release.

With his other hand, he fisted my hair and pulled me back against him. The arch of my body took him deeper still, his fingers never letting up. His pace held steady until my legs trembled so hard I nearly collapsed.

His strength kept me upright, holding my weight easily as he slowed, drawing me closer. In one fluid motion, he lifted me with him, his cock still buried deep inside me. I had no idea it was possible to feel so aroused and so weightless at the same time.

He turned, carrying me with him, and sat back on the couch with a thud and a crack. I couldn't help but giggle, my breath breaking into a moan as my weight settled. I was straddling him backwards now, my knees nestled into the cushions at his sides, my ass flush against his sculpted abs. His hands held me firmly in place as his hips began to roll beneath me, deep and steady.

"Fuck, Kia—don't stop." My voice was ragged, desperate.

I reached between us, teasing my own clit, my fingers brushing against the hard heat of him as he worked his cock inside me. Matching his pace, I moved with him in a slow, building dance of need and desire, my breath syncing with the pounding of my heart.

His fingers laced over mine, curling wickedly against the center of my clit adding to my pleasure. The coil low in my belly wound tighter with every stroke, every roll of his hips, until it was all I could do to hang on.

I growled and cried out his name—"Kia!"—just as his groan vibrated against my back.

"That's it, Sunshine," he breathed, his voice a low command. "Cum for me."

And I did. My world unraveled in that moment—threads of gold, green, and red twisting together as my body clenched around him. His release followed, hot and pulsing, filling me full. Magic was spilling through me in a rush so intense my vision blurred.

For one breathless second, everything snapped open. I could see Thalos in bed. I could see myself through Kia's eyes. I could hear them both—their thoughts bleeding together with mine.

One word thundered through me.

Fuck!

I slammed it shut. My magic burst outward, burning hot and bright, then sealed everything tight. If I looked back at Kia, he'd know. He'd see the gold blazing in my eyes. But I locked it all away. Concealed myself. Concealed Kia. Concealed Thalos.

The bond wasn't gone—it could never break—but now it was mine alone. Untouchable. Dangerous. If they ever learned what I had just done, they'd see it as betrayal. Maybe it was. But I wasn't about to be fate's puppet. Not when freedom was this close.

Kia rested his head against my back, breath ragged, as we stilled together. The storm outside had faded to a soft patter on the roof.

With shaky legs, I rose. I kept my eyes half-closed, pressed one light kiss to his damp forehead, and stepped away. I tossed him a blanket.

"Good night, grumpy. Don't forget the lantern." My voice was low, unsteady.

Then I walked off, leaving him naked and covered in the aftermath. I closed my door with a long, steadying sigh and stood there in the silence. I leaned against the wood, pretending not to hear the faint echo of magic still humming in my veins, or the whisper in my gut that told me I'd just crossed a line I could never uncross.

I'd just fucked him and left him there. I didn't know how he'd take it, only that I hoped he'd keep his word and be gone by morning. If he lingered, it would only make this harder.

I dropped onto my bed, sprawled on my back, staring up at the ceiling. Naked. Breath shaky. My hand clutched my stomach. A single tear slid down my cheek.

"Just us now, little one." I whispered softly in the dark.

I could feel it, her, the flicker of new life inside me, growing even now. But I also felt the threads of my fated bond with both Kiaza and Thalos, thrumming like a heartbeat that wanted out.

I wouldn't let it. Not ever.

Chapter 14

Thalos

Steam curled up from the basin, ghosting over the mirror as I leaned on the vanity. My shirt hung open, loose over my shoulders, and the cool air from the open window brushed damp skin. I splashed water over my face again, letting it run down my neck before wiping it away with the edge of a towel.

The council meeting had been days earlier, but the restless energy clung to me, and my sleep had been restless. Not the kind that came from politics or strategy. This was deeper, buried under my ribs, humming like a low chord that refused to fade.

Her name.

Lyria.

I'd heard it once in Kiaza's voice, low and raw in my mind, but it had lodged itself there like a hook. Since then, I couldn't shake the strange weight of it. I could still feel the echo of that moment, a shift in the bond we shared, subtle but undeniable. Something between us had changed... and not just between us.

I braced my hands on the vanity, leaning forward until my reflection stared back, green-eyes, farrowed brow, and unsatisfied. I was used to longing for Kia when we were apart, used to the ache that came with distance. But this—this wasn't the same.

This was wanting someone I'd never met. Someone who'd only come to me in fractured dreams and fleeting visions.

The worst part? In those moments, she didn't feel like a stranger at all.

Her laugh came to me sometimes, light, sharp, threaded with mischief. Other times it was the warmth of her skin against my palms, the scent of rain-damp earth tangled with something fresh and slightly floral like fresh cut hay, or a meadow of flowers. I'd see her in flashes: sunlight glancing off deep chestnut hair, the curve of a smile that promised trouble, the stubborn tilt of her chin.

Even still, I knew the intoxicating feel of her magic.

I shouldn't. I couldn't. Yet it brushed against me in those dreams, wild and unbound, with a pulse that made my own power stir in answer.

It was the same now, faint but present, as if she were just beyond reach. I gripped the edge of the vanity tighter, chasing it, but the sensation slipped away, leaving me with nothing but the echo.

I told myself it was nothing. Just the byproduct of too much distance from Kia, of the strain this endless search had put between us. But deep down, I knew better. Whatever was happening, it wasn't one-sided. She was *real*.

Though for reasons I couldn't name, I needed to find her.

The soft chime of the breakfast bell cut through my thoughts. I straightened, fastening the top two buttons of my shirt, and glanced once more at the man in the mirror. Still unsettled. Still restless.

By the time I stepped out into the corridor toward the great hall, my expression was as smooth as the marble beneath my boots.

Why could I only catch small glimpses of her? Why couldn't I reach Kia? Why was the bond so muddled? Fear slid beneath my skin and gripped my heart with flashes of what might be happening, of them needing me. My hands flexed, claws threatening to break through before sinking back beneath my skin. These halls could hold a Drake of my size, but I preferred not to shift unless forced, not when control was everything. Still, the primal pull etched itself deeper through me, like something calling to my very soul.

The scent of roasted root vegetables, bacon, eggs and fresh-baked bread reached me halfway down the corridor, pulling me from my thoughts. Once I stepped into the castle's kitchen, the hearth was glowing, casting its golden light across the long table where Renae sat with her son, both mid-laughter over something she'd said.

"Los," she greeted, her voice warm and familiar, the way it always was when we shared a meal away from the great hall. Her son, Sam grinned through a mouthful of bread and gave a quick wave before ducking his head.

I slipped into the chair across from them, the rough wood grounding beneath my palms. "Smells good," I said, reaching for a loaf still steaming from the oven.

"It's nothing fancy," Renae replied, sliding a plate of eggs scrambled mixed with potatoes and peppers, and large slices of bacon toward me, "but it'll fill our bellies."

The warmth of the meal settled into my chest as we talked. Nothing of politics or war, only small things. Sam asked about horses. Renae teased me about my poor appetite at formal dinners. For a brief moment, the gnawing tension in my chest eased, dulled by the simple comfort of food and company.

The peace lasted right until the kitchen door slammed open. One of the castle's young runners skidded to a stop, breathless and wide-eyed.

"Message for the King," he blurted, then caught sight of me and added quickly, "Queen Novalyn will arrive by midmorning." It was only an hour past dawn but that gave little time for me to prepare.

My half-eaten plate cooled on the table, eggs and vegetables forgotten. A faint, electric hum of anticipation rippled through me, part political urgency, part something I couldn't yet name.

Renae shot me a look over the rim of her mug, one brow raised. "Well," she said, setting it down with a soft clink, "looks like breakfast just got less relaxed."

I pushed back from the table, the chair scraping softly against the stone floor. Sam looked up, bread crumbs dotting his cheek, but I only ruffled his hair as I passed. "Duty calls," I said with a faint smile.

The truth was less gentle. My chest already carried the weight of what was coming.

The halls of the castle carried me forward, the murmur of servants quickening as word of Queen Novalyn's arrival spread. By the time I reached the throne room, a pair of maids were already drawing back the heavy curtains, letting the light of morning spill in.

Beyond the tall windows, the mountain valley stretched wide and sharp, the sprawl of trees threatening to change into their fall colors any day stood tall and seeding flowers still clinging to the ridges. It should have steadied me. Instead, it only reminded me how precarious the balance truly was.

Council members began to filter in, their voices hushed but clipped with urgency. I took my place at the center, the mantle of king consort and acting sovereign pressing heavy across my shoulders. We spoke quickly, circling the same questions: what words to meet her with, how much to yield, and how much to guard.

Already, I could feel the shape of the meeting shifting before she ever stepped foot inside.

The throne room's large wood doors opened wide and I watched as Queen Novalyn entered, as the whole room fell silent. She moved like living light refracted through glass, every angle of her form catching and bending the colors of the world.

Her skin was as pale and smooth as moonstone. Along her cheekbones, temples, and the sharp line of her collarbones, prismatic crystalline ridges grew in delicate lattices, as though the earth itself had sculpted her in shimmering quartz. These lines glowed faintly, fractured with inner fire. Iridescent veins of violet, gold, and green that pulsed softly whenever she spoke.

Her hair, cropped short and silvery-white, caught the glow and scattered it like a crown spun of ice. Her elongated ears, tipped with facets of gemlike growth, gave her an unearthly regality, half flesh and half mineral beauty. The gown she wore, woven of fine threads like veins of light, clung in luminous layers of embroidered filigree, refracting against her crystal lines so that she seemed half woman, half prism, entirely sovereign.

Her eyes were pale yet piercing, the faintest shade of diamond blue, with a sheen that mirrored the crystalline veins at her brow. To look at her was to be dazzled and unsettled, for her presence carried both fragility and indomitable strength, it was an unspoken reminder that beauty could cut sharper than any blade.

Queen Novalyn arrived not alone, but flanked. Two rogue Drakes walked at her sides, their human forms cloaked in the blue of the Bravarn faction—a bitter reminder of broken loyalties. Behind them, two humans kept close. A woman dressed in the rich violet of Velmorin, her posture rigid though her gown flowed around her, her eyes sharp, silently observant. Beside her, a tall, slim man in the regal red of Rauthen, his smile too polished, too thin, as though it might crack under its own false weight.

The air in the throne room thickened as they crossed the threshold. My people stiffened. Even the light from the valley beyond seemed harsher, gilding the edges of tension in gold.

I stood tall, every muscle trained to hold steady, even as the unease coiled tight in my gut. Whatever game Novalyn meant to play, she had brought her pieces with her. While I made the first move.

I stepped forward, bowing my head just enough to acknowledge her sovereignty without surrendering my own. When I spoke, my voice carried steady, trained, though I felt the weight of every gaze pressing into my back.

"Your Majesty," my unwavering voice echoed slightly, my eyes meeting her pale, diamond-blue ones. "On behalf of the Drakarian throne, I welcome you to our halls. It honors us that you would travel so far to hear our terms, and to consider what an alliance might yet mean for our peoples."

Her lips curved, not quite a smile. The crystalline ridges along her temples pulsed faintly, like the flicker of a heartbeat under stone.

"King Consort," she replied, her voice smooth as cut glass. "We shall see if your terms hold the weight you claim."

The rogue Drakes moved behind her, restless. My councilors bristled but held their tongues. I straightened, letting the mountain light pour over me, steadying myself in its clarity. This meeting would decide far more than trade or borders—this was moves in a game none of us could afford to lose.

Queen Novalyn swept forward, her gown whispering like crystal shards across the stone floor as she took the guest throne placed opposite mine. Her entourage flanked her, careful but predatory, the rogue Drakes' sharp eyes tracking every movement in the chamber. She settled gracefully into her seat, crystalline ridges glinting in the sunlight.

I inclined my head, careful not to let eagerness sharpen into demand. "My thanks for answering so swiftly, Your Grace. What I ask is simple, though not easy: withdraw your kingdom's aid from Morgryth and his traitors, and rein in the human railways pressing into the mountain valleys. Both paths threaten not just the Drakarian, but all who share these lands."

The Velmorin delegate—the woman in violet silks—leaned forward. "You speak of Morgryth as if he were ours. He is not. We tolerate him because he disrupts our enemies but he just as often disrupts our trade. To withdraw aid is to invite his wrath at our doors. Tell me, Consort, will you shield our trade paths when he strikes them instead of you?"

Her question hung like a drawn blade. I did not flinch. "I will shield them because if he razes your trade, he weakens the very walls that hold him back from me. His wrath is not yours alone to bear—it is ours together. The choice is whether we face it side by side, or one by one."

One of the Bravarn Drakes in blue gave a guttural laugh. "Pretty words coming from a king that can't stop his own kind from dwindling to whispers. You beg them to halt the rail when it is human hands laying steel. What are your whispers to their iron?"

I breathed once, letting calm anchor me. "Iron disrupts more than my kind," I said, voice quiet but steady. "It scars the ley-lines that all magic kind draw upon. The Abyssians feel the seas churned to unrest. I am sure the Crystalian's have felt it in the core of their ores. Even your kin"—my gaze slid deliberately to the Drake—"have felt the dissonance when your wings falter in flight. You may not wish to name it, but the iron burns us all. Allow it to spread unchecked, and you will find yourselves just as severed as we."

The Rauthen man in crimson flicked his fingers in disdain. "Then propose an alternative." his tone oiled with self-satisfaction "Trade halts without the rail. Our people starve while yours hoard the mountain passes."

I folded my hands on the table and let the silence stretch. Where Kia would have thundered back with fire and threat, I let the weight of stillness do the work first. My voice, when it came, was even—quiet, but deliberate enough to leave no space for dismissal.

I leaned forward, palms flat on the table. Not force—never force—but weight. "I do not ask you to halt progress. Only to reroute it. The valleys that thread through Drakarian lands must remain untouched. We will open alternative passes for your merchants and grant escorts through them. Safer routes, without the price of severed magic. Trade flows, life continues... and our world does not rot from within."

For a moment, silence reigned. The Velmorin woman's eyes narrowed as though weighing the bargain then whispered softly to the Queen who nodded. The Bravarn Drake grumbled low in his chest, unconvinced but quieted.

Queen Novalyn's crystalline gaze never left mine. "You argue for bridges," she said, soft but piercing. "Yet every bridge demands both sides step upon it. Tell me, Consort—what pledge do you offer in return for ours?"

My claws itched to unsheathe, but I kept them stilled, instead opening one palm across the table as if in invitation. I met her eyes and allowed the faintest trace of a smile. "That the Drakarians stand beside you when Morgryth comes. That our wings shadow your halls, our magic shields your kin. That your people will not face the looming threats of this coming storm alone."

Her lips curved, sharp and knowing. "Bridges and storms, Thalos Emberlyn. You speak like one who has learned patience. Let us see if patience can hold against hunger and fire."

The Rauthen man in crimson leaned forward, a sharp smile cutting across his narrow face. "All fine talk of wings and ley-lines, but tell me—what good is your protection, Consort, when your kind clings to old ways? No blackpowder. No rifles. Drake fire and steel swords are nothing to a bullet and gun."

The words cracked like a whip across the chamber. Even the Bravarn Drakes stilled, their amusement curdling into unease.

I let the silence hold, before I rose slowly, letting the noon sun spilling through the tall windows catch the subtle shimmer of power glinting over my skin. "You are correct," I said evenly. "We do not wield your blackpowder. We do not use your guns. But do not mistake our restraint for weakness."

I raised one hand, palm outward. The air quivered, barely perceptible, yet every shadow grew longer even as the sun did not change, the shadows stretching like grasping fingers they became solid brushing against flesh. "Your bullets tear flesh of the unexpected. What real use are your weapons," I asked softly, "when that iron refuses to answer your call, when your powder dampens, when your rifles misfire in your own hands?"

The man's smirk faltered. I let the hum of my magic fade, drawing breath slow and measured.

"Our power is not just brute force," I continued, voice calm, each word weighed with deliberate care. "It is the weaving of currents unseen. A soldier with a gun may fell one man or even a Drake. But someone with enough magic who bends the ley-lines may silence an army before the first shot is fired. That is the protection I offer. That is the choice before you."

The Velmorin woman's fingers tightened together, crystalline rings flashing. The Bravarn Drake shifted uneasily, boots twitching against the stone floor.

Novalyn's crystalline gaze sharpened, faint prisms scattering across her cheek. "Bold words," she murmured. "But words must become bonds. Tell us, Consort—will you swear it? That when the guns rise, your kind will meet them not with silence, but with this storm?"

My voice was steady and pointed. "You ask if we will raise arms in human wars. No. That is not our way, nor will it be. The Drakarian do not bleed for crowns that are not our own."

The Rauthen man's lips curled, triumphant, but I lifted a finger before he could speak. "Do not mistake clarity for weakness. Our concern is one name alone. Morgryth. His wrath threatens us all, and it is against *him* that my people will stand. Against his shadow, we guard the ley-lines, the skies, and the heart of this realm."

I paced a half-step, letting the long windows spill light across my shoulders. "Safe trade routes... Those I can promise. Our wings will guard the passes, our magic will weave protection along the caravans that honor the accords. The mines and caves of the western ridge, long closed, will be opened again. Only to your people though, Queen Novalyn. Let them have what crystal they need. But in return—" I met her prismatic gaze, "—we ask only that they cease driving rails deeper into our lands, and refuse aid to Morgryth. I can not stress enough that the iron is disrupting the currents we all depend upon. If the humans continue pressing those lines, they will not only weaken the Drakarian, but yourselves."

The Bravarn Drakes shifted, exchanging a glance. The Velmorin woman tipped her head, interest flashing in her violet-hued eyes. Even the Rauthen envoy bit back his smile, though his knuckles whitened on the armrest.

Queen Novalyn leaned forward, crystal facets along her brow catching the light in fractured rainbows. For the first time, she smiled. "A fairer offer than I expected, Consort. Trade routes, protection, and the western ridge..." Her voice lingered on the last words, testing them like fine wine. "You sweetened the deal well."

I inclined my head. "Peace demands sweetness, else it will never take root."

Soon just the scratching of quills echoed through the chamber as parchment was passed, marked, and sealed. The accords, simple in words, heavy in promise, now bore our names. When the last stamp pressed wax against vellum, the chamber seemed to exhale in unison.

I rose, meeting the Queen where she stood offering my hand to her. "May this alliance keep our people safe, Queen Novalyn. May it hold through the many years to come."

Her crystalline fingers, cool and faceted with prismatic lines of quartz, clasped mine. Her smirk curved as she leaned close enough for her voice to be meant only for me—though I knew half the chamber strained to catch it.

"Too bad we cannot seal such accords with a bond and marriage," she murmured, rainbow shards of light dancing from the crystals etched into her cheekbones. Her gaze flicked past me, toward the empty high seat beside mine. "Though you and Kiaza... you make for a most dynamic pair. Perhaps your bond will be enough to keep all this together."

I did not flinch, though the words cut closer than she could know. Instead, I let the faintest of smiles play across my lips and inclined my head. "What we build together is not so fragile as to need just strong binding, Your Majesty. Words and honor will hold—so long as we all mean them."

Her smirk deepened, unreadable, and she released my hand.

The council stood, the meeting officially ended, but the echoes of her parting barb lingered—like the aftertaste of steel on the tongue. The council chamber emptied slowly, voices trailing into the hall as attendants gathered parchment and extinguished lamps. The scent of ink and hot wax clung to the air. Queen Novalyn swept out last, her crystalline gown catching the afternoon light in fractured prisms, her smirk still etched in my mind.

I lingered a moment longer, fingers tracing the grain of the oak table where the accords lay. The words were signed, the promises sealed, yet her parting remark gnawed at me. *Dynamic pair. A bond.* The ache of Kiaza's absence pressed beneath my ribs, sharp and unrelenting. Beyond him, another bond, that kept slipping from my grasp each time I reached for it. I felt its echoes, haunting and near, but never the satisfaction of holding it.

By the time I left the throne room, the corridors felt too narrow, the walls too close. My chest tight with unspent breath, I climbed to the highest gallery, where wide doors opened onto a balcony carved into the mountainside. Beyond, the valley stretched vast and quiet, evening mist curling over the ridges, the wind carrying the thin cry of hawks.

I shed my emerald cloak, let it fall to the stone, shedding all my clothes in a pile until I stood naked and exhaled until the air trembled with the resonance of my magic. Smoke moved around me, my green scales rippled over skin, wings unfurling wide, catching the nearly setting sun. For a heartbeat, I hung there, caught between the weight of duty and the pull of freedom.

Then I leapt.

The wind roared in my ears, the cool bite of mountain air cutting through the last of Novalyn's smirk, the last of council formality. Here, in the open sky, there were no accords, no alliances, no questions of bonds—only the steady rhythm of my wings and the endless stretch of blue that belonged to no one but me.

And for a time, I let myself be nothing more than that.

Chapter 15

Kiaza

The blanket she'd tossed at me clung damp to my skin, doing little to hide the evidence of what we'd just done. I lay there naked, chest still heaving, staring up at the ceiling while the storm outside broke apart into silence.

She'd been... incredible. Too incredible. For a heartbeat, I swore I'd felt something more, some flicker of magic threading between us. But no—that was impossible. She was just a human, tucked away alone in the woods. A simple human. Besides, I must have overwhelmed her. Why else would she leave me like this?

A shiver rippled through me, and a sharp *meow* drew my gaze to the floor. Fergus blinked up at me, tail coiled neatly around his paws, his eyes narrowed in something that felt far too much like judgment. Another cry left him, scolding, accusing, as if he knew the exact line I'd just crossed.

I dragged a hand down my face, shutting my eyes against the rush of memory. Her voice, her scent, the way her body had molded against mine as though it belonged there. Foolishness. Reckless, ruinous foolishness. She was just a woman. A human. One who had no place entangling herself with me, or with the fragile survival of my people.

But still... The memory of her lingered somewhere deep inside me, like fire in my veins.

I exhaled hard, forcing the heat out of my chest. At first light, I'd be gone. I couldn't afford this. Couldn't risk losing myself to something that would only weaken my resolve, that would distract me from my mission.

Yet when Fergus gave another low meow, I swore the damn creature was mocking me, as if even he knew the truth: leaving wouldn't be as simple as I was trying to make it. The storm's hush pressed in against the walls, broken only by the faint creak of timber and the cat's soft purr. I forced myself to breathe steady, to rein in the ache of her that still burned through me.

My gaze drifted around the cottage, it was small, warm, cozy. The kind of place no king should ever find himself in. Yet it wrapped around me like I belonged here and not in the curved stone halls of my castle high above everything.

An easel stood by the window, rough-hewn from logs, a canvas stretched tight across its frame. Flecks of color splashed across its creamed surface unfinished. Clay figures of creatures crowded the sill, crude yet alive, their shapes softened by touch. Multi-colored Feathers dangled from twine, catching in the draft, their shadows dancing over hand woven baskets full of wool and yarn in various states of process. In the far corner sat a small wooden stool and a spinning wheel worn smooth by use.

Crystals lined the hearth in little clusters, catching the firelight in fractured glimmers, and bundles of herbs hung drying in the rafters, their scents mingling into something earthy, sharp, and soothing. It was beautiful, simple, practical. It was no grand hall, nor hoard of riches, yet there was power here. Not in gold or politics, but in the way every corner carried her hand.

I swallowed hard, the weight of it pressing into me. This wasn't just a shelter. This was a life. Hers. A life I had no right to step into, no right to want this. No right to imagine Thalos and I laughing around the kitchen island as she stirred warm soup, and I cut vegetables the wrong way. No right to imagine a life free of duty, and complicated treaties. One where Thalos would always smile and smell of grass, and I would secretly love the stubborn old ass that lived in the barn. One where Lyria's belly would swell...

NO...

At first light, I would leave. I told myself again and again. Even as Fergus leapt onto the end of the small broken sofa and curled into a ball, I knew the lie for what it was. The floorboards creaked faintly beyond the closed door of her room. I stilled, breath caught, listening to the soft shift of her weight before silence claimed the cottage again.

My clothes lay scattered on the floor in front of me, hers tangled with them. I bent to gather them, fingers brushing against a sliver of dark indigo cotton. Her scent clung to the fabric—wild, sharp, and sweet all at once. I lifted the panties to my face before I could stop myself, inhaling the essence of her. It seized something inside me, a low growl escaped through my snarling teeth, there was a hunger that had nothing to do with flesh alone. A need I didn't understand, that I couldn't place as if it was something I had forgotten and my memory had failed me.

I clenched my jaw, forcing the heat from my chest as I tugged on my trousers. Still, I tucked the little scrap of fabric into my pocket, a thief, ashamed and unwilling to let it go.

Fergus leapt from the floor with a questioning meow, head butting my hand until I scratched between his ears. The cat purred, content where I was not.

I settled onto the broken couch, the rough wool blanket pulled half-heartedly across my hips. Restless thoughts circled me, every shadow whispering her name. Eventually, exhaustion claimed me—not in peace, but in a sleep that held her scent, her fire, her hold on me, closer than I wanted to admit.

The first pale wash of dawn pressed against the shutters when I opened my eyes. Fergus was curled at my feet now, purring softly in his sleep, while the rest of the cottage lay hushed in the storm's aftermath.

I finished dressing in silence, tugging on my boots, sliding my shirt over my head. The scent of her still clung to my skin, teasing, daring me to turn back. My gaze fell to the closed door down the short hall. Her room.

I stood there longer than I should have, hand half-raised to the latch. A single glance, one last word—part of me ached for it. She'd left me first, retreating behind that door without looking back. If it hadn't mattered to her, then why should it to me?

My hand dropped. I turned away. Better to leave clean, with no trace of goodbye to weigh me down. The thoughts clawed at me though, I knew I needed to find the last female of my kind, not play house with a human, and Thalos he would be worried.

Outside, the storm had quieted into a damp hush. The magical mist clung to the fields, curling in pale ribbons around the fence posts. I breathed deep, letting the scents sharpen in my chest—wet earth, pine resin, the musk of deer bedding somewhere close. My Drake senses stirred at once, clawing for the freedom of flight, but I shoved them down. Flying so near her cottage risked leaving a trace, besides the fog high above covered the whole of the space and I would lose myself in it.

So I walked.

The path wound through thickets heavy with rain, droplets sliding cold against my shirt, I felt it through to my chest, as branches snagged at my shoulders. A hawk cried high above, circling the ridges, and the sound raked at me. Something about it felt too free, too honest.

Every step away from her home left me rawer, the distance carving deeper lines in my chest. Yet the forest steadied me too. My claws threatened to break the skin of my palms as I flexed my hands, but the rhythm of walking, my boots pressing into mud, breath fogging the air, it kept the storm inside me from breaking loose.

Hours passed like that. The land rose beneath me, sharper, rockier, until I reached the jagged foothills that shielded my camp. Here, the air tasted of stone and iron, bitter on the tongue, and the trees grew sparse, clinging stubbornly to the cliffsides. I followed the narrow cut of a ravine, boots crunching on loose shale, until the clearing came into view.

The remnants of my camp waited there—a cold fire pit ringed with dark stones, my gear stowed beneath a canvas tarp tent. I let the weight of my bow and arrows fall from my shoulders and drew in a long breath of mountain air.

A few days more, I told myself. A few more days of searching, then I'd return to Thalos, to the spire, to the duties that mattered. I wasn't sure how much longer I could really risk being away.

The sun had dragged itself high, burning its way through the thick fog above and leaving the rocks slick with damp dew. My stomach tightened with hunger I'd ignored too long. I gathered dry kindling from beneath a ridge, coaxed a flame to life, and soon had a small fire snapping back at me.

The smell of rice simmering in the pot mingled with the rich smoke of cured salmon set on a flat stone by the coals. Simple fare, but it grounded me, steadied the hollow that had opened wide inside.

As the food cooked, my thoughts drifted where they always did, back to Thalos. I wondered if he was pacing the throne room floors, the weight of crown and council pressing into his shoulders. He had always carried burdens differently than I—patient where I was quick to strike, clever where I was blunt. His strength was quieter, but no less sharp. I missed it. I missed *him*.

I pictured him now, seated in my stead, holding the fractured council together while I knew the Abyssians would push their endless demands. I could almost hear his voice, calm and firm, his eyes glinting with that wry light he saved only for me. Did he resent my absence? Or did he understand, better than anyone, why I had to leave?

A breeze curled down from the ridgeline, cool against the sweat at my temples. It carried the smell of pine and the faint bite of frost, and with it the reminder that autumn was nearly upon us. The passes would harden soon, the weather turn treacherous.

I wouldn't be able to linger much longer. Even if I didn't find her. The thought cut sharp as a blade. I placed my hand in my pocket and felt the piece of Lyria I had stolen, as my thoughts were pulled back to her and how she would handle a harsh winter alone. I shook my head, pushing the thought of it away.

Stirring the rice, I laid the salmon on top and let the fire's warmth seep into my hands. The sky above the trees had begun to pale, a cold, brittle blue that whispered of autumn's edge. Yet the hollow in my chest was colder still. Somewhere beyond these mountains, Morgryth hunted too. The thought that he might already be nearer to her than I was gnawed at me more savagely than hunger ever could.

Memory rose unbidden, sharp and merciless. Days when he was not yet my enemy. Days when he was *everything else*. I saw him as I had when I was small, him leaning against the wall of my chambers, arms crossed. That faint smile tugging at his lips as he watched me push carved animals across the stone floor. My mother's laughter was there too, low and melodic, her hand resting lightly on my hair as I babbled some nonsense about the wooden stag defeating the bear. Morgryth had chuckled, deep and rich, like he belonged in that moment as much as she did.

I had run to him often back then. He would catch me beneath the arms, swing me high, or lift me to his shoulders until the world seemed vast and endless and mine. He was my father's right hand, his shadow and strength. He had been there the first time my wings unfurled, when I leapt into the sky and faltered. It was his voice, steady and sure, that told me to try again. He had been *family*.

And still... he had killed her.

My hands clenched around the cooking stick, knuckles whitening. Had he planned it even then, while I looked up at him with blind trust? Had the seed of hatred already festered behind his eyes? Or had he loved her, in his way, and let that love rot into something jagged and cruel? I would never know, and that unknowing cut as deeply as the truth.

I could still see it—the day her body fell. My mother, radiant and fierce even in her human form, struck down in a storm of blood and screams. His hands, the same hands that once steadied me, that once carried me on his shoulders, they were the hands that ended her life. I had stood frozen, too young to understand, too powerless to stop it. All I could do was watch as he tore the heart from the only light I had ever known.

Grief lanced through me, sharp enough to steal my breath. But beneath it, rage smoldered. Rage that had never left, that had been carried in my marrow every day since. He had not only killed her, he had made me watch. That cruelty had shaped me, carved me into what I was now. Though duty weighed heavy, even as I swore never to spill the blood of my own kind, save for one. For him.

That one truth pulsed louder with each beat of my heart: If fate ever brought us face to face again, I would not hesitate.

Not for my crown. Not for my people. Not for the shadow of the boy I once was. For her. For the mother whose eyes he closed forever.

I lifted a bite of fish to my mouth, chewed slowly, unshed tears burning my eyes, and told myself again. *Just a few more days.* Then I would go home. Back to Thalos. Back to the spire. Back to the duty there. No more chasing ghosts.

Chapter 16

Lyria

The leaves had shifted into a blaze of gold, orange, and red. The sheep and goats alike wore coats grown thick for the coming cold. I bent over the last of the spring fleeces, scrubbing them clean to prepare for spinning and felting. A large clay pot simmered over the open fire in the yard, the lye biting sharp into the boiling mix of water and goat's milk.

I worked the lanolin out of the wool in a broad wooden pail—the same one I used for washing clothes—my hair tied back in a braid that kept slipping loose. The mingled stench of lye, wool, and smoke curled into my nose, potent enough to churn my stomach. I paused, swiping the sweat from my brow despite the cool wind threading across my skin.

Dosha rounded the corner, a basket balanced in her arms, her lavender hair streaming wild in the breeze. In her bright, lilting voice, she called, "I think I gathered enough marigolds for the dye."

I tried to breathe through my mouth, fighting the nausea clawing at me, and gave a curt nod. "Yes. Good." The words came too sharp, too breathless. Dosha tilted her head, concern flickering in her eyes—just as I dropped the fleece and bolted for the bucket on the porch. My stomach gave way, heaving violently.

"Woah! Are you all right? Did you eat a spoiled egg again?" Dosha set the basket down at once, hurrying to my side. Her hand rubbed firm, soothing circles between my shoulder blades as I shuddered through the last of it. She caught my hair back from my face, steady as always, while I wiped my mouth on the back of my sleeve and shook my head.

"It's not eggs." I gave her a sly grin. Nearly two full moons had passed since Kiaza stumbled into the quiet peace of my forest, and the child inside me grew steady and strong.

Among magic-born, we could shape when, how, and with whom we conceived, unless fate had other plans. Magic had always given us an upper hand over the non-gifted, though it wasn't without flaws. Fate could still play its cruel tricks, reminding us we were never fully in control. For the most part though, children came when we chose, not as carelessly as they did for humans.

Now, though, I couldn't ignore my mother's warnings. Humans, in their greed, had tried to snuff us out—first the Faelethians, then the Drakarian kind. When Kiaza spoke of his people having no more females left, it carved the truth into my bones.

It gave me more reason not to tell him. Not to reveal who I truly was. Because if I did, I knew that what would follow would be a gilded cage. A tower where I would be kept to breed hope back in the land.

I wouldn't do it. I *wouldn't*.

"No? Then what is it? Are you ill?" Her smile turned sly, knowing. "I haven't seen you in a while with the harvest keeping me busy... but there's something different about you. Tell me." Her voice lilted more playful than scolding as she handed me a damp rag. I pressed it to my lips, wiping them clean, before leaning back with a breath I wasn't sure I wanted to release.

"I may have had… a visitor a few weeks ago," I said slowly. Dosha fixed her gaze on me, sharp and unrelenting, as if she could pry the truth out of me with her eyes alone.

"A male Drake stumbled into my fields. Literally." I sighed, pushing to my feet, retreating to the half-finished tasks I'd abandoned. The lye pot simmered, a harsh, acrid scent rising as I stirred the dark mixture. I lowered an egg carefully into the liquid and watched it float, Dosha's silence burning hotter than the fire at my back.

"You didn't think to come find me and tell me? Lyria… did you two—make love?" Dosha's teasing tone was all the confirmation I needed to know she approved. She never judged me. She knew every facet of my life, every secret, and once, long ago, we had even imagined being each other's forever. It seemed I had no control over my bond, so fate had other plans. She deserved that kind of bond, longed for it like anyone would, and so what we had gently faded.

Now, every day, I struggled to contain the magic inside me, the shared magic tied to two powerful men who had no idea who I was, or that we were bound for the rest of our lives. A whisper in the back of my mind taunted: *How long can you truly keep this from them?*

I pushed it aside and forced a wide smile. "If you mean did we fuck, the answer is yes. I may have also took the opportunity to get the daughter I've always wanted."

My hand slipped lower, pressing against the rough fabric of my apron and the thick wool layers beneath, until it came to rest over the faint swell of my stomach.

I lifted the egg from the pot, its surface still slick, and together we used leather-covered mitts to drag the steaming cauldron from the fire to cool.

"So," Dosha asked, her tone laced with curiosity and a spark of mirth, "who was this Drake, and why was he here?"

I set a fresh pot onto the fire, the metal clanging against the stones, and poured water in until it hissed at the heat. "Hand me the marigolds," I said, nodding toward the basket. "We'll start the dyes next. He was—"

The words caught. Stilled in my throat.

My head snapped up.

Over the treetops, thick black plumes rolled into the sky, blotting out the pale autumn sun.

"Dosha..." My voice broke, raw. "The village!"

The acrid stench hit a heartbeat later—charred wood, burning thatch, and underneath it the unmistakable, metallic tang of iron and blood. The wind carried it straight into my lungs, into my bones.

Dosha dropped her basket where she stood, marigolds scattering across the dirt as her eyes widened in horror.

My heart slammed wildly against my ribs, faster than my legs could carry me. We ran, clothes and hair whipping in the sudden gusts, feet pounding over the ridge line of trees. My pulse roared in my ears, every step heavier, louder, the smoke thickening with each breath until it clawed down my throat.

No time. No thought. Instinct seized me. My body stretched, cracked, reshaped as fire surged through my veins. Scales rippled down my arms, wings tearing free in a spray of magic as the world tilted beneath me.

I launched into the sky, the air splitting with the force of my wings. The treetops fell away in a blur of green, the horizon drowned in billowing smoke. Below where the only people I had known as my family lived, where laughter and life had filled the streets only yesterday. Now flames devoured rooftops, and shadows moved like wolves among the fire.

A scream ripped free from my throat, half-human, half-Drake, shattering against the wind as I tucked my wings and dove headlong into the smoke, toward the burning village.

I saw them, men with rifles, their muzzles flashing, the crack of gunfire shattering the air. Beyond them, three Drakes swept low at the far end of the village, belching flame that caught on thatched roofs and small wooden huts until the world seemed to burn.

Faelethians scattered in panic, some in their unicorn forms, manes streaming in the smoke, others clinging desperately to human flesh as they clutched children to their breasts and fled. Shots rang out, iron slugs ripping into bodies with sharp, merciless percussion. The bullets didn't always find their mark, but enough did. Blood spattered across trampled earth, soaking into the soil as mist and smoke curled together, choking the air.

I surged forward, wings beating hard against the gale of fire and fear, my body straining with the single purpose of tearing into them. I would rip their throats out, break their bones, make them pay for every scream echoing through the smoke.

And then I saw him.

The largest of them all. A red Drake, his hide scarred and roughened with age, scales jagged and knotted like old wounds made flesh. His eyes—ruby, molten, cruel—locked with mine through the chaos. A snarl split his face, lips peeling back to reveal teeth before his form folded inward. Bones cracked and shifted, wings melting into broad shoulders until he stood before me on two feet, sword sliding free from the sheath across his back.

He radiated power. A predator unbothered by the flames devouring the village around him.

"HOLD YOUR FIRE!" The command ripped from his throat like thunder, carrying a weight that was more than voice—it was magic. It surged outward, wrapping around every soul in reach.

The world froze. Men stopped mid-trigger, Faelethians halted in mid-bound, the crackle of flames suddenly louder because everything else had gone still. My own body stiffened, muscles seizing. I strained against it, claws quivering uselessly against the ground.

My magic screamed inside me, begging to answer, to break his hold. To unleash what I had locked away. But I knew what that would mean—if I let it go, I would shatter the mask I had clung to. The bond I'd hidden, the truth I'd buried... all of it would flood free.

"Ah... you must be her." His voice rolled over the battlefield like smoke, smooth yet edged with something feral. Around us, the world hung in place, even the flames captured in mid-lash like a war painting. Only he moved, striding forward with deliberate grace. "I am Morgryth the Drakarian King."

The Drake was tall and large even in his human form, his presence filling every inch of the space between us. Age had carved its mark into him, but it had not diminished his strength—it honed it. His skin was a map of scars, each one telling of battles survived, wars won. Dark hair peppered with gray was pulled into a thin, severe braid down the center, the sides of his head shaved clean, his thick beard trimmed sharp to make the cut of his jaw even more brutal.

Rough fingers reached for me, calloused tips dragging slowly over the shimmer of my scales where smoke and light kissed them. The touch was too familiar, too certain. Rage flared hot in my chest. He had come here—to my home, my sanctuary—and slaughtered those I loved. I would not stand here idle.

I let my magic surge, no longer containable. It roared in my veins like wildfire breaking free. The bond flared to life, pulsing through me—red heat from Kiaza, steady as a forge, green storms from Thalos, wild and unyielding. Their magic filled my lungs until I could barely breathe.

With my eyes squeezed shut, I whispered across the bond, my voice trembling against their spirits. *"I am sorry."*

Then I broke.

With a single, explosive breath, I shattered the hold that bound me. Power burst outward, ripping the stillness apart as my form collapsed inward, scales folding, wings dissolving, claws vanishing into hands.

I stood booted in the dirt before him—woolen sweater askew, thick apron spattered with lye and lanolin, a wooden spoon clutched in my fist holding as a weapon. The battlefield reeled back into motion around us every scream, the raging fire, the chaos. In that moment, there was only him and me.

I raised my chin, fire in my throat, and pressed the spoon's worn edge firmly against the leather of his chestplate. My voice cut through the roar of flames.

"If by *her* you mean the woman who will bring you to your knees and eat you whole—" I bared my teeth in something between a smile and a snarl. "—then yes. That would be me."

He smirked, unyielding, even as his men pulled back and the Fae warriors gathered at my sides, their blades raised, their breaths ragged in the smoky air. An invisible line formed between us, a battlefield boundary drawn not in blood but in will.

"Look," he drawled, voice smooth as oiled steel, "instead of all this violence, why don't we strike a deal, Princess?" The word dripped with mockery, yet it curled with a dangerous allure. His tone was far too calm, far too unbothered, as if the chaos were nothing but a backdrop to his theater.

He spread his arms slightly, as though offering peace. "Come with me freely, and we walk away. No more fight. Your pretty little ponies get to live peacefully, hidden away from the world. You become my queen. And the bloodshed stops here."

I nearly spat in his face. The retort burned on my tongue, but then my eyes caught on the horror unfolding behind him.

Aiyana.

The elder of the Faelethians. The one who had been there for me when my mother's grave was still fresh. The one who had taught me to wield my hands, my claws, my heart. She stood rigid, a rifle pressed to her temple, silver hair tangled in the smoke, her bright eyes steady but terrified for me. For us all.

Behind her, foals. Several of them bound together with coarse rope, pulled closer by jeering men. Their small bodies stumbling, their cries cutting sharper than any blade.

He leaned closer, his breath hot against my ear, his voice a venomous whisper meant only for me.

"But if you refuse..." His tone sharpened, deadly soft. "No matter what you do to me, they will keep coming. Again and again. Until everything you love is ash and bone, wiped away like the world has always believed their kind to be. Extinct. Forgotten. Gone."

My throat tightened. My pride was a blade, honed sharp, begging to cut him down. Though the screaming foals wide, tear-bright eyes locked me in place. The bond inside me screamed to break free, Kiaza's fire and Thalos's storm clawing at my ribs. So I forced it down. Blocked it. Smothered it.

My hand hovered instinctively over my stomach, trembling as I shielded the life within. I swallowed the rage, the grief, the terror that threatened to consume me. I would let none of it show.

I lifted my gaze back to his—into those merciless, ruby eyes. Into death itself.

With all the bitterness of a blade sinking deep inside me, I gave a single, quiet nod.

Chapter 17

Thalos

The thin, delicate parchment crumpled in my tightening grip as I reread the words scrawled across its surface: *Our scouts have confirmed that Morgryth and his men have entered the Ironwilde. No further scouts are willing to follow. We will watch for any sign of his return and inform you.*

A low growl built in my chest. Outside, clouds thickened into a bruise-colored sky, drowning the council office in a grey half-light. My shadows stirred restlessly at the edges of me, eager to spill free. Conflict always unsettled me, not because I feared others, but because I knew too well how easily one could lose control and how quickly a quarrel could turn into carnage.

That was the truth of my gift. Peace and war, two sides of the same blade. I could still a room of bickering generals with a single breath... or unleash a storm of fear and watch brother turn on brother, mother on child. I chose peace, nearly always. I had only let vengeance take me once, when I was still young. I didn't regret it, but I had spent my life wishing I could forget.

Lantern light spilled across the chamber, almost blinding after the gloom. Maids moved quietly, trimming wicks and setting flames in place, while men tended the great hearth until it roared with orange fire. Warmth washed over the maps and scattered reports that cluttered the once glimmering stone council table. I leaned back in my chair, wood groaning under my weight, and pressed my fingers to my temple, rubbing against the steady ache building there.

"I know they were granted access to those caves," an exasperated voice carried from the hall, sharp with indignation. " However, we didn't approve of any construction of structures there." Footsteps echoed against the stone, drawing nearer.

"Well, I'm not saying you *did*, but including the caves in this treaty was your bloody idea," came the booming retort, rough as a hammer striking iron. "And you should own that this has gotten out of hand."

"I will do nothing of the sort," the first voice snapped as its owner appeared in the doorway. Lord Vare, Treasurer of the Peaks. His velvet doublet strained against his rounded belly, and his bejeweled fingers clenched the folds of a parchment so tightly the ink threatened to smear. His pale cheeks flushed an angry pink, the sweat on his brow gleaming in the lantern light.

Beside him, General Harth cut a far different figure. Broad-shouldered and built like the mountain itself, his long braid of iron-gray hair swung across a breastplate dented from a dozen campaigns. His scarred jaw worked as he ground his teeth, arms folded tight, every inch of him a man accustomed to shouting over battlefields rather than council tables.

They marched into the room still arguing. Their voices swelled around me like the clash of two dull blades, sparking but never cutting clean.

Lord Vare slammed his parchment against the table, jowls quivering. "We cannot fund *both*, Harth! Winter will strip our granaries bare. The people need food, not new steel strapped to their backs!"

Harth's growl rolled over him, deep and unrelenting. "When Morgryth's men come crawling back from wherever they are hiding in the middle of that same winter? What then? Will you feed the bastards bread and hope they choke?" His fist hit the table, rattling the inkpots.

They went on, their words tangling into each other—coin and steel, tolls and rations, winter and war. The argument blurred, the sound smearing into one ceaseless drone.

My chest ached.

Kia. The faint pulse of his magic where the raging fire of it should have been. I reached for the bond, desperate for more than just a flicker, but it was like clawing at mist. Empty. Cold. Then came the thought of her inching its way in, of her eyes, her warmth, the echo of her magic also in the distance. Within a breath my thoughts were flooded with memories of his voice, steady and anchoring. Without my bond, I was adrift, drowning in rooms like this one.

My shadows swelled along the edges of the chamber, crawling toward the vaulted ceiling, whispering at me to let them loose. I gritted my teeth, forcing them back, but the pressure behind my ribs only mounted, coil by coil.

"...then raise a toll on the southern passes," Vare spat. "We can't simply drain the coffers to line your army's scabbards."

"We should be *demanding* coin from our allies," Harth snapped. "If they want Drakarian protection so badly, they should pay their share. My men need armor, not promises!"

"ENOUGH!"

The word tore out of me like thunder, shaking the air, silencing them both. For a heartbeat, the chamber went still. My fingers clawing into the arm of my chair.

I stood, shadows snapping back into me as I shoved the chair hard enough that it scraped across the stone floor. Neither man dared speak. Neither dared move.

Without another word, I strode from the council chamber, boots striking heavy against the polished floor. The maids at the hearth scattered out of my way. My pulse hammered in my ears as I made for the corridor, each step echoing like a drumbeat.

By the time I reached my chambers, my jaw was locked so tight its ache blended into my head. I shoved the door shut and braced myself against it, dragging in a ragged breath. I lifted my hands slowly, fingers trembling with fine, betraying shudders, as an outward echo of the storm clawing through me.

Tonight, I would take no more counsel. No more voices. No more emptiness. Just the comfort of my cold bed that still smelled of him, the suffocating weight of dreams with her, and the bitter hope that tomorrow I might find them both again.

Stripping myself bare, I took slow, deliberate steps toward the wide, waiting bed. I had never felt so utterly alone, and I wondered if this was what dying felt like—the crushing weight in my chest, the hollow ache where Kia should have been. The hunger for him gnawed at me raw, yet grew even more ravenous when flashes of Lyria broke through, unwelcome and uninvited.

My thoughts spiraled, consuming themselves with questions I had no answers to. Were they safe? Would I even know if they were dead? The room pulsed with shadows, swelling and ebbing like a second heartbeat as I slid beneath the down quilt, its warmth doing little to ease the chill seeping into my bones.

As I had done hundreds—perhaps thousands—of times before, I reached for the tether, that frail string of magic still binding me to Kia. The glittering ruby path once was a rush of heat that had blazed like a river of molten fire, unbound and free. A constant in my life for so very long, our bond unshakable. Now it was nothing more than thin wisps of smoke, unraveling into nothing, slipping through my grasp.

Frustration twisted inside me. I rolled over, clutching his pillow to my chest, breathing in deeply the lingering scent of woodsmoke, iron, and something wholly him.

At last, sleep dragged me under, and I fell into its heavy, merciless dark.

I jolted upright, magic ripping me awake. Dawn's first light spilled across the chamber, but my shadows moved faster. They stretched, writhing up the stone walls, clawing through the windows, reaching further than they ever had before. Needy. Hungry. Searching.

My back arched as the shift tore through me, scales breaking over skin in a rush of emerald fire until I was more Drake than man. My breath came sharp and ragged.

Kia. I pushed, desperate to find the bond, only to meet emptiness. Nothing but a hollow void. Just faint, out-of-reach echoes.

It had been nearly a hundred days since his voice brushed my mind, since his presence steadied me. Ninety-eight days exactly. Only fleeting glimpses—moments when he was with her, our queen, our fated mate. He had bound us, or perhaps it was she who had bound us. Or maybe fate itself had twisted the knot. None of us truly understood how magic chose, only that it lived in us, bled through us, demanded of us.

Right now it demanded *them*.

My magic surged, frantic, wrapping me in coils of shadow and scale until my chest ached with it. I couldn't breathe, couldn't think, only *feel*.

Kiaza. My rock. My king. My whole fucking world. Where are you?

Desperately, I clung to the bond, to the fragile threads of our shared magic. Lyria's magic was still cold, distant, fading like a dream I couldn't hold on to. The loss of her burned, but worse was the silence of no Kia, no anchor, and all of me began to snap and splinter, my control unraveling into storm and shadow.

Darkness folded over me, thick and unrelenting. I stood in the center of my chamber, claws gouging the stone floor. The bed splintered behind me, one swipe of my back talons snapping the carved frame clean in two. My wings curled in tight, pressed hard to my chest. The chamber was vast, yet suffocating prison in my Drake form.

"Please Kia" I tried to force the words through the tether, jaw locked so tight it ached. *"Our magic—what's happening?"*

I staggered toward the tall windows, the glass trembling with each ragged breath I drew. I tried to pull in calm, tried to tame the storm boiling in my veins. But my magic refused. It thrashed, wild and unyielding, nothing like calm—nothing like peace.

"Thalos."

Kiaza's voice hit me like molten stone, steady and unyielding. Loud and clear.

I froze. My head whipped around, heart hammering. He stood there in the chamber doorway, flesh and bone and flame, chest heaving from the climb. He unleashed his magic and it pressed against mine, the heat of him pushing into the cold chaos that tore at me, grounding and unyielding.

"I'm here," he said, voice rough but steady. "Breathe, Los. You're not going to lose yourself."

I tried to answer through the bond, but it was useless—the tether was sealed, muted, cut off. My mouth opened, a growl tearing loose instead. Shadows writhed over me, frantic and wild.

Stone shattered under my claws. *"I can't—"* It came out broken, raw.

Kiaza crossed the room in three strides, the heat of his red flames rolling off him. His hand pressed flat to my scaled chest, his voice commanding as only his could be. "Yes, you can. Anchor here. To me."

His fire wrapped around my shadows, searing through the frenzy, tempering it. I gritted my teeth, wings shaking as I forced myself to focus, on the heat of him, the strength of him.

"You are not alone. You never truly are," his voice was low but fierce. The words burned like truth itself. "We've held kingdoms together. We've held each other together. You will not break now."

I dragged in a breath, deep and shuddering. Slowly, the shadows recoiled, shrinking back into me, claw by claw, breath by breath. My scales dimmed, light bleeding through until the green gave way to flesh again. My knees buckled.

And arms caught me. Solid. Familiar. Him.

We crumpled together on the stone floor near the window, my chest heaving against his.

"Gods..." My voice rasped aloud this time, words rough in my raw throat.

He wrapped me tight, with his body, his warmth and his steadiness. His breath brushed my hair as he whispered, "There you are, Thalos. My storm."

I shut my eyes, trembling, pressing my forehead to his shoulder. As the weight of his words sank in, I whispered back against his chest, "And you... my fire."

"I'm home," the roughness in his voice softening into warmth. Then he drew in a long, steady breath, brushing against my head as he held me tightly. "And we have much to discuss."

I dragged in air filling my lungs full, the storm inside me finally ebbing. My hands curled into the fabric of his shirt, grounding myself in the heat and weight of him. Slowly, I lifted my gaze.

His amber eyes burned down at me, flecks of ruby still glowing, they were fierce and unyielding as always. Yet beneath it I saw something else, haunted, guarded.

My throat tightened, words clawing up raw. "Yes, Kia..."

He stilled.

"About Her?" My voice was a rasp, the name sticking to my tongue. "Lyria... our queen?"

I felt the sudden tension ripple through him, every muscle going taut, as he sucked in a sharp breath.

Chapter 18

Kiaza

I found the tree I had marked the day the bond went silent—when Thalos slipped beyond my reach. My palm pressed against the rough bark, tracing the carved lines where I marked our binding rune. It wasn't real magic, not the kind that tethered souls, but it was our symbol. A promise, a home, a place where my fire had been sealed to his shadow before the eyes of our people.

The relief of touching it nearly buckled me, though it soured in the same breath. I was coming back empty-handed. Defeated. I hadn't found her, the last female, and the cost of chasing her was written in every unanswered echo when I reached for him. Each time I pushed thought, word, or even a spark of feeling through our bond, all I got in return was silence. Hollow silence.

Was this what my father had felt after my mother was taken? That gaping wound where a bond once thrummed? No, my grief had at least carried a faint pulse of Thalos. I at least hoped he was well and just the magic here concealed me. I think it would be worse. If there was nothing. Now I understood, in a sharp, gutting flash, how a bond could unravel a king. How love, once severed, could be the death of all reason. I better understood my father's loss of my mother and why it had claimed him too.

My fingers trembled against the bark as I pressed my forehead to it. Images spilled through me—his laugh, his warmth, the way he steadied my raging fire in me.

And then her. Lyria. The thought of her pushed sharp and unwelcome, though something in me clenched at the knowing, *No she is just a stupid human*. I growled low, shoved it down, and stepped forward out of the Mist of the Ironwilde.

The barrier clung like smoke and ice, brushing scales I didn't wear yet. It had hidden her well. Too well. What if I was already too late? What if Morgryth had reached her first, torn her away while I stumbled in fog and false hope? What if she was gone—and worse, what if Thalos was too?

I pressed on, leaving the Ironwilde's mist behind, boots finding the rough-hewn road where weeds split the cracks and the wooden signs leaned, their paint long since faded into ghosted words. The pack on my shoulders dragged at me, every step heavier than the last.

I reached for Thalos again. Nothing but distance. The bond still felt thin, weak, like a fraying thread stretched too far. My brow tightened, the worry gnawing deep. Why couldn't I feel him? Why couldn't I reach him?

I was out now, beyond the shrouded magic of the Ironwilde and still the silence pressed in like stone.

Fear snapped through me like lightning. I threw off my pack letting go of the magic I had tethered to it as it snapped to full size discarded along the path, just as my body convulsed, bending, breaking, reshaping. Scales rippled, claws dug into soil and stone, fire filled my chest until it roared out of me. I couldn't hold it back my fear, my need of him, I shifted, wings tearing wide, the ground shattering under the weight of my fury.

I launched skyward, beating into the noon light, tearing through cloud after cloud, I would continue until only the Peaks of Skyforge stood ahead. The Cliffs of the Evereach and Drakarro Spire. Home. My throat burned with a sound too close to grief, too close to rage.

I didn't care what snares the humans had set, what black powder they might aim skyward, what twisted iron gnawed at my magic. Nothing would stop me.

If I came back to a lifeless body, I would burn the world for it. If I came back to his breath still steady, I would never let him out of my arms again.

Because I could not live without him. Without us. Without our bond.

My wings beat harder, faster, as if the very weight of everything might crush me if I didn't outfly it.

I soared over the sprawl of the town, iron rails cutting through the world below. The closer I drew, the more the metal gnawed at me, magic draining from my veins, my wings growing heavy, trembling as if they might give out and send me crashing into the earth. Every beat burned. Every breath felt like it might be the last.

But I refused to fall. I refused to give in. Thalos waited—he had to.

I pushed through the pain, through the hollow ache as my strength bled out of me, until at last the pull of the iron slackened and the air lightened in my chest. My body sagged with relief, though the bond remained nothing but silence.

Night would claim the sky long before I reached the cliffs, yet still I drove myself onward. I had to make it home. I had to know why I still couldn't feel him.

"I'm coming, Thalos," I forced the words into the void where our bond used to burn, voice breaking in my own head. *"Just... please. Be alive."*

Need. Longing. Desperation. Each wingbeat carried all of it, driving me toward the only thing I couldn't live without.

I had flown through the night, the stars swallowed by storm clouds that thickened the closer I came to the Spire. The cliffs finally broke through the horizon, jagged black teeth rising above the sea of trees in the forest below the mountain peaks. My wings shook with the strain, every muscle burning as dawn bled pale light across the sky.

Thalos.

I felt him—wild, unsteady—his magic cracking against the air like lightning. The bond wasn't whole, but his presence was undeniable, raw and storming. My chest tightened with dread but relief that he was alive.

I forced my aching body higher, talons gouging into the cliffside as I landed, the stone shattering beneath my weight. I folded my trembling wings tight against my back, scales retreating in a painful rush until I stood human covered in dust in the cold dawn. My chest heaving as sweat dripped down my spine soaking into my shirt clinging to my skin.

The Spire loomed before me, its towers wreathed in shadow. His shadow.

"Thalos," I rasped, pushing forward. My magic surged with every step, flaring to answer his chaos whether I wanted it to or not. Fear clawed up my throat. Not fear of him—never of him—but of what my absence had done. What I had broken.

I charged through the carved halls, servants scattering at the sight of me. My red flame licking from my palms. The closer I drew to our chambers, the more the air thickened—charged with storm, shadows writhing along the walls like living things.

The door splintered under my hand, and there he was.

Shifted. Out of control. His scales shimmered with fractured green light, shadows lashing the room in violent bursts that cracked stone and split wood. His eyes burned too bright, unfocused, lost.

My heart clenched. *Gods, what had I done to him?*

He snarled, claws raking deep into the floor, wings beating once against the walls with enough force to send dust raining down.

"Thalos!" My voice thundered, though inside I shook with guilt.

I stepped forward, boots scraping across shattered stone. Every instinct screamed to grab him, to force him still, but I didn't. I let my magic burn through me instead, hot and steady, reaching for him—not the chaos, but the man beneath it.

"I'm here. Breathe, Los," I commanded, voice rough but steady. "You're not going to lose yourself."

His gaze snapped to mine, shadows quivering. I held it, even as every crack in my soul screamed at me.

This was my fault. I had left him. I had betrayed him. Worse—I had touched another, given myself to her. A human. And now the bond we had carried for centuries was fractured, bleeding.

He looked pained, his mouth opening as if he wanted to speak and a loud growl crashed out of him, strained and mournful. As if he felt that he couldn't take back control. I rushed forward till I stood right next to him. I reached for him then, my hand on his chest, steadying him.

Inside, my own storm tore me apart—fear, rage, guilt, desire—all tangled and raw. I wanted to fall to my knees, to beg his forgiveness, to tell him everything. I couldn't. Not yet.

Despite all the emotions warring in me, I forced the words out, fierce and unyielding. "Yes, you can. Anchor here. To me."

The shadows writhed, a storm within him, then faltered. His claws scraped deep furrows into the stone, but his breath came slower. His wings sagged against the weight of his exhaustion.

Letting the heat of my fire push against his shadows I met his magic with mine holding everything he couldn't. "You are not alone. You never truly are," my voice low and full of fire.

"We've held kingdoms together. We've held each other together. You will not break now." Commanding him loudly and sending him all my strength, even as I broke inside myself.

"Not while I live." I whispered,

For a heartbeat, the storm stilled. His magic recoiled, shadows folding back into his body. The glow of his scales dimmed until I could see him again—my Thalos, panting, trembling, but there on unsteady legs. I caught him into my arms as we both fell to our knees on the crack stone floor.

"It's over," I lied under my breath, for both of us. "You're safe. I'm here." Deep in my heart, I knew nothing was safe. Not him. Not me. Not us.

"Gods..." Thalos rasped aloud, his voice rough.

I held him tighter, my arms locking around him as though sheer force alone could keep him from unraveling again. His body trembled against mine, and I pressed my face into his hair. The scent of him—pine, spice and storm—hit me like coming home after being lost too long.

"There you are, Thalos," I whispered, the words cracking in my chest, equal parts relief and ache. "My storm."

He shut his eyes, forehead pressing hard into my shoulder, clinging. His voice came softer, breaking against me. "And you... my fire."

The words nearly undid me. My throat tightened, my chest burned. Fire and storm, we had always been halves of the same whole. And I had abandoned him. Left him to drown in shadows while I wandered the mist chasing a ghost. Worse—while I let myself fall into the arms of another.

"I'm home," I managed, roughness scraping my voice before it softened into truth. Home. The word tasted bitter and sweet all at once. I drew in a long breath, brushing it against the crown of his head as I held him tighter, tighter than I should. "And we have much to discuss."

His hands curled into my shirt, clutching like I was the only anchor left to him. Gods, maybe I was. The thought gutted me.

When he finally lifted his gaze, emerald green eyes meeting mine, I almost faltered. They burned at me, fierce and unyielding, yet beneath it something I couldn't place a kind of knowing.

"Yes, Kia..." he rasped.

I stilled. Dread coiled sharp and heavy in my gut.

"About her?" His voice cracked, Then he breathed out softly. "Lyria... our queen?"

The name struck like a blade between my ribs. My breath caught, my body went rigid, and every muscle locked tight in horror, shock, fear. How had he known? Thalos's eyes on me cut deeper than any sword. Why had he called her Queen?

I sucked in a sharp breath, haunted by her smile, her warmth, and her touch. I reached for him with our bond but it still felt cut off, and tears burned in my eyes threatening to fall.

"How...How did you know?" I wouldn't let him go, I didn't move. I didn't want to ever let go again.

Thalos reached up and touched my cheek, a smile forming proud and bright and guilt settled into me deeper. "You found her, Kia just like you said you would, and you're safe." His voice sounded so relieved. My confusion furrowed my brow, found her.

Thalos's hand didn't leave my cheek, his thumb brushing across my skin like I was something fragile. His eyes burned into mine, bright with conviction.

"She's the one, Kia," he said, voice quiet but certain, the words falling heavy as stone. "Lyria. The last Drakarian. I've seen her in dreams. Felt her through us. And now..." his smile softened into awe, "...we're bonded. All three of us. Fated."

The air left my lungs. My chest hollowed. "Bonded?" The word scraped raw out of me.

He nodded, as if it were the simplest truth. "Yes. I feel her in the threads of us. I know you must too. Where is she, Kia? Why isn't she with you?"

The question tore something open in me. My throat closed, panic slamming into my ribs. *Bonded. Fated.* Gods above, I hadn't felt it. Not once. Not truly. I thought she was—fuck—I thought she was *human*.

The memory of her laugh, the smell of her skin, the way she had moved against me—everything hit at once, twisting sharp into fury and shame. She had lied to me. Or worse—I hadn't seen. I hadn't *scented* her. Hadn't known.

"I should have known!" My voice cracked, breaking out of me like a roar. I shoved off Thalos's hold, staggering back as the chamber spun. "I should have felt her, scented her—something! Gods damn it, I should have *known* she wasn't human!"

Thalos blinked, confusion cutting through his calm as he stood with me, shadows trailing faintly in his wake. "Kia... what are you saying? She's not here? Not with you?"

Guilt slammed hot into my gut. "I didn't know!" I raked both hands through my hair, tugging hard, as if pain would ground me. "She concealed herself—hid from me. And now—fuck—I left her behind, Los. Alone. Vulnerable. In the Ironwilde."

His eyes widened, the steadiness faltering as the storm inside me spread to him. He whispered it like a curse, disbelieving. "Kia... you *didn't bring her with you?*"

"No!" The word ripped out of me, fury and fear tangled so tight I could barely breathe. My chest heaved, heat sparking under my skin, fire threatening to break loose. "I failed her. I failed *you.* Fuck, if Morgryth finds her first—"

Thalos's hand caught my arm, gripping hard, his own confusion laced with urgency. "Kiaza. Look at me. We'll find her. We *will.* But right now—calm yourself before you lose control like I just did. Together we will figure this out. Tell me everything."

I met his eyes then, green reflecting back at me steady and unyielding, and for a moment I almost shattered. Because he believed. Because he still believed in me, even when I couldn't.

Chapter 19

Lyria

Iron bit into my wrists, raw and chafed from days of marching. Each step dragged more dirt into the seams of my boots, my cotton overalls had long since torn at the hems, my apron crusted with mud and blood. The weight of the shackles didn't hold me, not truly, *they couldn't*. Though the constant pull of iron leeching at my magic, left me heavy, dulled, tired in ways I wasn't used to.

We had crossed days of forest, Morgryth's shadow looming over us whether he walked ahead or behind, his men circling like carrion crows. Now the trees broke open, and for the first time in my life I saw a human town.

The sight stopped me cold.

Stone and timber houses crowded the narrow street, chimneys belching smoke that hung thick with the smell of coal, tar, and roasting meat. Lanterns swung from posts, their glass cloudy with soot. It wasn't the buildings that rattled me—it was the *people.* Dozens. No, hundreds. The street teemed with them, more faces than I had ever imagined pressed together in one place.

The noise was loud with a constant thunder of voices, vendors barking about root vegetables, hawkers waving bolts of cloth, children shrieking as they chased a wooden hoop down the muddy path. The clang of hammers struck from a smithy, sharp against the hum of chatter. A dog snarled at the soldiers as we passed, its master dragging it back by the scruff.

Then I realized *all eyes were on us.*

The crowd parted slowly, like water around clustered rocks. Whispers rose, sharp and hungry.

"Prisoner?" An old timer spat.

"Look at the chains." A young boy ran by speaking to another.

"Who's the girl?" A man jeered.

I kept my gaze down, letting my tangled hair fall forward, hiding the burn I felt in my cheeks.

A child tugged at her mother's skirts, pointing with wide, curious eyes. "Mama, she's pretty." The mother's hand snapped down, yanking the girl back with a hissed, "Don't look at her!"

The soldiers shoved me forward. I splashed through an ankle deep muddy rut, filth soaking up my pant legs. Above me, laundry lines sagged with patched linens and faded shirts that stank of lye. Faces peered from windows—sallow, sunken, suspicious.

Then came the braver ones.

A man in a red-stitched vest stepped forward, spitting at the ground near my feet. "Is that sweet thing for sale?" he sneered. "I will give you a couple good golds. I could make good use of her."

His words sliced sharper than the iron on my wrists. My fingers twitched, magic straining, begging to answer. It would take so little to silence him, to silence *all of them.*

I couldn't.

Not yet.

I pressed my hand subtly to my belly, my heart hammering. I had power enough to tear these chains apart, to torch the soldiers around me, to disappear into the wilds before any of them could scream. Timing. Patience. Those things mattered more than pride. I would not risk my daughter. Her safety outweighed everything—my anger, my magic, my very life if it came down to it.

The soldiers barked at the crowd to move back, their rifles catching the last of the sun's glow, black iron glinting like a threat. I caught the stink of powder in the air and swallowed my revulsion. This was their world—noise, smoke, iron, blood.

And now I was walking in the center of it, shackled like a prize.

I lowered my gaze and kept walking, silent as a blade waiting to be drawn. We walked up the steps into a small inn squeezed between two other buildings. The soldiers tugged me through into the small entry.

The inn reeked of piss and ale, its wooden beams sagging beneath the weight of years of over use. Morgryth's men shoved me through the common room, their boots thudding heavy on warped planks as patrons turned to stare. The hush that followed us was louder then the chaos of the crowd outside. Whispers trailed behind, speculation mingled with fear, until we climbed the narrow staircase and the noise dimmed to the creak of steps and the pounding of my pulse.

At the end of the hall, Morgryth himself opened a door and guided me in with a mockery of courtesy.

The room was simple—a bed draped in woolen blankets, a small hearth throwing shadows across the walls, and a copper tub steaming in the corner. The scent of rose and soap clung to the air, foreign and sharp against the dirt and blood of the road. A folded dress lay on the chair beside it, dark green, cut finely at the waist.

He shut the door behind us. The click of the latch was louder than it should have been.

"Take them off," he murmured, stepping close. His hand rose, brushing the iron around my wrists, and with a flick of his fingers the shackles fell away. They hit the floor with a dull, final clank that echoed through my bones.

I rubbed at the raw skin, relief warring with dread.

"You'll find I reward obedience," he continued, his voice low, a rasp that carried the weight of storms. He plucked the dress from the chair and held it up, silk shifting like a serpent in his hands. "A queen should not look like a vagrant. And you are mine, Lyria. My queen."

I stiffened, refusing to flinch even as his eyes raked over me, glowing ruby red, predatory, gleaming with hunger that had nothing to do with desire and everything to do with possession.

"I don't want your dress," I said flatly, though my voice came softer than I liked.

He only smiled, a slow curl of lips that promised danger. "Oh, but you'll wear it. I've searched lifetimes for you. Across oceans, through wars, through ash. Do you know how many whispered rumors I chased, how many ghosts I followed, hoping it was you?" His hand lifted, calloused fingers brushing the blood coated strands of my hair back from my face. The intimacy of it made my stomach twist.

"You are the answer to every dream, every hunger," he went on, his voice deepening, softening in a way that might have been seductive if not for the malice coiled beneath it. He gestured to the steaming tub. "The innkeeper drew your bath. You'll take it. You'll let me cleanse you. Let me see you as you are meant to be... No dirt, no rags. Only the last queen of the Drakarian."

I bared my teeth in something that wasn't a smile. "You think a bath makes me yours?"

His laugh was low, dangerous. He stepped closer, close enough that the heat of him pressed against my skin, his shadow swallowing mine. "Not the bath, little flame. The bond. And it *will* be mine. Whether you resist or not, fate has already shown you to me."

The air seemed to tighten, my magic clawing against the weight of his. I wanted to strike, to rend him open where he stood. Instead, my hands curled into fists at my sides, the reminder of the child inside me anchoring me to stillness.

He lifted the towel from the chair and draped it over his arm as though he were some patient lover instead of a monster who had burned villages to find me. His gaze softened, almost tender, but it only made the chill in my spine sharper.

"I will make you my queen, Lyria," he whispered, his lips close enough to my ear that his breath ghosted against my skin. "And together we will remake the world in fire."

I stood there unmoving as he crossed the room, dipping the towel into the steaming bath and wringing it out with slow, deliberate care. His gaze never left me.

"Take off your clothes," he spoke quieter this time, as though it were not an order but an inevitability.

"No." My voice cut like flint.

Morgryth's eyes narrowed, but his smirk lingered. He reached past me, trailing the damp towel across the back of my arm as though to coax, not command. "You will let me," he murmured, "because you know what happens if you don't. Your... Pretty ponies." His smile sharpened on the word. "The Faelethians. Do you want their bones to litter the fields as ash? Or will you bathe, and sit with me, and make peace?"

The fury in me sparked bright and hot. Still, my hands trembled as I untied the straps of my apron, letting the blood stain soiled canvas slip down into a heap at my feet. I peeled away each layer, one by one, until nothing covered my skin, my round curves. His stare devoured me, his chest rising like a predator savoring the trap.

I turned, stepping toward the bath. My body felt raw under his gaze, but I forced my shoulders back, head high. The steam curled up from the copper basin, scented faintly of rose. I put one foot on the wooden step, as if I were yielding—then spun.

My hand shot out, grabbing him rough and merciless between his legs, squeezing his cock through the fabric of his trousers. He jolted, his smirk cracking, his body bowing forward at the sudden grip.

Leaning in, I let my lips curl into a smile. My magic pulsed out in a sharp thread, just enough to sear, to remind. His eyes flared wide at the heat thrumming into him from my hand.

"Let me remind you who I am," I whispered, low and deadly sweet. My thumb pressed harder, and his breath hitched, his composure fracturing. "You only have me here because I allow it. Because I chose not to burn this town and bury you into the dirt."

His growl rumbled deep in his chest, but I held his stare, unflinching. My magic sparked brighter through the fabric, and he shuddered, equal parts pain and arousal twisting his jaw tight.

I leaned close enough that my breath ghosted over his lips. "Never forget, Morgryth—I am no one's prize. And if you mistake me for prey again..." My nails pressed harder, the crackle of my magic licking up his spine through my touch. "I will show you exactly why queens are feared."

I released him suddenly, the heat of my magic snapping back into me. He staggered half a step, his smirk crawling back over his mouth, sharper than before.

And yet—I saw it. The flicker of wariness in his eyes.

His stagger slowed into a deliberate step back, his smirk crawling wider, teeth glinting in the lamplight. He adjusted himself with a slow, unapologetic palm, never breaking my gaze.

"Ah... there it is," he murmured, voice velvet over steel. "The fire I've hunted all these years." He inhaled deep, as if savoring the echo of my magic still crackling between us. "You think you've reminded me of your power? No, little flame. You've reminded me why I chose you."

My jaw clenched, nails biting into my palms. "You didn't choose me."

His chuckle rolled low, dark, as he prowled closer. "Didn't I? I've flown over every mountain, torn through every ruin, searching. The world whispered of a hidden ember in the mist. I knew it was you. And now..." His fingers brushed along the rim of the bath, trailing steam between us, "you're finally here."

I didn't flinch, though the air thickened with the weight of his intent.

He leaned in, his mouth grazing the shell of my ear, his words meant for me alone. "Defy me again, and I'll paint the earth with the blood of your precious ponies. Fight me, and I'll break you in front of them. But... stand beside me, Lyria, and I will raise you above them all. Queen of Drakes. Queen of humans. Queen of everything that crawls and bows."

His hand slid brazenly down the curve of my arm, stopping at my wrist where the iron cuff had left a raw mark. His thumb pressed over it, firm, as though testing how much of me he could bruise into submission.

"You're mine," he whispered, not as a plea but a vow, his hot breath spilling over my cheek. "And the more you claw, the tighter I'll hold."

I lifted my chin, refusing to yield even when the iron burned against my skin, even as my magic pressed hard against the cage of my body, begging to burst free. My smile sharpened, a mirror of his own.

"Then hold tight, Morgryth," I said softly, dangerously. "Because if I ever decide to slip your grasp, you'll never survive the fall."

His laugh was sharp, wild, and too pleased. He stepped back, spreading his arms as though he'd already won. "Good. Good. Keep your teeth, little flame. I wouldn't want a lamb. I want the Drake."

He gestured at the bath, steam still curling upward, his grin a blade. "Wash. Rest. Tomorrow, the world will begin to see what we already know...That you are mine."

I let the silence stretch between us, my heartbeat steadying into something sharp, something cold. He wanted a show of obedience? Fine. Let him think he'd won.

Without a word, I turned ready to bathe. His gaze followed, greedy and sure of himself, but I kept my face calm, detached, as though none of this touched me.

The steam curled against my bare skin as I stepped into the bath. The water lapped at my ankles, then my thighs, heat prickling through me until I sank slowly down, submerging in its warmth. I tipped my head back, closing my eyes for a moment, letting the rising mist veil my expression.

Inside, my magic begged for release, the bond with my mates sealed though, it felt restless. I felt it all humming like a coiled storm just beneath my skin. He thought he had me chained. He thought this was control.

Morgryth leaned against the doorframe, arms folded, eyes fixed on me as though I were already a crown set on his head. "That's better," he drawled. "Obedience looks good on you."

I smoothed a wet strand of hair back from my face and smiled, slow and deceptively soft. "Does it?" My voice was honey. "Then I'll let you enjoy the view... while it lasts."

His smirk deepened, pleased by what he thought was surrender, unaware that every beat of my heart was counting, measuring, waiting.

I let the water cradle me, outwardly calm, my hands drifting lazily through the ripples. Beneath the surface, every breath, every heartbeat was a plan forming. For my family. For my child. For myself.

Because if he thought I would be his queen, he had already made his first and final mistake.

Chapter 20

Thalos

My smile only widened as I listened to Kia recount his time with Lyria in the Ironwilde. His scowl was so sharp it nearly folded his whole face, and yet the frustration in him made me want to laugh harder. She had unspooled him in ways no one ever had, and gods, I loved that about her already.

Strands of his damp hair clung to his temples, one slipping forward to shadow those strong amber eyes, still glittering faintly with ruby sparks from his magic. He looked both ragged and untouchable, a king even in his sulking.

"She literally told me," Kia growled, pounding his fist into the bathwater with a sharp splash, "that if I was looking for Drakarians, I was in the wrong *cabbage patch*."

I barked out laughter so hard it shook my shoulders, the sound startling even me. I hadn't laughed like that in... gods, I couldn't remember how long. The release felt strange, welcome, and almost painful, like air filling a hollow chest after being starved too long.

"And that wasn't your first clue." It came out half chuckle, half teasing. That earned me a smoldering glare, only half hearted.

I had been the one to insist we slow down. That we clean up the wreckage of our reunion, that we rest, eat, and breathe before chasing off into the mist. Kiaza wanted to fly us both back to Lyria the moment he realized who she really truly was, wild with fire and need. I knew it wouldn't be that simple. I hadn't told him yet though that Morgryth had already entered the Ironwilde. I knew it would only fuel his rage, his recklessness. Right now we didn't need reckless.

We were drained, bone-deep, soul-deep exhausted. Charging after her now would break us both, and he knew it even if he hated hearing it. We needed a plan. We needed clarity. We needed her safe, yes, but also we needed to not hand over all our cards to the enemy.

I leaned back against the edge of the stone tub, water lapping at my shoulders, watching the man I loved more than life stew like a youngling denied his third breakfast. "I know patience isn't your strength, Kia," I said softly, smirking, "but it's why you have me."

Kia finally let his shoulders ease, the heat of his frustration dimming. The ripples in the bath stilled around us, and for the first time since he'd returned, he simply reached out, his hand warm, steady, fingers brushing against mine under the water. His thumb traced the inside of my wrist, tender, careful, like he thought I might flinch away.

"I'm sorry," he said, voice low and roughened with guilt. His gaze flicked down, amber eyes shadowed with regret. "For leaving you so long. For... for being with her. For breaking the bond. I..." His jaw clenched, the words catching, like they burned him to speak aloud. "I should have been here. With you. Not chasing ghosts and... and betraying what we have."

I turned toward him fully, catching his hand before he could pull back. His skin was calloused, familiar, as I twined our fingers together. A smile tugged at my mouth, not sharp, not amused, but soft, the kind that lived only for him.

"Our bond isn't broken, Kia," I murmured, my voice steady even as shadows stirred beneath my skin. "It never could be. You didn't betray me. You couldn't stop the fates any more than I could."

His eyes lifted, searching mine, the storm in them softening.

"You found her," I continued, my chest aching with truth. "She was always the missing piece. The third thread in the cord we've been waiting for. There was no mistake in it, only fate. And fate has always been stronger than either of us."

He breathed out, long and shuddering, and I saw the fire in him falter into something fragile. His hand squeezed mine like he was afraid to let go, afraid I might still pull away.

I leaned closer until my forehead rested against his. "You came back to me, Kia. That's what matters. The rest... the rest is only what was meant to be."

The silence that followed wasn't empty. It was full, of the weight of us, of her, of the bond now stitched between all three of our hearts whether we were ready or not.

His breath ghosted across my lips, shaky but warm, and the distance between us seemed unbearable. My shadows hummed at the edges of my skin, restless, reaching for him the way my heart always did.

Kia's hand slid up, cupping the side of my face with a reverence that made my chest ache. His thumb brushed over my cheekbone, and his fierce, unyielding eyes were full of something raw, something I had only ever seen when he stripped the weight of kingship away.

"I don't deserve you," he whispered, voice breaking like stone under a hammer.

I caught his wrist, pressing my lips to his palm. "You're mine, Kiaza. You always will be. And now... so is she. This was never about deserving. It was always about fate."

His forehead dropped against mine, and I felt the tremor in him, the relief, the anguish, the hunger. Then his mouth found mine.

The kiss was slow at first, almost uncertain, like he thought I might still push him away. But I pulled him closer, my free hand sliding over his damp hair, pressing him into me. Heat sparked between us, as inevitable as breath.

Kia shifted, the water lapping against the sides of the bath as his chest pressed to mine. The tension in his body melted under my touch, his fire blending into my shadows until the storm inside me eased into calm. I parted my lips, and his tongue swept against mine with the kind of desperation that spoke of months apart, of nights without touch, of longing that had nearly unraveled us both.

A soft sound slipped from me—half sigh, half plea—and he swallowed it like it was salvation. His hands moved, rough and sure, one gripping the back of my neck, the other sliding down to my hip, anchoring me against him as if he feared I might vanish if he let go.

The world narrowed to the taste of him, the strength of him, the steady thrum of his magic pressing against mine. It wasn't about claiming, or about forgiveness. It was about finding each other again.

When we finally broke apart, gasping, our foreheads still pressed together, I whispered against his mouth, "You came back. That's all I'll ever need."

Kia's answering smile was small, pained, but real. "And I will always find my way back to you."

Gong.

216

The deep chime of the noonday meal bell echoed through the stone halls, jarring and impossible to ignore. We both froze, lips still brushing, foreheads pressed tight.

Kia let out a frustrated growl, half curse, half laugh, and pulled back just enough to look at me. His amber eyes were molten, threaded with flecks of ruby that hadn't yet faded. "Of course," he muttered. "The gods themselves couldn't stand to give us peace for more than a moment."

I laughed softly, the sound catching in my throat, before pushing a hand against his chest. "Come on. If we ignore it, Renae will storm in here herself with a tray, and I'd rather her not see all *this*."

He sighed, the weight of duty returning like a cloak. Still, he pressed one last lingering kiss to my forehead before standing. Water slid down his chest as he reached for a towel, and my shadows stirred restlessly at the sight, hungry for more. I forced them quiet, reaching for my own clothes.

We dressed in silence, but it wasn't the old silence—the strained one that had haunted me in his absence. This silence was warm, steady. It felt like a truce, a promise unspoken.

The more I thought about it, the clearer it became, Kia hadn't simply just not realized who Lyria was. She was shielding. An ancient trait, rare and dangerous, most often gifted to females of magic. The ability to conceal not just themselves, but their very essence, sometimes even others, if their power was strong enough.

I remembered the old tales whispered in my youth, of Shields who could vanish entirely, standing before you unseen, their presence erased as if they'd never existed. My father had called it *true concealment.*

217

Now I believed it. She was bonded to us, and yet she kept that bond shuttered, closed off. Whatever her reasons, she was hiding from us. However, I didn't think she understood how far it reached, or how much it was tearing us apart.

When we stepped into the corridor, heading toward the kitchen where the meal would be laid out, I slowed. My hand brushed his, stopping him just before the carved doors.

"There's something you need to know," I said, my voice low.

Kia turned to me, brow furrowing. His shoulders straightened in that instinctive way of his, like he was bracing for a blow.

I held his gaze, letting him see all of it—the trust, the fear, the hope. "Morgryth has already entered the Ironwilde. Our scouts saw him. I didn't tell you before because…" My throat tightened, but I forced the words out. "Because I needed to trust that we would face this together, that you wouldn't run off half-cocked chasing him alone."

For a heartbeat, his anger flared, the heat of it surged against my skin, his jaw tight, fists clenching at his sides. His fire rose sharp, wild.

Then, just as quickly, it ebbed. His eyes softened, his hands loosening as he stepped closer. He exhaled, slow and controlled, and nodded once. "Together." His voice was rough, but steady. "We'll make a plan. We'll stop him. I won't risk losing you… or her."

Relief loosened something knotted deep in my chest. I gave him a small, crooked smile and pushed the door open. "Then let's eat. Clear heads make better plans than empty stomachs."

Kia huffed a laugh, following me inside. "Spoken like a true king."

"No," I corrected, brushing his arm with mine as we moved to sit. "Spoken like someone who knows you think better when you've had bread and meat in you."

That earned me the smallest grin, but it was enough.

Chapter 21

Kiaza

"Do you remember the day we met—the day our bond was sealed?" Thalos's voice was soft, his hand trailing down my arm as he leaned against the worn wooden kitchen table beside me. We'd finished our meal in quiet; Renae had given us more than enough food, then disappeared, leaving us the space she must have known we needed.

"I do." My reply came as barely more than a whisper. I couldn't stop staring at him, at the curve of his mouth, the depth in his eyes. Gods, I had missed him. Missed him wholly.

A fond smile touched his lips as his fingers traced slow circles on my bicep. "You had already been ruling for centuries then... but you'd started to give up. On yourself. On everyone around you. Your anger was so raw, so..."

"Out of control," I cut in.

He nodded, his fingers tangling in my hair, gentle but grounding. "Yes. But not when I saw you out on that cliff, jaw set like stone. My father had just brought me to the Spire for the first time, I was still so young, barely a man. And you... you looked determined to fall. No one else seemed to notice, but I did. Everything in me screamed to move, to get to you."

His breath hitched faintly, his gaze locking with mine. "I can't explain it, that pull. Even as my father shouted for me to return, I couldn't. I knew I needed you, and that you needed me, in that moment. When I caught your hand, just as you stepped to the edge, I pulled you back so we stood there together. One breath from falling."

My throat tightened. My voice rasped as I forced the words out. "You asked if I wanted to jump with you."

His smile bloomed, radiant. "I did. Because if you were going to fall, I wanted to fall with you. Not to end my life—but so we could fly. Together. Whether it was with both of us in our Drake forms, or me carrying you above the ground—I wasn't going to let you go. Never again."

A flush crept over his cheeks then, his smile tugging crooked as he bit his lower lip. With a rough, playful tug to my hair, he leaned closer. "But you said, 'Don't be silly.' And then you whispered that you'd rather get lost in the sheets with me instead."

A laugh escaped him, soft and breathless. "My father was so furious with me that day. But... I think he grew to accept us before his end."

I nodded, pulling Los closer, capturing his lips with mine. Kissing him like it was the only way I could thank him for that day, for every day after, and for every day still to come. His grip in my hair tightened, and I growled into his mouth. Gods, I had missed the taste of him, the feel of him. I couldn't wait for the day when we shared these moments with Lyria, when the three of us would finally be whole.

My magic reached instinctively for her, groping through the darkness between us, only to find nothing. Empty. Cold. I turned inward, clinging to the bond with Thalos, but even that felt more like a trickle than the roaring flood it should have been. Desperation burned through me. I gripped his waist tighter, pressing against him, needy and raw. I needed him close, his steadiness, his constant tether in my heart, my mind, my soul. My magic.

"I... need... you..." The words came out strained, slow, thick with heat. "Now."

His lips parted on a pant, his breath catching. He mouthed one word: *Yes.*

That was all I needed. I tore his shirt open and shoved him back against the table, kissing down the hard plane of his chest, worshiping the man who was my anchor, my world.

Dropping to my knees before him, I looked up. His green eyes blazed down at me, his breath ragged, golden hair curling in wild strands across his crown like the king he was. His hands gripped the edge of the table so tightly his knuckles whitened.

"You are my King, Thalos. Now and forever." My voice was rough with devotion.

I ripped open his trousers, freeing the thick length of him, already straining for me. I dragged my tongue from base to tip, circling the crown, savoring the salt and heat. His moan tore through the air—raw, glorious, unrestrained. His hand found the back of my head, pulling me closer.

I smirked, teasing him with only the flat of my tongue, planting small kisses down his shaft, making him wait, making him tremble. Only when his hips bucked did I finally close my mouth over him, cheeks hollowing as I drew him deep into my throat. He shuddered violently, his breath fracturing into ragged gasps.

Slow. Deliberate. Controlled. I moved with intention, showing him patience he had always claimed I lacked. Tonight, I would prove him wrong. Tonight, I would worship him until there was no doubt who he belonged to, who we belonged to.

I worked him with my mouth, my tongue swirling around his rigid, throbbing length. His fingers gripped tighter in my hair as I slid his pants to the floor, leaving him fully exposed to me. Anchoring myself with one hand on his hip, I worshiped his cock, savoring the salty-sweet taste of him as his panting broke into desperate whimpers.

My other hand slid along the inside of his thigh, spreading him wider, teasing until I reached the crease of his ass.

"Please, Kia…" His voice cracked with need, and I smiled around him. Gods, I loved hearing my name on his lips, pleading and raw with want.

I let my fingers linger in soft, taunting touches as I moved my mouth faster, more eager, drawing out every moan.

"Kia…" His gasp broke into a prayer. Yet here I was, the one kneeling in devotion at the altar of the man I could never live without. The man I wanted for all eternity.

My own resolve wavered with every shuddering plea. The strain in my pants grew unbearable, my cock twitching at the thought of burying myself inside him, of taking him right here on this table. A growl rumbled in my chest as I swallowed him deeper, feeling his entire body reverberate with the sensation.

"Gods, Kia—fuck—I need you inside me, please…"

I pulled back, slick with both of us, smirking as I pressed one teasing finger inside him. "Really? And here I thought *I* was the impatient one."

He tugged my head up, breathless, a matching smirk curving his lips. "Don't be an ass. You want me just as much as I want you."

He wasn't wrong.

I surged to my feet, still teasing him with my hand, and crushed my mouth to his in a rough, hungry kiss. Plates clattered and a basket of bread hit the floor as I grabbed him by the nape, turned him, and bent him over the table. My breath rasped hot against his ear.

"Tell me again," I whispered, voice low and sharp with need. "Tell me how much you missed me."

His head fell back against my shoulder, his voice wrecked, full of heat and longing. "My world was cold and barren without you. You're the fire that keeps me warm. Now, Kia—please. Fuck me."

His words undid me. I freed myself, my cock aching, and guided my hardness to his waiting entrance. His hands clenched white-knuckled on the table as I thrust deep and slow, groaning at the tight, scorching heat that wrapped around me.

"More, Kia..." His voice was breathless.

My heart hammered as I drove into him again, deeper, fully sheathing myself inside his body. I pressed my lips to his ear, voice ragged and claiming. "Mine. Forever."

His hips bucked to meet me, eager, wild, surrendering. The world fell away as our rhythm built, magic tangling around us, shadows and fire merging. My hand slid around his cock, stroking him in time with my thrusts, until every moan, every gasp, belonged to me.

Slamming into him fully, I held myself there suspended in bliss, spilling inside him with a guttural growl, I clung to him, shaking. "Mine."

My right hand traced slowly up his spine, a soft caress after the storm, while my other stroked him to his release. His cry broke against the wood as he spilled hot across my fingers.

"Yours," he gasped, breathless, undone.

I kissed the sweat-slick line of his back, murmuring against his skin, "I love you, Los."

He turned to me, cheeks flushed, lips trembling with a smile. "And I love you too."

I leaned back in the chair, pulling Thalos into my lap. We held each other in the afterglow, breath still ragged, skin damp. And then it hit—sudden, violent—like a floodgate crashing open inside my mind.

My magic surged. His did too. I felt it in the way his body stiffened against mine.

Flashes ripped through us. Burning thatched roofs. Gunfire cracking like thunder. Screams splitting the air. The stench of smoke and iron. It was so real I swore I stood in the center of it. Yet I couldn't move, only watch. A captive observer.

Beside me, Thalos's voice shook. "Kia... are you seeing this?"

"Yes," I rasped, my eyes wide as the frozen vision stretched around us. "How is this...?"

We stood side by side in the middle of a battlefield stilled in time. Fae warriors —Faelethians fought in human and unicorn form, their faces strained with terror and defiance. I had only ever heard stories of them, never seen one alive. Until now.

And then my gaze snagged—on him.

Morgryth.

The scarred red Drake stood in his Human form hand outstretched at the far end, his body caught mid step, blood covered leather armor, a snarl carved into his face. Rage and helplessness clawed through me.

"Look," Thalos whispered, pointing.

A medium-sized copper-gold Drake stood near the heart of the battle, her scales shimmering even in the frozen chaos. Her deep brown eyes locked on mine—eyes I knew. Eyes I couldn't mistake.

"Lyria..." My throat closed.

As if answering the name, her human form shimmered into being, stepping free from the battlefield. She walked toward us, unreal and radiant, an infuriating smile curving her lips.

Her hand lifted, warm against my cheek, her touch both tender and mocking. "Hello, my grumpy king," she whispered. "I need you."

Then she turned, her other hand cupping Thalos's face with equal reverence, admiration burning in her gaze. "Both of you. But only this once, okay?"

Her eyes returned to me, soft, sad, like a goodbye.

And then it all shattered.

The vision snapped away, leaving only the kitchen, only us. Thalos sat naked on my lap, our bodies still tangled, but the air between us had changed.

We stared at each other, silent. We didn't need words to understand.

Morgryth had her.

And now, no matter how much it burned in our veins to act, we would have to wait, and make a plan, because rushing headlong into his jaws would only mean losing her forever.

Chapter 22

Lyria

Shouts and boots stomping up and down the corridor jarred me awake as dawn broke. Babes wailed, dogs barked, and somewhere a rooster crowed—its echo twisted my stomach, a cruel reminder of just how far from home I was.

At least Morgryth, *the self-proclaimed king*, had left me locked alone through the night. I'd pulled the thin shift over my freshly scrubbed skin, curled on the hard bed, and slept fitfully, as restlessness had become my constant companion.

Now, I tugged the green silk dress over my head, lacing the bodice just tight enough to make the swell of my breasts sit high at the neckline. My gaze lingered on the pile of my ruined clothes, the ones I had stitched every seam of myself. With a sharp breath, I tossed them into the small fire smoldering in the hearth. The cloth caught quickly, smoke billowing thick and acrid until I coughed and choked on the air.

Probably not the wisest move.

The latch clicked and the door slammed open.

"Good Gods', woman...ya plan to burn the whole village down?" The gruff man stormed inside, dousing the flames with a bucket of cold bathwater.

Yes, actually.

I only shrugged and murmured, "Sorry."

His eyes cut toward me, they were deep cobalt blue with a faint flash of glowing aqua. A Drakarian. Morgryth's, no doubt. Slick black hair clung to his brow, and a jagged scar cut the line of his jaw. I tilted my head, studying him as if he were the one under lock and key.

Sitting back on the bed, I began braiding my freshly brushed hair. My tone was casual, almost sweet. "So...you're a Drakarian, yes?"

His head snapped toward me, then toward the hall. "What's your name?" I pressed, smiling pleasantly.

Morgryth had been careful until now. Only human soldiers touched me, handled me. That hadn't been by chance. It was strategy. He didn't want to risk disloyalty. Understandable, really.

"Draven," he muttered at last, voice low and uncertain. He shoved a hand through his hair. "And yours?"

I finished the braid and stood, stepping closer. I wanted him to see I wasn't just a prize on Morgryth's leash, I was flesh, blood, *will*. I held out my hand. "Lyria."

His brows rose. After wiping his palm on his trousers, he took my hand, it was hesitant, almost reverent, and shook it softly.

The door swung wide, boots clicking sharp against the floorboards, spurs chiming with each step. Morgryth strode in dressed in a crisp black button-up and trousers, every inch of him polished and predatory. At his side shuffled a small, trembling woman balancing a wooden tray in shaking hands.

Morgryth's snarl cut the air the instant his gaze landed on Draven. The younger Drake recoiled, stumbling back three steps.

"Sorry, sir," Draven stammered. "You said to keep watch…"

Morgryth's hand clamped the back of his neck, iron-strong, and he flung him into the hall like refuse. "I did not tell you to *enter*. Nor to *touch* what is mine. Do I need to remind you what mistakes cost you?"

Draven sprawled against the far wall, eyes wide, hand instinctively brushing the scar carved along his jaw. His breath hitched. Without another word, he scrambled down the corridor and vanished.

Morgryth turned back to me as though nothing had happened, smile full of teeth, arms open wide as if greeting a lover. "Little flame," he purred, ruby eyes roaming my body. "You are radiant in emerald. Richness suits you, it was what you were born to wear."

His fingers closed around my wrist, tugging sharply enough to make me stumble. I spun under his grip, forced into a full turn like a doll on display. I clenched my jaw and pasted on a small smile, refusing to give him more.

The young woman lingered, eyes downcast, as Morgryth's attention shifted to the tray she carried. On it lay three raw hearts, plump and slick, blood pooling beneath them. Sheep, I guessed from the size, rams, maybe. I'd butchered enough livestock to know. The organs glistened, heavy with unbled gore, their iron stench already thick in the air.

"Fresh hearts for breakfast," Morgryth said smoothly, lifting the plate himself. "They fill the belly, strengthen the blood… prepare the womb. My own mother swore by it." His tone curled like a knife, mocking tenderness wrapped around malice.

The girl scurried away the moment his hand freed her of the plate, leaving us alone.

I stood frozen, bile rising hot in my throat. Did he truly think I would eat such a thing? The smell alone made my stomach churn. When he held the plate near my face, the metallic reek hit like a blow.

I broke, spinning toward the bucket by the bath and retching what little remained in me.

"Come now, Lyria," Morgryth said, voice sharp and scolding, like a mother berating a child. "You cannot tell me living among those savages made you weak. Surely you've consumed flesh before."

I wiped my mouth with the back of my hand, forcing myself upright. My knees still trembled, but I planted my feet firm, meeting his gaze with a saccharine smile.

"Civilized people cook their food, Morgryth," I said sweetly, my voice a little raw from retching. "We season it, roast it, stew it. We don't gnaw on it raw like wild beasts."

His eyes narrowed, the plate still hovering between us, dripping red onto the floorboards.

I tilted my head, braid sliding over my shoulder, and added with a shrug, "Unless you're admitting you're no better than a beast."

The smirk that tugged at his scarred mouth was full of menace, but I saw the flicker of amusement there too—he liked defiance, twisted as it was. It gave him more excuse to "break" me.

Inside, my hand itched to press against my stomach, to reassure myself that the little spark within me was still safe. Instead, I clasped my hands in front of me, nails digging crescents into my palms, and smiled wider. He would not smell my fear. He would not see my secret.

Morgryth's smirk deepened, "We all have a beast inside us little flame."

He sat the plate down on the table and lifted one of the hearts with his scarred fingers, blood still slick and dripping. Without breaking eye contact, sank his teeth into it. The wet tear of flesh filled the silence, the sound gut wrenching.

He closed the distance between us. Then, slow and deliberate, he leaned to me, pressing the torn edge of the heart against my lips. The warmth of it, the iron tang, hit me all at once, pointed. I tried to turn away, but his other hand clamped hard around the back of my neck, forcing me still.

"Eat," he rasped, low and almost tender, as if the word were some intimate command. "You will learn, little flame. My queen does not deny me."

The blood smeared across my lips, thick and hot, pooling bitter on my tongue. My eyes burned, not with tears but with rage, and I let him see every bit of it.

Finally, he pulled the heart back, set it down on the plate with a wet slap, and the table wobbled. His tone softened, almost casual, though the weight beneath it was unmistakable. "You will have nothing else until you learn and hunger is a fine teacher."

I spat, red and slick, straight at his face. My voice shook with fury as I hissed, "Never."

The blood ran down his cheek as he wiped it away with a single finger, slow and deliberate, smearing it across his jaw. He chuckled darkly, the sound vibrating through the room as he licked his finger clean of it, then turned toward the door.

With his hand on the latch, he looked back over his shoulder, that predator's smile curling his mouth. "We'll see how you feel about that in a few days."

The door shut behind him with a final, echoing thud, leaving me with the stink of blood in my mouth and the fire of defiance in my chest.

I stomped across the room, bare feet slapping against the floorboards, and seized the pitcher of water from the table. Tilting it back, I rinsed the blood from my mouth and spat into the basin, the metallic tang still clinging to my tongue.

Returning to the bed, I sank onto its hard edge with a heavy sigh, both hands cradling my stomach. *I will find a way out of here. Out of this place. Away from this king.*

I stretched out on the unforgiving mattress, the rough quilt scratching against my skin, and closed my eyes. For a moment I simply breathed, forcing myself to stillness, to focus. To plan.

Kiaza had called himself king of the Drakarians. Morgryth claimed the same. Something in me believed Kia more—his words had carried a weight, a truth—but was that only because I had bonded with him? With them? I'd seen Thalos too, in a place that looked like some kind of grand castle.

I sighed. None of it mattered. King or no king, I was no queen. I didn't want thrones or crowns or power. I wanted my simple life back—for me, for my daughter.

Fate didn't seem to care what I wanted.

I reached inward, to the bond. Two threads red and green twined inside me, pulsing faintly. My magic purred at the thought of them, at the dangerous temptation of letting them in.

I thought of Kia, the burn of his touch, fire that seared but never harmed, the kind of heat that made you feel safe, seen. Then Thalos, his steady calm, cool but storm-shadowed, the weight of thunder pressed into every breath.

The thread belonging to Thalos flared stronger, and my breath hitched. I couldn't hold it back.

"Lyria, please. Don't block us out." His voice cracked through me, and my whole body trembled. The wave of his magic lapped against me like a relentless tide, steady, patient. I bit my lip hard, panic threading through me. This was why I'd closed the bond again in the forest, because now they knew. They could *feel it*. They saw me.

I couldn't let them in fully. Not when they might sense what I'd done. The secret I carried. The betrayal that burned deep within me.

I shoved myself upright and pushed hard, forcing the bond closed again. *No.* I didn't need them to be whole. I didn't need them to save me. I wouldn't give in to these unnecessary things. I wasn't anyone's chosen one. Not now. Not ever.

The room door slammed open. Two human soldiers stepped inside, iron chains rattling in their hands.

"Put these on," one barked, tossing a pair of laced shoes at my feet. His shadow loomed long across the floor.

The other carried a waxed canvas sack where he dumped the plate of bloody hearts, his face twisting with disgust at the mess. I complied and slipped the shoes on and tightened the laces. Straightening my back, I stared them down, fire still thrumming in my chest.

"Time to leave, princess." The soldier spat out.

Iron closed cold around my wrists, biting into skin as they dragged me upright. We left the inn, boots thudding on the boards, the world outside loud with morning bustle.

The only sound I heard was the hollow grumble of my own hunger. It would gnaw at me for days, maybe longer, but I clung to it like a promise. I would not break.

And if I ever did, it would only be for her.

Chapter 23

Thalos

The maps sprawled across the council table blurred together, ink lines of ridges and rivers twisting like veins under candlelight. My plate sat forgotten beside me, half-picked clean, the scent of roasted lamb now dulled to nothing against the sharp tang of ink and wax.

Kiaza leaned over the table, broad shoulders tense, his eyes fixed on the snow crested peaks of the Ironwilde. He'd been silent through most of the briefing, but the moment the council reports ended, his jaw locked.

"We're wasting time," he said, voice edged like a blade. "If Morgryth's already inside the Ironwilde, then we need to go. Now."

I shook my head, pushing a marker across the map to trace a valley route. "Running blind into mist won't save her, Kia. We need more than your fire and my shadows. We need information. And maybe even an army behind us."

His hand slammed the table hard enough to rattle the cups. "What good are plans if we can't act swiftly, she doesn't have time for all this." he swept his large arm above the table.

Maybe he was right. We had taken days, listening, learning what we could from scouts from lore. I just didn't feel in my gut that running blindly into the magical mist of the Ironwilde was going to work. My chest tightened, but I kept my voice level. "I do know, if we rush in and fail, we waste even more time. He already has her in some way. Do you want to give him both of us in one move?"

The silence that followed hung thick, heavy with everything we weren't saying. His anger burned, but I could see it wasn't anger alone—it was fear. The same fear tearing through me every time I thought of her.

Before he could answer, the heavy oak door creaked open. A messenger slipped inside, a young Abyssian boy with skin still slick from the sea, his hair damp and wild. He clutched a sealed note, salt staining the parchment.

"Your Majesty," he stammered, bowing low. "From Driftshore. Urgent."

I broke the seal and read. The words cut deeper with every line until my throat felt raw.

Morgryth.

Seen in Brakthollow town.

With a woman in chains and an apron.

The parchment crumpled in my grip as I looked up at Kiaza. His gaze locked on mine, fire sparking in the molten amber of his eyes, and I already knew what he was going to say before the words left his mouth.

"Yes. He has her...and they're out of the Ironwilde now." My voice came flat, controlled, though my insides roared.

Through the bond, I felt her—Lyria. She was so close it was like she stood just beyond the chamber doors. I closed my eyes and reached, letting my magic stretch outward. *Lyria... please, don't block us out.* My shadows carried the words to her, brushing against the storm of her. Rage. Fear. Reluctance. Determination. A thousand fragments of her beating heart.

238

Sudden silence. She pulled away again, severing me from her, and the loss carved through me. I longed to follow, to be her calm as I had always been for Kiaza. But I knew. She didn't need my peace. She would need my war, my shadows.

"Well then, let's go get her." Kiaza's snarl cut sharp through my chest. His voice was iron wrapped in fire. "I'll kill him. For everything he's done."

I forced myself steady and placed a carved pawn on the map spread across the table, pressing it into the parchment town marked with inked lines of rail and road. "Nat has eyes on him. We'll know where he takes her, where he settles. Once we see his path out of the Ironwilde, we can choose where to intercept."

"Then we bring Lyria home." Kiaza's voice softened on the word *home,* though his jaw remained taut. He leaned over the map, his brow furrowing as he traced possible routes with his finger, each one a thread of vengeance.

I stepped close and laid a hand on his tense shoulder, squeezing firmly until he glanced at me. "Kia... we bring her home only if that's where she chooses. Wherever she decides that home is."

It was a reminder he didn't want, but one he needed: she had closed us out, turned her back on the bond. She hadn't wanted us, not yet, not in the way we wanted her. And no matter how unbearable that truth felt, we had each other. Together, we could honor her choice.

"Yes," he said finally, voice low and raw. His eyes lifted to mine, and in them was something few others ever saw—tender vulnerability, a wound he couldn't name. "But Los... Why didn't she tell me? What did I do wrong?"

I pulled him into my arms, pressing my cheek to his temple. "It's not about fault, Kia. It's... complex. One day, we'll earn her trust. I believe that."

His arms wrapped around me with desperate strength, and for a moment the world outside faded. It was only us—the bond, fractured but alive. When we finally pulled apart, we turned back to the table. To the map. To strategy. To the fight waiting just ahead.

We spent hours into the night bent over maps—armies, numbers, choke points, logistics. Every path led to sacrifice, but at last we settled on an ambush in the coming days. Moving pieces on a board was simple enough; moving lives would take preparation, and no margin for error.

When at last we staggered away from the table, exhaustion clinging to us like smoke, we made it to our chambers. I curled into Kia's chest, his warmth seeping into me, his steady breath grounding the storm inside my ribs. For a moment, it was only us, his heart against mine, his fire wrapped around my shadows.

Even as I held him, a truth gnawed at me. If I was successful tonight, it might be a long time before I lay here again. Perhaps never. I knew him too well—I knew once he learned the whole of it, nothing would stop him.

I lay beside him, watching the rise and fall of his chest, the faint glow of emberlight catching in his hair. Every fiber in me screamed to stay here, in his arms, where I belonged. But I knew the moment he woke and saw what I meant to do, he would stop me. Or worse, he would follow.

And this... this was mine to bear.

I pressed a lingering kiss to his shoulder, letting the warmth of him soak into me one last time. Then I slipped free of the covers, dressing in silence. My shadows stirred, eager and restless, curling around my arms and whispering against the stone walls like a storm barely leashed.

I reached to the top of the wardrobe and pulled down a small wooden box, its edges worn smooth from years of touch. The lid creaked softly as I opened it, and there it was—the stone. A shard of rainbow iridescence, bound in simple wire, glowing faintly as if it still remembered every hand that had held it before mine. The pendant hung from a strip of black leather, plain yet heavy with meaning.

My fingers lingered on it for a breath before I lifted it free and slipped it around my neck. The cool weight settled against my chest, grounding me, breaking me. A single tear slid down my cheek, hot against the cold resolve hardening inside me.

Pulling my hood up to shadow my face, I drew in one steadying breath. Then I slipped out of the room in silence, leaving behind warmth, safety, and the man I loved, walking instead into darkness.

By the time I reached the courtyard, the night air bit sharp and cold. I shifted, the emerald fire racing over my skin until wings spread wide, blotting out the moonlight. One beat, and I was in the air, carried on wind and cloaked in shadow, racing from the spire before doubt could claw me back.

Hours later, I landed in the wastes beyond the Rauthen stronghold. Natrix was waiting, the hood of her cloak drawn low, a grin sharp as any blade flashing when she saw me. Two of her Abyssians flanked her, lean and cruel-eyed, the salt of the sea still clinging to their boots.

"Took you long enough," she purred, hands on her hips. "You sure you want to do this without your king?"

My jaw tightened, and the shadows around me deepened into a rolling fog. "He doesn't need to see what I'll have to do."

Her grin widened, all teeth and menace. "Good. Then let's show the Rauthen that it's your name they should whisper in the dark."

Together, we moved. Through the sleeping streets of the Rauthen capital, past iron rails and crooked alleys, toward the fortress that stank of Morgryth's presence. My heart pounded with every step, torn between fear, fury, and the faint thread of her bond thrumming in the distance.

Lyria.

I wrapped myself in shadow, the city vanishing beneath its veil. By the time we reached the black gates of Morgryth's keep, the night itself seemed to bow to me.

Chapter 24

Kiaza

"Get this army together and ready today, General. I don't care if they're barefoot and in their godsdamned nightclothes—We follow Thalos's plan and we march to the Ruathen waste at first light tomorrow." My voice thundered through the council chamber, rattling the stone.

General Harth stood at rigid attention, unflinching as always. He had borne my rage since I was young, never once blinking, never cowering, never speaking back. He was the rock I had beaten myself against countless times, and he stood steady now, taking the blazing fire of me as though it were nothing. I hated how much I needed that steadiness.

"For ruling a kingdom full of only men," I snarled, the words leaving smoke in their wake, "I seem to be dealing with nothing but children."

I stared down at my fist clenched tight around parchment and cotton. Thalos had left me a note. A godsdamned fucking note. Telling me not to go after him, to gather the armies instead, while he went off to do some unspeakable shit he thought I couldn't help with. And fuck our bond. Because that little fucking beautiful witch had blocked it, leaving me blind and aching. So here I was, yet again, left with my cock in my hand, useless as ever.

I didn't like it. Not one fucking bit.

I'd make myself very clear to both of them, this shit wouldn't fly again. No more secrets. No more shielding me from the things they thought I didn't want to face. I didn't need protecting. All I wanted was them, safe, alive, and in my arms where they belonged.

"Go deal with the preparations. Leave me." I exhaled smoke through my teeth, and General Harth bowed before slipping from the room.

I dropped into the wooden chair with a thud, dragging my fist to my face. The scent clung there—Thalos and Lyria tangled together, lingering on the parchment and her dark cotton panties. Fuck. Why had I kept them, like clutching scraps of them would conjure them back into my arms, into my lap?

Thalos—gods, he knew better. Or I thought he did. He'd always held me steady, always been the one to pull me back from the cliffs. But this time? This time he'd needed me to hold *him*, and I hadn't seen it. I'd let him walk away alone.

And Lyria. How had I been so godsdamned blind? How hadn't I seen her for what she truly is?

A growl ripped from me as I stood, shoving the precious scraps of them, the two people I loved most in this wretched world, into my pocket. Both out of reach. Both slipping further from me with every passing breath.

I stormed from the room, the chair legs screeching against the stone as I left. The corridors echoed with my heavy steps, fury radiating from me like heat. I slammed into the kitchen, the scent of stew hitting me like a wall.

Renae stood at the stove, ladling broth, humming softly while rain drummed on the windows. The sound was maddeningly normal.

"You hungry, dear?" she asked without turning, her voice gentle as ever.

"Am I dense?" The words broke out before I could stop them, raw and honest.

Her shoulders shook with a quiet laugh. She turned, spoon still in her hand, and gave me that knowing look that stripped me bare. "Dense? No, love. You're in love. And terrified."

It hit me like a blade to the gut. I swallowed hard, jaw tight. "Terrified?" The snarl in my voice was weak, thin, like smoke without fire.

She propped a hand on her hip, wooden spoon still in the other. "Aye. Because you can face down armies without flinching, but the thought of losing the two who own your heart has you pacing like a caged bull. You think your anger hides it, but I see right through you, Kiaza."

I dragged a hand through my hair, gripping until it hurt, my chest rattling with a growl I couldn't hold down. "I just... I can't—" The words cracked. My throat burned, my eyes stung. "Fuck, Renae, I can't lose them. Not him. Not her."

She softened, but her voice stayed steady. "Then stop acting like the world's ending every time they're out of reach. Love them enough to trust them. Love them enough to fight smart, not just hard. That's what'll keep them alive. Not your temper."

My fists clenched on my knees, the ache in my chest threatening to split me apart. For a moment, I thought I might break open completely, sob like when I was a child next to my mother's lifeless body. I swallowed it down, holding tight to what pride I had left.

She turned back to the stew, humming again, as if nothing had been said. But her words rang through me like thunder, leaving me raw, hollow, and too close to breaking.

Renae ladled steaming stew into a bowl and set it in front of me with a firm clatter. The smell of herbs and rich broth curled up into the air, grounding, stubbornly ordinary in the middle of my chaos.

"Fill your stomach, Kiaza," she said, voice steady as stone. "You can't fight for love on an empty belly. You'll need your strength—for them, for yourself."

I grunted, more growl than thanks, but I took the spoon. The stew was hot, the flavor heavy and earthy. Every mouthful filled a hollow I hadn't known was gnawing me raw.

As I ate, my mind drifted where it shouldn't. Back to her. Back to the cottage. To the way I had left her without a word at the break of dawn, giving her no time to explain, no time to trust me, or open up to. How had I made her feel? Did she feel like I did now? Alone. Unneeded. Empty.

Was it my fault she hadn't reached out? Had my leaving carved that silence into her?

I banished the thought from my mind, choking down another spoonful. No. She'd closed the bond herself. The moment it snapped into place, she shut me out. Shut us out. That wasn't me. That was her choice. She'd left me, gods damn it, left me with nothing but her scent on the blanket while I was sprawled on that broken sofa, naked, and my cock still aching. Acting like I was nothing more than a passing thought.

The anger came back sharp and hot, curling through my veins like fire. Better anger than that hollow ache. Better rage than despair.

I finished the bowl in silence, the spoon rattling once against the bottom before I shoved it aside. Without a word, I stood and stalked down the corridor, the storm outside still lashing the windows as if it carried my fury for me.

By the time I reached my chambers, my hands were trembling. Not from hunger. Not from exhaustion. From everything I couldn't name.

I slammed the door shut and the sound cracked through the chamber like thunder. My back hit the wood and I slid down until the cold stone met me, legs folding useless beneath my weight. My hands shook as I pulled the note free again, the parchment already creased and worn from how many times I'd read it.

I am sorry, Kia. Please, I beg you, read this and stick to the plan. Even if it's the last thing you ever do for me. I received word that Morgryth has taken her to his fortress in Rauthen City. An army cannot save her there. Too many people, too many lives lost. I have to do this. I am the only one who can. And I don't want you to see the unspeakable things I am going to do. I need you and the army to meet us in the Rauthen Wastes tomorrow at dusk. We will bring him out to you. I love you, my fire. I will now be her shadow. —Los

The words blurred. My vision blurred. The parchment crumpled under my grip as the first tear burned hot down my cheek, then another, until they came like rain. All my rage, all my fear, all my hurt, all my love, everything I had buried and wrapped in armor, it finally broke loose.

I dragged in a breath but it came ragged, and I pressed the note against my chest as if holding it closer could somehow bring him back.

I was tired. Tired of clenching my jaw, tired of hiding the cracks, tired of pretending I didn't feel the grief clawing me hollow.

I let it come.

The sob tore raw from my throat, shaking me so hard it hurt.

I had been so consumed with my own fury, with my need to *fix* everything, to *control* everything, that I hadn't seen what was right in front of me. I hadn't seen how far Los would go to protect me from himself.

And now he was gone.

I failed him.

I failed Lyria.

I failed my kingdom. My people.

I failed my mother. My father.

I failed them all.

For a long moment, I just sat there in the silence, letting the weight of my failure crush me. It would have been so easy to let it end here. To drown in this grief and never rise again.

But no.

The ember inside me flared. Rage. Love. Fire.

I curled my hand into a fist over the note. My jaw locked until my teeth ached, and I forced myself to my feet, legs trembling but unyielding.

"No more," I rasped, voice raw, and smoke curled from my lips with each word. "I will not fail them again."

I let my magic surge, rising in me like a tide that refused to be stopped, the hearth's flame roared in answer. I spoke with power, "Los, Lyria... I will trust you, because I love you. And I will burn the gods-damned world to ash before I let anything keep either of you from me."

I tore the note in half. Not to discard it, but to mark the vow in my bones.

Tomorrow, in the wastes, I would meet them.

And if Morgryth thought he knew fire, he had never met mine.

Chapter 25

Lyria

The train jolted beneath me, wheels grinding on iron rails that sang like nails dragged across my bones. The shackles at my wrists already leeched at my magic, but the rail itself was far worse. Its very hum stripped at my magic, pulling it thin, ragged.

Morgryth seemed to sense it, of course. He lounged across from me in the dining car, perfectly at ease, as if the rattling of the carriage and the smoke choking the air were his throne room. He smirked when I winced, fingers drumming the table.

"Don't fight it, little flame," he said, voice a low purr. "The trick with iron is to lean into the drain. Accept it, and it steadies. Resist, and it'll rip you hollow."

I glared at him but sat straighter, forcing calm into my breathing. I would not give him the pleasure of seeing me falter.

A waiter scurried in, clearly nervous, carrying a plate and the waxed canvas sack. Morgryth waved him off, and the man nearly tripped over himself leaving. With deliberate care, Morgryth opened the bag, pulling out the three raw hearts, their blood still full enough to drip down onto the porcelain plate before sliding it across to me.

"You didn't finish your breakfast," he said, as if it were the most natural thing in the world.

I kept my hands folded in my lap. "I told you already…I cook my food. I don't eat like a wild beast."

He chuckled, sinking his knife into a seared steak on his own plate, blood running down the cut as he lifted it to his mouth. His teeth tore through the flesh with practiced ease. "Wild beast or not, strength is strength. My mother swore by hearts. It kept her womb strong. Kept her sons alive. She bore nine younglings in her life, I was the youngest." He chewed, eyes never leaving mine. "Perhaps you'll learn."

The scent of the raw meat filled the car, thick and metallic, and bile rose in my throat. I clenched my jaw until it hurt. I would not yield. Not to him.

He leaned back, casual, as if we were old friends sharing a meal. "The humans fear me. Fear is respect in its truest form. They give me their guns, their trains, their factories. They open their gates, their banks, their homes. They bow, because they know what happens if they don't. More than some kings can say."

I stared back at him, defiant, though my magic flickered under the weight of the iron. My control slipped, just a ripple, just a whisper of what I concealed, and his eyes sharpened. He smirked, tongue darting over his teeth, and he sniffed the air.

"Interesting, little flame," he murmured. "The iron really does gnaw at you. Weakens your grip on those lovely secrets you clutch so tight."

I pressed my lips together, tasting blood where I'd bitten too hard. My heart pounded against my ribs, and I forced my magic deeper, smothering it down, sealing the bonds as tight as I could. Keeping my magic, my daughter, and my bonds concealed.

I feared his smirk meant that he'd felt enough.

The rest of the journey rattled on, every turn of the iron wheels leeching more from me. By the time the train screeched into the station, my skin felt too tight, my magic frayed thin as thread ready to snap.

Morgryth rose with slow, deliberate grace, fastening his black coat and running a hand down his salt and peppered beard as though preparing for court. He offered me his hand like some doting suitor. When I didn't take it, his smirk only widened.

Instead he picked up the lead of chain. "Suit yourself, little flame. You will still walk beside me."

The doors clanged open.

The world outside bursting with loud shouts, the bray of horses, the hiss of steam clouding the platform. Soldiers in crisp red Rauthen uniforms lined the rails, rifles in hand, their boots clicking as they fell into formation. Banners bearing the black-and-crimson insignia of a five pointed star and a sword placed in the top point blade point the sky, snapped overhead in the cold wind.

Beyond them, a crowd of humans pressed close, their faces pale with awe and fear. Mothers held children back, men tipped their hats nervously, women whispered behind gloved hands. I felt their stares rake over me. At the chains at my wrists, the green silk dress stretched across my body. Some saw a prisoner, and others saw a slave.

Morgryth thrived in it. He stepped forward, head high, pulling me along by the iron shackles so everyone could see. His voice rolled out, loud enough to carry above the clamor.

"Behold!" he roared. "The last female of the Drakarians. My queen-to-be!"

The crowd gasped, a ripple of fear and fascination sweeping through them. Soldiers shifted, uneasy, though none dared move.

I lifted my chin, refusing to bow under their stares. If he wanted to parade me like a prize, then I would stand tall and look every one of them in the eye.

Morgryth basked in it all, his hand tightening on my chain as he tugged me forward down the platform. "Remember this day," he called out, his voice booming across the station. "The day a new age began, and the world bent to its rightful king."

I smiled, not for him, not for them, but for myself. Let him boast. Let him revel. He thought this was his triumph.

Even though I was already plotting how to turn his stage into his downfall.

The iron gates of Morgryth's fortress loomed like a set of jagged teeth, black stone walls rising high above the city streets. Soldiers lined the path, their armor gleaming wet in the drizzle, their faces unreadable as the crowd roared behind us.

I walked stiff-backed beside him, each step a battle against the draining weight of restraint. The fortress swallowed us in shadow, the cheers muffling into echoes against the stone.

Out of the corner of my eye, I caught movement. Draven. He lingered just inside the archway, a bundle in his fist. As Morgryth raised his arm to wave grandly to the crowd, Draven slipped close, his hand brushing mine so quickly it could have been an accident. Something rough pressed into my palm.

I looked down at my hand, dried jerky pieces filled it.

His lips barely moved as he muttered, "Sorry," before melting back into the shadows of the wall.

I blinked, clutching the jerky in my fist until my nails dug into it. His kindness moved me, maybe I had allies here after all. I didn't let the gratitude show on my face, though.

Morgryth didn't notice. He was too consumed with his theater, dragging me deeper into the fortress, through winding halls, and up spiralling stairs, lit by smoky sconces until we reached a tall door carved with a snarling Drake.

His chambers.

The doors creaked open, revealing a vast room of black stone softened only by rich furs, a heavy bed draped in crimson sheets, and a balcony overlooking the city. He finally let go of the chain, turning to me with a strange look, half possession, half something softer.

"Have you ever been bonded before, little flame?" His voice dropped low, quieter than I'd ever heard it.

I stiffened, wary. "Why do you care?"

He chuckled, though there was no real humor in it. He moved past me, entering the room fully, a scarred hand across the length of his beard as though searching memory. "Because I have."

The words hit the air heavy. For a breath, the barbaric king seemed smaller, his eyes shadowed with something like grief. "Once." His jaw worked, the line of his mouth tightening. "And she was everything. Until she wasn't."

A flicker of sadness. Real. Unexpected. Then, as quickly as it came, the mask slid back into place, sharp teeth in a predatory smile.

"Now it doesn't matter. Because I have you. And you'll be mine in every way that bond failed me." He stepped close, his fingers brushing my hair back from my face, gentle, and yet cruel.

Inside, I cringed even as I held tight to the jerky in my palm. My thoughts drifted to Kia, Thalos, and to the bond I refused to open.

No matter how soft this monster's tone was or sad his eyes, this was still my cage.

I didn't move when his hand brushed my hair back. I wanted to recoil, to scorch him where he stood, I knew I had to play this carefully. Instead, I tilted my chin and met his eyes.

"So you've been bonded," I said softly, letting the words linger. "And yet... here you are. Alone."

His smirk faltered just a fraction. I saw the shadow behind his glistening red eyes, something wounded and raw. "She was weak. She thought herself stronger than fate." His voice hardened, clipped. "She chose another path. A mistake she didn't live to regret."

The air between us grew colder. I folded my arms across my chest, letting defiance bloom where fear wanted to take root. "Or maybe she chose freedom."

That hit. His jaw flexed, and he turned his back to me, pacing toward the balcony doors. For a moment, he just stood there, framed by torchlight and the storm-dark sky beyond, his broad shoulders tense, as though he carried more than a kingdom on them.

Finally, he spoke, low and certain. "There is no freedom in refusing fate, little flame. There is only what is written, and who is strong enough to claim it." He turned back, his smile returning sharp and predatory. "And I will claim mine. Through you."

I let out a short, humorless laugh. "You think bonding to me will fix what you lost? That I'll fill whatever hollow you've been dragging around for centuries?"

He stepped close again, so near I could see the thin scar cutting through his beard, the faint lines of age spidering around his eyes. His voice was soft now, intimate. "Not fix. Replace. Make better. You're the last of your kind, the strongest flame left in this dying world. And when we are bound, no one will ever take you from me. Not anyone."

The words slipped from his lips like venom, deliberate, testing.

My heart stuttered, but I forced a smirk, hiding the tremor in my chest. "Funny," I whispered, leaning in just enough for him to feel the heat of my breath, "because if fate were truly on your side... you wouldn't need chains."

His eyes narrowed, dangerous and amused all at once. He liked the fight. He liked me defiant. That much was clear.

I could use this, I would use his desire to have me, bond to me. I might even let him think he was winning. Even though I wore his chains for now.

One thing held true, bonds weren't his to decide.

Morgryth sat down at a long table that sat to one side of the room with two chairs. He leaned back in his chair, eyes narrowing on me as if weighing how much truth I deserved. "Tell me, little flame... Do you know of the factions? The humans you hide from aren't one people. They're five." Clearly he was changing the subject as I moved to sit in the other chair. Casual as if this was just friends speaking over tea.

I tilted my head, braid falling over my shoulder, and forced a smile that was all teeth. "Why don't you enlighten me, then? You seem to enjoy the sound of your own voice."

His laugh rumbled low, sharp as gravel. He stood and moved to the window, gesturing at the sprawling city below, smoke rising in plumes, banners of red draped from rooftops. "The Rauthen," letting the word hang like a drop of venom. "Silver tongues and sharpened smiles. Merchants, nobles, spies. They bow to whichever side fattens their purses. And they bow to me now. Fear," he added with a smirk, "is a kind of coin."

I forced a smile of my own. Coins could be stolen. Fear could be broken.

He turned back, pacing slow, deliberate. "The Caldenys are cold, clever little rats. They build their toys of iron and steam, break magic into pieces and pretend they can build it better. They make the guns that can pierce our scales. They believe we're problems to be solved." His lip curled, but I caught the gleam in his eye. "Useful rats, though."

His hand brushed the back of the chair where I sat, close enough for me to feel the heat radiating from him. I forced myself not to recoil.

"The Velmorin," he continued, voice lowering, almost reverent. "Dreamers, seers, dripping in purple silks, tattoos, and incense. They whisper that Magicborn are sacred, that your bloodline carries prophecy."

I nearly snorted. Prophecy? Over my dead body.

His gaze sharpened, pinning me. "They'll worship you if I let them. Or I'll burn them if they don't."

My stomach knotted, but I gave him nothing but a sweet, mocking hum.

His smirk widened as if he enjoyed the challenge. "The Bravarn," his tone turning almost fond. "They understand strength. Leather, scars, brute force, that is their worship. Many of them already follow me. They believe Drake blood belongs in their veins, and through me, they will claim it."

I stiffened but kept my face smooth. His words cut deeper than he knew.

Finally, his tone shifted, dangerous in its calm. "And then there are the Durnathi. Survivors. Endurers. The desert and tundra bred them hard. They'll sell herbs, smuggle goods, trade where others starve. Some pity our kind. But pity is weakness."

My hand twitched against the skirt of my gown. *If pity was weakness, then I'd take weakness a thousand times over. Pity meant someone still cared if a child lived, if a people endured. It meant we weren't forgotten.*

He circled me once more, crouching so that his eyes leveled with mine, his voice dropping into a near whisper. "Together, they are a hand. Five fingers. Separate, weak. Together? They hold the world." He tilted his head, his smile turning razor-sharp. "And with you at my side, little flame, I'll clench that fist until every kingdom bends."

I held his gaze, heartbeat pounding. "What a shame," I whispered sweetly, "that a hand can just as easily be cut off at the wrist."

For a moment, just a flicker, the smile slipped from his face. Then he chuckled low, straightening with a predator's grace. "Careful, my queen. You're sharp now, but iron wears down even the keenest edges. We'll see how long your tongue stays this defiant."

Inside, my magic burned, coiled tight against the leeching iron. I kept my expression calm, even amused, while inside I promised myself one thing.

He might think he held the fist, but I was the weight that would break it open.

I crossed my arms over my chest, feigning a pout of patience until his words finally ebbed into silence. "If you're finished with your sermon, I need to use the privy."

One of his brows arched, a sharp line of amusement tugging his mouth. "So civilized." He gestured to a guard near the door. "Take her. Don't give her more freedom than a piss."

The man grunted, iron keys jangling as he unlocked the heavy door. I rose, smoothing the silk of my dress with deliberate calm, hiding the tightness in my hand where I'd been clenching Draven's offering the whole time.

The guard led me down a narrow hall to a cramped washroom, the air damp and stinking faintly of mildew. He shoved me inside and waited outside the door, chains rattling at my wrists as I finally lowered myself onto the rough seat.

The moment I was alone, I pulled my fist open. The jerky Draven had pressed into my palm was warm and crumbled from the pressure, but the smell hit me like salvation. My stomach twisted painfully, growling loud enough I was sure the guard heard it. I tore into it with my teeth, chewing greedily even though the salted meat scraped my dry throat.

Tears pricked my eyes, not from weakness, but from the raw relief of filling the gnawing void in my belly. I pressed my back against the cold wall, savoring each bite, and swallowed hard. It was pitiful, scraps. But it was mine.

When it was gone, I tended to my needs quickly, then washed my face in the cracked basin, letting the cold water shock me back into myself. I studied my reflection in the warped metal mirror above it, paled, eyes burning with defiance. I wiped my lips clean of salt and straightened my spine.

The guard banged on the door. "Done?"

I smiled at my reflection, wolfish. "For now."

I opened the door, the taste of jerky still on my tongue, strength trickling back into my limbs. Small victories, I reminded myself. One bite at a time.

When I returned, Morgryth was already again seated at the long table, a silver goblet in one hand, the other tapping lazily against the wood. A second place was set across from him. The smell hit me first, thick, coppery, cloying.

On the plate waiting for me were the same hearts. Only now, their edges were turning dark, the blood pooling sluggish and sour. The stench curdled my stomach worse than hunger ever had.

"Sit," he ordered smoothly, as though he were inviting me to a feast instead of torment. "It's still fresh enough. You'll eat, and your strength will return."

I lowered myself into the chair, my face calm though bile burned my throat. He watched me with that predator's patience, waiting.

I let my hand drift over the table, casual, fingers brushing the stem of the silver knife laid neatly beside my plate. My grip closed around it, smooth and quiet, the weight grounding me more than any meal could.

I lifted my eyes to his, steady, and let my lips curl into the faintest smile. "I told you more than once today...I don't eat like a beast."

His smirk widened, sharp, teeth flashing. "And yet, little flame, every beast learns its place."

The spoiled hearts sat between us, reeking, untouched. The knife was warm in my hand, hidden now in the folds of my silk gown.

I refused him still, though this time, my refusal was more than defiance. It was intent. The thought burned steady in my chest. *Let him believe he held me caged, because I already held my freedom in my hand.*

Chapter 26

Thalos

The fortress loomed against the storm-split sky, its sharp towers rising like blackened teeth gnawing at the clouds. Lightning licked across the heavens, casting the stone in brief, hellish light. Every strike made the walls look older, hungrier, like the fortress itself wanted to devour me whole.

"Remember Nati," I whispered into her ear. "When it's time to go, fall back to the waste where we meet Kia." She nodded quick and quiet.

Nat and her two guards melted into the treeline, their cloaks drawn tight, faces half-shrouded. I caught the gleam of their eyes in the dark, sharp as predators on the hunt. They would circle the walls, keep watch, and cut off any reinforcements. The inside, the belly of the beast, that was mine.

I breathed in once, deep. Then I let the shadows rise, knowing that once I fully unleashed them they would no longer hide beneath my calm. Under my storms.

They crawled up my arms first, coiling like serpents, tightening around my chest until my heartbeat became their rhythm. My skin dissolved into smoke and night. I wasn't flesh and bone anymore, I was silence with teeth.

The first guard didn't even turn. Darkness swallowed his throat, and he dropped soundlessly, torch hissing into the damp dirt. The second guard gasped only half a word before my shadows clamped his jaw shut. His body sagged into the stone, limp. Every strike was swift, merciless. Every torch I snuffed bled the fortress darker.

The air inside stank of iron and mildew, damp stone steeped in old smoke. My boots barely whispered across the floor as I slipped down corridors that wound like veins.

Room after room. I dropped guards, silencing people forever. The reality of it was something I pushed deep down.

Storerooms stacked with grain, the burlap filled with wheat, corn, and rice. Two guards slumped into grain sacks, their last breath smothered by burlap and shadow.

Sleeping men in barracks lined with straw-stuffed cots, sour with sweat. They didn't even stir as my shadows claimed them. Hallways where the torchlight guttered in iron sconces, my shadows twitching with every draft.

Not her.

Every chamber scraped me raw. Every door I opened and shut behind me wound the tension tighter, until it felt like barbed wire cinched around my ribs.

Where was he keeping her? Where was Lyria?

Her name pulsed through me with every step. A drumbeat, a prayer, a wound. The bond throbbed in my chest like it wanted to tear free and drag me to her. I couldn't tell where my heartbeat ended and her call began.

If Morgryth had touched her—if he had so much as breathed wrong near her—I would paint these walls black with his blood.

A low growl slipped from my throat before I could stop it. My shadows answered, bristling, the hunger in them pressing at the edges of my control. I shoved them down, forced myself forward.

The stone rumbled beneath my boots.

At first I thought it was my shadows snarling under my skin. No, this was deeper. A vibration that shivered through the walls, climbed my spine, rattled my teeth.

And with it—her.

A flicker, faint but real. Her magic brushed against mine, gold, bright, and burning. The bond seized me, yanking tight, and suddenly I knew. She was here, and where.

I took the stairs two, three at a time. The higher I climbed, the thicker the air grew, choked with the weight of her magic pressing against the stone.

At the landing, I stopped. My palm pressed flat to the wooden door, rough-hewn and carved with an ancient Drake. The pull on the other side was undeniable. Stronger now. Alive.

A muffled sound carried through, low voices, guttural. A growl. Then a moan that ripped my stomach into knots.

My shadows snapped against the doorframe, swarming, and before I could think better of it, I shoved the door open in silence.

And froze.

There she was, Lyria.

Straddling Morgryth on the bed. His scarred hands clamped around her hips. Her face turned down, unreadable.

My chest tore open at the sight. Rage, grief, disbelief all at once.

Then I saw it.

Her hand. White-knuckled, hidden behind her back. A knife, gleaming faint in the firelight.

Her body coiled. Ready.

"Lyria!" My roar shattered the silence.

Her head snapped toward me. Her eyes widened. And in that single heartbeat of distraction, the knife plunged, straight into his chest.

Morgryth's roar shook the glass panes as blood gushed dark and hot across the sheets. His grip spasmed once, then fell slack. His body buckled back against the mattress, scarred face twisting before his eyes rolled white.

Dead. He had to be dead.

Lyria froze, her chest heaving, the knife slick in her hand. My name trembled on her lips as her magic broke free.

The world convulsed.

The fortress heaved as if the earth itself woke in fury. The floor cracked under my boots, stone splitting in jagged lines. Lanterns crashed from their hooks, flames spilling wild. Smoke and fire tore through the chamber, tapestries devoured in a heartbeat.

"LYRIA!" I lunged for her, but the ground ripped apart beneath me.

The quake spread, splitting walls and tearing open the ground beyond the fortress walls. I heard the city below crying out in panic, the collapse racing outward like a storm breaking free.

Her scream split the air as her eyes blazed molten gold. Her skin cracked with light. Scales ripped through, wings bursting free as her roar thundered through the collapsing tower.

The force of it hurled me back. Shadows tore through me, rending me into my Drake form. My green wings snapped wide, catching the storm-wind as fire devoured the walls.

The fortress crumbled around us, stone and flame crashing into the abyss below. Morgryth's bloodied body vanished beneath the rubble.

Side by side, we tore into the sky, wings cutting through smoke and storm, fury and fire lighting the heavens.

The storm swallowed us whole.

Wings beat against the night, mine woven of storm and shadow, hers blazing gold like molten earth risen into the sky. Each stroke tore us higher, away from the ruin and fire below. The fortress crumbled in on itself, stone and smoke collapsing into a grave no one could have survived. Morgryth was gone.

The bond surged and broke free from whatever hold was on it.

Kiaza's presence crashed into me, hot and sharp, his voice raw with fear and fury. *"Thalos—what happened? Where are you?"*

The words tore through me, but beneath the stern questions, I felt something else. Relief. His blazing fire eased at the edges, no longer clawing with panic, as my heartbeat bled into his again. He had feared he'd lost me. His fire wrapped around my shadows, steadying me in the sky.

Before I could speak, before I could even drag breath, she answered.

Her voice blazed through the bond, fierce as fire yet unyielding as stone. *"I did what I had to."*

The force of it reverberated through every tether, setting them alight. For the first time, the bond wasn't jagged, wasn't torn by distance or silence. It was whole—Earth, Sky, Fire striking together.

Her next words seared into me, indelible. *"I am owned by no one."*

Desire surged with it, molten and aching, threaded through with raw relief. I felt her solid as the earth beneath us, felt Kiaza's flame burning steady, felt my own shadows stretching wide across the storm. The hollowness that had gnawed at me for months eased, filled by her grounding strength, by his fire, by something greater than all of us.

Kiaza's silence came after, not empty, but weighted, deep as thunder waiting to break. Worry hummed in him still, but it was laced with aching relief. For the first time in too long, he could feel us both. Alive. Connected. His presence brushed mine, rough, unsteady, but anchoring, like fire warming stone beneath a restless sky.

I turned my gaze to her. Truly saw her. Scales gleaming like hammered bronze, wings cutting arcs of gold through stormlight, her eyes blazing molten and free. The bond thrummed fierce and whole. She was not broken. She was not anyone's to claim.

And I wanted her with a hunger that stole my breath.

We flew into the storm together toward Kiaza. Toward the collision that waited when the three of us finally came together.

The wind tore at my face as we broke from the stormfront, but I forced myself to draw breath. The air tasted of ash and stone dust. Below us, the earth lay fractured, split open in craggy lines that bled smoke. Whole streets had been swallowed. Roofs had caved in. Fires crawled across what little still stood, their glow a smear of ruin against the night.

Screams carried up faint through the wind. Human voices. Panicked. Dying.

I had been so consumed by her, by the bond, by the blaze of freedom, that I hadn't seen it until now. Not truly. The destruction sprawled beneath us like a wound torn into the world.

Guilt climbed sharp into my chest, cutting through the hollow place that had only just been filled. For the first time, my shadows recoiled instead of reaching forward. Every crack in the earth, every plume of smoke, every broken body was a reminder, this was what we were capable of when the bond snapped free. Not just salvation. Catastrophe.

Dread coiled under my ribs.

The bond thrummed still, whole and unbreakable, but it couldn't silence the truth pressing down on me. Humans would see this. They would come. They always came when the Magic born left scars.

The earth remained cracked even beyond the city, split into ridges that stretched toward the horizon. I followed the edge of the lines with my gaze, straight to where our forces stood waiting.

The army stretched like a dark tide against the broken ground. Torches flickered in the night, their glow glinting off drawn blades and raised shields. And there, at the front, with his wings spread wide above them all, stood Kiaza.

Black as the obsidian, eyes burning crimson red. His presence seared through me, storm and fire tangled tight. Relief surged so hard it stole my breath. Though, tangled with it was fury, sharp as steel, and hunger that scorched my veins. He had felt everything through the bond, every scream, every quake, every heartbeat, and now we came to him whole but carrying ruin in our wake.

Lyria flew ahead of me, golden wings beating arcs of molten light through the smoke-stained sky. Even from behind, she was resplendent, her scales catching flame light, her body cutting the storm like a blade. When her claws struck earth, the very ground seemed to bow beneath her.

Shadows snapped around me as I landed hard beside her, the fractured ground shuddering under my weight. Kiaza stepped forward, firelight painting his scales in shades of blood and night.

Gasps rippled through the ranks. The Drake soldiers bowed their heads bent to their knees, some in awe, others in fear. The whispers hissed sharp against the night air, *a female, a trueborn, golden.*

Eyes darted from Kiaza to Lyria, then to me, as if unsure whether to worship or flee.

I barely noticed them. My focus was only on Kiaza.

His eyes locked on mine, and through the bond I felt everything: his relief, his fear, his fury, his longing. It crashed into me like a storm tide. I wanted to take him then and there, my magic pulsing beneath my scales.

Then his gaze cut to her.

Lyria lifted her head, gold eyes blazing molten. She met his stare without flinching. Her words from moments ago still rang in me, sharp as brands: *I am owned by no one.* The bond thrummed as if repeating them.

Silence hung thick, broken only by the crackle of fires and the shifting of restless soldiers.

Natrix burst through the haze of smoke toward us, nimble as she leapt over fissures and cracks, her breathless shout cutting through the chaos. "Run! Fall back—go!" She caught sight of Lyria, pausing only for a heartbeat, before turning seaward and vanishing into the pitch.

Finally, Kiaza's voice cut the air, low, rough, threaded with storm and command. "Fall Back." His eyes swept the ruined city, the broken ground. His jaw clenched, ruby fire burning bright. "The humans will come for this. For us. We must return to Drakarro Spire."

The name rumbled through me like thunder. The Spire, the last true sanctuary of our kind. Home, carved into stone and sky.

Guilt pressed harder against my ribs, but beneath it burned something else. A steadiness. A belonging I hadn't felt in years. Earth, Sky, and Fire, bound at last.

I looked at her, then at him. My chest ached with the weight of it, terror, desire, relief all tangled tight. Whatever waited for us, whatever storm was coming, we would face it together.

And I prayed to every god still listening that it would be enough.

Chapter 27

Kiaza

Dusk bled across the horizon as we reached the outskirts of the city. The last light of day clung to the walls, bruised purple and ash-gray, the kind of color that warned storms were hunting. Mist rolled thick along the ground, curling through the streets like it wanted to swallow the world whole. Every breath carried iron and smoke, and beneath it, something older—rot, old blood, despair.

Our army stretched behind me, a living tide of wings and fire, their scaled bodies restless as they shifted, tails scraping stone, claws gouging ruts into the earth. Hundreds of Drakes, young and old, stood coiled and waiting for me to speak. They did not fidget like men. They did not chatter. They breathed, and the air itself thickened with the weight of them.

And I hated it.

I hated this silence, hated this waiting.

This had been Thalos's plan, with shadows and silence, slipping inside the fortress like smoke. He had insisted I hold steady here with the bulk of our force until he returned with her. His voice had been steady when he said it, but the tremor beneath his words had betrayed him. He had been as afraid as I was of losing her again.

The closer I got to this place made the weight in my chest heavier. Trusting him to go alone clawed at me. Waiting gnawed worse.

I was the Drakarian King. Fire and fury were my birthright. I was meant to burn a path through anything that dared stand in my way, to rend stone and shatter walls until nothing remained between me and what I claimed as mine. Tonight, though, I stood idle in the dark, wings furled, claws flexing uselessly in the mud, pacing like a caged beast while the two halves of my soul risked everything inside those walls.

Beneath the fury, the self-loathing cut sharper. I should have gone. I should never have let either of them be taken from me. My mother's blood had stained my hands the day I swore to protect my people, yet here I was, king of nothing but broken vows and waiting silence.

The soldiers shifted behind me, uneasy. The air itself felt wrong, thick with iron and smoke, the mist curdling heavier as the sun vanished. I had paced the torn ground until the grass was mud beneath feet, the bond stretched thin, frayed, faint as a dying ember.

Softly, the earth trembled.

It began as a murmur underfoot, stone rattling in shallow protest. Horses whickered, armor clattered, wings flapped, voices lifted in nervous question. The moment I felt—her spark, faint and flickering, Thalos's shadows coiled tight against it, I knew. My pulse slammed harder, straining toward them.

The tremor deepened. The ground itself groaned. I lifted my head and let my voice cut through the rising panic. "Hold steady! Ready yourselves!"

A drizzle slicked across my scales as I shifted, wings unfurling, hovering above the ranks. The storm thickened, rain drumming harder, wind tearing banners loose.

The army stilled under my command, though unease coiled in every heartbeat around me. I could feel it pressing at their throats, hear it in the ragged breath of men who had flown and marched for me but feared what this quake meant.

And then it struck.

The bond.

Magic ripped through the earth and sky, fire and storm, shadow and stone. The tether I had felt ragged and broken for months didn't just mend, it roared back to life. Snapping full into place. Whole. Alive. Blazing.

The force of it staggered me midair, wings jerking hard against the gale as if my body couldn't contain the flood. Relief hit first, sharp and searing. They lived. Gods, they lived. Their heartbeats thundered against mine, one steady, one wild, both fierce and undeniable.

Then came the rest. Thalos's storm-shadow grief bled into me, laced with guilt so sharp it stung my throat. Lyria's molten earth surged brighter, hot and steady, fierce enough to scald. Between them, I was torn open—every hollow I had carried since the night since I realized she was more than just human.

Desire followed like lightning through dry tinder, raw and uncontrollable. It ripped through me searing and heavy, twined with aching relief so strong it nearly bent me to the ground even while I hovered, wings thrashing against the storm. I hadn't realized how dead I had felt until they came blazing back into me, until the bond remade me whole.

Even as the wholeness roared, dread followed quickly behind.

The city below shuddered and broke. Towers collapsed into themselves, streets split into an open chasm, fire streaked skyward as though the world itself had been torn in two. Screams rose faint through the storm. The voice of death, and fear.

I clenched my jaw as I watched it crumble. There would be fallout. Humans would come for this. For us.

I reached for Thalos through the bond, fire surging down the tether. "*Thalos—what happened? Where are you?*"

In the heart of the storm, I waited for his answer.

Then came her voice, solid immoveable. Smooth as stone. "*I did what I had to.*"

The bond still thrummed wild in my chest, each heartbeat braided with theirs. It left me raw, torn open, but steady in a way I hadn't felt in too long. My lungs tightened when she continued, "*I am owned by no one.*"

Then the storm broke.

Shadows split the clouds as wings tore down through the smoke-stained sky. Once bright emerald now inked with black, thunder rolling in his wake. The other gold, radiant even against firelight, scales gleaming like pools of forged sunshine.

The sight of her stole the air from my lungs, even as fire tore through me with hunger. Still my eyes locked only on them.

Lyria landed first, talons sinking into fractured stone. She lifted her head high, golden eyes blazing molten. She met my stare without flinching, her presence thundering through the bond. Fierce. Unbroken. A blaze that would bow to no one.

Thalos hit the ground beside her, shadows curling around him, his gaze finding mine. Relief surged hot through the bond, but guilt threaded sharp with it, like barbed wire coiled beneath his ribs. He carried ruin in his wings as much as he carried her freedom.

She was alive. They both were. The bond sang whole at last.

The army gasped—not in words, but in sound. A shudder rippled through the ranks, a hundred throats rumbling deep and low, wings rustling, talons scraping stone. The ground itself trembled under the weight of their bodies bowing. Some lowered their massive heads until their horns pressed into the mud. Others folded their wings tight in reverence, scales clattering like armor in the rain.

The sound was a hymn. Raw. Ancient. Draconic.

A young Drake at the front loosed a startled cry, half-roar, half-keening wail. His scales flickered between shadow-black and cobalt blue, form rippling uncertainly as he fought to hold steady in the presence of what he beheld. His commander cuffed him with a wing, forcing him still, though even the older beast bowed his head, smoke curling sharp from his nostrils in short bursts of awe.

Not all bent in worship.

On the edges of the formation, several Drakes reared back instead, wings flaring wide, growls guttural and sharp. Lightning flashed across their scales as they paced, restless, torn between fear and reverence. One bared his teeth outright, lips peeled back in instinctive warning—until the bond heat rolled off me, pressing obedience into their bones. He snapped his jaws shut and lowered his gaze.

The storm swallowed their voices until it was nothing but a wall of sound. Roaring, keening, hissing. Awe, fear, worship all braided into a single voice that made the air itself quiver.

Golden. Trueborn. The last female lost but not forgotten.

And through it all, she stood unflinching. Lyria. Talons buried in fractured earth, wings arched high, eyes blazing molten gold that met every bow, every growl, every shiver without falter. She let them see her—fierce, unbroken, undeniable.

Their awe pressed heavy. Their fear cut sharp. Reverence swelled like a tide until I could barely breathe beneath the weight of it.

My chest ached. Fire clawed against ribs already tight. The bond hummed, alive and whole, yet the sight of her—the sight of them both—threatened to split me apart.

I dropped to the ground with a heavy thud, claws splitting earth as I shifted back, bone shrinking, fire burning away into flesh. My boots struck cracked stone, mud splattering up my legs. The army fell silent, the rain hissing across their scales. Every gaze fixed on us.

I wanted to roar.

I wanted to rage.

I wanted to demand why they had risked everything without me. At the same time, I wanted to fall to my knees in gratitude that they still breathed.

Both truths burned so deep they nearly split me in two.

For the first time, I believed my people might survive.

I lifted my head and looked beyond them. Smoke rolled upward from the broken city. Flames still licked the horizon. The earth itself lay fractured and splintered, bleeding ruin into the night. The destruction stretched wide enough that even our army could feel its weight pressing down on them. Their eyes were full of awe for Lyria, but also fear.

If this was what magic could do, what would the humans make of it?

I clenched my jaw and let the fire rise in me, magic burning as I stepped forward.

We cannot remain here, I thought to myself. Having seen what has been unleashed. The humans will come. They will see ruin and call it proof that we must be hunted down.

A ripple of unease stirred through me. I felt it echo in the bond, Thalos's shadows bristling, Lyria's magic flaring defiant.

Natrix appeared shouting something about fleeing and I bared my teeth, letting my voice cut sharp as steel. ""Fall Back." I looked over the ruined city, the broken ground. My expression tightened, again. I raised my hand, flames guttering to life across my knuckles. "The humans will come for this. For us. We must return to Drakarro Spire."

The army moved as one, voices lifting in assent, wings unfurling, weapons sheathed. Some faces were tight with fear, others alight with hope. But all obeyed.

I turned back to them, Thalos with his storm-shadow eyes, Lyria radiant in her golden scales. The bond hummed between us, fierce and whole.

We fly together now, I told them through the tether, fire curling into storm and earth.

I shifted as I leapt skyward, the storm swallowing me whole. Wings snapped wide, catching the rising gale, the heat of my fire trailing in sparks across the blackened clouds. Behind me, the army followed, a living tide of shadows, fire, and scale.

The sound of them... gods.

It wasn't just thunder. It was the voice of a storm given flesh. Hundreds of wings battering the sky, their beats tearing clouds apart. Black and green and molten gold streaked through the storm, a banner written across the heavens.

We flew through the night, the storm bleeding slowly into quiet. Rain eased, the clouds thinning, paling. Ahead, the horizon cracked with light. Dawn spilled slow over the world, staining the sky bruised violet, softening into rose, then blazing molten gold.

It painted Lyria's scales until she was the dawn itself, wings cutting arcs of fire through the paling night. Thalos's shadows wove beside her, stormlight clinging to him, his form both terrifying and beautiful as he matched her wingbeat for wingbeat.

I flew with them, black fire burning along my wings, I started to feel complete, at ease, even as I knew the war had just truly begun.

Below us, the Whispering Forest unfurled in deep crimson and golden orange, the trees swaying, their ancient branches becoming bare. Beyond, the cliffs of Skyforge rose sheer and rugged, catching the newborn sunlight like blades. And nestled in them, carved from black stone and sky, Drakarro Spire awaited.

The sight of it, my home, our sanctuary, hit me with the weight of inevitability. Whatever storm we had unleashed, whatever ruin we carried in our wake, this was where it would break. Here, in fire and stone, we would either hold...or fall.

I dropped hard to the solid ground, the shift ripping through me in a blaze of heat and shadow. Bone shrank, wings folded into nothing, scales burned away until only flesh remained. Drizzle plastered my dark hair against my skull, rivulets running over my skin, steam rising faint where fire still bled from me.

Thalos landed beside me, his green scales dissolving into shadow as he shifted. He was breathless, chest heaving, eyes wild with everything we had just endured. I reached for him without thought.

Our bodies collided, wet, shaking, alive. His mouth met mine in a fierce, bruising kiss, all fury and relief and hunger tangled together. Desire surged hot and heavy through the bond, a wildfire roaring in my veins. His hands fisted in my hair, my grip bruised his shoulders, neither of us able to let go now that we finally had each other whole again.

The bond sang, molten fire and restless storm winding together, grounding in the golden earth at the edge of my awareness. For the first time since we'd been torn apart, I felt steady. Complete.

A sound made me break from Thalos, my breath ragged.

Lyria stood only a few paces away, golden scales dissolving as she shifted. Her body shimmered in the filtered new daylight, as wings folded back into her skin, leaving her naked, bare and unflinching under the weight of our stares.

She didn't cower. She didn't try to hide. Her gold eyes caught mine, then Thalos's, heat flaring bright in the tether between us. For a moment, she only watched—me with his storm-wild mouth still pressed close to mine, his hands gripping me like I might vanish if he let go.

Then she snorted, one brow arching "As much as I enjoy the show," she said, her voice low but steady, "I'd like some clothes. And food. Preferably before you two decide to set the ground on fire with your need."

Thalos huffed a laugh against my shoulder, though his eyes still burned molten green when he looked at her. My mouth curved despite the hunger tearing through me.

Gods, she was everything. Fierce, unbroken, and still able to cut through me with a single sharp word.

I let my forehead rest against Thalos's for a moment longer, desire still thrumming between us, before I forced myself to release him. The army was watching. She was watching. And though the bond seared, demanding more, I nodded toward the soldiers.

"Clothes. Food," I ordered, my voice rough. "See to her at once."

The nearest men scrambled to obey, their eyes wide, unable to look too long at the miracle standing naked before them.

And I knew—this was only the beginning.

Chapter 28

Lyria

The spoiled hearts sat between us, turning darker at the edges, their copper stench cloying in the heat of the chamber. Morgryth's smirk held like a blade balanced on a fingertip—so sure, so steady, so convinced the weight would always tip his way.

I knew what he wanted, truly, more than me to eat these damned hearts. So I would play a game I knew I was all too good at, concealing my true intentions.

I let my fingers skim the rim of the plate, then drift lower, to the silk at my sternum. My mouth softened into a curve I'd used on hunters who thought they'd cornered a doe. "You're right about one thing," I murmured, letting my gaze lift and hold his. "I am hungry. Just... not for this."

I saw a hint of amber flickered in his crimson red eyes. His attention sharpened. Predators always did when prey stopped running.

"Oh?" he purred.

I drew a slow breath and slid my thumb under the bodice seam. The green silk loosened with a whisper, breath easing in my ribs. I felt the iron bite at my wrists, dimming and leeching, even as my magic flared but the line of his focus cut across it like a torch to fog. "Something else calls to me," I said, and I let heat thread my voice, a heat I owned. "Doesn't it to you?"

He stood in a single, fluid motion. "Yes, and we shall feed it."

The shackles clicked. His hands were quick, eager, the keys flashed, the lock gave, and iron fell away. The absence was a shock, pins and needles skittering up my forearms as blood and magic crept back into space it had been denied. I kept my face gentle, inviting, the pulse at my throat steady. Inside, every nerve bristled like a forest before lightning.

"Better," I breathed, and stepped into him.

I guided him by his lapel as if we danced. My lips grazed the scar along his jaw, not tenderness but precise distraction. He moved where I put him, a king who couldn't imagine anyone else leading. Here I was taking what I wanted and needed safely in this locked room.

His coat fell to the floor. Leather vest clasp undone, it fell to the floor next, then the buttons down his cotton shirt. I wove him backward with the ease of water finding the riverbed shaped for it, toward the spill of crimson on the bed.

The knife was just the weight of it in my skirts. I let silk hide steel as I pressed him to sit on the mattress, then pushed him backward, furs sighing around his shoulders.

Torchlight slicked over muscle and scars, over pride and want. He reached, but I caught his wrists, set them down to the mattress with a warning press of nails. Not yet.

He laughed, low. "So my little flame chooses to burn with me." He relaxed back on his elbows watching me.

I unlaced the bodice letting my full breast that had grown some, plunge past the opening bare and nipples peaked.

I slid the knife from the fold of my skirt into the sheets where I planned to kneel.

Letting the dress fall from my shoulders, the silk pooling at my feet like the shedding of a lie. Naked, I climbed on to the bed towards him. His breath shortened, victory glittered in his eyes. He thought this was surrender. He always would.

I kissed down the rough skin of his hard chest, as I counted his breaths, one, two, three...

I undid his belt and opened his pants, freeing his rigid length, and I climbed astride him. I felt the cool silver blade under my shin as I settled my weight, letting his cock sink into me.

I set the pace, slow, deliberate, coaxing his focus to narrow and narrow until nothing existed for him but heat and breath and the illusion of worship. His hands rose again. I pinned them again, until he learned the shape of my control, I moved. He followed.

The storm outside pressed its palms to the glass. Rain freckled the balcony doors. Smoke from the sconces crawled the ceiling in soft black ribbons. I could taste iron still, faintly, but the shackles were gone. My magic tested the edges of its cage with the caution of an animal sniffing open air. It hummed where it had been clenched, a trembling, low, dangerous sound.

He watched my face as if it were a prophecy unfolding only for him. "My queen," he said, strangled soft, and the words were a brand I would never wear.

I rolled my hips and kept his gaze until the moment his eyes slid shut, pleasure pulling him blind. Then my fingers slipped beneath the sheet. The knife's hilt found my palm like an old friend. I held it tightly behind my back, his hand finding my waist moving fast pushing hard, I let out a moan to encourage his fall into the depth of my seduction.

Not yet, I told the magic in my blood. Not until the scales tip and stay.

I bent to his ear, my breath a thread. "You were right about fate," I whispered, letting my lips brush his skin, letting him think it was devotion. "I can feel it."

His mouth parted. "Lyria—"

A shiver of something cut through the room. The stone under the bed thrummed, a vibration too deep to be heard, only felt. The rails in the city. The iron lines. The whole fortress had a hum. I'd felt it since we crossed its threshold. But this? This was different. It was a thread, green -red, tugging from somewhere below from halls and stairs and a door like a heartbeat behind a wall. My name moved along it, faint but real.

Lyria.

Thalos.

For one bare sliver of a breath, my chest broke open. The world sharpened and narrowed at once. I knew the shape of his voice in air and in bone, I would have known it if I'd been blind and buried in soil. He was close. The bond that I had held thin and flickering for months, twitched like a drowned ember catching a tongue of wind.

Morgryth's eyes opened at the same instant, startled, because he'd felt it too. He turned his head, listening. His hands tightened against my hips.

"Who..."

Now.

I drove the knife down.

Steel slid between ribs with a wet, sobbing sound. His roar tore the chamber, broke glass, and shocked birds from the city eaves. He surged up, a bear under a rain of spears, but my weight and the angle pinned him, and I pushed until the hilt kissed his chest, until heat poured over my hand and my thighs.

"Lyria!"

Thalos's shout ripped the doorway, a thunderclap of my name. The door I hadn't heard open stuttered against the stone. His voice didn't stop me; it steadied me. If there was a tremor at all, it was only to shove the blade the last, merciless inch.

Morgryth's fingers clawed at my wrist. I wrenched free and shoved his shoulder with my other hand, driving him back into the bed as the wound gushed. There was a wildness in his eyes I had never seen, shock cracked by something like grief. Pain cracked by something like recognition. It flickered and died.

My magic broke its muzzle and the world ripped open. Everything I had held back, all that iron I had forced down, I could conceal no longer, it all ripped out of me in a scream that wasn't pain and wasn't relief—it was a birth. Magic burst out of me as the earth in its core answered as it cracked open wide and its mouth consumed everything under me. The very air flinched. The floor arched. Cracks raced from the bedposts, as lightning broke through the roof.

Tapestries caught fire and ran up the walls. The balcony doors blew inward, rain and ash and ember swirling. Somewhere far below, the city answered, stone splitting, voices lifting. I felt the earth like a beast knocking off a rider it had tolerated too long.

Through it all—through flame and storm and stone—the bond crashed through me.

Fire. Storm. Stone.

Kiaza's heat roared in, not rage alone but the ferocious, shaking relief of a flame that had feared it burned alone. Thalos's sky poured over me, not only wind and thunder, but the steadiness of rain finding the ground it had searched for. The damn I had built for months broke loose and the bond claimed me with a single, blinding click. It hurt, and it healed, and I sobbed at the force of it as my body answered with light.

Scales pushed from skin. Wings unfurled in an explosion of breath and muscle. My vision refracted, every flame a star, every raindrop a hammered coin on black velvet. I reared, fully Drakarian and screamed my name into a world that had tried to deny it.

Morgryth slid sideways in the bed. The sheets were a river of red. His hands twitched once and stilled. The chamber tilted, stone thundered, and beams fell. He vanished into the collapse, into the mouth of the fortress I had turned into a grave.

I launched through fire and rain. The wall gave before me, stone shearing like wet parchment, and the night took me in its cold teeth. Wind rammed my chest, then caught my wings. I beat once—twice—and the city rolled beneath, fractured and burning, and I didn't look down again.

A shadow burst from the ruin after me, in green-black, wings spread wide, storm snarling in his bones. Thalos. The sight of him slammed joy into me so hard I staggered in the air, then steadied because he was there…He was there.

"What happened? Where are you?" Kiaza's voice lashed the tether, hot iron, hot fear, the kind of terror that only love makes possible.

I turned in the wind and hurled my truth down the bond, into fire and storm both, my voice bright as a white-hot brand.

"I did what I had to. I am owned by no one."

We rose. Storm swallowed our bodies and polished our edges, rain hissing along my scales, water beading and racing off in lines like veins of light. Thalos drew even with me, his eyes ringed in thunder, his presence a roar and a homecoming. He didn't touch, he didn't need to. He was there. The sky was mine.

Behind us, the fortress folded into itself, coughing stone and flame. The rails split, the city groaned. I felt the earth's ache and did not flinch from it. There would be a reckoning, and I would meet it. Not in chains. Not as a slave. Not as anyone's trophy.

We climbed until smoke became a smear and the cold bit my teeth. The bond sang in three voices and one chord—Earth, Sky, Fire—new and ancient, fierce and strangely quiet in its center. Desire threaded it: Kiaza's heat licking at my spine, Thalos's storm curling under my ribs. Relief settled like a mantle at my shoulders. For the first time since I'd hidden my name in a borrowed forest, I was whole.

Chapter 29

Thalos

Drakorra Spire loomed like a shadow of the gods themselves, its cliffs veined with firelight that bled from cracks in the mountain, its towers carved straight from the rock. The flight back had been long, the army strung out behind us like a black ribbon against the dawn, but when we reached the landing cliffs, silence fell.

No human army could breach this place. The cliffs themselves were wards, the Whispering Forests a labyrinth of illusions, and beneath us the molten heart of the Veins of Fire burned hotter than any forge. This was home. The last true bastion of our kind.

The soldiers settled into the outer chambers, their murmurs carrying awe, fear, reverence. Kiaza landed hard at the front, his presence drawing every eye as he began to bark orders, his voice echoing off stone and sky. He moved like the Spire itself had been waiting for him to return—each step a reminder that he was still king, still fire.

But I watched her.

Lyria.

She walked into the mountain as though it belonged to her. The cloak slid from her shoulders when the heat of the inner halls met her skin, her hair falling damp and tangled down her back. She should have looked exhausted, battered, half-broken after what she'd endured. Instead, every line of hers were steady curves. The fortress bowed to her without knowing it.

I followed her through carved halls lit by skylights until we reached the central space, called the garden valley. Light poured through the open crater, painting the stone in green and gold, streams whispering over rocks that glowed faint with runes. She sat at the edge of a pool, steam rising from a bowl cradled in her hands, and ate with the steady determination of someone reclaiming a piece of herself bite by bite.

I sank down across from her, the grass cool under my palms, shadows settling behind me like a cloak. The bond thrummed, steady now, whole, filling spaces I hadn't realized were hollow until she'd stepped into them.

Her eyes lifted once, catching mine, molten bright in the morning light.

"How long?" I asked. as I let my finger play slow with the edges of the grassblades.

Her brow furrowed faint. "How long what?"

My voice went soft and low, "How long did he have you? Parade you? Starve you?"

She dipped bread into broth and chewed before answering. "Too long."

The bond wavered at the edges of the word, slippery, evasive. She didn't want me to feel more than that.

I didn't press. Not yet.

Instead, I leaned forward, elbows on my knees. "When the bond snapped whole again, it nearly dropped me from the sky. I thought I'd imagined it at first. I'd forgotten what it felt like to be steady. And then it was you. Earth, the piece we've been missing."

Her spoon stilled. For a breath, her heat flared through the tether, warmth, fierce and real. Just as quick she covered it, her gaze dropping back to the broth.

"You and Kiaza would've managed," she muttered. "You didn't need me, still don't."

"That's a lie," I said, sharper than I meant. She glanced up, startled, and I softened.

"We were unraveling without you. Kiaza was burning himself down to embers. I—" My throat tightened. "I was wind with no ground to touch. We need you. That isn't weakness. It's truth."

Her jaw clenched, and she tore another piece of bread. She didn't answer.

I let the silence stretch, broken only by the stream's trickle and the murmur of soldiers beyond the chamber. Through the bond, I felt her strength, her defiance, but also a wall. Something heavy and hidden. She let us feel her, but she kept the heart of it locked tight. I could understand why she kept secrets, walls, she didn't know us, trust us not more then just instinct.

So I asked what truly mattered. "What do you want, Lyria?"

Her head snapped up, her brown and gold eyes sharp as flint.

"Not what he wanted. Not what fate wants. Not even what Kia or I want. You." My voice dropped. "What do you want?"

Her lips parted. Her breath caught. For a moment, I could feel her magic swell, and open as if she was finally going to let me in. Instead she turned away.

"I want..." She shook her head. "I don't know yet."

The bond vibrated with it—true and false tangled together.

I didn't call her on it I just noted it silently. Her voice. The way her eyes wouldn't meet mine. The way her magic curled inward instead of out. She was hiding something. Protecting something.

I leaned back, letting my shadows drift across the grass. "Then when you do know," I said softly, "tell me. Tell us. Whatever it is...it matters."

Her gaze flicked back to mine, her lips parting like she might. For a heartbeat, I swore she would tell me.

Kiaza's voice cut across the valley, commanding troops to the western cliffs, sending riders to the Whispering Forests to strengthen the border lines. His voice was steel and fire, the sound of a king shouldering the weight of survival. And just like that, her mouth closed. She turned back to her food, eating in silence as though the question had never been asked.

The bond betrayed her. A tremor. A weight.

And I knew, whatever truth she carried, it would shake us as surely as that fortress falling to ash.

She had nearly finished her meal when I reached into the neckline of my shirt. My fingers brushed rough stone, cool even in the warmth of being against my skin.

I hesitated. It had been mine since boyhood, my mother's last gift before they took her. A chunk of rainbow stone, veined with light, wrapped in copper wire and strung on worn black leather. She had pressed it into my palm and told me, *"For when you need to vanish, my stormbird. Every flame casts a shadow. Every shadow finds its refuge."*

I had never truly believed the legends, not until Lyria's magic had kept the bond from us, right now I truly believe she was a shield.

I slipped it free of my head, and held it across the space between us. The sunlight caught in its surface, shimmering faint hues—red, blue, green, gold—as if it held all elements at once.

Her brows lifted, curious, a small smile playing on her lips. "What's this?"

"A stone," I said, a little rough. "Not just any stone. My mother's."

She set her bowl aside, her cloak slipping a little at her shoulders as she leaned forward. Her hand brushed mine as she touched the pendant, and the bond flared at the contact, bright and hot.

I swallowed. "It's said rainbow stone can cloak magic essence. With the right will, it can hide fire, storm, even earth itself. My mother swore it helped shielders channel their concealment. She gave it to me to survive. And now..." I pushed it closer, my voice low. "Now it's yours."

The gold glowed in her eyes as they searched mine, sharp with surprise. "You'd give me this?"

"I would give you anything," I said, truth threading raw through the words. "But this... this might keep you alive if you ever need to disappear again. I don't want you caged. Neither of us do. If you choose to vanish, to be unseen, we'll respect it because it's *your* choice."

For a long moment she stared at me. Through the bond, I felt her emotions clash—gratitude, suspicion, something softer she kept trying to smother. Her throat worked, but her voice came out steady. "You trust me with something this precious?"

My faint smile grew softly. "No. I trust you because you are this precious."

Her breath caught. She looked down quickly, lifting the leather cord over her head, settling the stone against her bare skin. The copper wire glinted faint where it rested at the hollow between her breasts.

Through the bond, I felt her magic shift, curling in new patterns, like the stone had tuned it. Softer, harder to reach, as I had to strain a little more to feel the edges of her.

She looked up at me, her voice quieter than before. "Thank you, Thalos."

I nodded once, shadows curling close around me, though my chest felt tight and my magic felt hot.

I reached out without thinking, shadows softening at my back. My fingers brushed her cheek, just a whisper of touch, the warmth of her skin startling against the cool of my hand. For a breath she leaned into it, eyes molten, the bond humming low and aching. I almost leaned in to kiss her, because gods, I wanted that more than anything in this moment.

I didn't and she pulled away.

The space between us closed a heartbeat later, Kia came in, his boots striking stone, his presence burning like a forge in the garden valley. He slid down beside me, close enough that his thigh pressed to mine. His hand settled there, hot and steady, fingers curling possessively against the muscle. The contact rooted me, and I leaned into him without hesitation, my shoulder brushing his as my shadows curled around him. My shadows had become a living extension of me and my will, though it seems they also lent themselves to my instinct as well.

Lyria watched us, her gaze unreadable, as she casually picked her bowl back up. She cradled it in her lap like it created a wall between us..

Kia's amber eyes locked on her, unflinching. His jaw worked, the muscle ticking, fire rolling hot under his skin like it wanted out. He had been patient through my plan, patient through the army's awe, patient through the fragile quiet we'd carved out here. Though, patience was never truly his strength.

His voice came low, rough with heat. "Why," he said, the word more ember than sound, "didn't you ever tell me who you are?"

The bond flared with his demanding question, anger, yes, but threaded with fear. Also with hurt, with the raw ache of a king who had carried ashes too long only to the find gold he was searching for had been hidden right in front of him all along.

I felt Lyria stiffen, her hands clutched around the bowl in her lap. For a moment she didn't answer, the silence thick as the molten air that rose from the Veins of Fire below the mountain.

I held my breath.

Lyria's fingers tightened around the bowl until her knuckles whitened. She set it down carefully on the grass, as though buying herself a heartbeat of silence before she lifted her head.

Her golden eyes locked on Kia's, bright as hammered metal, unyielding. "Because I didn't owe you that."

The bond jolted with the force of it, the hard truth striking clean. His shoulders went rigid, the heat rolling off him so sharp I could almost taste ash on my tongue.

"I nearly burned myself hollow looking for you," he said, voice low, each word dragged through flame. "I left Los, and tore the world apart because we thought you were lost. And all the while, you were there. Gardening. Hiding."

Her chin lifted, defiance carved in the line of her throat. "I was living my life, yes. I won't apologize for that."

The words landed heavy, solid as stone. Through the bond I felt a flicker of her recent memories, the hunger and chains, iron rails humming against her skin, Morgryth's hand in her hair, the knife clenched in her palm. She had not been safe, not truly, not ever, and she felt it.

Kia leaned forward, his hand tightening on my thigh, his fire sparking dangerously close to rage. "You could have told me…"

"No." Her voice cut like a blade. "I could not. You see a queen. A mate. A savior for your dying people. But I am not a prize to be claimed or a banner to be raised. If I had told you… if I had let you see me… do you know what would have happened? Every faction, every rogue, every kingdom would have hunted me faster than they already have. I would have still been chained. Only this time, with your hand on the key."

Silence fell hard.

Kiaza's breath sawed through his chest, eyes burning ruby, but beneath the fury I felt it through the bond, hurt. The wound of being denied, the rawness of love twisted against secrecy.

I steadied against his heat, shadows curling around him, my hand covering his where it still gripped my thigh. "Lyria," I said softly, my gaze on her. "He isn't wrong. We needed you, still do. But neither are you. What you endured… gods, none of us can fault you for guarding yourself, for those vary reasons."

Her eyes softened at that, only slightly. Then she looked away, toward the glowing runes carved into the garden stone. "I told myself I would reveal the truth when I could do it on my own terms. Not when anyone—king, council, or fate—forced it from me. Mine. Or not at all."

The bond thrummed with it, earth solid, immovable, unbending.

Kiaza rumbled low, fire barely contained, but he said nothing more. His silence was thunder waiting to break.

And I knew, as I watched her tuck her cloak tighter around herself, that she wasn't just speaking of her identity as the last female. She was speaking of something else too, something she still kept hidden, even from us.

The silence stretched until it felt like the whole Spire was holding its breath. The stream in the garden gurgled softly, the only sound against the weight between them.

His jaw flexed, his eyes locked on hers like he could burn the truth straight from her skin. The fire in him coiled hotter, hotter, until even my shadows bristled, ready to smother if it burst.

Then, at last, he dragged a breath through his teeth and let it out slow, smoke without flame. His hand loosened against my thigh, though it still shook faintly with the force of restraint.

"You should have trusted me," he said, voice low, rough. The edge was still there, but beneath it was something quieter. "I would have bled the world dry before I let anyone cage you."

Lyria didn't flinch. She only drew the cloak tighter around herself, golden eyes steady. "And I would not have let you."

Another beat of silence, thick and sharp. Then he leaned back, gaze tearing away from her to fix on the runes glowing faint in the garden stone. His mouth pressed into a grim line. "Fine. You lived. You chose. You're here now."

I could sense it through the bond, reluctant acceptance, smoldering, not forgiveness but a step away from the edge.

I pressed closer to him, letting my shoulder bear some of his weight, shadows curling around him until the trembling eased. His amber eyes slid to mine, and for a heartbeat, I saw the storm of relief under it all.

He turned back to Lyria, voice clipped, almost formal. "Please, no more hiding. Not from me. Not from him. Not from this bond."

Her lips quirked, the faintest ghost of a smile, sharp as a blade. "We'll see."

The bond stirred, vibrating with defiance and longing all tangled together.

His eyes narrowed, but he didn't argue. Instead, he rose in a single powerful motion, steam rolling off him like heat haze, and barked orders to a passing soldier to tighten the patrol at the gates. His voice carried, all command again, leaving the air between us heavy with words unsaid.

I stayed seated, my gaze on Lyria as she bent to finish the last of her bread. She ate with steady hands now, though through the bond I felt the tremor of everything she hadn't spoken aloud.

I knew Kia had accepted her answer—for now. I feared though his fire would come for the full truth eventually.

Chapter 30

Kiaza

The corridors of Drakorra Spire swallowed me whole as I stormed through them. The stone walls light by torches and the air was thick with the heat from the Veins of Fire far below. All the stone channels had been opened to keep the cold of coming winter at bay. My soldiers gave me wide berth. They knew the sound of my temper when it was clawing to be let loose.

I needed space. Needed silence. Needed the steadiness of our chambers, the one place in this fortress that didn't feel like it had questions that would go unanswered or have answers I wasn't ready to hear.

My boots struck the carved steps hard Shadows twitched at the edge of my vision, Thalos's presence still humming faint through the bond, quiet but steady. I wanted him. I needed him. His shadows leaching out of him was an odd sort of comfort, one I hadn't known I needed. The feel of him completely enveloping me was soothing even as my magic was getting harder to keep under control. My flames came easier than ever, and it unsettled me. I flexed my hand as flames licked up for the tips, before I snuffed them out. I stepped closer to our room, finally looking up just before I reached the door.

Her voice caught me. "Are you planning on staying this grumpy with me forever?"

I stopped cold.

She leaned against the archway, cloak loose around her shoulders, chestnut hair falling in soft curls against her cheek. Her eyes gleamed in the torchlight, not cowed, not hesitant, mocking, almost. Teasing.

Grumpy.

The word was so absurd on her tongue that my lips nearly twitched before I caught myself. I turned, slow, arms folding across my chest. "Grumpy?" I rumbled, my voice low with the fire I still hadn't banked. "That's what you call it?"

Her mouth curved into a sly smile. "What else should I call it? You stormed out like a sulking child denied sweets."

Heat flushed through me, anger, yes, but threaded with something hotter, sharper, dangerous in an entirely different way. My jaw clenched, but the bond betrayed me, I felt her amusement sliding into me, warm and golden, daring me to bite.

"You think this is sulking?" I stepped closer, the stone under my boots echoing. "I call it restraint."

"Mm." She tilted her head, eyes bright, playful. "Looks a lot like pouting from here."

A growl rumbled deep in my chest. My arms dropped, fists curling at my sides, not in fury, but to stop myself from grabbing her and pressing her against the wall like my body demanded. She knew it. Gods, she knew it, and that smile of hers only widened.

"Careful, Sunshine," I said, my voice rough, slipping closer until her breath brushed mine. "Keep taunting me, and you'll find out just how little patience I have left."

Her laugh was soft, low, wicked as any weapon. "Maybe that's exactly what I want...Just for tonight."

The bond flared—fire meeting earth, gold and red colliding—and I had to bite back the groan that rose at the surge of want flooding through me.

She straightened, her hand brushing the stone wall as she slipped past me, close enough that her cloak brushed my thigh. She glanced back over her shoulder, eyes molten.

"So," she said lightly, as though she hadn't just set me alight, "are you coming to pout in your room, with Thalos? Or are you planning to keep stomping through the Spire like a thundercloud?"

My breath caught, my temper forgotten, my chest burning in a way that had nothing to do with anger.

Grumpy, sulking, pouting—she was lucky I didn't throw her over my shoulder and carry her there myself.

The heavy door to our chambers creaked open, shadows curling soft around the carved stone. Los looked up from where he sat near the window, his shadows inviting us in. The faint light from the room glinted off the copper and rainbow on a leather cord now resting against Lyria's breast. Thalos's necklace. His mothers. Now hers. I couldn't tear my eyes away from her, had they always been so full and firm. Gods she stirred something I couldn't deny my cock twitching.

"See?" Lyria's voice was bright with mischief as she stepped inside, cloak trailing across the floor. She flicked her gaze between us, brown eyes dancing. "Thalos isn't nearly so grumpy."

Before I could speak, before I could warn her not to toy with me, she crossed the space and leaned down, pressing her lips to his.

It wasn't soft. It wasn't shy. Her mouth claimed his with the same defiance she'd just thrown in my face, her fingers sliding into his golden hair, her body pressing against his shoulder. And the entire time, her gaze stayed on me full of mischief.

Fire ripped through my chest.

Not rage. Gods, not even jealousy. Desire, molten and sharp, watching her take him, watching him respond, shadows rising to meet her heat. I felt their kiss in the bond, the flare of it sliding into me, licking at my veins until my breath came harsh and heavy.

She broke the kiss slow, a wicked smile curving her mouth as she pulled back just enough for her breath to mingle with his. She looked down at his surprised expression, then she glanced at me again, eyes blazing gold.

"Well?" she asked sweetly, tilting her head. "Still thinking about pouting?"

I should have growled. I should have snapped, taken her mouth myself, reminded her whose fire burned hottest. Instead, my lips curved, heat curling into hunger so deep it ached.

"I think," I rumbled, stepping closer until the floor trembled faint beneath my boots, "Sunshine, it's a good thing you're so strong, because you like to play with fire far too much."

Los's hand lingered at the back of her neck, his lips parted, his eyes storm-bright and dazed from her kiss. Shadows curled off his shoulders like smoke, restless, hungry.

And she turned her head, slow, deliberate, until her gaze caught mine again.

"Well yes, I've always liked to play with fire." she teased, her voice low, breath still mingling with Los's and she looked into his eyes. "And dance in the rain."

My restraint cracked. I closed the distance in five strides, fire rolling under my skin until the very air shimmered. Her smile widened as if she'd been daring me to do it all along.

I caught her jaw in my hand, my thumb brushing the corner of her mouth where Los's kiss still lingered. Her skin was hot, damp with a bead of sweat. She didn't flinch, didn't shy, she leaned into it, golden eyes blazing at me like she wanted to be consumed.

I kissed her.

Gods, it was nothing like I'd expected. Fire should have devoured earth, but instead her strength held, solid and unyielding, meeting me flame for flame. She tasted of sweet berries and broth and defiance, and when she nipped my lower lip, I growled into her mouth, the sound tearing from my chest.

Thalos rose from the chair behind her, his presence wrapping around us both. His hand slid over my shoulder, steady, grounding, as his lips brushed her throat just beneath her ear. The bond flared as our magic twisting together until it was impossible to tell where one ended and the other began.

Her gasp shuddered between us, hands bracing against my chest, not to push me away, but to steady herself. I broke the kiss only to trail my mouth down her jaw, tasting the salt of her skin, while Los's shadows curled tighter around us, his mouth claiming the hollow of her throat.

She laughed, breathless, wicked. "And here I thought you two were going to stay mad at me forever."

"Mad?" Los murmured against her skin, his voice low thunder. "More like suffering."

I pressed my forehead to hers, breath harsh, the bond thrumming hot between us. "Not forever, Sunshine," I growled. "I could never stay mad at you."

Her lips parted, eyes softening for just a heartbeat, just long enough for something deeper than desire to pulse through us. Longing. Need. Belonging.

I had them both here, in my arms, in my room, and soon in my bed, just where they belonged. I didn't want this to be only for tonight, though part of me feared it might be all she would give. The thought clawed at me, but I shoved it aside. Instead, I lowered my mouth to kiss Los where his lips pressed to her throat, her cloak slipping from her shoulders to the floor.

I tugged off the simple cotton dress off her shoulders next, it slid to the floor, pooling at her feet with the cloak. I pulled her closer, pressing her bare curved body flush against mine. Her skin burned hotter than fire, the bond crackling between us.

Los's mouth still worked her throat, her shoulder, his shadows curling possessively along her hips, and along my spine. Every sound she made, every gasp, every laugh, shot straight through me.

I caught her mouth again, harder this time, teeth grazing her bottom lip before sucking it between mine. She moaned into me, fingers knotting in my hair, tugging just enough to draw a growl from deep in my chest. My hand slid down her spine, tracing the curve until I cupped the swell of her ass, grinding her against the hard line of my arousal.

"Fuck," I hissed against her lips. "You feel like you were made for this...for us."

Her hands tugged my shirt upward, baring me inch by inch until I let it fall away. I seized her hips again, dragging her closer, and felt Los press in behind her, his heat hard and insistent against her back. My palms shifted lower, teasing between them, brushing her body against the rigid strain of his cock still caged in his pants.

I worked open the buckle of Los's belt, the click sharp in the charged silence. She leaned back to claim his mouth, the kiss hot and hungry, while I trailed fire down her throat, my hand sliding into his pants to stroke him. His ragged gasp was swallowed by her lips.

I nipped at her earlobe, my voice a low growl against her skin. "Do you feel how much we want you, Sunshine?"

She broke the kiss with a breathless laugh, her fist tangled in my hair, tugging my head back until her molten gaze locked on mine. Her smile was wicked, daring, a challenge and a promise in one. "Then take me, my Kings."

I didn't need more than that.

I lifted her easily, her legs wrapping around my waist as though they had always belonged there. Los's hands slid down her ribs, then lower, his fingers brushing the insides of her thighs, his fingers working between us now, teasing her. She gasped, arching between us, torn between his touch and mine.

Los's guided us back towards the new plush bed, covered in soft furs for winter, the newly carved logs cradling them. He moved onto the end of the bed. Shadows trailing along my body sending a shiver up my spine.

We laid her down together, as if the bond, our magic guided us. Her hair fanned across the sheets, dark with flecks of gold in the low light, her breasts rising and falling as she looked up at us with molten eyes.

I climbed onto the bed, caging her in, my mouth finding her nipple while Los took the other. She gasped, her back bowing, and the sound shattered what restraint I had left. My hand trailed lower, parting the wet heat between her thighs, finding her already soaked.

"Gods, Sunshine," I growled, circling her clit with slow, deliberate strokes. "You're dripping for us."

Los laid along her side, he kissed up her throat, shadows licking where his mouth left her skin. "She wants to be ruined," he murmured, his voice vibrating through her as he slid his hand over mine, pressing my fingers harder against her as our fingers teased her entrance pushing slowly. "Doesn't she?"

Her answer was a broken moan, her hips lifting into our hands.

I pulled back just enough from her breast, to watch her face as I pushed two fingers inside her, slow at first, then curling until she cried out. Los held her open for me, his eyes wild and hungry, the storm in him barely restrained. As he captured her nipple in his mouth again.

The bond surged, thick with heat, and I felt everything, her pleasure sharp and bright, Los's hunger threaded with mine, my own desire molten and pounding.

"I need you now," I rasped, pulling my fingers free, freeing my throbbing hard cock from my pants and dragging the tip of it through her slick center Los's fingers following along.

She reached for me, fingers trembling as they wrapped around the back of my neck, dragging me down until our foreheads nearly touched. Her voice was a desperate whisper, raw with need. "Then don't make me wait. I want both of you... together."

Her other hand slid down blindly, finding Los, wrapping around his thick length. She stroked his cock with greedy, desperate pulls, her whimper vibrating against my lips as if the urgency alone could keep us both tethered to her.

A chuckle rumbled out of me, rough and low. "Not tonight, Sunshine."

And then I drove into her in one steady, merciless thrust, burying myself to the hilt. The sound she made nearly undid me, the cry of someone giving in and claiming in the same breath. Her hands clawed at my shoulders, nails biting deep, anchoring herself as I pulled back and slammed into her again.

Los shifted at her side, shadows clinging to his skin as he gripped her thigh and spread her wider for me. His mouth devoured hers, swallowing her moans, kissing her like he'd die without it, while I fucked her deeper, harder, every stroke dragging another desperate sound from her throat.

The three of us tangled together. Sweat slicking our bodies, shadow and fire wrapping tight, breath and heartbeats crashing like thunder. She was earth beneath us, grounding us, holding us steady even as she trembled apart. Los was storm, wild and relentless, feeding the fire I poured into every thrust, until the bond between us burned white-hot, searing through marrow and magic alike.

Her climax broke like lightning, sudden and savage. She screamed against Los's mouth, muffled but fierce, as her body clamped around me, squeezing tight enough to wrench a groan from my chest. I buried my face in her neck, teeth scraping her skin, voice rough and undone.

"Lyria—"

Her name left me like a vow, ragged and holy, and gods help me, I knew in that moment I never wanted to let her go.

Chapter 31

Lyria

The bond clawed at me, hot and unrelenting, dragging me closer to them both. Their mouths on my skin, their hands steady and hungry, it was everything I had sworn to resist. And yet tonight, I couldn't. Not when every thread of me had been starved for so long. Not when I could finally breathe again.

I promised myself this would be only for tonight.

Just one night to give in. To let storm and fire take me, to let shadows curl against my skin and burn away the ache of being alone. Just one night to pretend I belonged to something bigger than myself, to them, to us.

Tomorrow I would tell them the truth. That I couldn't stay. That I wasn't meant to be a queen. That my life wasn't only mine anymore, because my daughter already lived beneath my ribs, quiet and waiting, and she deserved a future without chains, without walls.

For just tonight, gods, tonight I would give them this.

Their bond pressed into me, flooding through my veins in heat and want. Thalos's shadows slid like silk around my waist, tugging me closer, drawing me into the storm of him. Kiaza's fire flared lower, sparking between my thighs, his breath searing my shoulder as his growl scraped raw against my ear. Every nerve lit where they touched me, each caress a spark setting tinder alight.

I arched between them, my whimper breaking free, half-desire, half-relief. My thighs trembled, slick with need, and I didn't hide the sound. I let it rise, let it spill, let them know I wanted, that I craved.

"Lyria," Thalos murmured, storm-wind rough, his lips brushing my swollen mouth. The syllables cracked through me like lightning finding its mark.

Kiaza's mouth trailed fire down the line of my shoulder, his teeth catching my skin, claiming, searing. "Ours," he growled, the word branding me through the bond as surely as if it had been carved into my bones. Then he spilled into me, hot and full, and my hips jolted at the rush, his fire searing through all three of us at once.

When he pulled out, the emptiness struck sharp, a hollow ache clawing at me. I whimpered, needy, desperate for the fullness again, desperate not to lose that heat.

Even with Kiaza's chest heaving, his fire still crackling under his skin, and my body trembling from the quake of release, I couldn't stop touching him. My fingers roamed over the ridges of his muscle, stroking his damp skin, grounding myself in the bond that thrummed steady and whole now, no longer stifled, it was free, I let be.

My eyes stung. Gods help me, part of me wanted to believe this could last. That I could stay here. That I could belong.

I turned, catching Kia's mouth with mine, swallowing his ragged groan even as Thalos's hand slid lower, rough and sure. His palm cupped me, then his cock pressed against the curve of my ass, sliding lower, finding the soaked heat of me still pulsing from Kia. The stretch of him made me cry out into Kia's mouth, my body clenching greedily around him as he filled me.

The bond flared, sparks and shadows, fire and stone colliding until I could hardly think, until I wasn't sure where one of us ended and the other began. My body arched, caught between them, pinned and lifted all at once, my hands clutching at Kia's sweat-slick skin, nails digging, desperate to hold on.

Thalos fucked me deep and hard, every thrust dragging a cry from my throat that Kiaza swallowed, their hunger and magic burning through me, their need tearing me open in ways I had thought I'd buried.

I clung to both of them, drowning in sensation, in heat, in the bond made whole. And even as my body shattered around them, even as I whispered their names like prayers, I promised myself again, it was only for tonight.

One night.

And then I would walk away.

Thalos's thrusts shook me, each one harder, deeper, until my body gave itself over to him without resistance. My cries tumbled into Kiaza's mouth, muffled and devoured as if he couldn't bear to let them escape into the air. His fire rolled over me in waves, hot enough to sting, branding every part of me he touched.

The bond writhed between us, not a tether but a living, pulsing force. Their need coiled inside me like a second heartbeat. Thalos's storm crashed against my spine with every push, relentless, breaking me down into something raw and undone. Kiaza's fire lit along my throat and breasts where his mouth dragged, teeth scraping, tongue soothing, claiming me as if I were both sacred and doomed.

I couldn't tell whose hands were whose anymore—shadows stroking along my waist, fire searing down my thighs, calloused fingers pinching my nipple until I gasped, arching higher, needing more.

"Fuck, Lyria," Thalos growled, voice cracking into my shoulder. "You're so tight..gods.."

"Ours," Kia snarled once again, against my skin, his palm sliding down to press on the soft swell of my belly above where Thalos drove into me. The pressure made me clench around him, the sensation too much, too sharp, tearing another scream from my lips.

I was breaking open. Not from pain, not from pleasure alone, but from the bond that surged like a stormfront inside me. Their magic filled me until my own answered, earth rising up to meet storm and fire, my body glowing with it, burning with it.

My climax hit so hard my vision whited out. My cry was ragged, desperate, my nails raking down Kiaza's back as my body locked tight around Thalos. He groaned, deep and raw, spilling into me, hips jerking as shadows clawed up my thighs like they didn't want to let me go.

Kia wasn't finished.

His hand pressed Thalos back just enough to spread me wider, first his fingers then his cock hot and heavy against my soaked opening. I sobbed at the pressure, at the stretch that came again as he pushed inside me, thicker, brutal in his need. He growled low as he buried himself to the hilt, the sound vibrating through my chest. Thalos moved in rhythm matching Kia as if they were one.

"You're ours," Kia rasped, his teeth grazing my jaw. "Say it."

I choked on a moan, my head shaking even as my body trembled with want. "Just tonight," I gasped, the words tearing from my throat. "Just tonight—"

"Liar," Thalos murmured, his lips brushing my ear, his voice a storm breaking low and certain. His hand wrapped around my wrist, pinning me against the furs as Kiaza drove into me again, each thrust slamming the breath from my lungs.

312

The two of them moved in tandem, their mouths finding mine, each other's, my skin, never letting me go, never giving me a breath that wasn't theirs. Their hunger devoured me, and I let it. Gods, I let it.

Because for tonight, I belonged to them.

Even as I screamed their names, even as my body shattered again around their relentless thrusts, even as they both let out ragged breathy groans filling me once again. I clung to the promise I'd made.

One night. Only one night.

As the bond surged, whole and unyielding, when our magics tangled so tightly I couldn't tell whose heartbeat was mine anymore, a part of me knew the truth.

I would never be free of this.

Chapter 32

Thalos

The heat of her body clenched around us both, wet, tight, almost too much to bear. Kia's cock drove deeper with mine, our rhythm jagged but desperate, both of us straining to give her more, to take more, until she was sobbing between us, her body trembling under the weight of it.

Her cries tore through me, raw and unguarded, her nails scoring my arm as if she could hold herself together only by breaking me open. The bond seared, white-hot, storm and fire colliding in the furnace of her earth until all I knew was us, three voices, three heartbeats, one blaze of need.

I felt myself fracturing, release burning sharp at the base of my spine. I groaned against her shoulder, teeth grazing her skin, shadows writhing wild at my back. "Fuck, Lyria...I can't..."

Kiaza's growl cut through mine, guttural, feral, his thrusts harder now, driving me closer to the edge. The three of us tangled, sweat and shuddering breath, and then her climax hit again—her scream muffled against my throat as she shattered, walls clenching down so tight it dragged me with her.

I came with a shudder, cumming into her as the storm finally broke. Kiaza followed a heartbeat later, a ragged roar tearing from his chest as his fire flared, heat and shadow and molten gold all colliding in her body at once.

Followed by peaceful silence only filled with our rasps of breaths.

I pulled out slowly, my chest heaving, my body trembling from the force of it. Kia shifted with me, both of us reluctant to leave her but knowing we had to. She lay between us, flushed and wrecked, hair damp with sweat, lips swollen, eyes molten gold still shimmering with the bond's glow.

I pressed my forehead to hers, catching her breath with mine, my hand cupping her cheek. "Easy," I whispered, softer than I'd been all night. My thumb brushed her skin, tracing sweat and tears alike. "You're safe. We've got you."

Kiaza's hand covered mine, rough and steady, his fire no longer burning but banked, warm. For once, he didn't snarl, didn't command, he only leaned down to kiss her temple, his lips lingering as though he feared she'd vanish if he let her go.

The three of us stayed tangled in silence, bodies damp and spent, magic humming low and steady between us. I drew the furs up over her, shadows curling to tuck them around her like a second skin. She let out a sound—half-sigh, half-whimper—and turned her face into my chest.

I looked over her, at Kia. His ruby eyes met mine, fierce even in their softness, and I knew he felt it too. A shift in the world around us, and not just our magic.

I pressed a kiss to her damp hair, tasting salt and smoke. My hand slid to her belly, gentle, grounding. She flinched, only faintly, but I noticed. My heart twisted, questions rising I didn't ask. Not yet.

Instead, I pulled her closer, my voice a low vow. "Sleep, My little glowbee. We're here."

And as her breathing slowed, as her lashes fluttered shut, I prayed the gods would let this night stretch longer, just a little longer. I knew deep down she wouldn't stay, not yet, maybe not ever.

Kia slipped in behind me, his body heat sinking into my back as his arms wrapped around us both. His breath ghosted my ear, low and unguarded. *"Los... I love you. Forever."*

A smile tugged at my lips. I leaned my head back into the solid weight of him, closing my eyes at the comfort of it. "I love you too," I murmured, voice rough but certain. "Forevermore."

My shadows stirred lazily, curling along the sheets, brushing against Kia's arm, against Lyria's thigh. For the first time since I had freed them, I didn't feel them as wild things straining at a leash, I felt them as mine. As *pieces of me.*

Curious how far they could reach, I let one slip free, reaching out into the stillness of the Spire. It slithered down the corridor, silent as mist, brushing against cold stone, stretching farther, farther, until it was in the kitchen. I closed my eyes, and suddenly I wasn't just lying in bed—I was *there.*

I felt warmth radiating from the ovens in the kitchen. Saw the wooden counter dusted in flour, a mound of bread dough resting under a linen cloth, rising slow with the heat. The space hummed with a quiet kind of life. My shadow coiled close, curious, and I reached with a tendril, brushing the surface of the dough. Soft. Warm. I felt it like I touched it.

A voice snapped me still.

"Who's there?"

Renae stood in the doorway, her eyes sweeping the room, suspicion sharp in her young face. "Show yourself. The kitchen's closed this late."

She turned a slow circle, gaze searching shadows I hadn't meant her to see. My chest tightened.

I pulled back, fast, recoiling the tendril into myself until it was only me again.

My eyes flew open. The kitchen dissolved into darkness, and I was back in bed with Kia breathing steady at my back, Lyria's soft hair fanned across my chest, both of them curled close in sleep.

My lungs ached as I dragged air into them, ragged and unsteady. The shadows whispered restless against my skin, curling and uncurling like caged serpents. I tried to hold them tight, as I once had, pressing them down with sheer will. *Not now. Not here.*

They pressed harder, their hunger bleeding through me. I couldn't tell if they longed simply to roam, to slip free through stone and sky, or if they craved what they had always known best, death. Their need coiled with my own unease until I could hardly tell where I ended and they began.

I clenched my fists in the furs, the thick pelts bunching between my fingers as though I could wring the restlessness from myself. All I wanted was the peace I used to know, the calm that lived inside my storm before the shadows became something I could never fully cage again. Now they writhed just beneath my skin, whispering, urging, hungry.

I pressed my teeth together, searching inward, reaching for the still point I had always trusted in myself. My shadows only hissed and coiled tighter, reminding me of every life I'd claimed, every ruin my hands had made.

Then she moved.

Lyria stirred against me, soft in her sleep, her hand sliding over my chest like she'd always belonged there. Her palm pressed to my heartbeat, steady and sure, and her magic bled through her skin into mine. It seeped into the cracks where my control faltered, quieting the gnawing hunger, soothing the storm that had roared so long inside me.

My lungs loosened, breath spilling out of me slow and deep. My chest eased under her touch as if even my shadows had no choice but to obey her.

Gods. How was I ever supposed to let her go?

I had heard her. When she said this was only for one night, she had meant it. She would leave. She would always leave. Kia wouldn't want to accept it, and neither did I, but wanting wasn't enough. We couldn't cage her. Not the one who had broken every chain laid upon her.

And yet...

My shadows knew what she hadn't said aloud. They whispered it to me every time her magic brushed mine, every time her body shifted in sleep. I felt it, pulsing faint and strong beneath her ribs. A heartbeat not her own.

Her child.

Our child.

The shadows told me the truth before she ever would. The life she carried beat fast, quick and fierce like her mother's already strong, already demanding. The sound of it echoed through me, a drumbeat I could never unhear.

I knew exactly when it had happened. The night in the woods, the night she'd lain with Kia, the night our fated bond had sealed itself in fire and storm and earth. She hadn't chosen because the world needed saving, or because magic was fading, or because anyone else demanded it. She had chosen because she wanted a child.

She hadn't told us. Because she never intended to.

She wanted to keep it for herself, wholly hers in a world that had taken too much.

It was unfair. It burned hot in my chest, stoked anger sharp enough that my shadows twitched again at the edges of my control. Even through the sting, I understood. How could she trust us with the truth when she barely knew us? Not in the way two souls should know each other before bringing a child into the world.

My own mother had chosen poorly the first time. I had borne the weight of that mistake, carried scars no child should ever have to carry. I had sworn no child of mine would ever suffer the same.

So I would let her go.

I would let her decide.

Gods help me, a small part of me hoped. Hoped she would tell us, hoped she would let us in, hoped she would see that she didn't have to carry this alone. I would cling to that hope, as tightly as I held my shadows, for as long as I could.

Her breath tickled my chest in sleep. Kia's warmth pressed at my back, his steady fire anchoring me. My shadows coiled close again, restless, but quieter now, because they had felt it too. That heartbeat. That spark. That promise.

As I lay between them, holding on to the fragile, impossible hope that she would stay.

Chapter 33

Kiaza

Morning light spilled through the Spire's high windows, pale and silver across the stone walls. I stirred, the ache of last night still in every muscle, the heat of it ghosting across my skin.

Thalos was curled against me, his head tucked under my chin, his breath warm and steady against my chest. Shadows clung to him even in sleep, curling around my waist like they feared I might rise without him. My hand rested there out of habit, fingers tangled in his blond hair.

The space on his other side was empty.

My eyes snapped open. The sheets were still warm where she'd been, the faint scent of her, earthy like rain touched soil with a hint of flowers, still lingered. My heart stuttered, panic striking before reason could catch it.

"Lyria," I growled under my breath, already pushing up, ready to tear through the Spire stone by stone if I had to.

Then the bond pulsed. Warm. Teasing. Her voice slid through me, laughter curling around the edges of it. *"Easy, Mr.grumpy. I'm not gone."*

I exhaled, tension bleeding out of me as I gripped the bedframe. *"Where?"*

Kitchen, she answered, her tone maddeningly casual. *"Renae is fussing over me, feeding me enough bacon and eggs to feed a small army. If you want some, you'd better get here before little Sam eats your share."*

I snorted, half in relief, half in exasperation. My chest still burned from the echo of that first moment of panic, but the bond thrummed steady, her presence warm and alive.

Behind me, Thalos stirred with a groan, his shadows stretching like a cat waking. He blinked blearily, rubbed his face against my shoulder, and mumbled, "Why are you growling at dawn?"

"She's not here," I muttered.

His head shot up, a storm flickering awake in his eyes. "What—"

"She's in the kitchens," I cut in, pinching the bridge of my nose. "Eating."

The corner of his mouth twitched like he might laugh, but wisely, he didn't.

Through the bond, her warmth pressed closer again. *"Are you coming, or are you two going to laze around all morning?"*

I swung my legs over the side of the bed, fire simmering low in my veins. *"We're coming."*

For a moment, I just sat there, elbows braced on my knees, staring at the empty space in the bed. The bond thrummed steady and alive, her laughter still humming through me, but the memory of that night pressed heavier than the stone around us.

Lyria had killed him.

Morgryth.

The monster who had haunted my bloodline since the night he tore my mother apart. The shadow that had ruled every fire I breathed since I was a boy.

I had sworn my whole life that his end would be mine to claim. That one day I would look into his scarred eyes and strike him down, and the ghost of my mother would finally rest. That vengeance would be my crown.

But it hadn't been me.

It had been her.

A flicker of shame burned hot in my gut, sharper than I wanted to admit. She had done what I could not. She had taken the knife, plunged it into his chest, and torn the world apart to be free.

And gods help me, I was in awe of her for it.

Even now, with the bond thrumming whole between us, I could still see her in my mind's eye: gold blazing through the ruin, her roar shaking the fortress as it fell. Earth, unyielding. She hadn't just survived him. She had ended him.

I dragged a hand over my face, breath shuddering out. Relief. Shame. Awe. They twisted together until I couldn't separate them.

Would they whisper it in the halls of the Spire? That the Drakarian King hadn't been the one to slay the tyrant? That the last female had done what the king could not? Would they see me as unworthy, a crown carried on her blade instead of my own fire?

One truth pressed cold and heavy in my chest, I hadn't avenged my mother. She had. A darker thought lingered, one I couldn't shake. If she could strike him down where I had failed... What did that make me?

The corridors of the Spire glowed faint with morning light, the air warm from the Veins of Fire far below. Thalos walked beside me, shadows brushing the walls with every step. His shoulder knocked against mine once, steady, grounding, though his eyes lingered too long.

"You're quiet, too quiet" he said at last, his voice low, still rough from sleep. "Are you alright?"

I grunted, but it wasn't enough for him. It never was. He had always been able to peel me open with a single glance.

"She killed him," I muttered, more to the stone under my boots than to him. "I swore my whole life that it would be mine. My vengeance. My fire. And she—" I shook my head, jaw tight. "She did what I could not."

Thalos's shadows stirred, but his voice was gentle. "And she survived what you never had to."

The words hit harder than I wanted them to. I didn't answer. Couldn't.

He let the silence stretch, then asked the question that knocked the breath from my chest. "Will you be okay if she doesn't stay?"

I stopped mid-stride. "Doesn't Stay?"

Thalos slowed too, watching me. His expression was unreadable, but his eyes were storm-dark, wary. "She's already said she doesn't want to be queen. She is holding back from us. What will you do if this bond isn't enough to hold her here?"

The thought slammed into me, hot and unwelcome. Of course she would stay. She was bonded to us, to me. She had chosen us last night, tangled in the sheets, her breath ragged against my skin. She was ours. She wouldn't leave. Not again.

But the bond hummed under my skin, and in its steady thrum there was a shadow of doubt.

Would she?

I forced my jaw to unclench. "She won't leave," I said, harsher than I meant. "She can't."

But even as I spoke the words, I felt the lie in them. The bond didn't chain her. It never could.

Gods help me, if she wanted to walk away, nothing in this world could stop her.

The kitchen smelled of bacon, eggs, and bread, warm and rich, a comfort I hadn't known I needed right now. The stone hearth blazed, pans hissing as Renae worked the stove with practiced ease, Sam perched on a stool nearby with his feet swinging.

There at the table sat Lyria.

Her hair was braided loose down her back, a simple cotton dress falling soft against her frame, sleeves rolled up. She had a wooden spoon in her hand and a bowl of batter in front of her, a dusting of flour streaked across her cheek. She looked... utterly at home.

My chest tightened.

Renae was watching her like a proud mother hen, nodding as Lyria stirred. Sam leaned in close, eyes wide as if the act of mixing batter was sorcery.

"We're making blueberry muffins," Lyria said as I entered, her voice bright, teasing. "Renae has the bacon handled, so I thought I'd show her a trick or two for the morning meals."

I couldn't help it. My mouth curved into a smile as I stepped closer. She arched a brow at me like she expected some gruff comment, but I only reached out, brushing my thumb across her cheek to wipe some of the flour away.

Her lips parted, rich brown eyes catching mine for a breath, the bond thrumming warm between us.

Behind me, Thalos all but bounded into the room, shadows trailing like an excited hound's tail. He swooped Sam off the stool in one smooth motion, spinning him high. The boy squealed, giggling, "Uncle Los! Uncle Los!"

Thalos laughed, nuzzling his cheek into the boy's hair before setting him back down, utterly unbothered by the floury chaos. Shadows licked playfully around Sam's arms until he squealed again, batting at them.

The sound filled the chamber, light and easy, and I felt something ease in me I hadn't realized was wound so tight.

Lyria shook her head, laughing under her breath as she returned to stirring. "I think he's more excited about muffins than the boy is."

Renae clucked her tongue. "He's always been that way. If it is about food, count him in."

I leaned back against the table, arms folding across my chest as I watched them all—Sam, Renae, my storm, and now my sunshine with flour on her cheek.

The bond pulsed steady, wrapping me in warmth.

This.

This was what we were meant for. Not fate. Not crowns. Not endless war.

Family.

She wouldn't leave this. She couldn't. Not when it felt like this.

Renae shooed Thalos and Sam toward the table while she plated the food. The smell of sizzling bacon and butter-warm bread filled the room, making even my stomach rumble.

Lyria brushed past me, carrying her bowl to the hearth. Her shoulder brushed mine, light but deliberate, and the bond sparked warm in my chest. She crouched beside Renae to scoop batter into small tins, flour still smudged across the back of her hand.

She looked up once, caught me watching her, and smiled. Gods, it nearly undid me.

"Sit, Kia," she said. "Before Thalos and Sam eat everything."

I grunted, but obeyed, dropping into the bench beside Los. Sam was already leaning against his side, shadow-tendrils playing at the boy's curls until he squealed and shoved at them. Thalos only grinned wider, his expression bright and careless in a way I hadn't seen in years. As a shadow dropped a piece of bacon into Sam's eager palms.

"You're going to spoil him," I muttered.

"He deserves it," Thalos shot back. "Unlike you." He reached for another slice of bacon before Renae slapped his hand away with the flat of a spatula. Sam cackled, clutching his own piece protectively to his chest.

When the food was finally set down with plates of bacon, bowls of eggs, baskets of warm bread and blueberry muffins, the room filled with the easy noise of eating. Sam's chatter. Renae's soft scolding. Thalos hummed some old tune under his breath as he tore into half of a muffin and stuffing his mouth.

Lyria slid onto the bench across from me, passing me a plate without asking. Her fingers brushed mine as she did, a shock of heat darting straight through the bond. She noticed it too, I saw it in the flicker of her lips before she hid it behind a bite of bacon.

She smiled, but her eyes strayed more than once toward the high windows, where sunlight spilled pale across the glass. She looked at it like it was calling her somewhere else. My gut tightened.

Sam leaned across the table toward her, eyes wide. "Do Drakes really grow their own food?"

She laughed, the sound rich and golden. "Only the smart ones," she teased, handing him one from the first batch she pulled from the hearth.

"Then Uncle Los isn't a real Drake," the boy declared with his mouth full.

Thalos feigned outrage, shadows flaring like wings as he clutched at his chest. "Betrayed by my own nephew! Kia, did you hear this?"

I smirked, spearing another piece of bacon. "He's not wrong."

That earned another burst of laughter around the table.

And I sat there, listening, letting it soak through me. The warmth of food. The bond steady and whole. The boy's laughter. Lyria's smile.

She wouldn't leave this. She couldn't.

This—this was ours.

But the thought curled sharp at the back of my mind, no matter how I tried to bury it, if she did leave, if she walked away, the bond would not stop her. I feared nothing in this world, not my crown, not my fire, not even my love, might be enough to bring her back.

Chapter 34

Lyria

The valley garden was the only place in Drakorra Spire that felt like home.

I trailed my fingers along the vine climbing the stone archway, its leaves cool and damp against my skin. The air was thick with the scent of soil and moss, laced with the faint sweetness of flowers that managed to bloom even in the shadow of the Spire. A stream murmured through the center, trickling over smooth stone, carrying the sound of water like a lullaby through the cavernous hall. Birds nested high in the rafters where sunlight spilled down in silver shafts, their wings flicking shadows across the garden floor.

If I closed my eyes, I could almost pretend I was back in the forest.

I could almost hear goats bleating in the distance, Pip braying stubbornly until I gave in and handed him a carrot. Cats chasing each other through the tall grass, knocking over baskets I had just set down. Ayiana's soft laughter curling through the mist as she braided flowers into her hair. The smell of damp moss and firewood, the sound of the lake lapping at its bank.

Almost.

But the forge-heat of the mountain below pulsed through the stones, a steady thrum that never let me forget where I was. This Spire was carved for kings. Not for me.

My hand drifted to my belly, pressing gently through the cotton dress Renae had lent me. It was loose and forgiving, a little too large, and for that I was grateful. Beneath it, the swell of my stomach was still small, easy to overlook if you weren't searching for it. But I could feel it. The firm curve, the spark of life thrumming inside me. My daughter. My secret.

This morning had been good. Better than I'd thought possible.

Breakfast at the long wooden table, Sam's laughter spilling over the sound of sizzling bacon, Renae fussing like a hen while Thalos spun the boy until his giggles filled the room. Kiaza smirking at me as he wiped flour from my cheek, pretending he wasn't as softened by it all as I knew he was.

For a little while, it had almost felt like I belonged here.

And gods, I wanted to.

Thalos—he would be a wonderful father. I saw it in the way he looked at Sam, shadows curling around the boy like a shield, playful but protective. He'd teach my daughter to laugh at storms, to dance in the rain, to be unafraid of the dark. And Kia—even with his hard edges and gruffness—he would teach her strength, teach her to fight for herself, to stand tall even when the world demanded she bow. He would hold her to fire, but he would never let her burn.

The ache of knowing she'd never have that cut deeper than I wanted to admit.

It had been easier when I didn't know them. When I thought I'd only given myself for one night.

Because as much as I wanted this—Kia's fire, Thalos's storm, the bond that bound us—I wanted something else more.

I wanted her to run barefoot to the lake in the summers, to drink milk fresh from the cow, to press her ear against a goat's belly and hear the miracle of life inside.

I wanted her to grow up with the Faeleathians, with Dosha and Ayiana, with the only family I had ever truly known. I needed to know they were safe. That everything I had endured, everything I had given, meant something.

And that meant I couldn't stay.

No matter the bond. No matter the love I felt here. A Spire in the clouds wasn't the life I wanted for her. A princess locked in a tower, no never.

I closed my eyes, inhaling the rich scent of damp stone and green. My hand lingered at my belly, protective. Already promising her what I could not promise them.

The bond stirred faintly, a ripple I'd learned to recognize. I knew who it was before I even heard his steps.

Thalos.

He lingered at the edge of the garden, shadows curled close around him, restless. He didn't speak at first. Just watched. Then he crossed the space between us, slow, his presence a tide I couldn't ignore. His hand rose, gentle, tucking a stray lock of hair behind my ear. His fingers lingered, brushing my cheek like I might vanish if he let go.

His eyes met mine, deep emerald but soft. "You're leaving, aren't you?"

My throat went dry. The words caught sharp in my chest, though I hadn't spoken them. I swallowed hard, pulling my gaze from his. "I don't know what you mean."

His fingers lingered a moment longer at my cheek before he let them fall. The bond thrummed low and steady between us, no anger in it, just quiet knowing.

His shadows whispered restless, curling against the stones like they knew the truth even if I wouldn't speak it. "You do. You've been planning it since the moment we tried to save you."

I forced a laugh, brittle. "I think you think you know too much."

He tilted his head, shadows curling along his shoulders, restless. "You want the forest. The goats, the river, the family you left behind. Not the Spire. Not us."

I pressed my palm harder to my belly, as if to hide the truth even from him. The ache in my chest sharpened. "This isn't about wanting or not wanting."

"Then what?" His voice was low, almost tender. "The bond is whole, Lyria. You're tied to us now. To me. To him." He stepped closer, the storm in his eyes quiet, searching. "And still I feel it—the part of you that doesn't root here."

The words tore at me. He was right. He had always seen through what I tried to hide.

I looked away, out toward the stream glittering in the garden light. "I can't be a queen in a stone tower. It isn't who I am. And it isn't the life I want for..." My voice caught too close to the truth, and I bit it back, forcing the words to shift. "For myself."

Silence stretched.

His shadows brushed against my arm, tentative, like the touch of a question. "And us?"

Gods. My chest ached so badly I thought I might break. "I want you," I admitted, the words ripped raw. "Both of you. Last night proved that. But wanting doesn't change who I am. Or what I need."

Thalos's jaw tightened, but there was no anger. Only sorrow, deep and quiet, like rain falling in the dark. He nodded once, slow, as though he'd already known what I would say.

"You'll go," he murmured. "I won't stop you."

The bond trembled at that, his truth laced with pain.

I turned back to him, blinking hard against the sting in my eyes. "I don't want to hurt you."

He gave me a sad, crooked smile. "You already have. And still, my little Glowbee, I would rather hold you for a night, knowing you'll leave, than to never hold you at all."

The words undid me. My breath hitched, and for a moment I nearly confessed everything, my hopes, my fears, our daughter, the real reason I couldn't stay. But the words lodged in my throat, heavy with fear.

So instead I leaned into him, let his shadows curl around me, let him tuck my head beneath his chin. His heart beat steady under my ear, strong and certain, even when mine faltered.

And I told myself again the lie I needed to survive, just a little longer for her.

Thalos's arms held me close, shadows curling soft as breath, when I felt it, another presence.

Heat.

The bond stirred a heartbeat before I heard his steps. Kia.

I pulled back from Thalos just as he stepped into the garden, broad shoulders filling the archway, fire simmering low around him. His amber eyes took us in—Thalos's hand on my arm, my face close to his chest, tears still on my cheeks, and for a moment, silence burned heavy between us.

He didn't speak. Just watched.

The weight of his gaze pressed down on me until the words tore free.

"I'm leaving."

The air crackled, heat sparking sharper. Kiaza's jaw clenched, fire rippling over his skin before he forced it back. "What did you just say?"

Thalos's shadows stirred, subtle but steady, pressing against his fire. "Kia—"

I lifted my chin, forcing the words out steady even as my throat ached. "I need to go home. To the forest. To the only life I've ever known."

For a moment, he only stared at me, like he hadn't heard. Then his voice came rough, low with something that hurt worse than fury. "After all this. After the bond. After last night. You still planned to walk away."

"I have to," I whispered. My hand drifted to my belly, instinctively. "This Spire, this crown, this war, it isn't mine. And it isn't what I want. It isn't what I am choosing."

His fire lashed sharp, grief tangled with fury. "You think you can just leave? Now? After I almost lost you—after I..." His voice broke, ragged, before he forced the words through gritted teeth. "I can't lose you again."

Thalos stepped forward, shadows brushing calm against Kiaza's fire. "Listen to her. She isn't betraying us. She's *trusting* us with her truth."

Kia's eyes snapped to him, fury sparking, but Thalos didn't flinch. Shadows spread across the floor between them, holding the fire at bay. Thalos's voice softened but firm. "Kia, trust."

I saw it then, the crack in him. The rage wasn't anger at me. It was pain, raw and twisting, and he didn't know how to carry it without turning it into fire.

"I can't..." he ground out, the words scraping from his chest. " Lose you again, Not after finally having you in my arms. Not after... this." His hand jerked toward the three of us, as the bond thrummed inside me, bright and alive.

Tears burned hot at the corners of my eyes. I wanted to run to him, to promise I wasn't gone, not really. Lies wouldn't hold him.

Thalos laid a hand on his arm, shadows curling gentle, steady. "We haven't lost her. Not yet."

Kia's gaze cut between us, fire flickering in his eyes, his jaw tight as he swallowed the fury down. He didn't move closer, didn't speak again. Though I felt it through the bond, all his grief, his longing, his desperate refusal to let go.

And I knew—this was only the beginning of the breaking.

Chapter 35

Thalos

The Ironwilde unrolled under my wings like a frozen sea covered in fog. White dunes of drifted snow, black ribs of shale, old pines bowed under rime. Winter had pared the land down to edge and bone. My shadows streamed behind me in long, thin banners, slipping over the ground as if they were smoke blown low by the wind. Cold burned the inside of my nose, every breath tasted of pine, wet snow, and deep earth.

Three months.

Three months since her golden wings knifed into the clouds and left the Spire. Since the bond had gone thin with distance but not empty. Since Queen Novalyn's note arrived, ink precise, threat unmistakable.

You broke our treaty. We will take what is due. This means war.

The council chamber had felt smaller after that. Kia's fire had licked the edges of the marble table while he read, and I watched the old stone sweat under the heat of his restraint. Natrix had stood unbothered at his shoulder, all dry humor and teeth, drawing quick maps on the back of reports while we counted the ways to bleed an invading army before they saw the cliff face. They made a good pair in battle, Kia's fury hammered to purpose under her ruthless economy. Every victory tasted of ash, because the Ironwilde wasn't a front, it was her home.

He hadn't wanted me to leave. Gods, he hated it. He'd agreed we needed eyes in the mist. Caldenys surveyors with iron stakes. Rauthen traders sniffing new routes. Hunters. Poachers. Things moved in this white world that had no right to.

What I hadn't told him sat heavy in my chest and lighter than breath at the same time, I wanted to be here when her time came. I wanted to catch the first sound her child made and to make sure danger heard me before it ever heard them. My shadows had known what she kept from us, one small heartbeat, quick and bright, tucked beneath Lyria's ribs. Kia had a right to that truth, and she had a right to her choice. Until those parted ways, I would carry both.

I banked lower, let the wind slide under my wings, and let the bond guide me like a taut gold thread. It thrummed warmer the farther north I flew. The mist gathered thick in pockets between the trees, spilled like milk down gullies, climbed old cairns and swallowed them whole.

There, smoke, thin and honest, from a narrow chimney. Fences angling across a white yard. A barn shouldering drift on its lee side. The little house I had carried in my head like a charm lay quiet under the weight of winter.

I circled once and dropped, snow kicking up around my talons. Shadows cushioned the jolt of landing. A flex of will folded wings into bone and I stepped out of the spray and shadows as a man, breath steaming, boots sinking in a clean foot of new snow. The cold bit my cheeks and burned. It woke everything that had been grinding for weeks.

I felt her before I saw her. The bond hummed bright and close, like a coal under the ash.

Across the yard, Lyria stood with a faelethian, her lavender hair tied back, sleeves shoved to her elbows, her cheeks bitten red by the cold. They bickered like kin while goats jostled their legs, complaining to the sky about snow on their feed. The chickens clucked around their boots, unbothered by weather or war, too intent on grain to care. Lyria bent, her cloak falling open enough for me to see the curve of her belly, round and proud. She laughed when the donkey—Pip, I'd recognize his stubborn skull anywhere—nudged her, and she pushed his head back with the heel of her hand, scolding him gently like a child.

For a breath, I forgot the cold, the war, everything. Just stood there and watched her be, here alive and laughing in a world that had tried to make her small. The sight rooted me like a stake in frozen ground.

Her voice struck through the bond, stern as a palm to the chest. *"What are you doing here?"*

She hadn't turned. Of course she hadn't. She felt me the way I felt the storm.

I kept my answer steady. *"What I promised. I came to be here for our child. For you both. To help. Nothing more."*

Grain trickled out of her hand slowly, then stopped. For a moment she didn't move. I saw the little plume of her breath in the air and the flakes caught in her hair. Her friend followed her stillness and lifted her head, gaze cutting the yard. Her eyes found me first. With quick strides I closed the distance my shadows trailing me.

"Shadow," she said, neither welcoming nor hostile, just naming the fact of me.

"Dosha. I assume." I lifted my hands, palms open. "You two need wood split. Fences tightened. The roof on the coop's sagging under drift." My breath smoked. "Let me work while you yell at me."

Lyria turned then. Her hood fell back a little, and her eyes found me. Gold, bright even against the gray of winter, steady enough to hold a man still. The line of her mouth was firm. She rested both hands on the swell of her belly in as much a claim as a guard.

"You should have told Kia," I sent gently. *"You still should."*

"I will." Her reply came on the bond like stone laid with care. *"In my time. When I choose. Not before."*

I bowed my head, not to concede the point, but to honor the line she'd drawn. *"Then I'll wait. And I'll stand with you until you do. Whatever comes."*

Her chin tipped a fraction. Permission. Dosha blew out a long breath and shoved the half-empty grain sack into my hands.

"If you're here, work," she said, already moving for the barn. "Pip ate half the fence yesterday. We need a post reset and the hinge back on the north gate."

Pip brayed as if to object to slander. Lyria snorted and stroked the donkey's forehead, and the ridiculous drama of my life collapsed into a laugh I didn't expect. The sound startled a pair of chickens off the roof, they flapped hard and scolded us all the way to the yard.

The morning fell into a rhythm I could live inside. Shadows held the ladder while I shoveled snow off the coop roof; they steadied the post-hole auger while I dug through hardpack and rock. I drove a new post into the frozen ground with a mallet that rang the bones of my shoulder, while Dosha braced it. Lyria handed me steel nails and glared at my face like she could keep me from overdoing it by the set of her mouth alone.

"You should let me..." I started.

She leveled me a look that could have frozen a river. "I am not made of crystal."

Dosha grinned. "Careful, Shadow. She'll make you knit if you keep fussing."

"I can knit," I muttered, and immediately regretted saying it as both of them turned with twin expressions of delighted predatory interest.

Lyria arched a brow, all sweet menace. "Oh? Blankets, then. For the baby. And you can fix the hole in Dosha's glove while you're at it."

"See what he's done," Dosha said solemnly to the goats.

"I brought this on myself," I admitted, and set another hinge pin with more care than was strictly necessary.

The world was white and quiet around the homestead, the kind of quiet that holds its breath. Under it, my shadows tasted other things—old iron in the creek, a far-off drum in the ground that could have been the ice settling or could have been something moving where no thing should. Every hour or so, the wind shifted and brought me the stink of coal smoke from the east, too bitter to be a hearth. Caldenys liked their fires big and dirty.

"We've seen men," Dosha said when I asked, low enough the wind could have carried the words off the yard. "Three days back. Red coats with black piping. Pushing a cart. They hammered stakes at the old trail cut."

"Rauthen?" I asked. "Or hired by them."

She nodded. "Left metal in the snow. The ground's wrong where they hammered it. The trees don't whisper there right."

Lyria's mouth tightened. "They came close the week I returned. They set a snare near the lake that would have taken a faun's leg clean." Her palm flattened against her belly again, a gesture so small and so fierce I couldn't have named it if I tried. "I cut it and left them a warning."

"What kind?" I asked.

"The sort no one mistakes," she gave a thin smile and crossed arms, with grim satisfaction riding the words.

I wanted to say "*You shouldn't be the one walking the perimeter in winter with the child so near.*" I wanted to make lists and lists of ways to make this place impossible to find. What I said was, "I brought warding salt. It'll keep iron stupid if we lay it right. And I can pull the mist thick around the ridge when the wind's right. They'll walk in circles until their courage melts."

Dosha grunted approval. Lyria's gaze softened a hair—not concession, but acknowledgment. She left us to our work.

"Tea," Lyria stuck her head out the door, after a while. As if the world had been waiting for the word, the wind used it to carry the smell of something warm out to us, sage and bitterroot and the faint ghost of honey. "Ten minutes."

I wanted to argue a fence never waits and cold doesn't care about kettles, but I was not an idiot. I followed.

The kitchen held the day in close. The stove snapped softly and threw a sweet heat that smelled like baked bread and old wood. Steam ghosted off two mugs on the table.

Snowmelt dripped in patient threads from a line strung over the door. A cat I didn't know had decided my chair was his; he blinked one slow green eye at me and did not move. Fair enough.

Lyria smoothed the knit over her belly. The dress Renae had sent fit softer now, the cotton gone smoother from washing. She reached for the cups and paused, a small crease appeared between her brows. Her breath hitched.

My heart stopped. My shadows jumped like dogs at a slammed door. "What was that?"

She inhaled slow, deliberate. The crease smoothed. The corner of her mouth kicked.

"Practice," she said. "Not the real thing."

I stared. "Practice—"

"Contractions," Dosha translated kindly, setting the kettle on the table in front of me so I'd have something to do with my hands. "Her body rehearses."

"I hate it," I said honestly.

Lyria laughed, low and bright in the little room. "I know." She poured and the smell of herbs went right to the back of my throat and untied a knot I hadn't realized was there. She pushed a mug into my hands and another into Dosha's. "Drink. Then you can go back to glaring at fences."

I curled my hands around the heat and let it burn the ache out of my fingers. The cat gave up my chair, jumped lightly to the counter, and looked at Lyria with the same expectation Sam did at the Spire when he decided he wanted a sweet. She flicked a crumb of something to him without looking. Her hand knew where he'd be. My throat tightened around the swallow.

"Los," she said, and the nickname curled around the kitchen like a promise and a wound at once. "You haven't told him."

"No," My voice was smooth and calm.

"You should bring him," Dosha added. It wasn't an accusation. A simple weather report.

I stared into the tea and watched the steam wet my lashes. In the bond, Kia burned steady and far like a hearth you can see across a winter field. I set the cup down.

"I want him here," I said. "I want him to lay his hand on your belly and to hear what I hear. I want him to know the way the world tips when that little foot kicks." I looked up. "And I want to keep my promise to you."

Silence. The stove ticked as wood shifted in the firebox. Outside, a plowbird scolded a hawk it couldn't possibly hurt.

"I'll tell him," she said at last. "Before the snow melts." A ghost of amusement curved her mouth. "So he doesn't try to chase me in the mud."

I huffed a soft laugh. "He would."

"I know." She sipped. Her lashes lowered. "I carry more than my own choice, Los. I know what telling him starts. I need a little longer to hold her close and quiet."

Her. The word hit me in the ribs. My mouth wanted to smile and to snarl in the same breath.

"Then I'll stand on your porch and kill anything that tries to stop you." with a cool calm and not joking at all.

Dosha clinked her cup to mine. "That's why he can stay," she told Lyria, and when Lyria rolled her eyes, Dosha's smile said she'd already won the argument for both of us.

Lyria step close to me. Her hand slid from her chest and she took mine, pressed it, without warning, to the side of her belly. Heat. Then a flutter, sharp and astonishing under my palm. I forgot the cold, the mist and every god I had ever cursed.

"Hello," I whispered, because my throat wouldn't let me be louder. "Hi there, little comet."

She rolled her eyes, but her smile was unguarded. "She's not a horse, Los."

"She's fast enough," I said, because the little heel jabbed my hand like she was already running.

For a long moment we stood there, drinking tea in the cozy quiet cabin, and I thought. *I could live in this one moment forever.*

Later, somewhere around midnight, as I lay on the small sofa covered in quilts, the bond pulsed once, curious, Kia half-awake in a chair with a map over his knees, Natrix muttering about supply lines and teeth. He felt me out here and didn't pull. He only warmed the tether like a hand on my shoulder and then went back under.

"Soon," I told the ceiling. "We'll tell you soon." The bond answered, warm, steady, stubborn as earth.

And under that, somewhere far to the east, something else answered too, faint and wrong, like a heartbeat echoing from inside stone.

I did not tell her that part. Not yet.

I tightened the shadow web I had spun another fraction and went to sleep.

The dawn came pale and brittle. My shadow-web hummed faint with the chill of frost, each filament holding steady. No fox had tripped them. No man had dared yet cross.

For a heartbeat, I let myself believe the valley would stay quiet.

Then the air shifted.

A low crack rolled through the earth, not from hooves, not from rails, but deeper, older. My shadows flinched like startled birds. The goats bleated in the yard, restless, stamping against the snow.

I ran outside in just my underpants, and turned toward the ridge just as the mist, the Ironwilde's shroud, lurched. It didn't drift or thin. It *sucked*. As if the very soil had grown greedy. Wisps pulled down in long, snapping ribbons, swallowed into the ground until the valley floor shone bare and exposed under the cold morning light.

Above, the sky split white. Sparks rained like falling stars, brief but bright enough to sear afterimages across my vision. The bond flared sharp with Lyria's alarm, the child inside her kicking hard, a ripple of fear and fury both. Kia's fire burned hot through me, my shadows became walls around us.

My chest went tight. The protection was gone.

Someone had torn the veil open.

And every enemy we'd held at bay would see us now.

Epilogue

The sea should have been mine.

Instead, iron shackles bit into my wrists, the weight of them leeching my magic until the tide inside me went slack. My throat still tasted of brine, raw from salt and screaming, though I had long since stopped wasting my voice on men who only laughed when I fought.

Snow flurried against the pointed crystalline cliffs, the sea below a black churn of foam and cobalt waves. The caverns of the coast glittered with their own cold fire, light refracting blue and violet across walls slick with salt.

The steamship's belly groaned as it ground into the cove. Chains rattled. The gangplank slammed to stone. Coal smoke choked the air, thick and bitter, drowning out the clean sharp bite of the winter sea.

They dragged me down the plank like cargo. Boots hammered against the rough cavern floor, the sound carrying too far, echoing until it was as though the walls themselves were announcing my humiliation. My skin prickled under the harshly refracted light off the massive quartz, painting my dark skin in cold hues, making me feel half-ghost, half-beast.

I forced my chin high. If they wanted a prize, I'd look like one, not some broken thing.

Two figures waited at the base of the cavern.

The first was a man of ruin. Taller than the rest, broader, his scars caught the crystal fire like fissures in stone. His body was whole, but whatever he had endured had left him monstrous. Hair iron-gray, tied back tight. Beard rough, peppered black and white. His eyes burned red, and the smirk that curved his mouth was the kind of smile that fed on suffering.

The second stood beside him, a woman made of stone and light. Her skin was pale, veins of prismatic crystal running beneath the surface in faint glow. Along her cheekbones and forearms, shards of gemstone jutted like blades. Her short white hair was crowned in silver, cold authority sharpened to a point.

The woman's voice cut across the cavern, sharp as a blade. "We traded gems enough to bankrupt three kingdoms for this one. Make her worth the price, Morgryth. I want the Stone Breaker. Nothing less."

Morgryth. So that was his name. The red-eyed beast.

Stone Breaker. The word struck me hard though I didn't understand it.. Did they think of me as nothing but a tool? A weapon to pry apart the world for them? Someone involved in tyranny? Rage flared hot in my gut, but the chains drank it greedily, leaving only the taste of blood on my tongue where I'd bitten too hard.

Morgryth moved closer. His shadow eclipsed me, his hand sliding into my tangled locks of inky hair. He ripped seaweed free, strands dripping in seawater, and lifted it as though it were a trophy. His breath scalded against my cheek when he bent close, his voice a low, poisonous purr.

"Such a rare pearl," he murmured. His red gaze cut through me like a hook through flesh. "You'll help us capture your sister."

My stomach lurched at his words. Sister, I had none, no one to call family. He spoke of her as though I should have known who she was. My magic arched as if in my blood carried a call and what answered in return was painful longing, sharp and undeniable.

His hand slid lower, rough palm pressing against my belly, and his smirk sharpened into something hungrier, darker. "And my grandchild that grows inside her. My legacy to claim."

For a moment, the cavern swayed. My knees wanted to buckle, but I forced them to lock, forced myself to stand tall even with his hand against me, even with his strange twisted words.

Inside, the sea still answered. Faint, faint, but there. The salt wind from the cavern mouth licked against my skin. The tide inside me stirred, shackled but not dead.

He thought me bound. He thought me powerless.

He was wrong.

I was Dalayna. Sea-born.

Water runs through stone, through fire, through shadow. Water endures.

Their pearl? No. I was tide and storm, and one day soon I'd remind them—no hand can hold back the sea when it breaks against the shore.

Triggers list
Content & Trigger Warnings

This book is an **adult dark romantasy (18+)** with high heat and heavy themes. Please use care for your own boundaries before reading.

Violence & War

On-page death and injury in battles

Graphic gore, blood, and dismemberment

Torture, captivity, and physical abuse

Murder of family members (including parental death)

War crimes: destruction, burning cities, enslavement

Emotional & Psychological Themes

Childhood trauma and grief

Survivor's guilt and vengeance

Manipulation and gaslighting

Captivity and loss of agency

Emotional breakdowns, panic, despair

Sexual Coercion & Captivity

Strong sexual coercion and obsession by antagonist

Forced nudity, humiliation, food restrictions

Forced bathing

Being paraded as a trophy/slave

Imprisonment with intent to break will

Forced consumption of gore (hearts/blood)

No on-page rape, but repeated scenes of **sexual intimidation, obsession, and degradation**

Sexual Content & Relationships

Explicit sex scenes (M/M, M/F, and polyamorous triad intimacy)

Rough sex, dirty talk, power exchange (all consensual within the main relationships)

Threesome dynamics and **bond-driven attraction**

Themes of **jealousy, possessiveness, and surrender**

Fantasy & Magic

Shapeshifting into creature forms and human forms

Dark and shadow magic

Bonding rituals that affect emotions/free will

Pregnancy & unborn child at risk

Religious/cult overtones in antagonist factions

Acknowledgments

Every book is built on the shoulders, hearts, and cheerleading of so many people.

To my family—you gave me the space, support, and stubborn love I needed to chase this dream. To my friends and critique partners—thank you for your eyes, your honesty, and your endless belief in these characters.

To my Alpha and Beta readers—you helped shape this story in its earliest, roughest drafts, giving it the spine and soul it needed to stand. To my ARC team—you are the real magic. Your excitement, feedback, and encouragement made the long nights and early mornings worth it.

To the indie book community, the authors, readers, and creators in my life, thank you for reminding me that stories connect us in ways nothing else can.

And finally, to you, the reader—thank you for picking up this book, for giving these pages your time, and for carrying these characters with you. You make the world brighter just by being here.

Small Business Thank You

This book was created by me, but it wouldn't have reached as many hearts without the support of small businesses who chose to stand beside me. Through direct PR sponsorships and collaborations, they shared their talent, creativity, and platforms in ways that left me in awe.

Your willingness to uplift my work, to share space with my stories, and to believe in this journey means more than words can hold.

Special thanks to...

Silky Gem Crystal Candy for your sponsorship. — https://www.silkygem.com/

Midnight Soapery for the continued collaboration. -- https://www.etsy.com/shop/MidnightSoapery

Beaded and Bound for the continued collaboration.— https://www.etsy.com/shop/beadworkbyber

Because of you, this book carries not just my voice, but a chorus of creative hands and hearts who make the indie community so vibrant.

About The Author

A.K. Neane (they/them) is a queer fantasy author who believes in the power of storytelling to create safe spaces and amplify diverse voices. Inspired by the comfort books have always provided, they craft immersive worlds filled with magic, complex characters, and the kind of representation they longed for growing up.

When not writing, they can be found wrangling their teens or goats on their small family farm, researching mythology, or diving into their next obsession.

Veins of Sapphire, Hearts of Steel is their debut novel, the first in the Destiny of Terraqua trilogy.

Stay connected for updates, exclusive content, and behind-the-scenes insights:

@A.K.Neane.Author

Coming Soon

The saga of the Drakarians is only beginning...

Book Two of the Asherium Series

Fire of the Ironwilde
Coming May 2026

Secrets will ignite, bonds will be tested, and Lyria's choice will shape the fate of kingdoms.

Also by A.K. Neane

The Destiny of Terraqua Trilogy

Veins of Sapphire, Hearts of Steel (**Book One**) – Available Now

Bloodlines of Ruby, Minds of Silver (**Book Two**) – March 2026

Other Works

A Road to Killing – December 13, 2025

Twisted in the Darkness: Bound by Shadows – Available Now

For updates, bonus content, and exclusive ARC opportunities, join the newsletter: https://linktr.ee/a.k.neane